Perfected

The Elected Series, Book 3

Rori Shay

Contents

*To all the brave girls, especially Marlena and Ellie,
who defy any stereotype that gets in their way.*

Part 1: The Coup

1

THE ROCKY GROUND AT my feet in East Country's internment camp is the only thing that seems solid. Three thousand of my captive people wait for my answer as Mid Country's two airrides hover overhead, the engines causing the air to suffocate with exhaust fumes. The citizens of East Country hold their breath, our shared anxiety so tangible it's almost a second layer of fog below the haze.

The past months weigh heavy upon my shoulders. Since accepting my birthright as East Country's Elected, each step forward has come wracked with consequences. I saved Griffin from hemlock's capital punishment but had to break the Eco Accords to do so. I snuck into Mid Country, finding out why they were determined to destroy East, but all of that knowledge came at the expense of my parents' lives. I managed to produce an heir only to have my baby stolen by Mid's Elected. I escaped Mid's prisons and launched a plot to free my people in East. But even that endeavor, a feat so close to gaining East's people their independence, now comes tinged with dire penalties too. Within moments of liberty, a lone communication from one of Mid's guards brought Calix, the enemy country's Elected, upon us with enough firepower to level everything we have left in East.

Griffin. My parents. My child. Vienne. Tomlin. All of my countrymen.

Everyone I love has either been torn from me, killed, or is under threat of annihilation.

My parents could never have imagined such an Electancy.

I look toward the border hill, stalling for time. Calix's threat—his so-called "offer"—lashes around my head, leaving me no good option. Either I leave with Calix as his Madame Elected and raise my son, Glory, as his, or I stay in East Country and Calix decimates my people. I can almost feel my brain contract under the pressure of the decision—two stone walls collapsing inward.

It seems like an easy choice. I give up Griffin and my country, and just like that, three thousand of my people, even the ones hiding in the marshes outside of the city's epicenter, are saved. The sacrifice of my happiness is certainly worth the lives of East's countrymen.

But even if I take Calix's offer of marriage and he doesn't bomb East, he's already said my people will be servants to Mid Country. Nothing will stop Calix from giving them the mind-numbing optogenetics treatment he administers to his own people. Do I relegate the men and women of my country to a semi-conscious life to keep them alive, or do we fight back now while we have a sliver of a chance but potentially suffer great losses?

Even as I consider an offensive stance, I glance up at Calix's elongated flat planes, the airrides, suspended over us. They create menacing shadows against the backdrop of the garish orange sunrise. Closing my eyes, the surprisingly quiet whir of the twin engines could almost be mistaken for a brisk wind. I can't allow myself to pretend the death machines aren't there, though. I don't have time for such luxuries, even if it's a thought that helps calm my nerves.

If I turn down Calix's offer of marriage, would East Country even have a chance to engage in combat? An answer of no from me now will bring Calix's bombs faster than anything else.

All eyes in East Country are focused on me, but I only glance at a few people while I consider the alternatives.

Glory stretches from within the cradle of Calix's arms. Mid Country's leader holds onto my baby possessively with thick-gloved hands, so much so, I wonder if the tyrant actually spares a spot in his heart for my boy. I see one of Glory's little legs poke out from under the blanket, and the movement almost causes me to leap forward and wrestle him away from Calix. That's *my* baby.

A quick glance at the guns pointed in my direction keeps me firmly in place. If I snatched Glory from Calix right now, it would start a rapid spray of gunfire that wouldn't only hit me, but most likely the baby that I've just tried to wrench free. So I stay in place, my feet feeling like they're growing roots into the hard-packed earth.

If I say yes to Calix's offer, I can remain with Glory. My boy won't return to Mid Country alone, waiting, perhaps indefinitely, for me to mount an insurrection and bring him back home. Glory is my future, and I'll be able to watch him grow up if I just choose the first option.

I hope for a fleeting glance at his face, but Glory and the ice-blue eyes that prove he's mine stay bundled in the fleece wrap. I settle for one more fleeting eyeful of his renegade foot, which continues to poke out of the blanket, as if Glory is also contemplating escape.

My eyes travel to my wife, Vienne, next. How can I marry another when I'm already wedded to Vienne, even if it was just a sham arrangement? Vienne moves a blonde wisp of hair from her forehead with one long finger. An uncharacteristic line of worry is etched on her brow right above the eyes. I'm sure she feels the brunt of Calix's cruel ultimatum as much as I do. She loves me. Everything I feel, I believe she mirrors inside her heart. Vienne's my best friend, and if I leave now, I may never see her again. I take a fraction of a second to memorize her face. Even with the many scars gained from searching for Mid Country's microchip, Vienne's face projects an angelic beauty. She wears the characteristic long, three-layered dress of East's Madame Elected. The bottom of her dress scrapes the ground, the light green trim now dark with weeks spent in the internment camp. Vienne tries to smile at me, but the movement is lost half-way up her face. No twinkle enters her eyes, and even the semblance of reassurance is caught in the edge of her lip, which quivers on the upturn.

I force myself to stop staring at Vienne and instead turn to my long-time mentor, Tomlin. His lips are pursed. He doesn't bother trying to smile like Vienne. He understands the gravity of my decision. As my parents' former advisor and now mine, he realizes the risks and downsides of being East Country's Elected. He's never placated me with falsities. He gives me the facts, even if they're cold in their cavity of truth. Tomlin is the oldest person in all of Mid. Older than even my father would have been. And now Tomlin's dying of cancer. I'll be missing his last months if I leave now. Because he's like my second father, Tomlin's absence will feel like I'm losing my parents all over again.

If he could convey the right choice to me, I know he would. I stare at Tomlin's face, my eyes unblinking as I read one possible answer on his face. I know he's the only one who truly understands the finality of each choice. And the reality, if I choose wrong. After a long moment, Tomlin nods. I imagine we're inside the Oval Office years ago, back when I was officially his student. He always told me to base my decisions on the good of my people, but what is best for my people now is a murky path, no matter what I choose.

I shake my head and look away. There's only one other person to see now.

Griffin lays on the ground, propped up on one arm, straining to help me even though he's been shot by one of Mid's guards. The man I would marry, if I'm ever released from the burden of my position, is severely hurt, and I can't do anything about it.

A spherical stain of blood soaks Griffin's linen shirt. The wound is still fresh, and even as I gaze at him for these few seconds, the pattern grows wider. His face is white, but his eyes are still bright and focused. I look from Griffin's steady stare to the red on his arm. He's always saving me. From his father's long arrow. From Calix's prison. And most recently from the guard's bullet that was meant for me. If I'm completely honest with myself, I don't think Griffin will be able to rescue me this time. If I choose to leave with Calix, Griffin's all but guaranteed to be the first person from East whom Calix puts under optogenetics. And that's *if* Griffin stays alive long enough. He's losing so much blood, I know without medical attention soon, optogenetics will be the least of our worries.

Upon our exchanged look, he gives me a crooked, albeit pained, smile—the same one I fell in love with at East Country's dance so many years ago. I know Griffin doesn't want me to feel guilty if I leave him. But does he realize that walking away from him now while he's hurt is like someone forcing me to rip my own heart from my chest? I *just* got him back. I can't bear to lose Griffin again.

"What's your decision?" Calix's voice punctures my thoughts—a steely knife, cold against the warmer images of my family members.

I swallow, feeling the hard lump of an answer forming in my throat. My whole body fights against my decision. Maybe my voice won't even allow me to get the words out. I look once more at the powerful sun, now higher in the sky than a moment earlier. It reminds me that the world will keep turning, with or without my decision. We are small creatures on this Earth. A hundred years from now there will be others making hard choices, and to them, it will feel like they're the first people to ever have to sacrifice anything. My choice is just one among thousands—no, millions—leaders have endured before me. No matter what I choose now, leaders will keep making hard decisions long after my people and I are buried deep in the earth.

I look from the sun straight into Calix's face. When I open my mouth to speak, the tone is surprisingly clear. I'm amazed at my body's ability to sound strong even as my insides are churning.

"Calix, what you're asking for is complete submission. Whatever I choose now, you've got to know I'll never stop protecting East Country."

Mid's Elected laughs. It's deep and guttural, starting in his belly and reaching out of his throat like the laugh has a life of its own. "I do realize that. But what of your choice? Will you come with me now or stay and be destroyed along with your precious countrymen?"

I already know what I'll choose. There's really only one viable option.

I take a deep breath, the yet unspoken words gathering solidity inside the fleshy, soft insides of my mouth. "I'll—"

Something long and thin slices through the air, leaving a zinging sound in its wake. In the utter silence of people listening for my answer, the air is quiet enough to hear this intrusion. We all turn on our heels to determine the cause, eyes circling to see where the noise originated.

There's a confused murmur among the crowd. My countrymen even look up at the airrides, crouching low, scared that Calix hasn't bothered to wait for my response. Maybe he signaled for the destruction to begin early.

But unlike my countrymen, I recognize the noise. I don't bother looking up to the sky. Instead, my head whips left and right, trying to find the target for the single-minded whoosh of a long arrow. When I see the telltale ring of red blood emerging from the weapon's embedded tip, I can't help but gasp. The arrow's aim was toward the *single, last* person I would have guessed.

The long arrow's barbed fin is stuck deep in Calix's chest.

A STAIN, MORE PERFECTLY circular than Griffin's, grows wider in proportionate size, so that no one would ever know Calix's wound started as just a drop of blood. Now the circle covers the size of Calix's whole heart, ruining his white robes with its red insistence. Calix stares down at the arrow in disbelief. Mid's Elected, once proud and steadfast, wobbles on his legs. I don't know who launched the long arrow or if there's another one about to finish the job, but I rush forward anyway. Calix doesn't look like he's about to drop Glory, but I don't want to wait for the inevitable. Who knows if another arrow is coming for Mid's leader. That one might not miss my boy, and I won't wait to find out if the launcher's aim was merely lucky.

"Give me Glory." My voice is a command, but it isn't harsh. I know what's happening to Calix, and for all the wrong he's done me, I didn't expect him to die like this.

Calix stares at me, his eyes round with horror and accusation.

"I didn't do this to you," I say.

Calix clutches Glory's blanketed body closer against his side, like my boy himself has the power to syphon off the blood leaking from his chest wound.

Voices bubble up in back of me, and I start to see Calix's guards raising their heavy guns. I only have a moment to grasp Glory before chaos reigns. The three-thousand-strong crowd of my people send the message of Calix's demise back through their ranks, their voices growing louder as news travels. I even hear a whoop of joy from somewhere toward the rear.

However, in direct opposition to the joy rebounding through my people, without Calix's instructions, Mid's guards grow more agitated.

I see them looking through the crowd of my countrymen to find the aggressor. In a moment, when they can't find the source of the long arrow, I imagine they will fire aimlessly at my people.

Grobe, East's former Technology Faction leader and the man who assumed East Country's Elected position during my absence, seems to realize this too and catches my eye. He's already gesturing with hand signals at a few of the bigger men from East. I know that in a moment they will charge forward and wrestle with Mid's guards. There will undoubtedly be more bloodshed, but since Mid's leader is about to die, I think we may win this fight. I wonder for a second if Grobe and his Technology Faction were the source of the long arrow—if perhaps Griffin's father, Maran, had a store of the projectiles hidden in my country.

But something in this explanation doesn't ring true. Mere feet away from Calix, I can see that this particular long arrow is different from the one Maran used on me. It's not crude and whittled. It's sleek black with razor sharp spikes on the handle—completely different from the ones I've seen previously. I'm about to say as much to Calix before he collapses, so that at least he'll believe me and hand me my child before the fighting breaks out and before his inevitable fall hurts Glory.

But as I move closer, the whole of Calix's heart seems to glow from the inside out. He convulses and stumbles toward me. Glory is squeezed between us both, but Calix holds onto him even tighter. The three of us make a strange trio, and I can't help bending under the weight. At once, I'm on the ground with Calix's body lying across my legs. Glory stays tucked under Calix's arm, and I fear Mid's Elected will crush my boy in his death grip.

"It's electrified!" Calix's chest jerks involuntarily as he chokes out the words. I don't know what he means until he says, "Don't get near the arrow." When I look at the buzzing tip, he adds, "It'll electrocute you. But I'm not a conductor." He points to his robe, which is sufficiently thick enough that it stops both me and Glory from being electrocuted along with Mid's Elected.

Calix is trying to protect us in his own demented way. But it's not good enough for me.

"Then give me my son!"

Calix groans and shudders as I see the tip of the arrow light up again inside his chest. His skin isn't thick enough to stop the arrowhead from glowing under the layers of cloth and singed flesh. The arrow is hurting

Calix but at the same time keeping his heart thumping for a few more beats. I know for sure this high-tech weapon isn't of my people's making. But I wonder who is trying to keep Calix alive for a few more moments.

"You're going to die!" I plead. "Just give Glory to me already!"

"I can't," Calix croaks in between pulses of electricity. "He's my only leverage."

I'm about to pry Glory from Calix's claw-like fingers, but a new sound stops the cacophony around us all. A metallic, amplified voice bursts through the noise, blanketing the internment camp with its volume. Its laughter. High-pitched, crazy cackling.

I stop pulling at Glory and look up toward the noise.

"It's over, Dear Brother. Your reign, false as it has been, is now finished!" Aaron, the true, if somewhat mentally ill, Mid Country Elected, stands at the mouth of the cave from which Griffin, Margareath, Cole, and I exited less than an hour ago. White hair lashes around his face in the wind, and his pink eyes are directed on his brother's quivering body. Aaron carries some type of mechanical cone, and each time he talks into the device, his voice is thrown out toward us, loud and all-encompassing. It's a trick I find particularly aggravating, as the words Aaron utters are so shrill, I can't block them out even if I tried. They collide like rocks inside my head, already threatening to bring on a blinding headache.

Aaron laughs again, and I can't help notice that Calix's eyes grow wider with each of Aaron's guffaws. If I'm surprised at Aaron's entrance, Calix is stunned. Even the original guards under Calix's leadership are baffled.

"That's right, little brother! I'm baa-aack. Come to my senses with the help of a few friends. And can you imagine how *astonished* I was to hear about your betrayal! Failing to annihilate the country that attacked us? Watching idly as our nuclear warheads were destroyed? Planning to *marry* our enemy?" Aaron spits after the last word.

An enemy? Right. One that saved Aaron's skin, is all. I should have let him fall to his death up on top of Mid's rocket launcher.

"Well, your time is finished," continues Aaron. "I'm here to announce my reinstatement as Mid's Elected and finish the job in East Country that you couldn't quite manage."

I close my eyes. Hope lies crumbling at my feet. My insides are devoid of strength.

Aaron lets the amplifier hang at his side and starts to walk out of the cave. I know I have just seconds left to save the one person who could potentially stay off Aaron's radar.

"If you *ever* cared about me, even a *little* bit, give me Glory now," I beg Calix.

Calix stares at me and then releases his hold on my son. The buzzing of the electrified arrow has ceased now, and I know Calix won't stay alive much longer. He passes me the squirming bundle, and before I can even turn, Tomlin is at my side. I pass Glory into his arms, and Tomlin whisks him away, anonymously far into the crowd. I fight the urge to look after my baby, as I don't want anything to turn Aaron's attention toward Glory. But yet again my heart lurches as I feel my boy's warm hand torn out of my own.

Calix's voice is failing, so when he speaks, I have to lean forward, almost nose to nose, to hear his words. "Of course I cared about you. Why do you think I asked you to be my wife?"

My mouth falls open, shocked, not exactly by the words themselves, but by the tender way Calix utters them. When Aaron arrives in front of us, looming overhead, I'm the perfect picture of a caring fiancée, holding Calix's head gently in my hands.

"Disgusting," quips Aaron, looking down at us, his sneer turning down the edge of his bottom lip.

I don't respond, just continue holding Calix who has started taking sharp breaths—ones that sound an awful lot like his last.

"Do you wonder how I got out of your prison, Brother?" asks Aaron, now bending down to look Calix in the eyes.

When Calix doesn't answer, merely clutching my hand hard on the intake of another ragged breath, Aaron continues, "I had sympathizers who took a bit more time coming around to my way of thinking than I would have liked. You, trouncing off to look for your would-be bride, probably pushed them over the edge." Aaron laughs, his high-pitched cackle ringing sharply into my ears.

I cringe, the anger in my gut bubbling up too fast for me to think twice. "I should have let you fall," I hiss at Aaron.

"What was that, Alicen? Or should I call you Aloy? Or maybe East's Elected?" He laughs again. "Oh, that's right, you don't even have that position anymore because you're a little *girl*!"

"Mac and all the rest of Mid were going to let you plummet to your death on top of the rocket launcher. I should have followed their lead," I say. My words are bitter, sour-tasting, in my mouth.

"Ah, dear ole Mac. You know, he was the one who led the brigade to oust me from that ridiculous solitary confinement and return me to my senses. Who knew it only took a short break from doctor visits to get my wits back?"

"Doesn't Mac deserve a parade in his honor," I sneer, the sarcasm dripping from my lips.

Aaron places a pinky on his chapped, peeling lips, a nasty smile growing wider on his face. "A parade would have been splendid, I agree. But unfortunately for Mac, I don't *reward* tardiness. He was a tad too slow on the reversal of his allegiance. So now he's making some of our cloned pigs a tasty slop in their feed trays."

The image of Mac's body ground up and fed to the hogs, flips my stomach in on itself. But I don't have too much time to dwell on the former foreman of the nuclear silo. All I can think about is how much power Aaron really wields in Mid now and what that means for my country.

As if to answer my unspoken question, Aaron starts ticking off his many backers on one hand. "I've got the army behind me. And all the weapons you didn't already manage to destroy. And the Elected position back. Hmmm . . . and what else? Oh, yes! And a slave country too! The entire breadth of East's people to do my bidding now as well." Aaron erupts into a tumult of gleeful chuckles.

I can't take it anymore. Some of the bile collecting in my stomach erupts into my throat, and I instinctively spit it out in Aaron's face. He winces as the small ball of liquid hits his right cheek.

"You're lucky you did save me up on the rocket launcher," he sneers. "Otherwise you'd be dead right now."

"Consider your debt paid," I say.

"Oh, you won't get the honor of my mercy again, that I can assure you."

"I don't want your mercy. I just want you to leave us alone. Go back to your country and leave East be."

"Actually, Aloy, that's exactly what I plan to do."

At this, my eyebrows rise. I don't trust a word from Aaron's mouth, but can this latest revelation somehow be true? Would he really walk away from us and be content to have just enacted revenge upon Calix? Does he know East had nothing to do with bombing his country? Will he truly free us?

"Yes, that's right," Aaron continues. "Unlike my brother I don't wish to subjugate all your people. I realize that in time you'd just find some way to break out of the optogenetics procedures now that you know how to circumvent them." Aaron looks like he's growing bored, idly playing with the nail of his index finger.

I allow myself to exhale sharply for the first time since Aaron's shown up. I hadn't realized I was even holding my breath until now.

"But . . ." Aaron's head jerks up, meeting my eyes, a light smile moving across his lips again. "There is *something* I want."

"What?" My voice is smaller in my throat, knowing Aaron's release of East was too good to be true.

"It seems Mid's women are infertile. Sad, really. Perhaps it has something to do with the mind control technique we've been using. Seems to shrink the ovaries, wouldn't you know? We're in need of women who haven't yet been touched by our optogenetics influence. Women who will help our population flourish." Aaron's eyes gleam as he looks at me, and I'm about to protest, to tell him he can't have anyone here, when his voice breaks in again. "Guards, seize all their women!"

All of them? My voice catches in my throat as I see Mid's guards already descending on East Country's women toward the outskirts of the crowd. Screams ring out as hands are clasped around arms and my people struggle against their latest captors.

"Absolutely not!" I shout.

"Who are you to tell me what to do or not do? Do you see the airrides above you? I am in control now!" yells Aaron.

I can feel my heartbeat in my throat and cheeks. "Take just me! I'll make plenty of babies for you! Boys to add to your Elected family lineage! You don't need the others."

I think I can hear a deep groan coming from farther back in the crowd, but I press onward with my resolve, shutting out the thought that Griffin is hearing me sacrifice myself to another man, yet again.

"I need all the women here!" Aaron laughs as more of the guards circle East's women.

"Just stop the optogenetics. Maybe your women will be fertile again!" I can hear my voice getting higher with hysteria as I grasp onto anything that might convince Aaron to leave my women alone.

"Unfortunately, I tried that on my own mother. She was never fertile again. And thus, useless. You heard I had my parents killed, didn't you?"

The lump in my throat grows, but I say, "She was older. Probably infertile at that point anyway, no matter the optogenetic procedure. Just give me a chance. I promise I will be a good wife." My last words catch with a slight begging lilt, but they're hollow, even to my own ears.

Aaron guffaws loudly, both palms pressing down on his knees as he rocks back and forth in his half-crouched position. "You should hear yourself! I really wish I had a recording device so I could play back your lies for you!"

"I'll do what you ask of me. I promise you." I shudder, knowing exactly what he would ask. "I'll make lots of babies for you."

"No. You're unsuitable to have more children because of the way your baby had to be pried from your womb. You don't even have the right organs anymore." When Aaron sees the horrified look on my face, he stops for a beat and looks at me closer, amusement and surprise flourishing across his eyes. "What? Didn't Calix tell you? They had to rip out your uterus."

I can't look at Aaron. I can't think. *That's* what Mid's doctors did to me?

There's one person who will know for sure. I blink hard and squeeze Calix's hand. He'll tell me the truth, if only through the glassiness of his eyes. He hasn't spoken for so long now, I doubt he'll be able to get out any words. I squeeze his hand again, trying to get his attention. But Calix's palm is limp in mine. As I look down into the face I'm still cradling in my hands, I can see I won't be getting any answers from Calix.

His eyes are wide, lips parted into a gaping O, a look of abject horror permanently etched along the lines of his forehead.

Mid's counterfeit Elected is dead.

4

"THAT'S DONE THEN," SAYS Aaron, also staring down at his brother. "What a shame." He smiles, the tone not matching the phrase at all. "Calix can join our parents and finally have all their attention just for himself."

"Maybe you'll unite with them sooner than you think." My words are bitter behind clenched teeth.

"I don't think so!" Aaron laughs, and then waves his arm wide over the expanse of my people. "Guards, round up all the women of birthing age! And tie up this one!" He points to me, and immediately two guards emerge to bind my arms behind my back with Mid's untearable nylon.

I haven't been constricted within the unbreakable rubber for weeks now, and the feel of the spongy material reminds me of my months-long confinement in Mid. I can't stomach going back to that prison again.

I struggle against the bonds, trying to jab my free elbows and legs into the guards, but they slam the butt of their guns into my side, and it throws me sprawling onto the ground. People are running and screaming all around me, and there's truly chaos. Through the legs, I see Griffin wrenched out of Vienne's arms and thrown to the side onto the ground like me. Vienne is bound behind her back, and she's forced forward into a growing pool of women who all try to fight back but are too easily rounded up into a tight circle.

East's men fight too. Grobe, with his long wooden pole, fences two of Mid's sentinels. A woman stands near him, sheltering someone smaller behind her and yelling encouragement toward Grobe. It must be his wife, East Country's Stargazer, Maggie. I have never spoken to her personally, but I've heard she can tell people exactly the day and time based on the sky's star formations.

I don't see Tomlin anywhere, and I hope in the commotion he's gotten far away with Glory. I don't know if Aaron realizes Calix brought Glory home. I certainly don't want Aaron looking for Glory, and I know that in the best-case scenario I'll be separated from my baby once again.

Everything is wrong. If I'd been given the chance to choose one of Calix's offers, all of this unnecessary fighting wouldn't be happening now. I try to get back up, even if it's just onto my knees, but the guard watching me thumps his long gun into my back, sending me onto my stomach once again. My cheek hits the dirt, causing my teeth to vibrate. An incisor slices into the fleshy skin inside my mouth, and I taste blood.

I hear a shrill, piercing yell and look over in Grobe's direction again. He's covered in blood, a ragged gash on his neck squirting in streams. Grobe lunges against his two adversaries, hurling his staff into the stomach of one. It barely bends the guard's thick armor, and then they're on top of him, putting a final bullet between his open eyes. Grobe's wife lets out an animal shriek, finally turning to run, pulling a girl along next to her. The guard straddling Grobe steps over his body and in one quick movement grabs Maggie by her skirts, causing her to fall forward. The girl reaches backward for her mother. I want to scream "run" to her, but a hand on my arm grabs my attention.

"Aloy." Griffin's voice is short of breath.

I whip my head around, eyes wide. "Griffin!" He's pulled himself along the ground from where he lay with Vienne, and no one paid attention since he was already wounded.

"We've got to get you out of here." He's panting with the strain of speaking.

I glance up at the guard above us whose face is thankfully facing away. Last thing Griffin needs is the end of the guard's gun in his gut. One more injury, and I'm convinced Griffin will lapse into unconsciousness.

"I don't think we'd get far," I say.

Griffin moans, and I can't help but see the line of blood dotting the dirt across the area he dragged himself. I scoot closer to him, hoping to put pressure against his wounds with my shoulder.

"Vienne . . ." He utters her name on an intake of air. "I couldn't stop them from . . ."

"I know." I can't see her through the crowd that's still battling. But as I look outward, it's clear East Country isn't winning this fight. Most of the men have been pushed backward, out of the internment camp. Mid's guards are pulling the perimeter fence back up, locking the men out and East's women in. The men who are left beat on the fencing, pulling at the links with all their might. Those whose hands cross through the fence have their fingers hit repeatedly with the guard's weapons. Some are even gunned down through the perimeter. Eventually, even the most stalwart fighters fall back.

Some of the women in the cluster stand, whereas others sit still, possibly shocked with the death of their loved ones. When the fighting diminishes, I can see Vienne, her blonde hair blowing in unruly wisps. She's one of the women still standing, staring into the melee, maybe looking for me. When we spot each other, she shakes her head. Neither of us can think of anything to do.

"Let go of me!" screams Grobe's daughter, who is pulled by her hair toward the circle of bound women.

"She's not even of age!" someone yells from within the group.

The girl is thrown against her mother. Maggie presses her body against her daughter as well as she can with arms tied behind her back. The girl is small, maybe only five feet tall. She's thin like all of East's people. Even with her tiny frame, the girl is striking, and I wish I knew her name. She rubs her head where the hair was pulled by Mid's guard. It's a deep black mane, straight and sleek. Her eyes are just as dark, glinting within her contrasting pale skin.

The commotion pries Aaron's attention away from one of his airrides. He speaks to a trio of guards and then walks over to East's women.

As if the girl's predicament is disturbing his tight timeline, he says, "Load them all into the airride already."

"No!" screams Grobe's wife. "Not her! You can't take my daughter. She's only twelve."

Aaron looks at the black-haired girl, not even a teenager yet, halting his gaze on her face. He picks up her chin in one hand, inspecting her like a piece of ripe fruit. "What's your name?"

The girl doesn't speak, glaring at Aaron with a stubbornness that I know won't please Mid's Elected.

Aaron consults a nearby guard and then pulls Maggie over by the sleeve of her dress. "What is your daughter's name?" His words are defined, each one a staccato of anger. Aaron presses one of the smaller guns into her back.

"Gretchen," she says, panting out the word.

"Gretchen," Aaron repeats, testing out the sound on his lips. He tosses Maggie aside so that she stumbles onto the ground. He takes the girl's chin within his hand again, this time holding it tighter. Aaron's voice rolls over his tongue as he stares at Gretchen. "Can you bear children yet?"

The girl refuses to give an answer, but Aaron automatically looks over to Maggie who shakes her head vigorously no.

Aaron continues to look over the girl, tipping his head to one side. He pulls a finger over her collarbone, lingering over the tender curve of Gretchen's snow-white neck. "Well, then we can wait a year or two to breed her. Take her as well," he juts his chin toward the closest guard.

"No!" Maggie's yelp rings out clear over the now reverent group. "I'll do double the duties! Produce my own share of babies, plus hers! Leave her here, and I'll do anything you like!"

Aaron laughs. It's a cool, low chuckle, different from the high-pitched ones he emitted upon entering East Country. "You? How old are you?"

Maggie gulps, and even from this distance I can see her shoulders starting to shake in defeat. "Thirty-nine."

Aaron's laugh languishes, reverberating off the mining hills to our left. "Too old! You have, what, maybe one baby left in you? Leave her behind," he instructs another guard. "I don't need the trouble."

Gretchen's mother screams again, and she doesn't let up until a guard thumps her over the head with his gun. She falls heavily onto the packed soil, an audible crack emanating from a twisted limb. She's unconscious but still hopefully alive. There's been no bullet put in her head, like they did to Grobe. At least not yet.

"Dispose of her," Aaron says. He doesn't spare Gretchen's mother another look as he turns to go and a guard steps forward to follow his instructions.

I expect the daughter to scream. To fall at her mother's side amid the fray. To beg them to let her mother be. But Gretchen stands stock-still, glaring at Aaron with her coal eyes.

I pull myself off the ground with Griffin leaning heavily against my side. The guard who was watching me turns, reminded that in the tumult, he's still in charge of his bound prisoner. He raises his gun to strike me again.

I call out before the guards can hit me or move Maggie. "Aaron, you're wasting my time! Take us already!"

It's enough of a distraction that the guard assigned to Gretchen's mother looks up.

Aaron turns slowly, raising a hand for everything to stall. "So quick to leave your country behind, Aloy? You won't be seeing it ever again. And when I'm done with you, you won't even *remember* it."

I shrug in his direction, Gretchen's coolness reminding me not to give Aaron the satisfaction of a heated response.

"I don't know exactly what you and my brother did together," says Aaron, "but there will be no more informal references to your new country's leader. You are to call me *Elected*!" Aaron walks in my direction and grabs the rifle from my guard. He uses the end to sock me in the stomach, pushing the wind out of my chest and causing me to double over.

Griffin tries to protect me but slumps over when I can no longer hold him up. "Stop," he groans. "Take me instead of the girl and Aloy. I can help you."

"You?" scoffs Aaron. "Help *me*? Please!" He throws his head back.

Griffin tries to stand up so his injury won't look so bad. But I can almost smell the iron tinge of the blood that soaks the back of his shirt.

"I can keep Mid's clone program going. And you owe me a debt for helping save your life on top of the rocket launcher too."

Aaron seems to deliberate on this idea for a moment, automatically staring at Cole who's sitting cross-legged under the rifle of a Mid guard. Cole's hands are linked together in his lap, a dutiful puppy hoping to please. I still can't be sure where his allegiance lies. Maybe to whomever looks like they're most in control.

"I don't owe you anything," says Aaron. "Letting Aloy live pays the debt for both of you, if not more. And why in the world, after the display you provided, would I want clones around who could impersonate me?"

"For the body parts," I say even though I wince at the thought. No matter where Cole's allegiance stands now, he upheld his part of the bargain in the campaign against Mid, and he doesn't deserve to be harvested. I say the words, but I don't mean them.

"I won't get sick. I have the purple pills," says Aaron. "You see, Griffin, you'll be of no use to me. You're a dead man, anyway. I'd say you have just a few hours until you bleed out." He laughs again and makes a small snapping gesture to the nearest guard. The man kicks Griffin's legs out from under him, sending him sprawling hard into the dirt next to me.

"But I wouldn't mind a butler who looks like my dear brother waiting on my every need. Just for old time's sake! Take the clone," Aaron says.

A guard grasps Cole's arm roughly, pulling him up. Cole plods along behind the guard as they make their way to an open airride. Cole peers back at me and Griffin, but he makes no attempt to run or fight back.

"No more delays!" yells Aaron. "Get the women loaded already. As Aloy so nicely reminded me, we're wasting time!"

Aaron glances in my direction and watches as two guards lift me off my feet, holding me under the armpits. He sees me lose the struggle, as my legs are pried upward, and I'm forced forward.

What he doesn't see is the second exchange between Griffin and me while we're still both on the ground. Our eyes lock, and I catch the three words he mouths before I'm taken away.

"Use Vienne's microchip."

I THINK I CAN hear Maggie regain consciousness, screaming after her daughter, begging them to leave her behind. But I block out the sounds of East as I step inside Mid's monstrosity. If I listen to Maggie's pleading or think about Grobe's fate, I'll crumble from the inside out. Instead, I look around me, taking in everything I can about Mid's technology.

The inside of the airride is cool and dark in complete contrast to the rays of light peeking through the thin windows. There are no seats, just a large open cavity that we're prodded into like cattle. We're silently sorted into lines, the butts of the guards' guns doing all of the necessary communicating.

The ramp into the airride closes, and Aaron takes his position toward the front of the vessel. A few of the women near me gasp as the plane rises into the sky. We stand in rows across the belly of the airride with white satchels of compressed air suspended in front and back of our torsos. Without the satchels across our chests, I'm sure we'd have stumbled forward. The airbags shift with the flow of the plane, feeling like pillows. It's not altogether uncomfortable, and under other circumstances, I'd even be enjoying my first flight. Up in the clouds it's almost easy to forget there's anything important down on the ground. Except that "almost" is a million miles away from entirely. I can't stop thinking about Griffin, Glory, and all the rest of my people back in East. What are the guards doing to them now? Is anyone healing Griffin?

Vienne is three quarters of the way in back, closer to Margareath than to me. When I crane my head to search for them, I see Vienne whispering something to Margareath who nods in return. I wonder what they're discussing and if Vienne really kept the microchip, not destroying it as she told me during one of our border meetings. If Griffin knew something I didn't, I'm sure Tomlin has the chip and is figuring out how it can be used to our advantage. We'll have to find a way to access Mid's surveillance hub to hear what East communicates.

I stare out the window as menacing gray clouds gather fast around the airride to our left. Another storm. I assume Mid's airrides are advanced enough to withstand the acid rains, but when I hear the pelts of hail against the roof, I see some of the women cower in fear. I call out, "Don't worry. They won't penetrate."

"No talking!" yells a guard.

I shut my mouth but know that my few words at least helped calm my countrymen. I start to close my eyes and get set for the ride onward. I have no idea what Aaron will do with me upon return to Mid, and these might be my last moments of semi-peacefulness. The look on Griffin's face as I left pierces my thoughts. I try to picture his amber eyes without their slant of worry and the hard muscles of his arms without a bullet hole struck through the shoulder. If I have to stay far from Griffin again, I at least want to picture the man who saved me in Mid, not the one on his knees left in East.

Mid left forty guards to round up the men of East Country. I wonder who is a healer of those left—who can fix Griffin's wounds. Not Tomlin. Hopefully, he made it back to the marshlands with Glory. Grobe is dead. Maybe Albine, Margareath's husband? I never did get to find out if he made it through Mid's initial attack.

"They shouldn't have taken Gretchen," says a voice to my right. I open my eyes and stare at the woman next to me. We're shoulder to shoulder, so she doesn't have to speak loud to converse with me. I nod, not knowing what else to say. I've failed my people yet again and have no other plan than an old microchip.

"I mean, losing both your parents on the same day? How awful!" The woman shakes her head. I recognize the lady as one of East's "talkers" who was in charge of spreading my father's speeches throughout the stands at our town halls. I search for her name within my memory and am pleased to remember it without much consternation.

"Amelia," I say. "You were good at your job."

"Call me Mel. And thank you."

I nod my head in acknowledgement of her nickname. "At least Gretchen's mother is okay. Maybe a broken arm is all."

"Yes, at least there's that. But Gretchen has seen more than her fair share of bad luck over the years. You'd think the Heavens would let it average out over different people rather than heap it all on one family."

I wrinkle my brow, trying to remember what Mel refers to. "What bad luck?"

"Ah, maybe you were too young to have given it much thought. You were only thirteen at the time, but Gretchen's sister's sickness was the talk of the town for months. She was the youngest ever to contract cancer."

The hair on the back of my arms prickles. Mel continues, "Gretchen was eight when Aurora miraculously overcame the disease. She loved her sister with a ferocity after that. Like any minute Aurora might be taken from her again."

I know exactly whose family Mel refers to. Aurora was the three-year-old recipient of my purple pill-laced cupcake. It wasn't a miraculous cure. It was my fake cold that enabled the stolen pill to enact its miracle.

I look away from Mel, hiding the faint outline of my smile as I remember. Then I glance back. "If Aurora was cured, why do you call it bad luck for Gretchen, then?" I ask.

Mel shakes her head. "Well, to not only lose her parents but her sister in the same day, she must be heartbroken."

"Aurora's in the marshland? Left behind, right?"

"Yes, she's still there."

"Well, that's good luck then, wouldn't you say?" I ask.

"Gretchen should have been with them, being only twelve, but she came back to fetch food for Aurora when they got the hawk's note. Thought she could sneak in and out during the distraction and bring food back for the children."

My head falls forward, a little more of my hope ebbed away with Mel's words. "The children are starving in the marshlands?"

Mel realizes the extra burden she's loaded onto my shoulders and finally stops chattering. She snaps her lips closed with affirmation.

The rest of the airride trip is quiet. When we can see Mid's city in the distance, many of the women gasp in surprise. It's the first time they're viewing exactly how our neighbor broke the Accords. Word of Mid's excesses was passed around after Griffin's and my return, but seeing the truth for themselves is much more telling. A few of the women gasp in surprise.

Aaron leaves the cockpit when the noise flows up to his seat. "Ladies, ladies, calm yourselves." His voice does not soothe. It riles my people even more. "You'll give birth in the most technologically advanced centers you've ever seen. You won't die in childbirth. Won't that be nice?"

He stops in front of Gretchen in the first row, and I wish I could see her face as she matches his stare.

"We offer the utmost of comfort as you lay splayed on our operating tables." Aaron's tinny laugh sounds like he's selling us some twisted, horror-filled vacation. He looks at us with one eyebrow raised, as if to see who wants to buy what he's hocking. When no one joins in on the laughter, not even the guards standing nearby, Aaron continues, "We even have something called *Anna Stejia* to keep you pain-free during the worst of it."

I grimace at Aaron's soliloquy. If he thinks some pain medication is enough to placate my people, he's got another thought coming. I wonder what he's got planned to keep the women in check and stop any uprisings. He can't have enough hospital prison rooms to house each of us separately.

I don't have to wait long to find out, because soon Aaron walks up the aisle to stand in front of me. "I realize you all may not look forward to spending the rest of your days as breeders. Maybe you thought you'd be having a baby with the love of your life as your partner." He draws out his words and rolls his eyes as he says them. "Or maybe you thought you were done pushing out pups. So you're not in the best of spirits arriving in my country, are you?"

A few of the women near me grunt in reply. One calls out, "Not so much."

I can't help but smile a faint line of defiance as Aaron looks toward me.

"Understandable. But I have something that may squelch your bad moods and keep you producing without any unnecessary backlash," he says.

I shake my head, actually looking forward to what ridiculous idea Aaron may have cooked up. Nothing will stop my women from fighting back, even if their legs are strapped down during impregnation.

"What? Aloy, you think me incapable of enacting a viable deterrent?" I don't say anything, keeping my eyes chilly on his. "Ladies, you love your Elected, don't you?" He waits a beat and then goes on. "I saw the way you all volunteered yourselves in her place earlier today. 'Me. Me. It's me.'" He taunts us with a falsetto voice, imitating East's women who said they were me when Calix's guards went searching. "Well, as you seem to love her so much, I promise to keep Aloy alive." There are a few murmurs of positive reaction from the women. "That is, *unless* even *one* of you defies me. Got that?"

Aaron walks around us, through the aisles, arriving behind me. "You keep producing babies, and I won't give Aloy my special medical and purple pill combination that'll drive her completely bonkers." Aaron grasps my bound wrists and squeezes, hissing into my ear. "I don't even know what large doses of optogenetics would do to someone who's swallowed purple pills her whole life. I only had one dose a month. But if anyone acts up and refuses to be the *bitch* they're meant to be, I'll give you one dose a week!" Aaron sneers out the last sentences, sending a wash of spittle toward my right cheek.

I don't give him the satisfaction of even blinking. I keep my eyes straightforward as Aaron releases my wrists and then walks back to the airride's cockpit, slamming the flimsy door behind him.

His words don't scare me. I already realized he'd use me in some malicious way. Why else bring me along if I can't even produce babies for him? If anything, his words just invigorate me further. I'll be damned if Aaron's going to impregnate even *one* of my people with the threat of my wellbeing hanging over their heads. I'll tell them to fight back no matter what. *No one* will lie still on my account.

THE DESCENT INTO MID Country is smoother than I imagine. I had expected jolts and to be thrown around as we hit the ground. In fact, most of the women suck in their breath, bracing themselves for impact. But the plane lands like it's on a pocket of air, pillowing down onto the roof of a high building with barely a thump.

The women handle the views well, none of them ever having been up so high. A few people look nauseated, white with the fear of heights, but for the most part, we're unscathed from the twenty-minute ride.

"Everyone out!" yells a guard at the front of the airride. I stare at the compressed air bag in front of me as it deflates and slides into a pocket in the ceiling. We're all free, except for the cords binding our hands behind our backs. But I can move front and back now, and I can't help bending down so that my spine stretches.

"Stand tall, ladies!" shouts Aaron from the doorway. "You're about to enter your new home!" Mid's leader looks like he's holding the door for us, but I know better than to think he has a chivalrous bone in his body. I'm sure he's just there on principle; if we don't step out fast enough, he'd probably push us.

The airride's hatch unlocks with a hiss, as compressed air collides with fresh oxygen. I didn't realize my head felt cloudy inside the plane, but after the door is open and I get my first breath of real air again, I wonder how we didn't all suffocate inside the airride.

The sky is still gray with heavy clouds hanging low. I hope they'll get us inside fast before the rain sweeps down again. Aaron stops me with one hand when I'm next to him. "Remember my promise," he says.

I meet his eyes. "You mean your threat?"

"If you'd like to think of it that way, yes." He chuckles. I'm about to step forward, but Aaron checks me again. "All of the other women are going straight to the hospital. But you and Cole are coming with me." I purse my lips, but don't say anything, instead proceeding past him as the line continues to move.

Building seven isn't the tallest structure in Mid, but it's one of the outermost buildings, convenient for landing. It has no guardrails along the top, so all of us are careful not to take a wrong step. We stick close together, as if crowding like salmon in a narrow line will stop any of us from being blown over the building's side by a strong wind.

I'm next to Gretchen before I even realize it. When I do, I can't help looking down at her little body. She's only six years younger than me, but she's a full four inches shorter, which makes me feel like I should protect her even more.

"I'm sorry about your father," I say.

Gretchen looks over at me but doesn't say anything.

I continue, "I know he and I didn't always agree, but he was a stalwart supporter of East Country, and I'm grateful for his sacrifice."

The girl looks away from me, staring instead over the horizon in the direction of our country. When she still doesn't utter a word, I'm compelled to keep talking, even though I don't think my words are helping at all. It just doesn't seem right to leave her without more of an assurance that I'll do what I can to save her from Aaron.

"I won't let them hurt you," I say.

This time Gretchen turns in my direction, her movement sharp as if she's tightening all of her muscles at once. "Just like you took care of my sister?"

I blink once, unsure of what she means.

"Griffin told me," Gretchen says. "The cupcake." Her voice sounds appreciative, but the fist forming at her side is more telling of her inner emotions. I don't know what to make of her. "She got the cancer again, you know, and now there's nothing you can do for her. No pills to give her. No family to hold her hand as she gets sicker."

I stare at my shoes, which are making soft imprints in the crumbling concrete and dust still swirling with the airride's landing. I can't offer any words of encouragement. I can't even tell her I understand—that my lifelong teacher Tomlin is descending into the depths of the same disease and I can't be with him either. Gretchen is already mourning, and nothing I say now will ease the pain.

And then a thought flickers in my brain. There is something that can help. And it's conveniently here in Mid.

My eyes alight as I lean in close. "We can help her. Mid Country still has purple pills. When we mount an insurrection, we'll steal them from Aaron and give them to Aurora." I don't bother explaining that it'll just take one pill to cure her sister. It sounds better to say we'll give Aurora as many pills as Gretchen would like.

The girl seems to consider this for a moment. "Do you promise?" Her dark eyes seem to grow larger, the pupils dilating as she stares at me. No wonder Aaron was infatuated with her. When she's intense like that, it's almost impossible to look away from her.

"I do." I've made so many promises already, I just add this one to the long list of responsibilities I carry on my shoulders. One more doesn't even tip the scales.

Aaron walks out of the airride behind the last of my people. He grasps Cole's elbow and leads him to the front of the group toward an elevator door. I wonder if the women will have as much trepidation about the elevator as I did upon arriving in Mid for the first time.

"You're coming with me too," Aaron says in my direction. He doesn't bother waiting for an agreement or even looking at me. He thinks I'll just trot after him obediently.

I do plan to follow Aaron without a fuss, but first I have to speak to Vienne, and this might be my only opportunity for a while. I find her face close enough within the crowd and push through to reach her side.

"Aloy, where is he taking you?" she asks.

"I don't know, but it doesn't matter. Even if it's back to the prison, I'll find some way to break out. It won't be like last time where I let them keep me confined for so long."

She's about to say something else, probably something intending to be comforting. It's just like Vienne to think about my feelings when she and the rest of the women are in just as much jeopardy as I am. I don't let her speak, though, continuing on without as much as a breath of air in between my sentences. "The microchip in East Country—you didn't actually destroy it?" I ask.

Vienne looks confused for a split second, but it's only an instant. I see the understanding reach her eyes before I have to explain further.

"Grobe had it. I'm sure someone in East took it off his body when he fell."

I lower my voice to a whisper, "I'm going to try to reach Surveillance to hear our people in East communicating through the chip, but if I don't make it, you'll have to do so. Find out how East intends to fight so that we can be ready to help. Our women won't just wait idly for rescue, but it would be good to know what East's planning so we can coordinate efforts."

Vienne looks at me with a touch of skepticism. "We don't know that they'll be able—"

I cut her off, already spying a guard moving in my direction to enforce Aaron's order. "Yes." I say the word with conviction. "They'll be able to combat Mid's guards and surmount an insurrection. I *know* it."

I can't let Vienne or anyone else sense anything but my complete and utter hopefulness. If I let even a fraction of doubt edge its way into my own mind, I'm afraid I'll crumble from the inside out. If East isn't able to mount a campaign, that means only one thing—Griffin didn't make it to lead the fight. I can't let myself even think about such a scenario.

So I stand a little taller and walk away from my best friend with my head held high.

7

It's just me, Aaron, Cole, and two of Mid's guards in the elevator as the box descends fifteen floors to the ground. When the doors open, I'm hit straight in the face with a stench of sweat. There are maybe two thousand people crowded at the opening. They start yelling as soon as Aaron steps aside and my face is seen.

"Kill her now!" they screech. "Show no mercy!"

I'm surprised by the crowd's insistence, but I shouldn't be. Last time I left Mid they intended to execute me for treason. I shrink back against the wall of the elevator. Aaron promised the women I wouldn't be harmed, right? I'm momentarily dizzy, thinking that it's entirely within the realm of Aaron's behavior to make such rash decisions. Say one thing and then do another.

However, Aaron steps in front of me, his arms out wide to his people. "My minions," he says, sweeping one arm across the expanse of the crowd. "Now, now. As your Elected, I beseech you to restrain yourselves. Yes, it would feel delightfully satisfying to have our enemy's head on a pike, but rest assured, I have plans for her."

The people reel in their anger but still look at me with stony, glassy eyes. They're like zombies, even more so than when I left. Like their degree of optogenetics has been heightened in my two-week absence.

Aaron pushes me forward, pointing at me like some kind of trophy he's just won for a fencing contest. An object to be displayed on a shelf— useless, yet coveted. "She will be a symbol. A show of our strength. We will not make a martyr of her. Instead, we will use her for technological knowledge. If she refuses" —he looks at me, his eyes glinting in the little light reflected off the stormy clouds— "then we will strike her down just as we disposed of her parents!"

The crowd roars in agreement, and the din hurts my ears. Even Cole makes a motion to cover his, burrowing his head against his chest. I almost forgot he was standing next to me, he's been so quiet, a captive mouse respecting a looming cat. He leans in close to me, his shoulder bumping mine so that I turn toward Cole's face. "He won't hurt you, don't worry," Cole says.

I shift my shoulder away from Cole, and in so doing, knock him to the side. I don't want the clone touching me. I don't need his pity. "I'm not worried," I growl.

If this *thing* beside me can see any hint of anxiety on my face, then I need to put on a better mask. I control the muscles in my cheeks so that my face goes slack. My eyes glaze as I stare straight into the crowd, daring them to come one inch closer to me. I won't flinch, even if they do. I won't have the women from East Country descending in their elevator to see me shaking in front of Mid's masses.

Griffin would want me to stay fierce. Tomlin would expect it. My father would accept nothing except my complete, unflinching strength.

"Let's go," says Aaron. The crowd parts for us as Aaron walks forward. We're flanked on either side by a steady stream of people, but no one dares touch me. We move toward building thirteen, where Calix lived in the penthouse. It was his parent's apartment, and when we step into the gilded lobby, I'm sure Aaron has overtaken the suite again. Where else would he live?

So I'm not being taken to the prison. At least not yet.

I try to imagine what Aaron wants with me up in his living quarters. As we walk, though, the way he rubs a thumb over my shoulder answers my questions more clearly than anything he could even say. His fingers play at the edge of my sleeve, fumbling with the fabric. A few of his fingers slide up the skin on my upper arm, and I wince, pulling away. If he hasn't been able to share physicality with anyone from Mid Country, will I be the vessel for his release? Without optogenetics, perhaps Aaron's needs are more prevalent, like a prisoner released after years in darkness. I'm already contemplating how I'll kick Aaron to get out of the situation and if that could yield repercussions for any of my people. Will Aaron take revenge on them for my non-complacency? And if I do act obedient, how will I turn off my mind so that he's hurting only my body, not my brain?

Aaron deposits the two guards outside the elevator doors when we hit the top floor. The hallway toward Aaron's suite is just as I remember it. Long with stark white walls. But there's a new rancid smell coming from the only door on this floor. At first it's just a slight tangy scent, but with each step, the air is heavier with an increasingly putridity. I'm not the only one who notices.

"I think your fruit has gone bad," says Cole. It's the first thing he's said straight to Aaron, and I'm just a little surprised Cole's first sentence wasn't something more along the lines of hero worship. His words actually sound chiding.

I sneak a peek and see that Cole's nose is wrinkled. Aaron turns to Cole, rounding on the clone with teeth exposed. His eyes are fiery, but there's something else on the Elected's features too —embarrassment.

"You job isn't to *think* anything, robot," says Aaron. "You're merely here to wait on me."

Cole doesn't seem to realize Aaron is peeved. He keeps talking. "Actually, Elected, I am not a robot. I am a clone, a real-live functioning hu—"

"Yes, a clone of my *brother.* I know. And that makes you *trash*! As such, your first job as my slave is to clean up the garbage in my apartment."

I can't help it; one of my eyebrows rises without even thinking. I don't need to direct any more of Aaron's wrath toward myself. But he sees the slight movement.

"What? You think something is funny, Aloy? You want to get on your hands and knees and lick the spoiled fruit off the floor, do you?"

I clear my throat and just look straight ahead.

Aaron continues, "I heard about your little obsession with our vitamin-laced oranges. I bet you wouldn't even care that they were rotten. You'd still lap them up!" His mouth is a tangle of lips, snarling in my face.

It's true I did like the neon pink oranges. But one at a time. The smell wafting from under Aaron's closed door is indicative of entire bushels of the fruit. I wonder what he was doing with so many.

We're in front of the gold doors in a couple more steps, and Aaron looks down at the biometric display. He pauses for a moment and then leans forward, opening one eye wide. Aaron steps back, satisfied, but when the door doesn't click open, his brow furrows, and he tries his eye again. Again, the door refuses to budge.

Cole glances at me behind Aaron's back, shrugging his shoulders. I don't acknowledge his gesture. Aaron tries one more time, and then slams his fist down against the bio-entry pad. A slow coolness works its way up my back, ending at the base of my skull.

Aaron doesn't know how to get in.

Aaron pushes on the double doors of his apartment. When he doesn't feel any slack, he leans his whole body into the job, his brow erupting in perspiration.

My voice is slow, as if the idea is dawning on me as I speak each next word. "You don't remember how your own technology works in Mid, do you?"

Aaron grumbles, glancing back at me with squinted eyes. "Just an error with the system. I *know* how it works. Biometrics, of course."

"But you don't remember the details. The entry pads take finger-prints, not eye scans."

A memory seems to strike Aaron, and he nods fast. His fingers fumble at the bio-pad again, trying one and then another digit.

"It's your index finger," I finally say when he's gone through his pinky and the thumbs on both hands.

Aaron presses the correct finger onto the pad, and the front doors swing wide. He steps through the entry with Cole close on his heels.

I stand in the doorway, staring inside. Hundreds, if not thousands, of oranges, half-peeled and quartered, lie in decomposing piles on the floor of Aaron's living room. Fruit flies circle the stinking mess, forming black shifting clouds in the air. I suck in my breath, the smell of the rot-ting fruit hitting me full in the nostrils. I don't think I'll ever be able to look at the vitamin-laced oranges again without gagging.

"But why—" I start. And then it hits me, another cold shiver reaching up my spine. "You're not completely cured after stopping the optogenetics procedures. You tried to eat as much of the vitamin-infused super fruit as possible, thinking that would help. But it didn't, did it? You still can't remember everything."

Aaron whirls around, striking me in the chest with one open palm. It doesn't hurt, but the force pushes me backward out of his apartment.

"Get out! I thought I might find something attractive in you, but my brother was completely wrong. You're *nothing* that anyone would want!"

With both hands raised, Aaron slams the doors in my face, and I'm left completely alone in the white hallway, nose still inches from the mahogany and gold plated entrance of the Elected's disturbing living quarters.

I DON'T HAVE TO wait long for company. I look down the long, white hallway, wondering if I'm free to go where I please, even contemplating running toward Mid's city gates and breaking for home. But no more than ten seconds later, two muscled guards unlatch unseen doors in the walls and flank me on both sides. One with bushy black eyebrows and a bald head pulls at the nylon bindings around my wrists, directing me down the hall back to the elevator.

"Make it tighter," says the second guard. Bushy Eyebrows complies, readjusting the rubbery bands until my wrists throb.

"Do you have any idea what's going on in there?" I ask them, jerking my chin toward Aaron's apartment. The two guards continue looking forward, silent. "It's not hygienic. Your Elected is crazy. Someone needs to monitor him." I sigh. "Help him, at the very least. He's messed up after coming off optogenetics."

The guards still don't utter a word, and I fall silent in step with them as well. If they don't care about their ruler, then I certainly shouldn't either. Except that he's a madman who now controls the women from my country, and I don't know how to get us out of his grip.

The elevator ride back down is fast. I brace myself for yet another onslaught of an angry Mid mob. But everyone seems to have dispersed, presumably returning to work in the various tall buildings all over the city center. The two guards lead me past the repaired former wreckage of Tower One. I can't help looking up toward its tip, which is immersed in the clouds above. The whole structure bends just slightly with the wind. I can't help wondering how the tower would fare if we're besieged by another set of earthquakes.

The last set of terrible natural disasters occurred before I was born, but my parents told me they were horrific, opening chasms in the earth's floor. My father even lost a childhood friend down one of the gaping holes. The quakes were enough to create new topography and landscape, which is partly how we ended up with more nirogene mines. Tomlin says it was "a blessing in disguise," but I can't agree. Who needs more nirogene when it's at the expense of the environment killing its own people? Nature is no nurturing mother, as far as I'm concerned.

Since the last onslaught of earthquakes, we've only felt slight tremors, which crack miniscule fissures in the clay walls of our East Country houses. Did Calix or Aaron ever think how their tall buildings would fare in another set of catastrophic earthquakes? Do they even care?

I could keep thinking about the possible effects of environmental disaster forever, but my thoughts are punctured by a more immediate need to pay attention to where we're heading. I won't let the guards take me to the prison again. I don't think I can stand another solitary confinement for months on end. Heaven help me, if we're moving in that direction, I'll throw caution to the wind and just start running. I bet I'd be faster than these behemoths anyway. They're so hulky with their guns and metal armor, I could probably beat them any day.

In fact, I'd be willing to take the risk now and make a blind run, but the consequences to my people ring in my head like a bell that tolls anytime I get any tempting ideas of escaping. The gong in my brain thumps faster now as we walk in what looks like the exact direction of the prison. My heart beats so hard I'm sure if I don't calm down soon it'll shatter the surrounding ribcage. Mid wouldn't possibly put me back in that room where they performed my surgery, right? They can't possibly . . . it wouldn't be humane.

"Stop shuffling your feet!" says the guard on my left. He's freckled with a buzz cut of ginger hair. "Move faster."

I take a deep breath and pick up my pace, finally rewarded when we pass the prison. "Where are we going?" I ask when I think I can speak words without my voice sounding like a squeak.

"With all of the other breeders, of course."

"But I thought I wouldn't be used for—" I catch myself mid-sentence, this new horror shocking. "They took out my . . . I can't have babies." It's one thing to help repopulate the earth, but to be used just for . . . It's too much to accept.

Bushy Eyebrows glances down at me. He squints for a moment and his cheek twitches. "Orders are just to put you with the others. Don't know the Elected's other plans."

Okay, so maybe I'll just be living with the other women. That would be a good thing. I count to five in my head, keeping my breathing steady enough for the intake to last through all the numbers.

The hospital is exactly as I remember it. White walls, just like the rest of Mid's buildings. But the smell of antiseptic is strong, and it sends a rush of memory through my nostrils straight into my head. This was where they kept Glory. Where I tried to rescue him the first time and failed. This is where they saved my son with new lungs.

The dichotomy of my thoughts about Mid's technology is torturous. On the one hand, I hate Mid Country for pulling my baby out of me like the gizzards of a chicken and then keeping him here in some terrible science experiment. But at the same time, it was Mid's technology that saved his life.

I'm led across the same main hallway Griffin, Margareath, and I took toward the incubation room. When I actually see the wide windows of the baby's nursery, I think the sight will hurt like acid being poured on already burnt skin, but my heart feels almost hollow. The nightmares that plagued me about this place turn out to be worse than the incubation chamber itself. There are no infants in the five plastic bubbles within the room. The wall into which Glory's machinery was plugged is empty. It looks like no one was ever here, the room is so clean and undisturbed. I wonder what happened to the nurse who was so determined we be caught that night. Did they punish her for letting us through her grasp or reward her for such a fervent attempt at stopping us?

The guards take a sharp left down yet another long corridor and stop at the third door in. I don't hear any voices and think maybe it's a trick. I'm not being led back to my people but into yet another hellish situation. But when Bushy Eyebrows opens the heavy metal door, four hundred sets of eyes turn to meet mine.

"Aloy!" Vienne rushes at me, throwing both arms around my shoulders. "Are you alright?"

Margareath moves near us too, a smile peeking across her face. "He couldn't perform, could he?"

So they'd all deduced the same ugly idea of Aaron's intention as I had.

"I was so worried!" Vienne says. Then she looks at my bound wrists, which are starting to chafe and bleed in the cinched-tight nylon. Vienne gestures to Bushy Eyebrows. "Well, aren't you going to release her?" The guard stares at Vienne for an extra-long beat. With Vienne's corn silk blonde hair past her waist and all the scars across her face and neck, she's a sight even the unobservant people in Mid can't reconcile. Gorgeous and grotesque at the same time.

"Yeah, you can't leave her like that forever. How's she supposed to sleep in those?" Margareath is insistent, taking a daring step closer to Buzz Cut.

"Are you disrespecting my authority?" He lurches forward, raising a fist, but Bushy Eyebrows grabs Buzz's wrist, mid-air.

"No need," the bald-headed guard says toward his colleague. "Save your aggression for their first escape attempt." Then he faces Margareath. With unblinking eyes Bushy Eyebrows says, "And that attempt had better not be you. Back. Down." I can't tell if he's threatening her or just trying to defuse the situation.

When Margareath doesn't move, Bushy Eyebrows takes a step closer to her.

"Hey," I say, my voice quiet. The tension in the room is thick, a dangerous layer that threatens to coat us all before we can even devise some wiser plan for interaction with Mid's people. I raise my chin toward Bushy Eyebrows. "We know you're in charge here, believe me." And then at Margareath: "And I'm fine. I appreciate you standing up for me, but if they want to torture me with a few more hours of suppression, I'm sure it's not without need." I look up at Buzz Cut. "These two brawny men up against all hundred and ten pounds of me. Could be quite a scuffle."

Bushy Eyebrows shakes his head, turning his face away from me for a split second. "Cut the bindings," he instructs Buzz Cut from under his breath. The second guard steps forward and produces a retractable knife, which, when extended, shimmers with the glint of diamonds. It slices through the nylon as if nothing were there, and my arms drop free to my sides.

My wrists throb with the sudden release of blood, but I refuse to give Mid's guards the satisfaction of seeing me hold them.

"Be careful, Aloy," says Bushy Eyebrows. "As I understand it, last thing you want is any scuffle that sends you straight to the doctors."

I stare after both guards as they leave the dormitory. Guards stand stationed outside our one dormitory entrance, but we're left alone inside the room. Vienne wraps a hand around my bleeding wrists, bending down to get a good look at them. The room around me rings with conversation as the ladies of East Country mill around me closer. The sounds are a dense din, but everything seems like background noise. I just keep staring after the guards who just exited.

If optogenetics is still a secret, how did the bushy eye-browed guard know *anything* about what occurs at the doctors?

9

WE SLEEP IN COTS lined up one next to another. The room is a cacophony of sounds: women shedding tears, using the restroom in the corner, preparing their beds for sleep, eating food Mid delivers via wall cut-outs, and just the general apprehensive conversation. I'm not used to so many people in such a tight space. Coming from my isolated position in East's White House and then being cocooned in Mid's solitary for four months, even the breathing of four hundred bodies resting near me renders it almost impossible to sleep.

When I turn to my side, eyes open in wakefulness, people stare back at me. When I get up to use the bathroom, fifty sets of eyes follow me.

Tonight, almost at the door of the commode, the soft pad of footsteps right behind halts my progress. "Look, I'm sorry, but I just need a little privacy," I say.

"Oh, I apologize." Vienne's voice is heavy.

When I turn, I'm looking into her creased brow. "No, wait," I say before she can turn around. "I didn't mean you . . . I just . . ." How can I admit to her that even though I love my people, it's hard being so close to so many of them at once. Even the words in my head seem spoiled.

Vienne just nods, indicating I don't have to explain further. Instead she asks, "Do you still dream about Glory?"

I expected Vienne to say something else—something comforting from her psychology lessons about understanding my need for space. But her question about Glory stops the breath in my throat. "Yes, all the time. Being here in the hospital makes it worse, I think."

For two nights I've tried to gather my strength, but even when I do fall asleep amid the snores and groans of four hundred bodies, the memories of Glory pour in and wake me with a fitful start. I just keep picturing him being eased out of his father's arms as Griffin takes a last dying breath. I dream about Glory growing up without me or Griffin. As an orphan. I have no way of knowing if either Griffin or Glory are all right. And the dreams of Glory that just used to show him in the incubator have grown more disturbing. When he grows up will he come to avenge his father, trying to show strength just like I've tried to do in avenging my Apa? I don't like the images of my baby grown up and fighting a foe I couldn't destroy.

Thus, in between nightmares, my fitful sleep is punctuated by trying to devise alternate plans for overthrowing Aaron.

"I like to think all our children are doing fine in East," Vienne says.

I know she's not only talking about Glory but also her daughter, Eve, who's hopefully still hidden in the marshlands.

"Eve is okay," I say.

"Mmmm . . ." Vienne looks away. "Aloy, I don't mean to rush you, but how many more days are we going to sit tight? The women grow more anxious with each passing day. I try to keep them calm, but with the threat of rape on top of everything else . . . it's . . ."

"Hard. I know. We'll act soon. As soon as Mid starts to use me for technology research, I'll somehow get to the surveillance hub. Maybe there's even a way to talk to Griffin and Tomlin through there instead of just waiting for their communication to us."

My voice sounds assured, but over the last two nights I've thought a lot about the chip. In all the discussions of the device, we never talked about two-way communication. All we know is that Vienne's conversations transmitted to Mid Country. I know nothing of an ability to communicate in the other direction. I don't think the microchip technology is even capable of such feats unless it can be hooked up to a speaker system and receiver, two pieces of banned machinery that I don't believe East Country owns.

I'm contemplating giving Vienne this news, but a soft knocking interrupts our conversation. We both look in the direction of the dormitory door, my eyebrows arched in surprise. It's got to be the middle of the night. Who would be coming to see us now? And what of the two guards stationed just outside?

I walk to open the door with Vienne on my heels and a few of the other roused women behind us. It seems wherever we go now, it's in a pack, even if it's just to the front door of our dormitory. When the person on the other side doesn't barge in, I take the liberty of trying the normally locked door myself. It cracks open without any resistance, and the sight on the other side takes my breath away.

"Ty!" I throw an arm around his shoulders and pull him inside before the boy can utter a word. "How'd you get out of your room? Are you all right?" The words pour out of me, and I'm rewarded by a tenuous smile from my former savior, the sharp-eyed thirteen-year-old boy who cared for twenty-three Mid Country children and who helped me, Margareath, and Griffin escape a month earlier.

"I'm fine," he says.

"Well, I'll be!" says Margareath throwing her legs over the side of her cot and joining us at the door. "Have you come to orchestrate our escape?"

Ty erupts with a small giggle. "I could manage hiding three of you in our wet linens, but I don't think I can hide hundreds in there."

"Hello," says Vienne extending her hand. Ty just looks at it, not understanding East Country's greeting ritual.

"They're not used to touching," I whisper to her, and Vienne instantly retracts.

"So nice to meet you in person, Ty. I've heard so much about you. I'm East Country's Madame Elected, and I want to thank you for what you did for my wife. I can't begin to—"

Ty cuts her off, shaking his head. "It was nothing."

I slap Ty on the shoulder, ignoring my own advice about touching the boy. "When we escape, you and the other children are coming with us."

"That's what I wanted to talk to you about," he says, a hand across his brow. "I only have three months left before I turn fourteen and am forced to start optogenetics. I was wondering when we might be bolting, now that you're here and all." His voice lilts up at the end, like he's scared I may say we're not leaving before his birthday.

"We're all wondering!" shouts a voice from the rear.

I ignore it and keep eye contact with Ty. "I'm working on it. But, tell us, how did you get out of your room?"

At this, Ty smiles so widely I can see the molars in the very back of his mouth. "I was tinkering with something before I helped you escape, and I think I've perfected it."

"What did you do?" asks Margareath, peering closer at Ty. She inches forward, circling his side to see if he's holding anything.

Ty doesn't answer. Instead, he walks to the door, pulling it back open. I'm about to tell Ty not to risk the guards seeing him in here, and to ask him how in the world he even got past the guards, and where in the heavens they are, when an orange-eyed nightmare of a robot stares back at us.

10

A FEW OF THE women around me, the ones with the best views, shriek. I jump forward, attempting to slam the door, but Ty stops me.

"The robot is mine," he says, his voice barely a whisper. I peer at Ty to see if he's sold us out. If he's somehow turned against us during our month's absence. Maybe they started his optogenetics treatments early. Maybe he's lying about hoping to escape. But the look on Ty's face is pure pride. He doesn't exhibit any of Mid's characteristic detachment. "Watch this," he says, pulling the robot inside the room. When the machine is fully planted within our walls and the heavy door is creaked shut once again, Ty commands it. "Come here!" Immediately the hunky metal beast takes two steps forward toward Ty. I suck in a long breath of air, not believing what I'm seeing.

"Sit down!" Ty commands next. The robot looks left and right, trying to find a seat. When one isn't close enough, the automaton drops down onto one knee and then intertwines its limbs to sit cross-legged on the floor. "See?" asks Ty. "I can make him do whatever I ask."

"Let me try!" says Margareath. She charges forward, facing the robot. "Stand up!" It doesn't move, and she stares at it, hands on hips, in frustration.

"It's only programmed to follow my orders," says Ty.

"This is fantastic!" says Vienne. "How wonderful!" She claps both hands to her mouth. "So that's how you evaded the guards outside."

"They leave every night. The robots take over after eleven p.m."

I think about that statement for a moment. If there are only automatons guarding us at night, and Ty can control them, our escape is immensely easier. Now we just have to figure out a way to contact East and get four hundred women through the streets of Mid without anyone noticing.

"How did you do it?" I ask Ty.

"I brought the robot into the optogenetics room," he answers, his face flushed with satisfaction.

"You messed with its mind." A voice in the back pipes up, indignant and clear. Gretchen wanders to the front of the room, stopping in front of Ty and the robot. Ty's mouth hangs open in response to the girl's blatant stare. She wears a meager black tank top and loose white linen pants, tied tight at the waist. Gretchen refuses to change into the shapeless brown robes Mid left on our beds. She's a tiny figure, but with her squinted eyes and jutted chin, Gretchen looks more imposing than her twelve years. Her voice doesn't help. It's sharp and accusatory.

"Yeah, I did," says Ty, mistaking Gretchen's attention for praise. His mouth opens into a large grin, the pride on his face as he looks from Gretchen to the robot too obvious. None of us foresee Gretchen's hand slapping him hard across the cheek. When it does, Ty is thrown off balance. He catches himself on a nearby table, staring at Gretchen and then at me, his eyes blinking furiously.

"Hey!" I say to Gretchen, my features hard.

"You're *one* of *them*!" she shrieks at Ty, pushing away my outstretched arm. "One of those awful doctors they threatened us with!"

"Shhhh!" says Margareath, grabbing Gretchen's arms behind her back. The girl thrashes, trying to get out of Margareath's grip. "He works with the doctors. They force all the children to do so." Then she stops and directs her words to Ty. "You aren't one of them now, are you?"

"Absolutely not!" Ty walks around the table. His eyebrows furrow, as if he's suddenly regretting his decision to show us the robot tonight.

I step forward, ignoring the scene Gretchen's created. I realize we'll need to get a handle on the girl. At best, hot-headedness is a liability in our predicament. At worst, it's a death sentence. At the moment, though, I focus on the robot still sitting on the floor in front of us with its blank orange eyes staring straight ahead. "Optogenetics works on machines?" I ask Ty.

"Yes, cool, ha?" The boy recovers himself, adjusting his robes and standing again next to the robot.

I stare at the automaton for one beat longer and then slowly let the smile starting in my lips make its way upward. New possibilities fly through my head. We could reprogram all of the robots with Ty's system. They could help me sneak into the central surveillance hub, for one. And then after that, who knows. Mount a revolution?

"How many of these robots can you program?" I ask.

"As many as I can get alone in the opto-rooms. Maybe one a day, if we're lucky."

"That's better than nothing," says Margareath, still holding a squirming Gretchen.

"I do have a few . . . procedures to help administer tomorrow," Ty admits. He looks sheepish, his eyes downcast, his foot absently shifting back and forth across the concrete.

Vienne picks up on Ty's sudden discomfort. "Do you have something else to tell us?" she asks him. Her face angles with the question, but she doesn't make any more attempts to touch the boy or move closer to him.

"I heard that tomorrow they're going to start taking each of you to the pregnancy labs," he says. Ty looks off at a distant wall as he says the words.

We don't need more of an explanation. The women all look toward me, as if I will tell them a way I plan to stop it. We knew it was coming, but hearing that the forced insemination will occur in just a few hours is hard to take.

When I don't say anything, Vienne responds, "It was going to start eventually." She catches Ty's eyes that appear to have fallen back on Gretchen. "We appreciate the warning."

Ty pulls his face from Gretchen's and says, "There's more." He turns in my direction, making eye contact again. "Mid is coming tomorrow to take you to the optogenetics lab too."

11

Vienne's voice, when it responds to Ty's announcement, is shrill. Very few times have I heard Vienne lose her temper, but this may turn out to be the worst. "Impossible!" She stamps one foot. "They said they wouldn't touch Aloy if we all complied! They haven't even given us a chance to show our obedience." She grips my arm with one hand. I don't know if it's to steady herself or me, but I certainly feel like falling to the ground, and Vienne's grasp is welcome.

Aaron *promised* he'd keep me out of the doctors' office, but apparently, after I figured out his memory problem, he's not abiding by any of our agreements now. I should have just kept my mouth shut. If he's putting me through optogenetics, then he's decided against using me for my technological knowledge. There's zero chance I'll have an opportunity to communicate with East's men in the comms hub. Now it'll definitely have to be the robots carrying out Ty's orders.

"I'm really sorry," Ty says to me. He's stopped looking me in the eyes again.

I just shake my head. If I open my mouth to say something, it might come out in a squeak, and I can't let my women know how afraid I am. I don't even know what I'd say if I attempted speech right now. Ask everyone if they wouldn't mind if I ran? Put them all in more danger so I could make a quick escape tonight and leave them all behind?

But Vienne says the words I don't dare. "You should go now." She points to the door.

I look at her again and then at East's women, who are now clustered in a semi-circle, which weaves in and out of the rows of cots. A part of me wants to take Vienne's suggestion—run now while the sun hasn't risen. Make my way to East Country. Somehow sneak in and tell the men when to mount their insurrection. Ensure my mind isn't erased as easily as chalk on a wall. The impulse to leave thumps in my chest, hard and rapid like one of Griffin's hawk's wings. But only the *idea* of an escape is appealing. The reality of leaving my women behind and risking their lives in exchange for my own isn't a real option.

"I'm staying," I say, my forehead now damp.

Vienne faces me, her head turned away from the rest of our people. "You know it won't be the typical optics appointment," she whispers. "Aaron's not giving you a dose to heighten your work ethic. His goal will be revenge." When I don't say anything, she continues. "Fight the treatment, at the very least, if you won't leave. Try to remember who you love." Vienne hisses her plea at me, the white of her teeth keeping my attention.

I force myself to focus on the way her mouth opens and closes as she speaks. If I dare stop staring at Vienne, I think my knees will start shaking. Knowing Aaron, I wonder if I'll even remember my own name when the procedure's finished.

Ty leaves the dormitory, his robot right behind. His head hangs as he glances back at us, even though he's given us the key to our eventual escape. Or at least the escape of all the other women. I probably won't want to leave after I've been sufficiently brainwashed.

When everyone finally shuffles back to their beds for the night an hour later, I find Gretchen among my people. "Hey," I call at her back. The hand she'd been twisting around a lock of black hair stills, and Gretchen slowly turns her head in my direction.

"You promised you'd get me home," she says, accusation flooding her words.

I look at the ceiling, rolling my eyes. "You'll still get home. With or without me. But there's some other things we need to discuss."

"Yeah?" she asks, her tone closed, already aimed at dispelling whatever I'm going to say.

"I know we're in a terrible situation and that your father was killed in front of you just days ago. Your mother was left in East, and you're still thinking of your sister. But getting in people's faces here, acting rebellious to Aaron, it won't be good for you. Stay under the radar, do you understand?"

"What does it matter to you?" Gretchen flicks her dark hair and bumps her foot into a nearby bedframe.

"We're trying to protect you so you're not picked as one of the breeders for a long, long time. Hopefully never because you'll break out by then. But don't get yourself noticed before we have a chance. There's more than one lady here who'd fall on her sword defending you. And you don't want to carry that guilt on your shoulders, believe me."

Gretchen looks away. I know I've at least piqued some degree of caution in her. "And" —I clear my throat— "I need you to look out for Ty."

Gretchen swivels around on the balls of her feet. "What?" The word erupts from her lips, enunciated on each letter so that the *T* could knock someone down if it had any more air behind it.

"He's all alone over there, leading those kids who are younger than he is. You're the only one his same age. When I'm—" I can barely make out the words.

"Incapacitated?" she provides coolly.

"Yes. When I'm . . . unable to look out for him, will you make sure he has someone to talk to?"

"Maybe an adult would be a better choice," Gretchen says, stopping her assault on the bed frame and instead picking at her nails.

"No," I say. "Someone his own age. You."

Gretchen doesn't speak, and I try to move my body into her view. Force her to look at me again. "He never had any parents here," I say, reminding Gretchen that she's still got a lot more than he does.

After a few beats of prolonged, defiant silence, Gretchen mutters, "Fine." She kicks the bedframe again.

"Good." I look at all the ladies wrapping themselves in the meager canvas blankets provided by Mid. "Try to get some sleep tonight."

Gretchen sighs, flopping down onto the nearest cot, unconcerned if it's hers or not. "You too. Maybe you'll like being able to forget about everything."

"Maybe," I say, and then walk back to my own cot, lying awake, thinking of everything I'll try not to forget tomorrow.

We're all awake, hours before any of the guards appear at our door. When Aaron looms in the entryway, gloating and filling up the room with as much pomp as he can muster, we're not surprised.

"Well, well," he quips. "Such a come-down from your own private quarters on the hundred and thirteenth floor in Tower One, isn't it,

Aloy?" His nose turns up so high, we all have a perfect view of the white hairs in each of his nostrils.

I walk from the middle of the room to where Aaron's situated himself with two guards flanking him. "I'd rather be there, or here, than in *your* private quarters." I pretend to sniff the air, imitating the look I gave when first entering his penthouse. If Aaron's going to drag me away this morning, I want to at least see the look of embarrassment on his face one more time.

Aaron's never been one to hide his emotions well, and I'm rewarded by his tight lips and glinting eyes. Mid's Elected shifts on his feet, his eyes hardening into two pieces of pink quartz. He spits out his next words. "Cole's done his job cleaning it all up. Pity you weren't fun enough to keep around for the job."

"I'd *never* clean up after you." My lips curl. I know I'm testing him. When Vienne walks next to me, placing a hand on my shoulder, I realize it's a warning—the same one I gave Gretchen last night. Don't goad our captors. Keep a level head.

"You're certainly a pleasure this morning, aren't you?" Aaron raises his pinky finger to his lips. "We'll have to do something about that, won't we?"

"I know why you're here," I say.

"Oh, do you?"

"Yes, it's been days since we landed in Mid, and you haven't yet used me as your technical advisor. You're not planning to do anything of the kind, are you?"

Aaron smiles. It's slight at first, but the movement makes its way across his face, all the way to his eyes. Their pink hue looks red, glistening in Aaron's excitement. "I've decided on a better use for you." Aaron pauses, picking off a fleck of peeling white paint from the wall. He flicks it from his fingernail, drawing out the suspense, not knowing that I already know his exact plans. "If I can't use your womb. And if I can't safely use your knowledge—because frankly you could just give me bad information like you did with the engineers under Calix's reign." He stops and watches me for a moment, squinting. "Yes, I do believe you put us back at least a few weeks with those shenanigans. So if I can't use you there, and I can't very well send you back to East, *and* I have to keep you alive to hang over the heads of your beautiful troop in here, well, then I just had to think of an alternate solution."

"You're going to give me optogenetics." I sigh on the words. Frankly, I'm tired of hearing Aaron's long, drawn-out soliloquy. He's enjoying this too much, and I'd rather he just get to the point.

Aaron's voice trills in happiness. "I *am* going to send you to the mind factory, but it's not for nothing, my dear. You're going to be part of some very important scientific research." He pretends to keep his laughter concealed, but it's making his chest shake and the lines around his mouth pinch upward.

Vienne bristles behind me. I feel her grip on my arm tighten. I know the word she's thinking even though she doesn't utter more than even a small gasp. *Run.* She wants me to flee now while the door is open. But I'm not backing off my promise to keep our people as safe as I can. I know if I try to escape, Aaron will order someone to be killed. I don't even want to think of whom. I close my eyes for a second, trying to get the picture of Griffin, Vienne, Gretchen, Glory, Tomlin, Margareath— or any of my people—out of my head. I wouldn't get far anyway. Not with Bushy Eyebrows staring at my forehead so hard he could bore holes through my skull.

"You say I can't remember everything. Well, congratulations. You're right!" Aaron claps a few long, drawn-out slaps of each pale hand against the other. He paces across the room, his fingers splayed on the side of his head, feigning deep thought. But the smile spread across his hollowed cheekbones shows he's still enjoying the drama. "It's the little things, you know. So annoying. I remember my role, my name, my history. But I can't remember the simplest things like the names of my guards. He points to Bushy Eyebrows near me and pumps a finger against his lips. Bushy Eyebrows, to his credit, just stares straight ahead.

"So," continues Aaron, "I need someone who's also taken the purple pills all their life to go through the same optogenetics I did. And then I'll stop the procedure and see what you remember."

"So you're not erasing my mind?" I ask.

"Alas, no. I'll give you the same dose everyone else gets. Just like I got. And we'll see if it does to you what it did to me."

I try to keep my breathing steady. This is a better verdict than the one I imagined, but I still don't like how frantic and confused the procedure made Aaron. While he went through optogenetics, he didn't even know he was Mid's Elected.

"Fine, let's just get this over with," I say. Maybe if I walk out with him now, he'll follow close by and forget about the first set of women set to begin breeding today. And if he's distracted by me, maybe he'll be less apt to realize Vienne and all the women left in the hospital will be helping Ty, any way they can, reimage Mid's robots to overtake the comms system.

"Guards," Aaron calls, and Bushy Eyebrows walks to my side, wrapping the blasted nylon rubber tight around my wrists. He pulls less tightly than Buzz Cut commanded him to do last time, but it still pinches my skin. "Let's move!" Aaron's tone is full of glee, and I think for a moment that I've succeeded in distracting him, at least for today. But then he stops in the doorway with me one step behind. He glances backward, and I see a slight tic of his right cheek. His eyes narrow, and his tongue licks his bottom lip.

"You there," Aaron points to Buzz Cut. "Pick the five most sensuous ladies. I'll be watching East's women today. Choose the ones who are most likely to . . . put on a good show." He grins at me, a cat who knows the mouse is beyond escape and unable to defend itself. "I like to see a little . . . struggling."

I almost can't take it. The urge to kick Aaron with my free legs is overwhelming. How much damage could I do with my hands behind my back before one of the guards puts a bullet in my head? But one look at Buzz Cut, whose gun points out toward the crowd of women, keeps me in check. I growl, and it merely serves to produce another laugh from Mid's Elected.

Buzz Cut complies with Aaron's order, scanning the crowd. His eyes focus on Vienne for one moment, but I see him grimace at her scars. He passes her over and instead picks five others.

I'm pushed forward by Bushy Eyebrows who prods me in the back with the butt of his gun. "Start moving," he says.

Aaron, his guards, and I march into the hallway, the white walls seeming to go on forever as we continue straight. I don't look back, but I can hear the yells of the first set of women selected for the day. I close my eyes and try to keep calm.

"What? Don't like hearing their pleas?" asks Aaron, pulling a long-nailed finger across my cheek and then up to my earlobe.

"Don't touch me! They're not pleas. Do you hear *any* of my women begging?"

"First off, you mean *my* women." He laughs gutturally. "And even if they're not beseeching now, they will be once they're tied down on the medical tables!"

"I despise you!" I spit at him.

"That may be, and it's one of the wonderful reasons I'm accompanying you today. Just to see what you look like strapped to a chair, awaiting my medicine. Do you think Calix would have enjoyed the show as much as I will?"

I don't answer this time—just keep my head down and plod forward, periodically being jabbed with Eyebrows' gun between my shoulder blades.

We stop in front of the children's nursery door, and I think Aaron will go in to gather help with my medical procedure. Instead, he turns to one of the guards and says, "Get them later after she's finished. I want to watch this one in private." We pass by Ty's room and walk around three corners before finally stopping in front of a yellow-painted door.

"Everything else is so white," says Aaron, reading my mind. "I just thought a little reminder about the sun's radiation would make my subjects a bit more compliant. Smart to be speaking to their subconscious, don't you think?"

I keep my eyes focused straight ahead, as if answering Aaron would be an imposition. He shrugs and opens the door to my nightmare. Inside is a black padded chair held off the ground by one central support pole. Around it are wires and numerous steel trays. A woman stands in the corner, her back toward us as she prepares something on a countertop. At the door's opening, she turns, her straight face giving rise to an indulgent smile when she sees Aaron.

"My Elected," she says, her voice smooth and buttery. The woman walks toward us, peeling off white latex gloves and tossing them into a sink to her right.

"Emma. A pleasure to see you, as always." Aaron nears the doctor and places a small kiss on her cheek. I watch in amazement, remembering that the doctors have not undergone any optogenetics. They are in on the ruse, in agreement with Aaron's idea that the procedure will give Mid Country a more enthusiastic workforce. Emma doesn't stiffen at Aaron's touch. Instead, she stays completely still, never losing the smile spread across her lower face.

The doctor wears a long, white lab coat and has almost matching blondish-white pixie hair that ends in sharp points in front of her ears. I watch as Aaron reaches toward her neck, at first thinking he is caressing her. But then I see he's pulling something up from under the doctor's coat. It's a silver chain, and on the end of it, lying right between Emma's breasts, comes forth the largest diamond I've ever seen. The jewel is at least two full inches wide, resting on an angle at the doctor's cleavage.

"Ahhh, so beautiful," says Aaron, admiring not the woman, but the stone she wears. "I like to see my gift to you displayed, Emma, not hidden within your gown."

She arranges the jewel on the outside of her medic's uniform, turning it so the light rebounds off its many intricate cuts. I think I see the hint of words bored inside the diamond's shape, but when the doctor turns, I lose my train of thought.

"Of course, My Elected," she says.

I don't like the way she supplies "my" before Aaron's title. It makes her seem all the more enamored with him, and that makes me hate the doctor even more.

"Only the best for my betrothed," Aaron says. He glances at me, feigning surprise as my eyes widen of their own accord. "Oh, didn't you know, Aloy? I'm engaged. Have to keep the Elected line going now that I don't have a dear brother here to take over if something befalls me." He laughs hard, holding himself steady on the doctor's arm.

She stays perfectly still, letting him laugh, acting as his support without even a blink.

"Shall we?" he asks the doctor, motioning for the guards to direct me into the chair.

"Yes, let's begin. Please, call me Emma," she signals to me.

I lift my head and stare her in the eyes. "I won't call you *anything!*"

Emma gives a sharp, small laugh, looking toward Aaron. "Not even *shrew? Harpie*, maybe?"

Aaron laughs along with the medic. "If she dared, it would be her own undoing," he says, picking up a thin, metal instrument from a side table and thwacking it across my thigh.

I suck in breath as the shock of pain reverberates up and down my leg.

"Oh, you mustn't harm her," Emma purrs, running a soft hand across Aaron's back. "I need her in good condition for the session."

"Whatever you require, Sweet." Aaron reluctantly fits himself and his layers of robes into a side chair to watch the proceedings. He settles himself, crossing his legs and placing both hands on his highest knee.

I can't help wondering if the dear, "sweet" doctor would mind that her betrothed planned to rape me earlier this week. Or that he's enthusiastic to see my women get forcibly inseminated. Would she still hang on his every word and preen as he watches her get the instruments of my torture ready?

Emma works with a few tools on the counter again until a trill sounds from a box on the wall. The doctor moves to the machine and listens into a receiver. After a moment, she says, "Yes, right away. I'll tell him." She puts the machine back together and then faces Aaron.

"My Elected, they must begin the insemination process now. The fertilization pods are the precise temperature to start."

"Dammit!" Aaron erupts, stomping his foot on the tiles. "Already? Can't they wait a few minutes?"

"Unfortunately, no," she says. "The procedures must begin now."

I see Aaron work though the conundrum in his mind: watch me for revenge or watch my women for pleasure? He can't tell Emma his quandary, so I get the intense satisfaction of seeing him squirm, uncomfortable once again this morning.

Emma, though, seems to understand Aaron's predicament and gives him ample room to extricate himself. "Aloy will have to undergo many of these optogenetics sessions to reach the level you were at. You will be able to watch any of them in the future. But there is only one chance to view five Mid babies be granted life."

Aaron weighs her words, and I can almost see the relief in his hands as they uncurl and flex. "Wise, as usual," he says. "All right then, I'm off to the labs. You'll be fine in here?"

"Of course," she says. "A guard will be right outside the doors to keep me safe."

"Yes." Aaron points to Bushy Eyebrows. "Make sure no one comes inside, do you hear me? This *must* go smoothly!"

"Yes, Elected," he says, nodding and then exiting to take his position outside the yellow room. The other guard follows Aaron out to the hallway.

Mid's Elected turns once more to look our way, eyeing up the cinched nylon straps the guards used to tie me to the chair. "Comfy?" he asks.

Then he chuckles and turns, his boots making loud clomping sounds as they echo through the otherwise empty hallway.

The doctor and I are alone in the room. She fiddles with a contraption to her left, and at once a bright light bursts outward, hitting me in the eyes. The light is so intense it seems to burn my retinas. I can't help crying out.

"Hmmm . . ." The buttery tone of the doctor's voice coats me like oil, thick and smothering. The room is hot, and I can feel my cheeks redden. My eyes refocus and fall to Emma's face. There is no longer a smile displayed there. She is stoic and apathetic, a cold statue moving closer to me.

"Shall we begin?" she asks.

12

I TRY TO COMPOSE myself, blinking hard, wishing I could rub my eyes at least. Circles of light keep flashing across my vision when the lids close. The doctor looks out the office door's small window, seems to be satisfied with whatever she sees out there, and then fiddles with something in another corner of the room before moving to sit near me. She holds a remote control in her hand, and I think it's a contraption that will induce the glaring light again.

I'm already scrunching my eyes closed in anticipation when Emma says, "I'm just turning on some music." She looks across the room at a box in the corner, fingering the remote from memory. Notes erupt in a sorrowful melody and there are words, but I'm too anxious to listen to the singer. "Did you have music in East Country?" Emma asks.

I don't answer her, refusing to make small talk. Plus, the pulse of light has induced a headache that already throbs behind my forehead with steady beats. Emma seems to understand and nods once before speaking again. "We used to have lots of music in our country when I was a young girl. Nothing through this equipment at first, of course." She points to the box. "It's a stereo." She almost seems to be smiling to herself, waxing poetic. "But people would gather at night and play all kinds of homemade instruments. You know, before we brought all this technology back. My friend, she had this little long-stemmed thing with wires. She called it a *ban-jo*. Don't know what ever happened to that gadget after my friend was treated with our procedures." The doctor is quiet for a moment, as if she's wondering where her "friend" is now. I wonder what the girl would think of Emma if she knew the truth about these medical treatments.

"Did you ever create music without technology?" Emma says again.

When I don't answer, Emma just stares at me. This question she won't let go, so I finally shake my head no.

"That's a shame," she says with a sigh, cocking her head. "Music is such a beautiful expression of self. Tells so much about a person. Like this song, for instance." She bends over the remote and the volume increases. "Do you hear what the artist's singing about? So poignant."

I close my eyes, trying to block out the notes. I don't know if this is some kind of trick. Maybe sound is one of the ways Mid brainwashes its people. I thought they used the light, but I can't be too sure. Emma keeps talking, not waiting for a reply this time. "It's by a man named Hozier. The song is called 'Take Me to Church.' Are you religious, Aloy?"

My head is down, but I open my eyes, glaring at Emma through the top of my eyelashes. "Can we get this over with already?" The sound my throat emits is hardening caramel. The light must have really affected me because my voice is slow and heavy.

"Oh, your head. Sorry about that," the doctor says. "Here take this." She walks to the counter and comes back to me, offering a cylindrical white pill in her hand.

"No," I manage to spurt out.

"Come now. It's nothing untoward. Not part of the procedure at all. It's just a pain relief pill. Acetaminophen."

I don't know what she's talking about, but I won't willingly put anything she offers into my mouth. I clamp my lips shut and shake my head back and forth, vehement.

"Fine, but it would stop the headache. Nasty side effect from the pulse I had to give you. Aaron had to see a big light to be sure your procedure started. I needed to begin with one of the biggest pulses instead of doing a gradual increase of light, like usual."

I breathe in, trying to control my thoughts. Of course they'd have to do the most heinous of treatments to me first. Of course.

"What do you think of the song?" she asks.

I turn my head away from her so that I'm focusing on the yellow walls instead of the doctor's relentless questions. She just won't let this song thing go.

She continues, "Well, I like it. You know, it's not really about being pious. I mean, it is and it isn't. It's about being told one thing by the people you trust, but knowing they must be wrong on some level."

I turn toward her. Is she trying to tell me something? Between the pounding and the flashes still echoing across my vision, I can't focus.

"It's about love, really," she continues. "Tell me, what do you think about choosing who you love?"

At this, I see an opening to tell her what I really think. I eke out the words, my voice still sluggish. "The man *you* love is crazy. Do you know that and still choose him?"

I may have actually gotten through to the doctor. She looks away for a moment, squaring her shoulders. So I push harder. Maybe if I anger her enough, she'll forget about my treatment. Or she'll just get to it already and stop giving me a history lesson on Mid. "Or, wait, is it because of the rock he gave you? Did he buy your love?"

Emma looks up at the ceiling. Then she pushes the huge diamond back inside the neckline of her robes, shielding it behind the fabric.

"Oh, come off it already," I say, slurring. "You must just want the power then. Is that it? 'Cause you can't very well want Aaron. Have you even seen what he's done to his apartment?"

The doctor turns to face me. "This isn't about me. If you want to talk about a Madame Elected so much, let's discuss yours then. Did you ever really love Vienne? What was it like to act as a homosexual in a society focused on childbirth?"

I won't answer any of her questions about Vienne. "Leave her out of this." My voice miraculously comes out clear and strong.

"Oh, so she *does* mean something to you." Emma smiles, but it's a tight-lipped line. "How much, exactly? Who would you be willing to destroy to keep her safe?"

My eyes widen, wondering where this line of questioning could possibly lead. Emma continues, "Ten of your other women? Your son? Where is he exactly? You can't honestly think Mid has forgotten about him."

"I wouldn't give up *anyone*. That's not how we show loyalty in East." My throat produces a growl on the last words. Do they intend for me to know how many people they plan to hurt before my mind is blown to oblivion? Why torture me with this information just to wipe the knowledge off my consciousness moments later?

"Yes, I want to hear more about your loyalty," Emma says. She leans forward in her seat, as close to me as she can safely get.

I sit up straighter in the chair, at least as much as the rubbery bindings will allow. "My *loyalty*? My allegiance is to the innocent. The ones who won't hurt others just for power or territory or whatever Aaron is after. The ones who sacrifice themselves to save others. Not those who'll ruin countless lives just for the sake of 'progress.' Not ones who *poison* others with brainwashing."

Emma leans back in her chair, crossing her legs. She nods to herself.

I bang my head back against the contoured plastic pillow on the chair. "Can we just get this over with already? Then you can go *be* with your precious Aaron?" I spit out his name—a toxic word.

Emma stands, and I think this is it. I shut my eyes again, expecting another onslaught of the light. I try to cram pictures of my loved ones inside my brain. Glory. Glory. Glory. Griffin. Griffin. Griffin. Vienne. Vienne. Vienne. I refuse to forget them easily. Mid will have to pull their memories out of my brain, one silvery thread at a time.

"Aloy," says Emma.

I feel her standing over me. I will not give Mid's doctor the pleasure of looking at her while she wipes out my thoughts.

"Aloy," says Emma again. Her voice is calm and still. I picture waves on a lake settling back down to a glassy surface after a storm. "Not everyone is *with* Mid's Elected."

My eyelids fly open. Emma walks over to the yellow door and knocks twice.

"She's ready," Emma says into the dark space as the door opens.

13

Bushy Eyebrows looms in the doorframe. "Are you sure?" he asks the doctor.

"Yes, I've asked her enough to know. She won't turn us in," Emma says.

Now I'm totally confused. I try to sit up again, wriggling on the seat. Bushy Eyebrows sees my movement and slices through one of the nylon bands across my shoulders with his diamond-edged knife. I watch the binding rip away and slap at the metal table. I swing my legs over the side of the chair, and all three of us stare at each other.

"What's going on?" I ask.

Emma holds onto the stereo's remote control in one hand and then sets it on the tray of steel instruments. "Just what I said. We don't all share Aaron's perspective. We're not all *with* him."

"Am I hearing what I think I'm hearing?" I ask.

"Sorry for everything I had to say and do to you earlier," says the guard. "You understand— keeping up pretenses." Bushy Eyebrows holds out his hand to me. "Name's Ollinear."

I take his hand, pumping it limply, too shocked to maintain a firm grip. "You two work together?" I ask.

Emma nods. "Ollie is my brother. I stopped administering optogenetics to him a year ago."

I stare at the guard, trying to discern with my own eyes if he's one of Mid's monotone people or if it's true he's in control of his mind. "And you . . . remember everything?"

Ollinear knocks on his temple with a loose fist. "Solid as a rock. No lost memories."

"Not like Aaron," Emma says. "Yes, to answer your question from earlier, I do know he's lost some of his functionality."

I raise a hand to my eyes. "So you're not marrying him?"

"Incorrect," Emma says. "I *am* set to marry him. It's just not something I've *chosen*."

"He's forcing you," I say. It's a statement, not a question.

"I'm the only female doctor in Mid. Thus, the only one who hasn't undergone optogenetics, and the only Mid woman who's still supposedly fertile."

"And you two are mounting an insurrection?" I ask, taking the big leap. I look back and forth from the doctor to her brother, waving a hand between them.

"There are more than just two of us," he says.

"Strategically placed," adds Emma.

"How many?" I ask. "What kind of rebellion are we talking about?" I lean forward, my hands glued onto each knee.

I'm still in awe of what's happening. A few minutes ago I was sure my memories were about to be vaporized. And now I'm talking to two of Mid's insurgents—the doctor who almost vanquished me a minute ago and the guard who bloodied my wrists bringing me into Mid's hospital dormitory. I rub my thumbs over the still-tender flesh of my hands, trying to reconcile the differences in the people I thought I knew and those who are standing before me now.

"Just three more," says the doctor. "And . . . I was hoping to involve Ty soon, once he came to my table for his first procedure in three months. I've been watching him carefully. He's smart as a whip. I think he could be a good asset." She pauses for a moment and looks at me with one eyebrow raised. "He helped you escape from the hospital last time you were in Mid, didn't he? Am I right?"

I don't easily implicate Ty, contemplating for a moment this is all a trap to root out East's plan. But I don't have to say anything because Emma continues, "Never mind. Don't tell me. I think I'm right, and that's all I need for now."

Ollinear lays a hand on his sister's shoulder. He gestures with a flick of his head toward me. "Did you make her swear she wouldn't give us up to Aaron in exchange for saving her people?"

"I didn't have to. She won't stab us in the back." Emma turns to me. "Will you, Aloy?" Emma doesn't really ask it. She smiles at me instead.

This movement of her lips looks much different than the placating, sugary sweet grin she distributed to Aaron. Now I think I'm seeing underneath the doctor's careful veneer. "Plus, what is Aaron's word anyway? Aloy knows even if he did promise safety for her countrymen, Aaron could change his mind anytime."

I nod, still dumbfounded by the two people sitting in front of me.

"So now we have six plus the four hundred women from East plus as many other people whose optogenetics procedures I can cease."

"That makes a lot more for the insurgency," says Ollinear, the hope gradually making its way to his face. He automatically assumes my people and I will join forces with them.

They're not totally off base. "What were you planning?" I ask. My hands are now neatly folded in my lap, mostly to ensure they won't shake. I cannot believe the change of events.

"We were hoping you might have some ideas," says Emma.

"I do, actually. But I still want some kind of assurance that this isn't a ploy. How do I know you're not just pretending to be on my side? And at the first opportunity you'll tell Aaron what my people intend to do?"

Emma considers this for a moment. Ollinear leans down, whispering in her ear. She nods and then looks up at me again. "Because I can provide you information you need. Something that proves we're on the same side. Information Aaron wants, which you could use against him when needed."

"Okay." My eyebrows rise.

"You tell her, Ollinear," Emma says. "It's yours to give."

The big man clears his throat and sits down hard in one of the metal swivel chairs. His sword's tip reverberates against the floor as it scrapes tile. "Aaron used to keep a code on him at all times—a sequence of three-letter combinations said to be the key to Mid's ultimate supremacy. When Calix took the Electancy, he looked for the legendary code but couldn't find it. Not on Aaron's person. Not in Mid's computer systems. Not with any of the bio scientists, as he presumed it would be. No sign of the original, nor any copies."

Emma continues the explanation, "Aaron wants the code now that he's back to being Elected, but he can't remember where it is. He only ever kept one handwritten copy, and he killed the scientist who initially discovered the sequence. So the one copy that exists is Aaron's only option."

"All along, he preserved the code on a scrap of paper hidden in an antique gun holster," says Ollinear.

I stop for a second, picturing the last time I saw Aaron while Calix was still in office. "A revolver," I say, the depth of understanding infiltrating my head. "Aaron held it when he looked for Calix in my apartment. And Calix took the revolver after that attack."

"Yes, it was confiscated, but not by Calix. By Calix's *guard*." The realization that I've seen Ollinear before hits me like a solid brick. Something about his bushy eyebrows and smooth head had been familiar, but between the threat of optogenetics and my people's forcible insemination, I hadn't recognized him fully. Emma's brother was there in my Mid Country apartment, helping pull out the thrashing Aaron on Calix's order.

Ollinear reaches into his lengthy robes to pull out the silver revolver Aaron threatened me with months ago. "And in one bullet socket, the fabled code, rolled up."

Emma looks at the scrap of paper in her brother's hand and then clasps his fist so that both their hands move the paper toward me.

I gaze at the sequence of seven three-letter combinations written in blue ink. I don't know what the letters refer to, but given how seriously Ollinear and Emma look at the paper, I imagine they're dangerous.

When I raise my eyebrows in question toward Emma she says, "It's part of the mutated protein code that differentiates people in East Country from anyone else in the world."

I can feel my heart skipping a beat, two beats. A grave wrinkle settling between her eyes, Emma continues, "Because of severe environmental factors, the people of East Country, West, or anywhere else for that matter, have unique metal concentrations in their blood. It means there's a distinct protein code for people from each country."

I nod, but the full importance of this information hasn't sunk in yet, and Emma can tell.

She wrings her hands together, folding the fingers over each other in her lap. "Biological warfare could wipe out an entire group if their code was known. A precise nanite in the water supply could affect only people from East. Or such a nanite could kill everyone with similar coding but skip over those with Mid's differentiation."

I don't understand what she means by *nanite*. I can feel my throat closing in on itself, the breath catching in my lungs. "One large bomb would be enough to wipe out my people. Why would Aaron need to kill us biologically?”

“Your people are scattered now,” Emma says, a hand reaching out to rest on my leg. “Aaron has always been paranoid that East’s spies are within his border, watching, waiting for his demise. The code would be a way of annihilating that threat completely. A way to ensure Mid wiped out any trace of East’s people for generations to come. Only those with Mid Country proteins would be safe or those who were born in Mid.” Her eyebrows rise in a sinister manner, and at once I know to what the doctors refer.

The babies my women are helping to create will be safe. But the women won’t be. I grasp on straws—anything to put holes in her theory. “But the women from East who are here. Aaron needs them for continued population growth. This code would kill them.”

Emma’s face drops even further, her jaw slackening and causing her cheeks to appear hollow. “I’m so sorry,” she says. “You don’t understand how this ‘insemination’ will work. Aaron doesn’t want your women to carry the babies themselves. He only intends to harvest their eggs.”

“Making the women from East Country . . . disposable . . . after he’s done with them,” I say. The words feel mealy in my mouth. A sour, rotting apple.

Ollinear leans closer to me. “We want you to have this piece of East’s protein code.” He puts the refolded scrap of paper into my palm, and I tighten a fist around the threatening letters.

“Do you believe us now?” asks Emma.

All I can do is look her in the eyes and nod yes. The medic, with Aaron’s diamond still protruding in a point from beneath her uniform, has got my complete and utter faith.

14

WHEN I RETURN TO the dormitory room, the first thing I notice is the hushed silence. Vienne kneels at the side of a cot, and I make my way through the crowd toward her. All around me, faces are anxious, either in solidarity with the women who were chosen today or in fear that they'll be next.

"Vienne," I say, tapping her on the shoulder. She looks up, probably surprised that I still even know her name, and tries to give me a small smile. But it catches on her lips, not making its way higher. Only her raised eyebrows ask the question of my mental capacity. I skip over the explanation for now and instead ask about my people. "What happened after I left?"

Vienne pats the woman lying on the cot and then stands, ushering me to a corner. "Their ovaries were removed. They could hardly walk when they were ushered back in after the surgery."

I inhale deeply, shaking my head. "So Mid's not just using the mature eggs from our people, they're stealing all future babies."

"Yes, it's a much worse situation than we first realized."

I know exactly what she means, but Vienne doesn't understand the full extent of our predicament. If, say, ten women are taken per day, we have just forty days until Aaron's use for us finalizes. And if Aaron somehow manages to re-map East's genetic code during that time, the entire population of my country is doomed. Instead of our insurrection needing to occur before Ty's initiation three months from now, the date just got moved up.

Sitting on the side of a cot, I tell Vienne everything about my optogenetics procedure, or lack thereof. She listens with her eyes closed for some of the story, but when Vienne does return my stare, I see she grasps the urgency with which we must gather forces.

"You can't act like you're fine," she says at last, a sigh escaping her pursed lips. "You need to look confused, as if the optogenetics treatment is proceeding as planned."

I nod, realizing that even my normal walk back into the dormitory was ill-founded. If Aaron is to believe Emma gave me a proper dosage, I'll have to slur my words, act mentally off-balance, and pretend to forget everything.

"So you need to be the one in control," I say. "At least in front of the guards."

Vienne nods. "And Ty should begin programming as many robots as he can to contact East as fast as he can."

We hash out more specific plans for the rest of the night, and when Ty sneaks into the room again in the middle of the night with his reprogrammed robot waiting within the doorway, we have the message for East ready for him. I tell Ty everything I can remember about the main surveillance hub Calix showed me. The place where I first heard Vienne's voice through the chip.

"A wall with multiple headphone ports in building four. Got it," whispers Ty as he leans on an overturned bedframe at the back of the room.

"I hope the robots you convert can get access to the surveillance room," says Vienne.

"Or can work the switches, let alone find the specific computers that communicate with your old chip," I say.

There are too many risks to count. As we talk through each one in detail, even I can see it's a long shot that the robots will be able to provide East's men a coordinated date to invade. Or that East's men will be able to overtake Mid's occupying guards and travel to Mid undiscovered.

Most likely we'll be mounting the insurrection by ourselves with just those people Emma is able to convert. But we plod on with our plans because Ty's use of the robots is the best weapon we have at present. Our only way of helping the rebellion.

We're still in the midst of hushed talk when, through the darkness of the room, we hear a loud yelp that jars many of the women in the room awake. It stops our heated conversation mid-sentence, and the three of us rise to look for the sound's origin.

When the yelp turns into a louder, pained cry, a murmur rumbles through the rows of dormitory beds as more of my women sit up.

Vienne finds the source of the squealing encased in a squirming mound of gray wool blanket on top of a nearby cot. "What in the world?" She pulls the cover down with a hard yank. A head of coal black hair shoots up, trying to recover itself.

"Just leave me alone!" the head says.

I know immediately whose voice just hissed at Vienne, and I'm there at the bedside in an instant. "What are you doing, Gretchen?"

"None of your business!" I can hear the pain in her voice, though, and bend down to look at her face. Gretchen is a bleeding mess, red dripping down her cheeks from a multitude of slanted lines. I grab her chin within the palm of my hand.

"She's cutting herself," says Ty from behind me and Vienne.

"Are you kidding me?" I hiss at Gretchen. Here I am trying to stop my people from getting hurt, and the girl is maiming herself on purpose?

By this time, most of the women in the room are awake, and Vienne turns on an overhead light. We've all gotten used to the convenience of the electricity, and hardly anyone breathes in a gust of surprise at the sudden display of light anymore. It's almost funny how fast they've become accustomed to technology.

When the room is illuminated, I turn from Gretchen to look at the vast number of faces staring back at me. What I see causes a gasp to stick in my throat.

Blood runs down the faces of dozens of my women who all look at each other with guilt oozing out of each monstrous gash.

"What is this?" I ask, but no one answers. Vienne stares at all of the bloody faces, looking from one set of eyes to the next. They've cut themselves with whatever sharp instrument they could find, producing grotesque wounds along their faces, almost in the same exact fashion as Vienne's. I can't tell what my wife is thinking. She stands there still as a tigress contemplating its next kill.

The women whose faces are still wholly intact start to ring out questions, accusing their neighbors, and a thunder of objections encases the room in noise.

"Be quiet!" yells Vienne at last, the tone of her voice causing all of the women to bite their tongues. I don't think they've ever heard her this angry. "Do you want the guards to come in here? Who started this?"

I still don't understand what's going on, but apparently Vienne does and she's not pleased. So I stand off to the side, letting her take control as we discussed just moments earlier. When no one speaks, Vienne walks back to Gretchen's bed and pulls her up by the arm. "Tell me right this instant whose idea this was."

Gretchen keeps her mouth shut and looks at the ground.

"It was mine." A woman in the middle of the room with lacerations in at least seven spots on her cheeks steps forward.

Vienne walks over to the woman, standing right in her face. "Is this how you deal with the threat of Mid's surgery? You don't have to outrun Mid? You just have to, metaphorically, outrun your own people?" Vienne asks.

The realization of what my women are doing hits me and Ty at the same moment. I hear him breathe out the answer next to me, muttering to himself. "They're trying to look like Vienne 'cause the guards didn't want to take her."

"I've never been ashamed of our people. Until now," says Vienne. She walks through the rows of our people, stopping at each bed where women with cuts stand, heads down. "Throughout all of our tribulations, we've stood together, and now when you think we don't have another option, you scar your face so that you will look less appetizing to Mid's guards than your sisters? So that they're chosen for harvesting before you?"

Vienne ends her procession at Gretchen's bed again. "And you've corrupted a twelve year old into following your foolish plans."

Gretchen looks up, catching Vienne's eye. "They didn't have to convince me. I wanted to do it. I'm done listening to you and Aloy. We don't stand a chance here in Mid just sitting around this room waiting to be dissected like pigs. I may not be old enough for Mid to take my eggs yet, but it'll be soon, and when the time comes, I'd like to look as unappealing as possible."

Vienne stares at Gretchen, giving the girl a wilting glare. "And you do this at the sacrifice of others who will go to the surgery table first, instead of you? That is *not* how we operate in East Country."

Gretchen finally looks away from Vienne, her eyes on the wall.

I can't take this. An outside entity hurting my people is one thing. But seeing my people turning on each other like hens in line for a slaughter, is altogether another.

"All right!" I say. "Enough. It's time to bring you all in on the plans."

15

I TELL MY PEOPLE everything in as soft a whisper as possible. My doctor's appointment. The code given to me by Emma. The next move we'll take with the robots. How I need to act confused. The chip in the surveillance room. I gesture as much of the plan as possible and use talkers in East Country's telephone fashion to send the message to all our people without Mid's possible surveillance overhearing our plans. I tell the women enough to convince them that we're not sitting ducks—that we'll take a stand and we have a plan. I speak until my voice is hoarse and the faces around the room stop looking like scared ducklings and more like the hard-as-stone, determined countrymen I remember from home.

When I'm done, I fall onto Gretchen's bed, sitting beside her on the blanket. "Don't ever cut yourself again," I say, shaking my head. Hopefully one day my own teenage son won't be as hard to handle as Gretchen. I roll my eyes and can't help but smile at the thought of being able to mother Glory in the future. I've been able to convince my people that there's a glimmer of hope, and obviously in speaking the plans out loud, I've convinced myself as well.

Ty stands to the side of us. "I should get back," he says. I nod, and he's about to walk away when he turns and whispers something in Gretchen's ear. I think I can see a grin shining through her features as she watches Ty exiting the room. The pupils of her eyes grow bigger and a flush covers her torn face.

I look at her with raised eyebrows. When the door clicks in back of Ty, Gretchen whispers, "He told me I'd be beautiful even with the cuts."

At this, I can't help smiling bigger. I stand, my fingertips squeezing her shoulder. "Go back to sleep." Somehow, I think Gretchen may be easier to deal with from now on. I can't help remembering what it was like to realize someone liked me. I picture Griffin's thumb grazing my cheek under the now destroyed oak tree near the White House. I can almost feel that kiss we shared in Margareath's enclosed garden. My fingers trace the contours of my lips, relishing the memory of Griffin's skin against mine. So much has transpired since the time I took office. So many atrocities. But so many good things too. The memories of Griffin both haunt and soothe me as I fall into a light sleep on my own bed across the room.

What feels like mere minutes later, the thump of heavy boots echoes through the dormitory, waking all of us who were still asleep. I try to wipe the sinewy images from my head as fast as possible, but the faces of Glory and Griffin stick hard, stinging the back of my eyes.

"Rise and shine, ladies," calls Buzz Cut who's graced us with his presence each morning so far. "We need ten more *volunteers*!" He laughs at his own joke, his shoulders shaking. But a few of the women in the room do accept the offer.

"Take me!" calls an older lady from the middle of the dorm room.

"And me!" yells another.

I realize that a few of the older women, those who've already mothered children in East and are past their best fertility potential, step forth. I watch, numb, as the spectacle of self-interest shown last night fades to this display of sacrifice. Vienne catches my eye and gives a grim nod. I know she's somehow been involved in the orchestration. While I fell into a hard sleep, Vienne must have been up all night furthering our efforts behind the scenes.

Buzz Cut meanders toward the first volunteer, looking her over, toe to head. "Hmmm . . . Mid's Elected does like blondes. But I think not. Look at the crook of your nose. Not the best that East has to offer."

I start to step forward, about to say something pointed. Something along the lines of "how dare you treat us like cattle," but I stop myself, remembering in the fog of waking that I'm supposed to be mute and confused.

"And you," says the guard, grasping the elbow of the next volunteer. "Who told you that you were good looking? Obviously someone who kept his eyes closed when you kissed!" He barks out a guffaw. He's hard and cruel now, but I bet Buzz Cut's bravado is easily crushed like diseased, rotten wood in the face of true authority.

I think the second female volunteer will keep still and suffer the guard's insults in silence, but when Buzz Cut stops snickering and looks at her again, she spits in his eyes.

The guard screeches, raising both fists to wipe the spittle. "This one! This one is going for the procedure today. Take her!"

Ollinear, who has been standing in the doorway the entire time, as if he doesn't want to be part of the callous nature of these affairs, finally walks through the threshold. He wraps an arm around the woman's waist, leading her forward. "Who else do you want, Vassily?"

"How about Scarface?" He starts for Vienne, and I have to hold myself around the waist so as not to run forward and snatch my wife from out of his sight. "She's pretty behind all those gashes."

"No, not her." Everyone turns to see Aaron striding into the dormitory. He wears a blue, velvet cloak pinned at the top with a gold leaf. It's ostentatious compared to the brown canvas shifts billowing over all of our figures and the black uniforms the guards wear. Aaron's like a circus ringmaster from the books Tomlin used to show me, except he can't grow any mustache curled at the ends. Aaron's hair is still white as snow with almost translucent eyebrows to match. Not a speck of other hair is apparent on the rest of his face.

"Mid's used East's Madam Elected enough for now," Aaron continues. "And I'd like to keep her as collateral to hang over Aloy's head, if need be. I'm not too sure Aloy has anyone else left in the world whom she loves." He ticks off my family members on one hand. "Her parents. Pity about them, really. Firing squad, nasty way to go. Griffin. So damaged. I wonder if he bled out and died. And her baby. Well, we'll find him, if he's still alive, that is."

I look at the ground, trying not to let Aaron notice the fire glowing in my eyes. If he could see inside my body, he'd know that all my muscles are as tight as bamboo shoots, ready to lash out at him the first chance I get.

"Grab whomever you want for today," he says to the guards. "I'm not going to watch their procedures. Today I'll see Aloy in the doctor's office, come hell or high water."

My eyes clamp closed and I can feel my palms grow hot and sweaty. How will Emma prevent me from receiving optogenetics now?

Ollinear grasps the top of my arm and leads me forward out of the room. I don't have a chance to see whom Vassily and the rest of the guards choose for today. Again I'm ushered out ahead of them, walking down the whitewashed corridor with Aaron at my side. I stare at the interlocking tiles on the floor, focusing on anything except the thought of pulsing light puncturing my retinas.

Aaron reaches toward me, gripping my shoulder above where Ollinear holds my arm. "Nothing to say, Aloy? Hmmm? Should be an interesting—" Aaron's comment is cut short by a tremor running under our feet. "What was that?" He glances toward his guards. A few of them shrug their shoulders, looking at each other.

"Earthquake?" offers Ollinear.

Aaron ponders this a moment and is in the midst of agreeing when a massive boom echoes around us. The floor shakes again, but this time it's more violent.

"Bombing!" yells Aaron, and the group of us is herded fast toward the first door we see. Ollinear and the other guards encase themselves around Aaron's body in what I presume to be standard procedure for protecting their leader. The ground shakes three more times and a wall to the left of us groans with the reverberations. Amidst screaming in the distance and the explosions rocking Mid Country, seeming to come from all directions, Aaron's hysterical voice peels through the mass of his bodyguards. "How did our sensors not catch this? We should have been two steps ahead of any attack. Someone will pay for this!"

The bombing lasts for no more than three minutes, but it's enough to pound Aaron into utter fright. When at last the guards move off of him, I can see Aaron's irises flying around like caged bats.

"*YOU!*" he bellows at me. "You come with me *now!* We're going to see the destruction you caused first-hand!" He pulls at my arm, not allowing his guards to intervene or escort me on their own accord. Aaron's grip is tight across my flesh, and I can already feel the point of his beloved revolver shaking in his hand against my back.

"Take it easy," I say, still trying to play the confused act but knowing I have to say something to defend myself. My voice tries to belie calm. I summon every atom of Vienne's psychology to ease Aaron back to sanity. He might not even mean to shoot me right now, but the gun is so loose and volatile in his fist, who knows what might happen.

We burst out of the hospital into the blazing sun. Rubble from the nearest building smokes, and a fire is sprayed with water by robots at another site. The heat of the sun, which I haven't felt in over two weeks, and the temperature of the scorching fires combine to produce beads of sweat on my forehead. Everything is chaos. People run in all different directions, but not together. Everyone is still separate even after this catastrophe. In East, if such a bombing occurred, I'd have witnessed families escaping together or at least children held in their parents' arms as they run from the fires. It's this thought that reminds me such a bombing did occur in East Country. I just wasn't there to watch it. In my mind's eye I never pictured that the devastation could look like this.

The screaming and sounds of groaning seem to coat all activity. Orange-eyed robots rumble past us on their way to stamp out more flames, circumventing people without even an acknowledgement. Guards look to the sky, watching the direction from where the airrides retreat eastward, silvery exhaust still lingering behind them. And there are bodies. On the ground not two hundred feet from us a man is being pulled out, legs first, from a burning building. A women moans in anguish at another corner, holding one side of her face with bloody hands.

"Do you see what you do to us?" Aaron screams at me. His mouth is by my ear, but he continues to deliver his accusations in high-pitched squawks. The ringing through my head is deafening.

"We didn't. I swear it!"

"No warning this time. No time to get people to the bomb shelters! You did this! Somehow you tricked our sensors so they couldn't detect incoming airrides!"

"How could I possibly have been involved—"

"Shut *up! Shut up!*" Aaron leads me toward a body lying around one corner. As we approach, all I see are legs sticking out of standard brown robes. But the closer we get, I see the man's arm has been blasted off, and there are pieces of tissue and bone lying in fragments all around our feet. The man's head is turned at an awkward angle, nothing that a live person could endure. I've never witnessed carnage like this. I wretch into the dirt, my empty stomach coming up with little except for frothy white bile.

"What a show! What a *show* you put on, Aloy! How dare you be ill viewing the mess you've made!"

A guard runs up to Aaron, speaking urgent, tumbling words, but I don't hear them. All I can see is the mangled body in front of us. The scent of burning flesh removes every other thought from my head. When the guard moves away from Aaron, Mid's leader turns to me once again. He grips both of my shoulders, shaking me.

"Why do you want our nirogene so badly? Why does East keep stealing it?"

"I don't know what you're taking about!" My voice is beginning to take on the same high-pitched tone as Aaron's. I try to focus my eyes on Aaron's as he continues to shake me. "My people are your prisoners. How could we be stealing or bombing *anything* right now. We don't even have the technology for airrides. You've seen our city. We have nothing of the sort!"

"So smooth. So convincing. But you must have them stashed somewhere!" Aaron lets go of me and paces in tight circles, his fingers drumming against his bottom lip. His gray, shiny boots are churning up dirt in tiny clouds that almost resemble the smoke billowing around us. "Maybe underground in those tunnels below the White House? In bunkers? As the former United State's capital, Washington D.C. had to have them hidden somewhere!"

"You know all of the nuclear bombs were used up in the world wars. No country had any left at the end. We're not hiding anything!"

"Maybe not nuclear deposits. But then regular bombs."

I shake my head, frantic to dispel Aaron's rage.

"Who's bombarding us, if it's not you?" Aaron's face is right up against mine. Our noses touch as he screams at me.

"I don't know! Maybe West Country? Maybe a country across the ocean?"

Aaron leans back, giving me a moment to breathe again. He hoots, pulling his hair as he tips his head back. "No. West collapsed a few years ago with the onslaught of massive earthquakes. And Europe? You speak of what was once Europe?"

"Yes, them! What about them? East was bombed too. It could be a foreign enemy."

Aaron's laughter turns to cackling. He continues turning in circles, like he'll burrow a hole down into the earth floor. "Don't you think we already considered that? There's nothing out there! We've flown airrides as far as our systems would allow, way over the European continent. Even up to Greenland, until ice coated the wings so we had to turn back. Everything is desolate there. Decimated by the nuclear attacks from a hundred years ago. Snow everywhere up north and piercing sun everywhere south. No life. You and your awful East countrymen are the only ones left with us in this world!"

"No, that can't be!" I put my head in both hands, trying to wrap my mind around the world Aaron describes. East has stayed in isolation for so long, but I've been sure this entire time that life still existed on other continents. Africa or Asia still must endure.

"It's true. We're the last of the human population, and you're trying to wipe us off the planet!"

"No! There have to be people still left out there, and they're the ones attacking Mid Country, not my people!"

"So tired of listening to these *lies!*" Aaron gestures to Ollinear and another guard, who've quietly sidled near us, watching our exchange with tight-lipped mouths. "Take her to the yellow room. And finish her off. Tell Emma, maximum dosage. I have to stay and deal with all this." He waves his hands in the air, gesturing to the smoke still puffing out of broken windows. "I want East's Elected a sniveling mass next time I lay eyes on her!"

OLLINEAR MANAGES TO ENGAGE his colleague with another task along our route back to the hospital, so he's the only one holding me during this chaos. "Pull that woman out of the rubble. Get all the corpses out of the way," he says. "I can deal with this puny girl by myself."

When we're alone, I ask, "Do you believe Aaron?" I cough out the words in between lungfuls of the sour smelling smoke. "About East Country creating all this wreckage?"

"I don't know what to believe." I hear the air hissing out of Ollinear's mouth as he breathes deeply. "I don't know what East would have to gain from our destruction. And it does seem unnatural that we should be the last two countries left on Earth."

I nod, taking that to mean he still believes I'm on the right side of the fight. "Before we see Emma, can we stop in Ty's room?"

Ollinear gives me a pointed look. "It'll be risky, but yes." We walk next to each other, Ollinear's hand loose around my wrist for pretenses sake. But no one is looking at us. Everyone runs somewhere, visibly shaken with the latest attack. The robots are the only ones who seem coordinated. Even the guards dealing with the carnage look disoriented, not knowing what to do first.

I see a woman limping in our direction, the tips of her hair singed dark. She crosses our path without looking up, aiming for the moving walkway that will make the trip to wherever she's going a bit easier, and it's at this angle I see she's cupping a severed hand close to her chest. I suck in my breath fast, the horror of this image hitting me hard in the stomach. My first instinct is to ask if the woman's okay—if she needs assistance—but I can't bring any attention to myself. Who knows how Mid's people would lash out at me right now. I keep walking straight, leaving the woman and her macabre hand alone. After that, I keep my eyes down, letting Ollinear lead me.

When we get to the room where Ty lives with the rest of the children, I see he's been pacing, waiting for some kind of news.

"Another attack." I try to explain, but even I don't have a good enough set of words to describe the scene outside the hospital walls. "Whoever did it is stealing nirogene."

Ty looks away, trying to discern what that could mean, but he comes up with nothing.

"Your robot has to communicate with my countrymen back home. *Tonight*, Ty. While there's disarray and less attention on the surveillance room." I'm more forceful than usual, placing a hand on Ty's shoulder to convey my earnestness. Everything is resting on Ty's reprogrammed robot, and it's a thinly threaded plan as is. If we can utilize the terrible chaos from today, perhaps we have a greater chance of communicating with East Country.

Ty nods. Unlike the older citizens of Mid Country, he doesn't shake off my touch or step backward to avoid it. Ty looks older than his years. Resolute. Grave. The robes hang on him, limp as if there is little of him ensconced in the fabric. I want to say something encouraging. At least tell him how appreciative we are of his help. However, before I can summon the right words, he says, "I'll send him now," and starts toward the linen closet where his creation is hidden.

"You still have the message, right?" I ask. The one Vienne and I gave Ty was explicit as to the date and time the men from East should arrive in Mid Country. If we're going to go through with an all-out coup, we need the extra numbers from East. And the timing has to be synced just right.

"You're sure your people will understand the code?" Ty takes the scrap of paper from within his robes, swaying it in the air. "What are these numbers again? Consillations?"

"The numbers represent positioning of *constellations*," I correct him. "Yes, everyone in East tells the time and date by the stars' positions. Plus, we have a stargazing expert in Gretchen's mother, Maggie. My people will know when I mean for them to arrive and strike." Conveniently, it's a code I don't think Mid can break. That art of telling time by way of the sky's stars and sun's position died for Mid when the country began relying squarely on technology.

Ty folds the piece of paper once down the middle and then again in the opposite direction. As he closes the precious message, I see the numbering along with a short phrase scrawled by my hand. As planned, the robot will broadcast all parts of the message into a transmitter until there is confirmation of receipt.

"Don't forget the last part." I add. The phrase I included below the numbers is critical, but I don't know if my desired recipient will be in any state to remember its meaning. All I can do is hope and try to imagine the best scenario. All other thoughts don't serve me well.

"Got it," says Ty. He's jumpy and ushers me and Ollinear out of the room before any of the robots or nurses can resume their use of the children. I try to look back at him with a faint smile, but he's already looking away, tending to some of the toddlers who grab at the hem of his robes.

With all the injuries and casualties, it's only a matter of time before I imagine Mid will redirect the older children from helping in the optogenetics rooms to assisting in the emergency operations. I dispel images of Ty seeing, firsthand, the effects of warfare in the hospital's bowels. Instead I focus on the task at hand.

Ollinear and I back out of the room with just a few looks toward the mass of children huddled together in a corner. I know they have no one to offer a few kind words or a good explanation of the devastation they're bound to see, but I have no choice except to leave all of that for later.

"Any other stops before we see Emma?" Ollinear asks.

I think for a moment. "Yes, it's time she and Vienne met each other." My wife and my newest comrade have yet to meet, but they've both heard an awful lot about each other. And it's almost with reverence that Emma speaks of Vienne. She knows all about Vienne's unwitting act of treachery against East Country for all those years. She's fascinated at how Vienne handled the news and she's heard about Vienne's scars from Ollinear.

Emma's brother and I stay close to the walls as the two of us head back to the dormitory to gather my wife, but no one slows us down in the hallway. They're too busy bringing victims into the hospital to care about a lone woman being escorted by Aaron's guard. Large sheets are laid out on the ground and bodies that no longer flail lie, one by one in rows. It's sickening how the carnage grows. It seems they'll never stop adding to the row now stretching farther down the hallway than I can see.

"Thank goodness we have gloves," I hear a woman's voice utter to another nurse. "I mean, *really*."

I look up and cringe, recognizing the nurse who kept me away from Glory a couple of months ago. I could wring her neck if I had a spare moment, but I can't waste the time and can't afford the scene. We edge past the onslaught of casualties being carted in on stretchers, keeping our faces turned away.

Upon entry to my dormitory, we're told that no one was taken for fertilization today due to the bombings, and I tell everyone, through way of talkers, what's going on outside our walls. I can see several women visibly shake, but the youngest, including Gretchen, are watched over by the elders. No one here will faint from a light heart. At least, no one with shaky legs will get a chance to falter. They'll be buoyed up by the women of East around them.

I omit the most gruesome facts but tell them the general idea. I gather up Vienne, whom we conceal by carrying her between us. She acts like a hurt Mid citizen, legs dangling limp beneath her. The ruse works well enough, and we're in front of the yellow optogenetics door before anyone's head turns toward us. Ollinear knocks once—a hard pound that almost sounds like a shelling in and of itself—and the door flies open.

"Oh, thank goodness!" cries Emma, pulling her brother into a tight hug. "I didn't know what was going on. I merely got a call from Aaron commanding me to stay inside this room and . . ." She looks at me, her features pinched.

"Yeah, I know. Finish me off."

Vienne peers at Emma with raised eyebrows, as if daring her to proceed with Aaron's directions.

"Well, obviously, I'm not going to . . ." Emma voice trails off as she glances back and forth between us, her forehead creasing.

Vienne retains her knitted eyebrows, as if she's not sure she can trust Emma, even if I've decided to do so. The doctor and my wife stare at each other, two prowling animals, sniffing out danger. "Aloy showed me the supposed genetic code you gave us," Vienne says. "I want to thank you both for it and the trust you place in us, but it could just be numbers on a paper. We would never know."

I've thought the same thing, but what other choice do we have but to trust Emma and her brother? I've said as much to Vienne, and I know she agrees. But she still watches for the telltale signs of lies emanating from

Emma and Ollinear's body language. Enlarged pupils. Excessive sweat. Darting eyes. Hunched shoulders. Vienne's taught me how to notice all of them, but she's still better at recognizing the subtleties than I am.

"They're real as the hair on my head," says Ollinear with a slight twitch of his mouth. I look at his bald head and hope he means the sprouting eyebrows that seem to take over his entire face.

Vienne stares down Ollinear too but finally sighs, and in the wake of the awkward silence, Emma takes this as my wife's acceptance. The doctor glosses over the mistrust, instead focusing on circumvention of Aaron's orders. "We'll have to coach Aloy on what massive optogenetics patients act like," she says. "Aaron thinks she's had a few small doses so far. So he hasn't expected her to seem permanently damaged. Now, though . . ." I look at the wall to keep from kicking something. Emma continues, "We haven't had many people get a full dose so quickly. A couple of criminals, perhaps. Mental patients. Let me look back at my notes." Emma fishes within a drawer and produces a sleek tablet on which she skims her fingertips. After a moment she glances at me. "You'll have to slur your words."

"I know that part," I say, pursing my lips.

"You must act as if you don't know me anymore," says Vienne, moving closer and grasping my hand. "At least not in a familial way." I look at my wife, the worry etched in permanent lines across her forehead. Gone is the lighthearted young girl who first brought me mint tea, hoping to ease the burden of my solitude all those years ago in the White House. Now she is scarred and anxious, but still profoundly regal. I hope one day when all of this is behind us, Vienne can return to being carefree. I imagine Vienne running alongside her daughter, Eve, the gossamer folds of a gown rushing up at her ankles as Vienne keeps up with a toddler.

"Or what you're doing here," says Ollinear, clearing his throat, bringing me back to the present. He drops down into a chair in the corner, his usual place during our meetings.

"Almost nothing will be a priority to you anymore. Well, nothing except science and technology." Emma wipes a hand across her brow, almost like she's embarrassed for all the people she steered in that direction over the past years. Perhaps it's partly that embarrassment that propels her to help us now.

I listen to the onslaught of their instructions, starting to tune out the words as images of the bloodshed I saw this morning lurk close behind my eyes. A limb lying on the ground, unconnected. The stump of a leg, blood still gushing. The woman holding her severed hand. I don't understand any of it. Why now? Why such widespread destruction? Even the earlier attack on Tower One seemed to only hit empty rooms. Nothing like this that actually killed so many people.

I cut Emma off mid-sentence as she's explaining how optogenetics causes an especially severe type of something called autism. I wave one hand as the other brushes across my brow in consternation. "The attacks in the past were all on targeted spots that didn't hurt many people, right?" I rub my temples as if I could develop the idea more fully once it's wrangled out of my head. "The rocket launcher. Tower One. This assault was different than any others."

The three of them stop talking and turn back to me. "What do you mean?" asks Ollinear.

"This bombing was all over the place. Uncalculated."

There's silence for a moment as everyone contemplates my words. Vienne's eyes fixate on the shiny green and yellow floor tiles but look up abruptly after a moment, large with realization. "The attacker seemed angry."

17

THE FOUR OF US mull over what the bombing could mean, but we don't reach a conclusion. We only manage to rule out the idea that Aaron created the attack to further implicate East. He seemed too genuinely surprised to have orchestrated such a device. Instead, by the end of our conversation, we turn back to Emma's plans for stripping her people of optogenetics, leaving the reason for the uncharacteristic attack still unanswered.

While Emma reduces her people's intake of optogenetics as fast as she can, Vienne will stand by to provide psychological help. When people are confused by Emma's explanation of Aaron's experiments, Vienne will step in with the soothing words she is well-trained at providing. As we can't very well eliminate optogenetics without an entire populace wandering around with misdirected confusion and anger, Vienne's skills will be essential. Plus, Mid's people require an explanation on how we're planning to fight back against Aaron's rule. And we need to know whether they're onboard.

If certain Mid countrymen refuse to help, unfortunately, those citizens will go right back under the pulsing light, with no memory of the information Emma and Vienne ever relayed.

Later that night, I can't help sifting through Vienne's words again as I lie with eyes open, face up on my cot. My thoughts are like flour, a few ideas shaking out only to end as a soft mountain that's easily blown away.

Why was the attacker mad? What was different this time? They stole nirogene like always, but why ruin so many buildings and kill people in the process?

Nirogene was stolen from Mid in earlier attacks. But this assault was something else entirely. Was it some kind of distraction? It just doesn't make sense, and I worry about what I'm missing.

"You'll make yourself sick if you don't get any sleep *and* don't eat." Margareath wanders over to me with a bowl of food in one outstretched hand.

"Thanks." I accept the bright pile of green beans she offers.

We both sit on the edge of my cot, and Margareath snags a bean out of the bowl. We crunch on the legumes together in silence. I'm still surprised at the flavor of vegetation Mid produces. East's planting tasted muted compared to Mid's oranges, green beans, and sprouts.

"I wish they'd at least let us outside. I could provide some kind of service helping them as a Grower or Healer," says Margareath. I remember back to the time Margareath worked in Mid as my spy within their planting group, using the skills she had learned in East Country.

"Yeah, right," I say, a mouth full of vegetables. "And risk you telling everyone they're being brainwashed?"

"I know. But the lack of sun or fresh air is driving me crazy."

"I'm sure there are vitamins in these greens, otherwise we'd all be a lot weaker than we are. Plus, I don't really think the air is all too fresh out there."

"You know what I mean. Being cooped up. I miss feeling free. I miss Albine and my kids."

I nod, knowing exactly what she means. "Our captivity will be over soon." Emma plans to take two hundred Mid countrymen off optogenetics a day, starting tomorrow. Even with Emma asking for more shifts and putting in eighteen-hour days, two hundred was the max number she could dare, and that gives us only seven thousand converts out of forty thousand total Mid countrymen. That is, if everyone who's taken off optogenetics even wants to join our side. What if they like what Mid's doing? Maybe they'd prefer not knowing the truth.

The day's exhaustion is starting to get to me, and Margareath can sense my mood as we finish off the bowl. "Want anything else?" she asks.

"No, I think I'm just going to get some sleep." I reach up to my hair, which is now past my shoulders, a golden, wavy crop that I can't help wringing within my fingertips. It's strange how I feel more weighted down with all these tendrils falling into my face. I've taken to keeping it spiraled back, securing a section of it with the mechanical bee's long stinger I found when first entering Mid Country over a year ago.

"Ah, I remember that," says Margareath, staring at the small pike I twist in my fingertips.

"It makes for a good hair clip. And a nice, sharp instrument if needed in a hurry."

Margareath tilts her head back with a quick chuckle. "And a nice homing beacon too."

At this, I sit up straighter, moving my arms back in front of me to look at the bee stinger. "What?"

"Well, without being attached, it doesn't make the bee move, naturally, but that's what it was used for on the bee."

I stare at the thing. "You sure I'm not being tracked having this tangled in my hair?"

"It shouldn't work without the bee's body as a counterpart. I used to kill all those fake bees flying off course into my gardens all the time when I was a Grower." Margareath stretches her arms wide, getting up from my bed. "Once you remove the stinger from the bee, the body can still fly around, but the parts don't track anymore." She pats me on the shoulder, yawning. "Well, g'night."

I nod as she walks back to her own bed, but I can't help staring at the stinger, still suspicious that it could somehow be keeping tabs of my whereabouts. So instead of putting it back in my hair, I stash it within the grout of a broken tile on the floor near my cot. Then, with loose hair now itching my cheeks and nose, I fall into a deep sleep, fighting hard to blot out the images of today's destruction and the unprecedented attack that niggles my brain with dozens of unanswered questions.

"Aloy." Vienne's warm hand holds mine, and it's such a gentle wake up, I hardly want to open my eyes.

"Mmm?"

"I waited as long as I could to wake you, but Ollinear and the other guards are here to take ten new women to the fertilization room, and Aaron may arrive at any moment. We need you to put on a good show."

I do as she instructs, leaning over as I try to stand, drooling a little and wiping the spittle on my sleeve. I keep my eyes unfocused and feign agitation when one of the women touches my arm. Thus, when Aaron indeed drops by to escort the ladies to Mid's examination room, the guards have good things to report.

"She's as batty as a rabid crow," says Vassily.

"Really?" Aaron's joy is written in his showy gestures. He swings his arms wide, claps a few of the guards on the back even though they wince at the touch, and even seems to do a little jig as he walks my way. "Got to see for myself!"

When Aaron's directly in front of my face, I can smell the orange-laced scent of his breath. It's still putrid bursting from his mouth, an over-fermented perfume. "What's your name?" he asks.

I stand dumbly, my eyebrows knitted together.

"Dunno, ha?" He pokes me in the gut, and I jump back a step, knowing that I shouldn't want to be touched. "You don't like that, eh?" Aaron continues poking me, and I scamper backward until I fall in a jumble onto a cot in back of me. "Got anything to say to me? You know who I am, right?"

"My . . . my Elected." I grunt out the words like they're hard to say. They are, in a way. Just not in the way Aaron imagines.

"*Very* nice! And what's the first thing you'd like to do now if I were to let you out of here?"

I think for a moment, rocking back and forth from one foot to the other and then blurt out the answer in staccato. "Do research for Mid Country. Work on the rocket launcher. Build airrides."

"Ahh, lovely!" Aaron waves over Vassily. "See what good things come of a doctor's visit? Isn't it wonderful to have the capacity to cure so many of our people?"

"Yes, Elected. What would you like me to do with her?" Vassily asks.

"Leave her here for now. I want to keep watch of her symptoms. Make sure she's all cured of the disease and cancer she brought with her from East Country." He lies coolly to Vassily. "Never know when we might need a little help in the rocket room, though, eh?" Aaron tweaks my chin between his thumb and index finger, squeezing me like I'm a child.

"Well, got to be off, now. Have lots of baby-making to oversee!" He's gleeful, like he's completely forgotten about the mass of his people who were hurt or killed the day before. Or like he doesn't really care.

"Elected," A new guard stands in the doorway as if he's not positive he's welcome but still has something important to relay. He takes one tentative step inside, thrusting a written note toward Aaron.

Mid's Elected turns a frosty glare toward the door. "What is it? Can't whatever piddly need of my people wait until after the fertilization? I've only been able to supervise one so far." His voice is a whine, high and sing-songy. Not at all befitting of a leader.

The guard bends his head in apology but keeps the note stuck out toward Aaron. The Elected rips it from his palm, flipping open the folded scrap of paper. The guard keeps his eyes focused on the floor tiles, as if he knows he'll be in trouble, just for having been the messenger of some bad news.

Sure enough, as soon as Aaron reads the scrawled lines, he flies into a rage. "A robot doing *what?* In the main control room? Fiddling with switches he wasn't authorized for?"

"I'm not sure, Elected. We're looking into it," says the guard, eyes still downcast. "With everything going on after the attack, we haven't had much of a chance to—"

Aaron picks up a nearby pillow, launching it across the room. If he was expecting a satisfying thwop or the pillow to hit one of my women, Aaron isn't rewarded. The pillow softly swishes through the air and skids across the tiled floor, almost soundlessly.

"Pieces of useless trash, those robots are, all of them!" he screeches. Aaron darts his head from side to side, looking for one of the said robots. Upon finding none on which to unleash his rage, he stamps his feet. The thud punctuates the air, a lone sound in a room of women sucking in their breath.

"Perhaps it was a malfunction, Elected?" says the guard, taking a step back so Aaron's flailing arms won't collide with his face.

I know for sure they're talking about Ty's robot, and I hope to the heavens, whatever Ty did to the robot's programming, it can't be traced back to him.

"What was it doing there?" Aaron asks, walking right up to the guard's face to ask his question in uncomfortable proximity. His pulse throbs within the veins of his temple.

The guard shifts but doesn't dare move backward. "We . . . we don't know, Elected. He was on the communication hub, but we stopped him before anything was transmitted or received."

My eyes scrunch, the news of our unrealized plans sounding like sharp buzzing in my ears. We won't be able to contact our men in East about a synchronized revolt. We won't be able to communicate with them to see how they're doing. We won't be able to do anything now. Not after a failure like this. Aaron's eyes will be all over us after this breach of security.

As if on cue, Aaron rushes back to my side. He rips my head toward his face, pulling me by my hair. "What did you do?"

I stammer, keeping up the act, even now. But I can see Vienne wincing from her spot across the room. I wish I could convey to her that I won't fail her, that I'll keep up this ruse even with Aaron screaming in my face.

"*What did you do?*" Aaron screeches at me again. The yells sock me hard, his breath punching my flesh.

"Nu . . . nu . . . nothing," I continue, gasping within Aaron's grasp.

A tuft of my hair tears from my scalp into Aaron's fist. He clenches it, rubs it across his cheek, stares at me with glowering eyes, and then *humphs*. He leaves my side, and I fall to the floor on my knees. A few of East's women run to me, but they stop when they see the side glare I give them. No one should help me now. Not when Aaron is so angered with me. I refuse to bring any of my women down with me.

Aaron turns his attention elsewhere. He walks up to the messenger, waving a finger in his face. "Burn them all!"

I gasp, thinking he means my women, but Aaron continues, "Get rid of all the robots. We don't know how many of them are compromised. Destroy them. Melt their metal for other purposes. More bombs!" He nods to himself, satisfied by his latest decision. "I want to see the specific communication hub the robot was found in front of. Take me there at once!"

Aaron's about to follow the messenger out of the room, waving a group of his guards behind him, but he turns at the last minute. He takes a moment to stare at the four hundred of us. "Take twenty of their women to fertilization today."

Ollinear stops, meeting Aaron's chilly gaze. "Are you sure, Elected? Twenty is over capacity for the lab."

Aaron focuses on Ollinear, looking at him from toe to head. Ollinear, to his credit, doesn't stir. Just keeps his stance, legs hip width apart, hands still at his side. "I said twenty!" He points to me, still lying with my legs underneath me on the cold tile. "Watch her like a hawk! If she even steps out of line, even just a fraction—if she doesn't eat all her vegetables at dinner, if she takes too long in the bathroom. Anything! Put a bullet in her head!" Aaron's gaze shifts across all of my people, taking an extra-long time to meet their eyes.

"And kill three of the men in captivity back in East Country," Aaron snaps.

At this, several of the women in the room gasp. There's a pleading "No!" that erupts from the back, but I can't tell who uttered it.

"Which three?" asks Vassily from the side of the room. His lips curve into an almost-smile, but the expression stops at his eyes. Even in happiness, I suppose Vassily isn't truly joyful.

Aaron shrugs. "I don't care. Radio our guards over there and tell them to pick whichever three they want. Whoever's the biggest thorn in their sides."

Vassily bows, turning on his heels to follow-through with the order.

"Enjoy the rest of your day, ladies," Aaron says, and then whisks a path out of the room, his heavy, velvet robes swaying in the movement.

18

TWENTY WOMEN ARE TAKEN in a line out the door to the labs. Only when Ollinear is the last guard still left inside our dormitory do I dare pick myself up off the floor. I rub my scalp where the hair ripped out. I allow Vienne to grasp my hand and squeeze it tightly. I know whom the Mid guards back in East will choose to kill. How could they not pick Griffin? If he's still alive, that is. There are just too many odds against him. The bullet wounds. This new decree by Aaron. The fog of unfocused grief spreads across my heart and lungs, the weight settling heavily. I shut my eyes, trying to push the thought that I won't ever see Griffin again from my mind. I can't let the belief rest too long in my head or I won't have the strength to push forward. And we must push. With everything we have left.

With a labored cough, I lean against a nearby bedframe. "We don't know when the three will be killed," I say to the women starting to congregate near me. "Aaron didn't give a date. It's up to Mid's guards in East." I pause, dropping my head again to stop a bout of dizziness. "Maybe they'll take their time. Maybe our men have already staged an ambush against their captors. We don't know. We have to keep faith."

Vienne vehemently nods her head to show agreement, but I see the shadow pass over her eyes. She doesn't truly believe my words, and neither do I. The murmurs of anguish thrum across the vast dormitory as my women try to guess who of East's men might currently be the biggest thorns in the sides of their jailers. Which of their husbands. Which of their brothers or sons.

A shout from the back of the room, however, squelches the cacophony. "Instead of just bringing Mid's people out of their medically induced stupor, let's use optogenetics to brainwash them!" It's Margareath's voice.

"They deserve it! We can't afford to wait for them to decide whether to join our fight. Let's just force them!"

Gretchen, who's been standing near Margareath, pipes up. "Yes! We'll create an army against Aaron with his own people. If they followed Aaron's stupid messages all these years, they'll follow something we slip in too."

A few other voices sprout out of the ensuing melee. My women now entertain ideas on how to brainwash Mid's people onto our side of the upcoming fight, having found an outlet to punish Mid's people for Aaron's latest decree against East. It seems to give them back a sense of control. I even hear one idea to convince Mid's people they're assassins, all with Aaron's face in their heads.

Vienne and I look at each other for a moment, my raised eyebrows meeting her blank expression. Even in the midst of our people discussing the best ways to perform such atrocities, Vienne remains unflustered. I'm intrigued at the latest idea of manufacturing assassins, thinking of the one particularly nasty nurse turning upon her Elected with a knife to his unsuspecting gut, but I see Vienne's slight shake of her head, and I know she thinks it would be the wrong choice.

Both of my hands are in the air before I even plan my next words. "Do you even hear yourselves?" I ask, raising my voice. "Are you saying we should sink to the depths of the same person we abhor?"

There are rumblings of displeasure across the room as I keep talking. "No matter what Aaron has done, we would be worse than him if we try to control the mental state of his people. Everyone is allowed a choice in the matter of battle. You take that away, and you take away their humanity."

"Not to mention our own humanity," adds Vienne in a quiet voice behind me.

There are a few more tense moments, as I'm not sure my words were enough to convince my people. But Margareath leads the conversation toward a different route again, throwing up another question into the air. "How are we going to reach East to tell them about the invasion?" Her voice is thick with frustration. I acknowledge her change of topic with a slight nod. Margareath lays a palm against the whitewashed walls and proceeds forward. "We don't have the robot anymore. We'll never be able to gather a significant force against Aaron if we aren't even sure how many of Mid's people will turn. We need East's men in the fight too."

"We'll convince most of the people Emma gets the chance to cure," says Ollinear, speaking for the first time since Aaron left. "Believe me, nearly all seven thousand will move to our side once they understand what Aaron's been doing to them."

"He's right," says Vienne, placing a hand on Ollinear's bicep. "Truth is a much more powerful tool than lies and brainwashing."

"Maybe," says a woman on my right. "But do you really think Mid's people will care about saving East once they learn they can get cancer if they don't stay under optogenetics' spell? What would you all choose?"

The other women chime in, the conversation picking up to shrill heights once again. A frail woman clings to one of the bedframes, spouting anxiety-ridden words, her voice a mere scratch. "What about the men in East Country? We still need them. No one will be on our side or protect us as well as our own countrymen can."

Margareath's voice rises above the group to answer the woman only she seems to have heard. "Protect us, Ursa? You think we'll be sitting idly by? No one will be in charge of *rescuing* us!" She cocks her head in my direction, and I nod in agreement. "We fight just like everyone else!"

"We still need to connect with East, though, right?" asks one of the older women toward the back. "At the very least to caution them when the coup is happening. We leave our men sitting ducks without *some* kind of warning." Even though she doesn't strain to shout over the crowd, her words reverberate around the room. She's right. We start an insurrection without them, and the men from East will be Aaron's first target with which to subdue us. "And I, for one, would like them by our side, even if we're picking up our own stones to throw," the woman says.

I take the opportunity to still my people with both hands in the air. "I agree. We need to stand as warriors, but I want East's men by our sides as well." I picture Griffin holding my hand as we head out of the hospital on our way to meet Aaron for the start of a coup. No matter how many times Griffin has stood in the crosshairs of a target, he's managed to gain the upper hand. I can't bear to picture him at the wrong end of Mid's guns now. He should be here, at his rightful place beside me and Vienne, for this latest, and most ambitious, plan against Mid. "I have an idea how we can still contact them."

In the end, the way we reach out to East is simple. Ollinear, who is still free to move about Mid Country as he likes, visits the fake forest on the outskirts of the city. He waits until a wayward fake bee buzzes near. Then he grabs the insect by its spikey stinger and hands it into the intrigued hands of Ty, whose programming of the orange-eyed robot may have failed, but who still has a way with animatrons.

"I promise I won't mess this one up," Ty whispers to me after sneaking into our dormitory one night later.

"It wasn't your fault the last robot couldn't fly under Mid's radar in the communication hub," says Vienne, standing behind Ty as he cracks open the bee's fuzzy body with a set of tweezers.

"And this one," I say, a wry smile spread across my cheeks, "will definitely fly."

Margareath's discussion about my unique hairpin the other night set my thoughts in motion, and now we're in the midst of inserting our handwritten message inside the bee's belly, preparing it for flight.

Margareath stands nearby, hands fidgeting in the wide pockets of her canvas robe. "I still can't guarantee it'll be able to fly all the way to East," she says.

"I know." I meet her eyes, trying to transfer a semblance of my own hope to her. The bee, carrying our message, and being routed by Ty's computer programming, is a faint bet, but it's the only one we have. There is no other option but to put our full faith into this inch-long plastic contraption. It's sadly fitting that the bee, a symbol of Mid's twisted sense of nature and what served as my first introduction to the country, should now serve as our communication tool. "But it's the simplest of solutions that sometimes work."

"We may never know if it worked," says Ty. He squints over his project, his thumb and pointer finger gripped hard to steady the tweezers.

"True," I concede. "After this we need to focus all our attention on Emma's work. We have less time than originally planned if Aaron keeps up his rate of sterilizing twenty of our women each day."

So far Aaron's kept good on that threat, and twenty of my people returned to the dormitory, worn out and gray-faced after a day in surgery. With many of the health professionals still focused on the aftermath of the bombing, there are fewer doctors administering the fertilization. Thus, the surgeries are hurried. One of my people even says she hoped they botched her incisions so there's a chance she could still have eggs left inside her ovaries.

The things we now wish for are not for the faint of heart. A botched surgery. A stash of guns, which Ollinear will deliver to our dormitory the night before the coup—to a group of women who have never picked up any weapon to inflict pain, much less one whose firing inflicts not a cut or a bruise but a quick death. And a mechanical bee flying over fifty miles, through an internment camp, and into the hands of our people . . . all in time to stage a synchronized attack against a man who has every technological advancement at the palm of his hand.

Everything we're relying on for survival is an extreme solution. No, the faint of heart are no longer tolerated here.

19

I SIT IN THE back of the dormitory, head bowed over a cot that now serves as my planning station. Fortunately, Mid's guards mostly stay at the front of the room, trying not to intermingle with us if they can help it, almost as if our misfortune is infectious.

We use the guards' discomfort to our advantage, creating a shield of bodies to separate me and my work from their prying eyes.

On the off chance Vassily or one of the other guards roams toward the back of the room, a complex game of telephone is whispered until it finds my ear. I bundle myself within a blanket against the wall, hiding all of the marks I've scratched into the white paint. So far the ruse is working, but each day, as I scratch out another war scheme on the back wall, I feel more like the broken medical experiment I'm supposed to be.

To others, my scratching would look just that—nails against paint, crazy lines made by a crazy woman. But to Vienne and Ollinear who communicate my markings to Emma, and who in turn communicates them to the people she releases from optogenetics, they aren't just faint marks. They're notes and strategies to raise a coup against Aaron.

How many people will it take to fight the guards in front of Aaron's building? How many to secure the doctors? What kind of weapons can we steal ahead of time? How can we keep as many of the unwitting Mid countrymen out of harm's way?

For a leader who's only thought of peace her entire life, each battle plan is a chisel cracking away at the very fibers of my being. My body is stone. When I've devised a new idea to defeat Aaron, my innards may still thump with life, but my arms feel cold as if just one more tap of a tiny rock hammer could shatter my entire being. I keep thinking of my parents. Would they be proud of me for waging an all out war . . . or disappointed?

"Hiya," says Ollinear, stepping through the people who surround me in a protective, tight weave.

I lean closer to the wall, not answering him right away. Instead I peer at my latest drawing of Mid's city center. Buildings two and three are tiny scratches in the painted concrete. I circle the first and etch a line through the second, then rub the outside of a fist across the whole thing and start again.

"It's time for your next treatment."

I've been scheduled in the evenings to attract the least amount of attention. Aaron doesn't want his people seeing me, almost as if I'm a symbol of his weakness. And the evenings work to our advantage, as it affords us a quiet space and time to discuss plans. If only Aaron knew what we were doing when I was supposed to be under his fiancée's treatment.

"Hmmm." I glance at Ollinear but don't move from my position, kneeling on the cot pushed against the wall.

"How long've you been sitting like that?" He nudges me lightly with the palm of his hand.

I finally look up from my work, blinking a few times in his direction. "I look that bad, ha?"

"You look . . . consumed."

It's been nineteen days since my first high-intensity optogenetics treatment and the attack on Mid. I've spent all nineteen either huddled against this back wall or hunched over my makeshift desk.

"Well, you know . . . planning for war and all." My voice is heavy.

"Come on." Ollinear helps me stand, and my knees crack with the change of position. "There aren't many guards still out, and we'll try to avoid the few milling around, but it's best we wrap you up." He pulls a nearby wool blanket over my shoulders. It's course and thick, and I tuck myself into it like a child with a towel after a bath. I know the blanket's just to keep me inconspicuous for our walk to Emma's office, but the warmth feels good across my back.

"Where's Vienne?" I ask, looking over the pool of ladies around the room. The women of East Country have been spectacularly supportive since Aaron's latest outburst, bringing me portions of their food, fluffing my pillow after I've risen in the morning, even washing my garments in the nearby bathroom for me. I'm supposed to act mentally ruined, and my people pretend at taking care of me. Except, in the last few days, with my eyes red from staring so long at my schemes, I get the feeling it's no longer a ruse. The only woman I don't see hovering near my side is Vienne, but I know it's because she's doing a job I devised. I rub my forehead, burying the heels of my hands into my eyes.

"Still with Emma." Ollinear's acted as Vienne's escort at dawn before most people are awake and at night after everyone's holed up in the tower apartments. I've stayed up late, waiting for Vienne to arrive back in the dormitory so I can review my day's strategy planning and hear how the optogenetic sessions proceeded. But I'm careful not to spend hours talking Vienne's ear off. Though she doesn't utter a complaint, I can tell sleep is what Vienne craves most when she arrives back to our dormitory. It must be exhausting trying to persuade confused Mid countrymen that what they've been told for years are lies.

"How's Emma doing with the triple shifts?" I ask.

"Tired. Same as you."

"I haven't been doing anything worthy of being tired. Just sitting in this room."

"Well, it's a kind of tired, all the same," Ollinear says, tapping his forehead to indicate thinking.

"S'pose," I agree and keep my head down as we pass through the exit door. Ollinear mumbles to the armed guards standing outside our dormitory, and then he walks me, gun pointed into my back, down the hallway. I know it's just for show, but it unnerves me anyway.

When we're three quarters of the way and my legs are finally starting to feel loose again, Ollinear catches me off guard. "The burden of planning for war doesn't have to be such a grim one. You're saving my people. Not killing them," he says.

I consider his statement for a moment and nod underneath the blanket. But fighting is fighting. Even if I've devised ways to reduce Mid's casualties: staging the attack after sunset when everyone's off work, or instructing Emma to tell Mid's people not to kill the doctors, just to capture them, I still know people will die. With each flick of my fingernail across the dormitory's grimy wall, I'm deciding who lives and who dies.

Which people do I leave at the city's gate to greet our men from East? If our men don't arrive or come too late, am I condemning that battalion to a sure death? And the people I've dedicated to disarming Mid's guards—that's ultimately the most dangerous job. Pitting heavily armed guards against a troupe of my people who are only armed with piecemeal weapons and sticks, I'm surely sealing their fates.

We arrive at Emma's office door and hear gentle laughter, which quiets the moment Ollinear knocks. I wait, leaning against the wall, still feeling the weight of my decisions. I try to picture which of the women, Emma or Vienne, was laughing. It's been so long since I've heard my wife happy, I don't even know the sound of her joy.

The door unlocks from within, and Ollinear walks in first, me tightly behind, almost connected to him at the elbow. Emma's hand rests on the top of Vienne's arm, a light touch that moves when we step inside, but I can't peel my eyes away from it. Vienne turns toward me, a smile still large across her face. Her eyes are warm, but upon seeing me, they change shape. Wider with a creased brow as accent.

"Aloy?" she asks, moving to my side.

"She's fine," says Ollinear. "But you might remind her not to skip meals." He directs his last words to Emma, as if she, in her role as doctor, is an appropriate person to advise me on this matter.

Emma starts to stay something, but I stop her. "I will. I will." I don't let them fuss over me. They have the same dark circles under their eyes. Instead, I delve straight into questions about the optogenetics release.

"We had ten out of two hundred refuse to believe us today," says Vienne. That's the typical percentage.

I do the math in my head.

"Not too bad, considering," says Ollinear, his last words lilting in a question.

"Yes, good work," I add, trying to remember to dole out the accolades I know Vienne and Emma deserve. Both are wearing themselves thin seeing so many people each day. But instead of looking as tired as I feel, they seem to glow. I stare into Vienne's face, having expected to see lines etched into her brow, same as mine. If anything, she looks more vibrant here in this small yellow-colored room than in the dormitory when we're back together at night.

Vienne's face is bright like a flower opening in the pre-dawn. For some reason, the realization causes my stomach to knot. "Is it hot in here?" I pull at the collar of my robes, only noticing a fraction of the wayward glance Emma gives Vienne. Before they can comment on my question, I ask, "How'd the latest resistance meeting go?" Ollinear has been staging small rendezvous with people who've taken our side. They meet in the underground bomb shelters or in secret, during the day at work, receiving instructions as to their roles in the upheaval.

"I spoke to an excellent resource today," he says. "One of the men with access to Mid's digital clock projection who's in a good position to help us." Calix once told me this projection helps direct the brain stimuli, which is part of Mid's optogenetics refresh. The light pulses from the projection, which Mid's people can see from any building in the city, keeping the monthly optogenetics procedure constantly updated with instructions for the brain. Ollinear continues, "He agreed to change the projection as a signal when we're ready to strike."

"A perfect synchronized start to the campaign," says Emma, clapping her hands to her chest.

"It doesn't matter what we write on the projection, really," I add. "Just as long as the pulsing stops. We could even turn the whole screen off."

"Except that a message would be more inspiring," says Vienne. "I'll put some thought into the best one."

I nod, and Emma keeps the report going with the most pertinent of sentiments from the people who've been taken off optogenetics so far. "Many of them want to see their children. They aren't pleased when we say that'll blow their cover. We just need them to keep up the act for less than a month, but it's like keeping hungry people away from food. And they're taking so long asking us questions, we almost can't finish each within the schedule. We need more people to talk to them, like Vienne's doing."

"More of my women?" I ask.

"I can't sneak that many prisoners out," says Ollinear. He rubs a thumb and forefinger against his temple.

"More children," says Vienne. "Or some of the people we've changed who work in the hospital."

They can't mean doctors, as those two hundred individuals are free-thinking without the optogenetics spell. "Nurses?" I ask. Vienne and Emma glance at each other, and this time I interject. "What's that look for?"

"We'll use some of the nurses, but speaking of them, we saw your favorite person today."

They both know about the nurse who stopped me from taking Glory back to East months earlier. Besides Aaron, she's the person I despise most in Mid. "We had high hopes for changing her mind, but she just didn't budge," says Vienne. "I'm sorry."

"Don't be," I say. "She'd obviously be in Aaron's corner with or without any brainwashing. What'd she say?"

"Threw herself toward the phone," says Emma. "Screamed like a banshee for her Elected."

Ollinear's hand clenches visibly, a tight red fist at his side. "And?"

Vienne laughs, and I instantly recognize the quiet sounds from earlier tonight as my wife's. "Emma isn't as delicate as she looks."

Emma grins and teeters into a slight bow. "She may not remember why she has a black eye, but it'll be a shiner tomorrow morning."

"Best news I've heard all day," I say. "What else?"

"There's a strong inclination to assassinate Aaron," Vienne says.

"What do you tell people?" I ask.

"That an attempt on one's own without a coordinated advance and an ability to disarm his bodyguards would prove futile and jeopardize our entire operation," says Emma, almost as if she's reciting a party line. She must have repeated it multiple times.

"And that I want to be the one to do it," I say, my eyes fixated on a crack in the ceiling.

"Well," says Vienne, shrugging one shoulder. My words pretty much end the conversation for the evening.

20

IN TOTAL, WE MANAGE to pull—and keep—around six thousand two hundred of Mid's forty-thousand countrymen off Aaron's brainwashing. I haven't slept in over twenty-four hours, as the night of our attack is now imminent. Ollinear's friend in the control room will replace Mid's clock projection at precisely eleven p.m. with the phrase Vienne concocted, "A new day is here." Six hundred of the optogenetically-free people will be used to capture Mid's two hundred doctors. Capture, not kill . . . I hope. Four thousand people will fight Mid's guards, and they'll be placed at strategic locations: outside Aaron's apartment in building thirteen, at the communications hub in building four, within the armory at building five. Four hundred will be spread throughout the towers' floors, keeping the rest of Mid's forty thousand people within their apartments through a computerized system-wide door lock. The rebels will also be on hand after we've successfully taken Aaron out of office so that Mid's people will receive aid while they're kept within the apartments throughout their optogenetics withdrawal.

It'll take about six weeks for the effects of Aaron's treatment to fully wear off, and the whole time, Vienne's will be the voice Mid's people hear over their apartments' speaker system. She and Ty will work the communications and surveillance hub to keep our prisoners abreast of what's happening the entire time. Our goal is to peaceably give Mid's people knowledge, both the good and the bad, and hope they understand why we've staged the coup. Tonight, Vienne and Ty are already in place, having been snuck out by Emma during the last medical exam.

Nine hundred of the optogenetic-free will dismantle Mid's weapons, starting the long process of melting the bronze and steel, so that even when Mid's people are freed from the apartments, the ones who still believe East is their attacker won't be able to fight us. At least not with such technologically advanced mechanisms.

Fifty people will be reserved for central processing, ensuring life systems for Mid's people in the towers continue. This includes food service, air, heat, and water. I've mostly saved these safest of roles for Mid's children, and Ty's already schooled them on what needs to be accomplished.

The last fifty people will be staged at Mid's city gates or at the entrance to the tunnel Cole and Griffin built. They'll be used to greet East's men, tell them what's going on throughout the city during the invasion, and usher them to positions of most need. That's *if* East's men ever received our cryptic message sent through the mechanical bee. And *if* they were able to overcome Mid's guards at the internment camp. And *if* they were able to traverse the miles of terrain at just the right time to reach us during the attack. A lot of ifs.

Throughout all of my planning, I kept Griffin's face in the back of my mind. Three of East's men were ordered killed by Aaron just a month ago. What if Griffin was one of them? Am I being selfish to wish that a man already dying of a bullet wound wasn't chosen over another of East's countrymen? But is it truly selfish to wish the man you love is still alive? I push these self-recriminations from my mind, choosing instead to believe no one was shot. Maybe Mid's guards decided not to carry out Aaron's order. It's a faint wish but one I need to cling to in order to move forward with today's plan.

There are so many wishes moving through my head like fish battling rapids. I wish I knew Griffin would be part of the group arriving in Mid. I wish none of what's about to ensue ever had to happen. I wish I could have convinced Calix and Aaron of East's innocence. I wish whoever is Mid's true attacker would have stayed isolated and followed the Accords. I wish my parents could see the leader I've become, for good or bad. I wish I were surrounded by everyone I love.

I stop on this last one and change my mind. No, I don't wish Glory or Tomlin or Eve were here. I'd rather they were safe. I hardly want Vienne involved in the ensuing melee.

I look down, trying to keep strength the only characteristic my women can ascertain from my face. They don't need to see my uncertainty. And they don't need to hear my internal voice, which keeps telling me all this is futile. Seven thousand against forty. East's unarmed men against Mid's gun-toting guards. And me against Aaron. The odds are not in our favor.

But we've planned. We've sweated over the intricacies. My women have practiced sling-shotting in the wee hours of the night. We've been given guns from Ollinear too, but there's been no opportunity to try them yet. Ollinear's found a few swords for us as well. Nothing fancy, but it helped to while away the hours, showing people how to step forward, plunging the weapon and slashing. The more rudimentary weapons are all we dare practice with inside the concrete dormitory walls, and even that's been in the complete darkness or under bedsheets in case Mid's surveillance is watching us.

Vienne's been gone more often, her voice hoarse and often lost completely when she does return. And I've belabored the numbers and positions of our rebel group so many times I can recite them from memory at any given moment.

So wishes need to be set aside for now. It's time for action.

I tug the laces of my boots in each hand, pulling on them tight as if my grip on the cloth strands could match the tenacity of my feelings. I don't bother with the farce of mental ruin anymore. I stand and move to the middle of the dormitory floor, fluid and straight-backed. All eyes are on me, and I keep the contact, staring from one person to the next. Margareath spins a gun in her right hand, almost cavalier in her hold. Gretchen holds a good-sized rock and then slips it inside her robe's pocket. In her other hand, she grasps a slingshot, its rubber bands lying lax now. I'm reminded of her aim just nights before when she pulled the rubber back until her shot against a faraway target was dead-on. The oldest of my women don't look old right now. Their faces are granite, their feet planted firmly.

"We've arrived at the most fateful of times," I call out, my voice meeting the ears of every single East citizen in the room. "We held fast. We suffered in silence. We recruited with truth on our side." A few whoops echo around me. "But it wasn't in vain. Now we stand up, not only for East country, but for the freedom of the known world as well." Nods and a chorus of yeses rain across the crowd. My voice grows quiet. "None of us wants to fight. We don't value war or aggression in East's culture. But we do value our way of life. And when someone cannot be reasoned with and will not back down, we will defend ourselves! Tonight we take the necessary action to reclaim what is ours."

There's a growl to my voice. The pent up buzz of inactivity we've all labored against runs loudly now within our veins. I shout the next words. "Our children! Our families! Our country!" There is an overwhelming roar of agreement throughout my women, and if the guards outside the door weren't already attuned to the shift in the room, they would be now.

We don't have clocks or watches in our un-windowed dorm, but I know exactly when eleven p.m. is upon us. As I say my last words, we hear two sharp bangs piercing through the unrest. I hate to think what just happened outside our locked door, but I know Ollinear had no other choice.

The door opens and our friend wordlessly stands in the unlit backdrop of the hospital. Vassily and another guard lie prostrate on the floor, their heads slumping against slack shoulders on either side of Ollinear. The gunshot wounds in their chests are fresh, blood spilling onto the floor and leaking into the dormitory.

"A new day is here!" I shout. On cue the women I've shared the last months with in this cramped and stuffy room burst from its confines, a belly ripping open to produce the most fertile of plots.

The crowd pushes through the doorway, leaving the two guards where they fell, half in, half out of the entrance. Maybe one of my women will come back to move the dead later, but we don't stop for them now. How much has changed in such little time. I isolate the part of my mind that remembers the rituals we provided for our dead in East Country. The stones. The prayers to the heavens. Even those who drank hemlock received these rights.

But we never participated in war before, and the rules are different now. More savage. My sequestered thoughts are purposely tamped back, my eyes moving their focus from Mid's two deceased guards to the rush of movement around me.

My women run past in an organized stampede. Gretchen meets my eyes for one split-second, and I give her a steely nod in exchange. She refused to go with the other children toward the life support processing in building two, instead signing up to meet East's men at the city's gates. I know her father, Grobe, will not be in the pack, as his death occurred at the hands of Mid months ago, but still I can sense her urgency to be closest to what's left of East when it arrives.

The taste of iron was fierce on my tongue as I realized many days ago that I could not stop Gretchen from making her own decisions.

Besides locking her back in this dorm, there is little I can do to guide her judgment once the fight begins. What she does and whom she chooses to fight rests in her own hands. She is still a child, yet now fully grown in the pit of two countries' turbulent affairs.

The room is suddenly empty, the sound inside eerie compared to the yells from far across the hospital. I can hear the second my people meet resistance. Their whoops and battle cries are shattered glass, cracking and splaying in all directions.

Ollinear stands just outside the door, and I stop for just one beat more to wish him good luck and make my final request of him. "When you meet with Vienne and Ty, tell them . . ." My words are hoarse but steady. "To proceed forward no matter what."

Ollinear agreed to guard these two instead of the person I know he'd rather protect during the fight—his sister. But Emma will have many people surrounding her as the doctors are confined. Her job against unarmed medics will be safer than Vienne's, we know. And so the sister and brother who started this revolution are to be separated in its culmination.

"I will," he says. There are more words on his lips, which he almost struggles to expel, but they burst forth, pointed and lean. "My Elected." Ollinear calls me a title long past my time. I could argue with him now. Not take the credit he gives me. This formal name doesn't belong to me anymore. Not in this country or my own. I gave up the right to be called Elected when I left my people months ago. But we don't have time for any minced words now.

I thump Ollinear on the arm and then run out of my confinement, on my own for the first time in months. I take off down the empty corridor, not toward my people who've turned to the left out of the dormitory to reach Mid's outdoors. Instead, I veer to the right in the direction of Emma's office, now deserted at this late hour.

Each door I pass means something to me now. The green one where I know the children are usually housed. One of Ollinear's volunteers ushered them to the appropriate station hours earlier, and there's another of Mid's guards slumped to the side of the entrance. A third casualty no one has had time yet to move. I know Glory's incubation room is to my right, down three other winding hallways. And the hospital's entrance, which Griffin and Margareath and I took to enter the complex months earlier, is two corridors away from that, to the right and behind me.

When I first arrived in Mid the whole country was a shell. Gray, distant, and unknown. Now that I'm familiar with its organs—the people, the buildings, and the landscape—it's like the whole place has rounded in my mind, filled-in and concrete. I know the twists of the hospital like the back of my hand, its winding maze of closed doors and dark hallways, now just a map toward my destination. I run without stopping or looking around to get my bearings.

Ollinear and my women, whom I can still hear behind me, are a big enough distraction that I'm ensured of easy passage toward the inner bowels of the hospital, as was part of the plan. Mid's guards, if not under duress from other groups of my rebels, will be caught up in the firefight with my people, not wandering in the deserted rooms at the hospital's rear where I run now.

I try to breathe in deeply, as I know this last minute will be all I have before the next set of our plans commences. I blink both eyes closed, holding back any nostalgia. I cannot let the emotion of what I've started overwhelm me. Not now when I'm so close to my own role in the plan. Not even after I've said goodbye, I'm sure, to at least some of my women for the last time. I say a silent prayer to the heavens that I will once again have the privilege of looking upon Vienne's torn, yet perfect, features. That Gretchen will meet the people from East and not a group of Mid's guards instead. That Margareath will come through the fight unscathed so she can rendezvous with her three children and husband.

As we planned, when I reach the too-bright yellow door of Emma's office, it's unlocked and the room is vacant. Emma is long gone, helping to rouse the doctors from their apartments and round them up into the city's epicenter. I can almost make out the sound of yelling from outside the hospital walls, but I am so deep into the building now, the hums are faint, almost dream-like. I slide into the office, barely opening the door wide enough to slink through and bolt its lock behind me.

The screen I've seen Emma use multiple times before is glass-like in its futuristic shine. The videophone lies still on the opposite wall, beckoning to me, as if the strange machine knows it could be both my salvation and undoing at the same time. I could just use the audio part of the communication device, but I opt for the full video so I can see for myself what's happening as I deliver my message. I type in Emma's fourteen-digit security code, and the protective security shield flashes open, yellow and black, a blink of a feline eye. My own face stares back at me, the video technology something Emma's taught me to use but which still baffles me in its mechanics.

When we wanted to speak to one another in East Country, we physically sought out the person. In this bizarre country, modeled after the world from years ago, people communicate through intricate pieces of metal and silicone. It is so stark; I still wonder how anyone converses through this technology in a way that accurately conveys feeling.

I type in the three-digit code to reach the person I now seek and then step to the side, out of the camera's view so all that shows are the yellow painted walls and the reclined medical chair lying vacant in the center of Emma's office. Five seconds count through my mind, each popping with the electricity of my held breath.

Answer! Answer! I repeat the mantra in my mind until there's a whoosh, and a picture of a gold-ensconced room springs onto the screen.

"Emma? What do you want?" The voice on the other end is hurried, and I see my tormentor step into view. "I've got a lot going on right now. Don't know if you've noticed the people gathering outside since you can't be bothered to leave that office of yours lately, but it seems we have some citizens who need subduing."

I don't speak, just keep staring at the screen, my back pushed up against the far corner of the room.

"Emma? Are you there?" Aaron's voice is a mixture of annoyance and fear. His eyebrows crest toward his pale hairline and the filmy pink of his albino eyes peer closer at the video feed. "Look, I don't have time for another update of yours about brain waves and such." He circles his palm in the air, trying to portray an air of unconcern, but it shows through anyway. There are already a few beads of sweat forming on Aaron's brow.

I pause to ensure my tone contradicts the heat of Aaron's features. It is a cold and calculating voice that speaks back to the man who's orchestrated the lobotomy of his entire population. I've waited weeks to show Aaron he's underestimated me and my people.

"Emma's not calling you. It's me." I wait a beat and then step into view.

21

ANGER STEAMS OFF AARON'S reddening cheeks. The veins in his temples leap as he stares back at me. "How . . . how . . ." He fumbles against the knowledge that I haven't been mentally eradicated in the optogenetics treatment. Someone's been lying to him, and I have to suppress my own satisfied smile as I see the notion just dawning on him. "What have you done to Emma?" he asks.

I'm momentarily surprised that Mid's Elected even bothers to ask further about his fiancée. I thought he just kept her nearby as a sign of prestige. A sort of marriage rite—that he could possess one of the only females in Mid Country who wasn't under the optogenetics fog and was, thus, still fertile. But perhaps he did care for her. The idea of telling Aaron that Emma's been against him for a long time flashes across my mind. I would relish the look on Aaron's already crimson face. But I hold back, foreseeing one possible outcome of tonight's events that would leave Aaron still in charge.

I won't risk Emma's life by giving away her position. If things turn out how I'd like, Aaron will know about Emma's defection soon enough, and I'll make him let her leave Mid. But if I lose tonight and Emma is stuck in this awful country, I will not send her straight to the gallows with my words.

"She'll be fine as long as you follow my instructions carefully," I say.

"So you had a hand in what's going on below?" He stares at me, assessing as much as he can from far away with a mile of optic cables separating us. "How did you get better from your treatment?"

He still thinks I had optogenetics, and he's wondering how I've managed not to break under the strain, not losing my memory after taking the combined mixture of light pulsations and the purple pills. I just shake my head, and I can see Aaron doesn't know if my movement means I won't tell him how I escaped the mental breakdown or if I won't tell him what's currently transpiring across his country.

"Guards!" Aaron yells. There's a scuffle as Aaron leaves the screen. But I know what's transpiring in his penthouse suite right now. I bide my time, keeping the videophone buzzing. Slowly, with a hint of a smile on his face, Cole's messy blonde hair inches into the picture. The clone still looks like the dead Calix's identical twin, even though his hair is inches longer than the former Mid Elected's locks ever were. His blue eyes sparkle back at me in triumph. Aaron is caught off guard with a gun held taught against his neck.

Cole, whom I at first refused to trust, who so grotesquely reminds me of his look-alike, Calix, and who holds my stolen genetics inside his veins, has been the secret key to our entire endeavor. I should have known that anything of Griffin's making would not disappoint me. Just the thought of Griffin causes a well to begin in my throat. I file away the feelings with so many others that will soon need to be expunged and pored over if I ever expect to get past all the grief.

The clone winks at me from behind the screen. Mid's Elected glances back and forth between me and Cole, his face growing ashen. Aaron tries to splutter out a call for guards, but Cole cuts him off. "Elected," he says, his tone sweet, no different than his usual drawl, "There's no use calling for them. They've been taken care of." Cole bobs his head to me, almost an acknowledgement of his own worth, and for the first time ever I smile a wide grin back at him.

"Good work," I say.

"What are you both attempting?" Aaron growls, his lips parted in a pant, the gun still wedged under the folded skin where jawbone meets neck.

"It's simple," I say. "I just want to speak to you."

Aaron grunts. "Fine then. Speak."

"No. In person and alone. A real conversation. One where you try, for once, to listen to reason."

"Absolutely not!" Aaron guffaws. "You think for a minute I'm going to meet with you alone while my country is clashing fifty floors below me? No, I am going to let my thousands of guards do their job and wipe you and your little . . . whatever this is . . . off the face of the planet. Then when your body is a simpering mound of flesh, dying with your wounds—of which I am sure by that time you will have many—then, and only then, will I speak to you." Spittle from Aaron's diatribe hits the videophone's screen leaving pinprick dots. Aaron cocks his head back, haughty, even in the face of Cole's gun. "And you," he says, referring to Cole, "probably don't even know how to use that thing."

Cole holds Aaron's antique revolver, the one so pertinent to our fight, but that I too am not quite sure Cole understands how to use. I don't even know if he realizes it hasn't contained real bullets for some time. Or perhaps since Aaron's reign as the current Elected, new bullets have been fashioned for the thing. Whatever the case, Aaron doesn't seem too pulsed by his situation, although to me it would seem dire.

I ignore Aaron's dismissiveness, instead pulling out my own form of weaponry, which I know will get his attention. I hold in front of the screen the small, worn strip of paper Ollinear and Emma gave me two months ago. A couple of the letters show through the video so Aaron can recognize his own writing, but I ensure my thumb and forefinger cover the others.

I read, "AUG. ACG. CGG."

"How in the world . . . ?" Aaron's eyes are alight, and a furrow embeds in his brow.

"Yes, it's what you think. I have your only copy of East Country's genetic code." I let my words sink in, reveling in the stunned expression settling on Aaron's face.

Aaron squeals as if he was just poked by something hot. He leans forward, grasping at the videophone screen with both hands. I see the tips of his fingers as he holds tight. My smile back to Aaron, as I pinch the tiny fragment of paper between my forefinger and thumb, is crooked and triumphant. Aaron opens his mouth to say something, but I stop him with my own words. "I'll give you the sequence, if you just join me for a conversation. Alone, where we first met. You remember where, don't you?"

At this, Aaron laughs deeply, his chest rising and falling with the effort. But there's an unmistakable gleam in his eye. He wants the paper. Calix told me his brother was, at heart, a scientist. A man who celebrated his own successes. Surely this code was Aaron's own discovery, and the loss of it was felt in Aaron's very bones. Losing both the paper and his fragile memories must have been an enormous blow.

Aaron lifts an eyebrow and says, "At the rocket launcher? Alone? You're surely joking."

"At what's left of it. Except this time we talk. About the future of our countries, what you're doing to your people, and who really is to blame for the attacks."

"You realize what you're holding, don't you? I could just overpower you, alone in the tower, take the paper, and obliterate everyone in East with my nanites!" Aaron snarls, the whites of his eyes shining with the idea.

"I don't think we stand too much of a chance, as it is, under your current rule. But I agree, what I'm offering is a dire plea for you to listen to reason." I don't tell Aaron that I intend to be fully armed and prepared for an ambush by him at the base of the launch pad.

I can see the yearning behind Aaron's toothy smile. "I've looked for that slip of paper, for you don't know how long."

"I do know. You kept it hidden in your revolver." I point at the weapon still stuck against Aaron's throat. "How upset you must have been to finally receive back the gun but find it was missing its most precious occupant. Your people removed the code from within the gun months ago."

Aaron's pink-rimmed eyelids flick fast with the fact that his own guards conspired against him. "Once I'm done with *you*," Aaron growls, "I'll kill all the guards who ever *touched* this gun."

I ignore Aaron's venomous comment, instead turning the slip of paper within my fingertips. Cole digs the butt of the revolver deeper into Aaron's neck. "You have ten minutes to get to the launch pad," I say.

Aaron grunts, glancing at Cole to his side.

"Ten minutes," I continue, "before I rip this little paper into bits and let it sail away over your rooftops."

Aaron grimaces. "How do you propose I get out of this building, through the crowd below, and into the rocket launcher without being waylaid by your crowd of rabble-rousers below."

Without guards flanking him, and having had Cole remove all other weapons from Aaron's apartment as he slept, I envision how hard it will be for Mid's Elected to move through the raucous crowd unscathed. If any of his optogenetics-free citizens see him, I don't think anything I've said in convincing the rebels not to assassinate Aaron will make a difference anymore. He'll be torn limb from limb.

I let the faintest of smiles creep across the corner of my mouth and say, "Figure it out."

If Aaron doesn't make it from building thirteen to the rocket launcher, ripped apart by his own people, it's a fate Mid's Elected most certainly deserves.

Abruptly ending the phone call, I scoop up a sack Ollinear and Emma saved for me here. It holds one of Mid's fancy guns, sleek-black and straight-edged. I've clasped it before in this room but never fired it. I understand how it should work, though, and I double-check that the catch is still fixed, leaving the gun disengaged. Last thing I need is for the weapon to shoot off as I hold it tight against my torso.

The sack also contains a lightweight gray, hooded robe. I pull the covering over my small frame, encasing myself inside its folds. The final item inside the sack is a miniscule earpiece. A sticker is easily lifted from its surface, helping keep the plastic object attached behind my left lobe. I pinch the gadget in its squishiest spot to engage the communication, as taught. The microphone isn't directly in my ear canal so as to obstruct other noises or make me deaf if the responder yells, but I hear Ollinear right away.

"Everything going according to plan?" he asks.

"Yes," I say. "He seemed to take the bait."

"Okay, then. Coast is clear for you."

"Thanks."

"Good luck," he responds and the static behind his voice ebbs as my rebel General clicks off again.

I left Aaron little time to think about an offense against me. Ten minutes is hardly enough time to find himself new bodyguards. Especially when our forces are fully engaging his guards as we speak. And it's not a lot of time to traverse the city's epicenter toward the ruins of the rocket launcher. All Aaron may have a chance to do is don some concealing robe, as I have, on the way out of his apartment.

Ten minutes, though, isn't a lot of time for me to move from the hospital all the way to the launch pad either. As planned, my route out of the building is clear now that my people have pushed through, emptying the hospital of the scant amount of guards it held earlier tonight. Thus, I run as fast as I can, knowing I'll be slowed when I reach the outdoors. I'll need to spend the majority of my ten minutes pushing through the rebels and captured doctors congregated in the city square, so any minutes I can make up by running faster through the empty hospital is time I can use outside.

As I move closer to the main doors, I hear the commotion of fighting grow louder. My rebels have started a chant of "A new day is here," and it's so loud I can feel the vibrations of their voices up the back of my spine. But the sound of gunshots also pierces the air, and the screams of the fallen or wounded continue their shrieks inside my head even after each dissipates.

I've been inside the stuffy hospital for so long that when I fling open one of the hospital doors and the cool air hits me, it causes all the hairs on my arms to stand on end. Snowflakes are starting to drift down from low-hanging clouds, blanketing the ground in a slippery dusting of white. The almost sheer gray robe, while sufficiently covering my features, is nothing against the blast of air that gusts harshly onto my exposed skin. One of the intricate flakes barely grazes the back of my hand and sends a sharp stab of pain through my nerve endings. Each snowflake, while beautiful, is composed of the skin-burning acid rain we tried to avoid at length in my home country.

People all around me pull the hoods of their robes up to withstand the stings of the flurries. I jerk the arms of my robes down to cover my fingertips and weave in and out of the yelling crowd, dodging past a group of citizens tearing down the city's main stage where my parents were killed. I try to block out the past images and keep my eyes on the terrain, ensuring I'm not hampered by a snow-covered obstruction in my path or a reaching arm. Everywhere I turn, our rebel forces fight Mid's guards. Men in black nylon armor, the signature uniform of Mid's police, pour out of each building, as if belched into the city's epicenter. My people are there to meet them, the ones with the weapons, stepping bravely forward to clash one on one.

Already I see a group of Mid citizens corralling the doctors into a tight ring inside the city's square as well. The doctors are thrust forward on Mid's moving sidewalks. Many of them stumble, trying to beg my rebels for release. Mid's rebels taunt the medics, peppering them with angry questions and barbs. "How could you do this to us? We'll see how *you* like being lobotomized!" I grimace at the vengeful barbs being tossed around. My intention was never to subjugate Mid's doctors to the same type of treatment they prescribed, but that will have to remain a discussion for later.

I turn away from them, running further into the crowd to reach Mid's rocket launcher at the other side of the city. I must make it to the rocket launcher before anyone spies Aaron. As much as I'd like to see Mid's Elected decimated by the crowd of angry rebels as he waits for me at the base of the rocket launcher, I have other plans for him. I'll give him a chance to see reason, but if Aaron won't listen and band together with East instead of against us, then . . . well, I'm prepared for that scenario too. I clutch the gun against my waist, feeling its blunt edge against the pad of my thumb.

My method of convincing Aaron was highly contested within our planning group. "Ridiculous" was the word Emma used when I first proposed the idea of meeting Aaron alone, dangling East countrymen's genetic differentiator in his face as bait. "Dangerous" was Ollinear's response. But it was Vienne who finally came around, agreeing with my methods. "She can't very well speak with Aaron in his apartment. Who knows what communication devices he has stashed there. He could call for reinforcements. We have to get him out of his safe haven. Aloy needs a neutral place—somewhere that will remind Aaron of his vulnerability and how much he owes her. Not to mention somewhere that reminds Aaron of the forces attacking Mid. A ruined rocket launcher isn't a bad spot."

The next point of my plan, though, was never accepted by Vienne. My conversing with Aaron alone always rubbed her the wrong way. "Keep some of the rebels with you," she'd begged.

"Aaron won't come if he thinks he won't get what he wants," I'd argued. "If he sees me surrounded by our forces, he'll forgo the code and focus his attention on rallying his guards. With me alone, Aaron may think he has a chance of snatching the paper fast and then returning to stamp out this coup. He won't think a few minutes spent meeting me at the launch pad will be enough to give us any advantage." I'd kept going, not letting Vienne, Ollinear, or Emma get a word in edgewise. "What Aaron doesn't realize is Mid's guards have relied on orders from their Elected for so long, that without his commands bombarding them, the guards will be left directionless. The few minutes we'll get with Aaron chasing the genetic code may be enough to gain some foothold. It's an advantage we can't do without."

Vienne had pursed her lips into a straight line. "Take off a serpent's head and the whole monster topples down." She'd understood.

Thus, we'd settled on stationing a squad of rebels around the rocket launcher's base, a few people with access to my headset feed. If I call for help, they'll intervene.

I pinch the device behind my ear again now, getting back in touch with Ollinear. I skirt around two men pushing each other up against the shiny silver walls of Tower One, listening hard for the telltale static of Ollinear's answer.

"Any sign of the men from East yet?" I yell above the fighting. My feet pound on the pavement, as I can't afford to stop running, even now as I wait for the answer I hold most dear. If I could just see the men from East and know if Griffin was alive or dead. Know if Glory was hidden away. Know if our plan worked and our men weren't slaughtered by Mid's guards. Then I could go through with the next phase of the plan, clear-headed. Not knowing any of these answers feels like a shroud, lingering in the back of every thought.

"Still nothing yet." Ollinear's voice shoots through the earpiece, out of breath. He too sounds as if he's running. Ollinear should be settled in next to Ty and Vienne, keeping watch over their work in the comms lab. I don't comment on this detail, but the thought nags.

"Tell me the second anyone sees them, all right?"

I know we have sympathizers staged in the towers' hallways, but there are no windows where they stand. Only Mid's optogenetically-impaired people inside their apartments have windows and a vantage to see if a band of men are running through the countryside to reach Mid's gates. And they obviously haven't mentioned anything to their jailers about it.

"Copy," Ollinear says.

The static grows soft again, and I keep running, eyes trained on the rocket launcher ahead of me. It's a mass of bent metal. After the last bombing, Mid hasn't had a chance to completely repair the building. The billowy fabric dome, which used to cover its top, is completely ripped away. Only fragments of the material blow in the wind—a sad, torn, and unintended flag.

Tomlin told me years ago that a white flag signified surrender. Many countries raised theirs to meet incoming bomber planes during the aftermath of the Eco-Crisis. But the world was so far-gone that even this old-fashioned plea of defeat wasn't accepted. Too many countries were too angry. The fighting was too harsh and orders too solidified to stop a bombardment with merely a flag; use of white fabric to signal surrender was abandoned. I don't know why Tomlin even bothered teaching me about it, as I'd never seen such a symbol in our time. If it wasn't even accepted back in the early turn of the century, why bother imparting the knowledge to me?

I stare up at the rags of white flying over Mid's rocket launcher under the heavy storm clouds. Mid's isn't trying to ask for a surrender—couldn't even possibly know of this old ritual. The white material is just a coincidence. But I can't help feeling as if it's some sort of sign.

I run harder, imagining Aaron's surrender to me. He'll have seen the clash of his guards and my people in the streets as he ran toward the rocket launcher too. Maybe Aaron will realize we're gaining ground and will accept my compromise here in this broken building where we first met. Stop the optogenetics. Let my people go. Quit attacking East. And we'll leave him be. I can only hope for such a simple outcome.

The bottom of the destroyed building is just in reach. Aaron is already here, apparently alone as we agreed, hiding behind one skeletal column of the rocket launcher. He squints into the darkness, as if trying to see me before I see him. I take a deep breath and am about to step out of the shadow to show myself when there's a deafening roar above us.

Everyone, including the fighters in the square, look upward as two monstrous Mid airrides burn fuel, hovering above us. They fall beneath the thick layer of clouds so they're right over our heads, overpowering everything with the sound of their engines. Plumes of silver smoke blow from their exhaust pipes, turning the dark sky an eerie pinkish color and causing my nose to burn.

People are fearful, even those I know to be Mid's guards. Everyone thinks bombs will rain down on Mid's open city center, leveling all those who fight below, regardless of side. How could the airride operators even discern who is who? I glance at Aaron who moves farther behind the column for safely. Even he seems to think Mid's next move is inevitable.

How could this be possible? I thought we staged more than enough rebels around the armory to stop Mid's use of their airrides. Plus, we've been secretly dismantling their hovercraft for weeks, removing necessary pinions and gears so that, even if Mid's guards broke through our wall of rebels, the airrides would be unflyable. But apparently something in our plans wasn't fool-proof. The two airrides barreling over us prove it. My stomach plummets down into my legs. We can't fight against two armed airrides. One would be enough to kill everyone in the city center plus dent many of the closest buildings. Two have enough firepower to decimate the entire rebel force.

The advantage we gained with the element of surprise is gone. Two airrides change everything.

I turn to see Aaron's expression again, expecting another gloating smile, but he's gone. I activate the earpiece with a single squeeze. "Ollinear!"

A second later my commander returns. "Aloy. Are you hurt?"

"No, but Aaron's disappeared. Run off into the crowd. Abandoned the genetic code!" I feel the heat rise to my face. This was my plan, my stupid idea, and now Ollinear knows I failed.

"All right. What was he wearing? I'll designate the squad around the rocket launcher to act as a search party."

"Purple robes, I think. Hooded." My eyes fly around the base of the launch pad, looking for anyone skirting away from the crowd. Then I look up once more at the airrides suspended above us. The squeals of their motors roar, blocking out the cacophony of fighting on all sides. It's with my chin raised to the sky that I notice a figure looming overhead.

Leaning out of an open fissure on a floor of the rocket launcher, way above my head, is Aaron. Even from down on the ground I can see the glint of a smile across his features. Aaron's arms wave maniacally, beckoning me to come join him.

"Call off the squad!" I call through the earpiece. "I've seen Aaron. He's up in the launch pad!"

Just like last time.

22

I KNOW INSTANTANEOUSLY WHY Aaron's moved higher, even if the structure is precarious in its quivering, damaged upper levels. He's maybe eight floors up and climbing further. At every higher level, Aaron leans out a window or a broken wall and gestures in my direction with exaggerated arm movements, grinning like a madman.

He's smart about his ascension, even if the launch building is rickety. If his two airrides unleash weapons inside the city center, everything on the ground will be within harm's way. But up here on the highest of the dome's teetering floors, Aaron will escape all of it.

I look up at him, my teeth biting my bottom lip so hard I taste the hints of blood rising right under the skin. He may have planned his airrides' onslaught and escaped the devastation in the town center. But he won't escape me.

The earpiece vibrates, and Ollinear's voice is firm in my head. "I'm close to you. On my way!"

Hopefully, I'll have finished my mission before Ollinear even arrives. I run forward, the fast-falling snow at my boots having gained a slippery inch as I stood looking for Aaron. Barbed wire and the leftover fence, which is now a mess of bent metal, still encircles the rocket launcher's base, but there are big gaps with which to step through. The barbs poke precariously close to the cloth backpack draped across my right shoulder, but I don't stop long enough to extricate it. I rip through the fence as fast as possible and arrive in the center of the base, looking up at the thick stairwell Griffin and I climbed to save Aaron in this very spot less than a year ago. Previously there was a door in front of the stairs, but that's been blown off its hinges, no sign of the impasse even lying on the surrounding tiled floor. A few minutes later, I'm heaving with the effort of a fast climb up five flights.

"I hear you!" says a sing-songy voice, emanating down through the stairwell's shaft. Aaron leans way over a bannister above me, his white hair blowing in the wind.

"Why don't you just come down then?" I ask, panting. "If you don't want to wait." Without leaving the hospital in over a month, my legs have atrophied in the cramped spaces. The exertion of the run from Mid's hospital, the dodge around fighters in the town square, and now a fast-paced climb, test my body.

Two more floors are below me before Aaron answers, "So one of your minions can just pluck me dead? No, I think it's better to meet up here. Nice and quiet, here."

I'm about to retort, when he sings another sentence over the steep bars. His words travel down to me in a gust. "And won't your body make such a satisfying plunking sound hitting the ground from this far up?"

At this, I hesitate. He's not going to listen to me. Nothing I say will make a difference to Aaron, especially now as he watches his airrides hovering near. He knows he's going to win. But he still wants the genetic code.

I stop on the eighth floor to catch my breath. I could just rip up the code and run. It would be easy. The thought sifts its way into solidity, working its way up from my tired legs and spent lungs to my heart, where it weighs like the heaviest of stones. I've already kept Aaron away from his guards and a commanding post. And wasn't that the purpose of this whole distraction anyway? To buy us some valuable time without Aaron directing his forces? To cut the monster's head away from its body?

My foot teeters backwards, suspended above a lower step. I'm almost ready to retreat, when the airrides rev outside, reminding me to stay on track. Maybe they're waiting for Aaron's signal. The longer I keep him occupied up here, the longer my people have to retreat below—run for the border land, hide within the tunnel Cole constructed, and generally just get away before the airrides start leveling those below.

My feet willingly find the top step, and I keep ascending. I don't stop again until I'm just one level from Aaron's position. He's stayed quiet for a few minutes now, but as I reach floor fourteen, I hear Aaron signing again. His notes sound twisted and demented with their high, off-key lilts.

The ozone's gone; it's all a shame.

Misused technology is what to blame.
When people learn to use it well,
Then use these words to mend the hell.

The rhythm of Aaron's trills are so familiar that I have to hold onto the handrail to keep from toppling over in surprise. The short stanzas. Reference to the hell of this environment. It's another verse of my mother's rhyme—the one she used to sing to me! It doesn't sound comforting as it did coming from my mother's mouth, but it's almost certainly the continuation of her song. I grasp onto the handrail so hard my knuckles turn white. The picture of Ama in my head, tucking me into bed, is a vivid portrait of reds and pinks. The pink of the sun setting outside my bedroom window. The red of my mother's lips as she sung her version of the song. I hear her words in my head, the same ones I've used to soothe myself multiple times since she left.

Lock your strength far away;
Save it for a rainy day.
When the sun no longer shines,
That's when you'll need this little rhyme.

"Where'd you hear that?" I whisper toward Aaron, meeting his gaze as I finally place my feet onto floor fifteen.

Aaron cocks his head, seemingly amused. "Oh, you like that?"

I can't answer him for a moment, wondering if he had contact with my parents while they hid in Mid Country. Does Aaron know something more about them? Some secret that will tell me why Ama and Apa didn't come find me if they knew I was here?

I inch to the side, my hand against the wall. Aaron doesn't move closer, but the look on my face must arouse his curiosity. "My mother made up the darkest of ditties, didn't she?"

I back all the way into the wall, almost tripping on my own feet. "Your mother?"

"Yes, despite what you think of our country, my mother took great care with me. She sang to me every night," Aaron says. He seems to think I was commenting on the parenting system in Mid, not that I was in any way referencing my own mother.

"Did . . . did she sing more of the song?" I ask.

Aaron gazes at me, one eyebrow slightly raised. "More? No." Then he seems to shake off the thought, possibly remembering he was the one who ordered his parents' death. Aaron snaps his fingers. His palm opens, and he wiggles the hand in my direction. "All right, Aloy. Don't you have a code to hand over?" His voice mocks me in its sardonic tone.

I ignore his question. "My mother sang that song to me too. Different words, but . . . " I blink a few times, trying to rid my head of the childhood visage, so fleeting in its comfort. If I dwell on my mother's image for too long, I'll grow soft, forgetting I'm here to dissuade a dictator.

"Oh, please. My mother made it up. A bedtime poem only for me. She told me so. That she'd made it up just for my ears. The ears of the future Elected. Her favorite." He flicks a lock of light hair off his forehead. His hands twirl a few times at his side and then settle, tightening into fists. "Give me the code already, and let's get this over with."

I move to the right, putting more distance between us. I can still hear the loud *whirs* of the airrides, threatening us with their proximity. I begin to think they really are waiting for Aaron's order. His people are probably trying to find him in the Elected suite as we speak. Hopefully, Cole's been able to head them off somehow . . . but maybe, Mid's guards have surrounded Cole, realized Aaron isn't where he's supposed to be, and have launched a manhunt for their precious ruler. Either way, Cole's not in the best predicament. And neither am I.

I must delay Aaron's orders for his airrides as long as possible. Get him caught up in a debate, at the very least. "Aaron, can you imagine how strong our countries would be if we stopped fighting each other and looked elsewhere for our enemy?"

Mid's Elected grunts and takes one step closer, beginning to bridge the few feet between us. "You always try to take the light off yourselves, yet you and your people are always the ones fighting us." He points through the gaping hole in the wall, down into the crowd below.

"All those years of attacks Calix talked about. It wasn't us," I say. "We don't have the technology. If you'd just listen to reason and help us search for the real aggressor!"

Aaron takes another step closer. I back up but realize I'm running out of space. The top floors of the cylindrical rocket launcher are smaller in circumference the higher the level, so floor fourteen is only about eleven hundred square feet.

"Your lies are so easy to dispel," Aaron says. "We've flown as far as a tank of nirogene and the sun's energy will take us. There's nothing out there. East and Mid are the only surviving civilizations."

I shake my head, adamant at dispelling his notion. The former United States couldn't possibly be all that's left of the world. And since I know East Country isn't the one bombing Mid, I'm absolutely certain we're not alone. Instead of disagreeing with Aaron yet again, I choose another topic. Anything to keep him talking. Aaron's anger, directed my way, means he's not thinking about the fight transpiring below. Which means more time for my people to escape the airrides' firing zone.

"You have to stop the practice of optogenetics on your people. Let them have a choice, for heaven's sakes!" I know my words are falling on deaf ears, but I say them anyway, knowing this will probably be the last time I have a chance to make my case.

"How long do I have to listen to this drivel?" groans Aaron, his hand rubbing his forehead. He takes another long stride toward me. I've been holding both the gun and the piece of paper close against my body, concealed underneath the long robe, but the gun could be extricated in a moment's notice. The smooth metal is cold in the circle of my fingers. If Aaron tries to wrestle the paper out of my hands, I already know I'll make a martyr of him. I just have to hold off long enough until Ollinear arrives. Then we'll overpower Aaron and make him call off his airrides.

"Give me the paper already!" Aaron's voice is a full growl. There's a roar outside, and we both turn to see the airrides' doors open mid-air. What's going on? Are Mid's troops tired of waiting for direction? Are they going to shoot manually into the crowds instead of dropping bombs? Were we able to disable the airrides in that one regard, at least?

My eyes are so focused on Aaron's steady advance and the hovercraft outside, that I don't notice Ollinear near the top of floor fifteen until his booming voice says, "Leave her be."

Aaron's white hair whips over his shoulder as his whole body turns to face his one-time guard. "*You!*" he snarls. "*You* took my gun and let the code fall into the wrong hands! Get back below ground and fight. I'll deal with you later." Aaron waits for Ollinear to obey, but my rebel General stands still. "Get the code off her." Aaron points at me and then looks back at Ollinear who still doesn't budge. Confusion and then realization crosses Aaron's features in a split second.

"So, you've stopped taking the doctors' medicine, have you? Abandoned your duties and your Elected?" Aaron asks, the vitriol dripping from his mouth.

"You're no longer acting as an Elected should," Ollinear says, quiet and even-toned.

Aaron turns sugary sweet, trying an alternate tactic. "Perhaps if you're just granted a few more hours in the Satisfaction Room? Eh?"

Ollinear still doesn't move a muscle in his face, the whites of his steady eyes reflecting the scant light outside. Ollinear holds up a gun in his hand, centering its aim on Aaron's chest, ignoring his Elected's offer. "You will no longer control the doctors. My sister included," says Ollinear.

Aaron sneers, his pursed, crescent lips splitting his face in half. "Your sister will preside along with me, and I'll have her be the one to put you back under."

Ollinear shakes his head. "She will not."

The three of us make an isosceles triangle with our bodies. Aaron and I are at the base, close to each other at the far side of the room with Ollinear standing as the topmost point. Mid's Elected seems to contemplate his options and then lunges toward me and the code, screeching in the effort. Ollinear launches forward, grasping his Elected with a muscled bicep around the throat. Aaron writhes under Ollinear's powerful grip. He can barely form words, but the sounds emanating are all threats and venom. An array of spit sprays from Aaron's mouth in his attempt to maneuver out of Ollinear's chokehold. It's not enough, though, against my strong rebel leader.

I move closer to Ollinear, avoiding Aaron's flailing arms. "I suppose in the end this turned out—" I'm just in the middle of telling Ollinear how timely his entrance was and how much I appreciated him following me, when there's a small human squeak emanating from below us. Both our ears perk. Even Aaron shifts so his head is cocked in the direction of the stairwell. There's a moment of quiet and then the small voice rings through the air again, as if all the fighting below is silent against the one word beseeching from a few floors below us.

"Ollie!"

23

"OLLIE!" RINGS THE FAINT voice again. Except this time, the sound is a fraction louder, as if the person is climbing the stairs toward us.

"Emma?" Ollinear rushes to the top of the steps. Aaron is dragged within his grasp, letting out malcontented grunts as his suede-shoed feet brush roughly against the hard tile.

"You hold right there!" comes another voice, the complete opposite in tone and strength from Emma's. I follow Ollinear to the top of the stairs and see the nightmare nurse pulling Emma by the nape of her neck, a long surgical knife stuck precariously close to the future Mid Country Madame Elected's jugular.

"No!" The word escapes me even before I can stop myself. The nurse who kept me from Glory and who refused to be taken off optogenetics pulls Emma tightly beside her as they both shuffle up the stairs, one step at a time.

Finally Aaron sees Emma being led by the knife up the stairs, and a guttural, primal laugh makes its way from his belly out through his O-shaped mouth. "My, my," he grunts toward Ollinear whose face is shockingly similar to that of his sister's. "What a quandary for you now." He coughs out the words, still within Ollinear's tight grasp. Aaron manages to twist so he's glaring up toward Ollinear. He lets loose another whiney snicker.

"Elected!" says the breathless nurse, keeping the knife trained on Emma. The nurse wipes sweaty brown hairs from her forehead with the back of her other hand. "I saw you at the top of the building, out a window. I was being corralled in the town square by this woman. She spoke to her brother while they held me, so I knew he and she are part of the force against you. I overpowered her and brought the traitor here for

143

your sentencing." She breaks off her lengthy explanation, winded from the climb.

Aaron lets out a long peel of laughter, shaking with excitement inside Ollinear's grasp. My General tightens his hold on Aaron's neck, but it's no use. The nurse pokes her knife into Emma's neck, and the sound that escapes the doctor's throat all but causes Ollinear to release Mid's Elected.

"That's right," says the nurse. "You just let our valiant leader go, unless you want to see Miss Pretty lying in a pool of her own blood!"

I stare at the foursome, trying to decide how best I can help. My gun slides within my sweaty palm, itching to show itself. Emma's pale, pinched features catch mine, and then I glance toward Ollinear. I could shoot, but unless I hit the nurse square in the head, she could still slice into Emma's neck before she died. And I've never held a gun before, so who's to say my aim is anything worthy of the situation.

Ollinear pushes the gun in Aaron's side closer so the nurse can see it. "You hurt her, and I'll shoot him."

The nurse seems to think about the threat for a moment and says, "You hurt our Elected, and I slice the doctor's neck. You don't have time to shoot both me and our Elected at once." What she doesn't realize, though, is that I have a gun hidden within my robes. So if timed correctly, yes, Ollinear and I *could* shoot both the nurse and Aaron at the same time.

The nurse instinctively moves her whole body behind Emma's, and just as I reveal my gun, brandishing it high, Ollinear drops Aaron to the ground. I gasp, realizing Ollinear doesn't think I'd be able to follow through and make an accurate kill shot, even in this small space. He might have believed in my strategies, but he doesn't believe in my fighting abilities.

My General takes two steps back, both hands in the air, surrendering. He looks at me, his eyes glazed. "I'm sorry, Aloy. My sister . . ."

I nod my head, still shocked at his sudden concession. Emma is now held directly in front of the nurse's body as a shield and Aaron takes the same tactic behind Ollinear, picking up his dropped gun.

"Drop it," the nurse orders me, but I don't comply, still holding the gun in my shaking right hand.

"What's your name?" Aaron asks the nurse, a touch of raw awe in his intonation.

"Dolche, your highness."

At this, I bristle. Aaron may be Mid's Elected, but no one has ever referred to him as royalty.

"You're just what the doctor ordered, Dolche," Aaron says, guffawing at his own joke. He dusts himself off and walks closer to Emma and the preening nurse, pulling Ollinear alongside.

Under Aaron's gaze, the nurse simpers, a blush spreading across her lower face. "Your highness. Oh, it is such a pleasure. An *honor!*"

Aaron lays a hand on Dolche's shoulder, running a finger across the rise of her bone. "You will be rewarded handsomely."

"Your well-being is my reward," she says with demure features, her eyelids flicking too fast as she dares not meet Aaron's steady gaze.

"Dolche. Dolche." Aaron rolls her name across his tongue. "Did you know that Dolche sounds like the old world Italian word for sweet?" Aaron runs a long fingertip up the nurse's cheek, and she gasps with pleasure.

"Italian, your grace? I've never heard of . . ."

"No matter," says Aaron. "You are sweet, though. So very sweet. I can think of a most fitting reward for you, the one person who aided her Elected in this most opportune of times." Aaron spares a withering look toward his future fiancée, reaches inside the neckline of her standard-issue medic's uniform and rips the diamond necklace off her throat.

Emma gasps with the thrust of the pull, coughing as the necklace is ripped savagely away. She tries to raise a hand to her neck but is stopped by the swift return of Dolche's knife.

"A diamond as big as this one deserves to reside on the neck of my future wife," Aaron says, handing the stone on its long chain to Dolche."

The nurse can hardly contain herself, almost hopping in place. "Oh my heavens!" she squeals. "Oh!"

"Now, what shall we do with these two?" asks Aaron, placing both arms around Ollinear's neck from behind in an almost-bear hug.

"Traitors," snarls Dolche.

I'd like nothing more than to shoot the nurse right here, but there's no angle that wouldn't also injure Emma. I catch a glance of Emma's eyes, and they're staring at me, imploring. For what, though? Is she asking me to shoot Dolche, even if that means she might be caught in the crossfire?

I don't understand why Ollinear doesn't fight back, doesn't knee Aaron in the groin and steal back his gun. Ollinear is inches taller than Aaron and much more muscled. But he stays where he is, staring at his sister with fearful eyes. I thought my guard was fierce, but it seems as though Dolche's inadvertently found Ollinear's Achilles heel.

I still don't know what my next move should be. Aaron is completely hidden behind Ollinear's large frame, and the second I even try to shoot Dolche or Mid's Elected, I know one of my friends will feel either the knife or the gun in their sides.

"My fiancée said to drop your gun," says Aaron, pointing his weapon in my direction.

"You'll just shoot us all, then," I say.

"No," says Aaron, his voice sounding like a grandfather's reprimand, low and coaxing. "No. I'll shoot you and Ollinear. But Emma I'll slice through with the knife!" His guffaws crowd the circular room, reverberating around us. Only when he finally stops laughing do I realize the edge I still maintain.

The genetic code. I still have the code in my hand, right between my sweaty palm and the gun's handle. I show him the paper now, waving it through the air, letting it catch the slight breeze from the open, bombed-out wall.

"Give it to me!" growls Aaron, immediately remembering the paper.

"Come get it if you want it so much." I bark out the threat, letting Aaron know that one move away from his human shields will earn him a gunshot wound, or maybe multiple.

"Oh, you'd like that, wouldn't you?" he asks, the words staccato and full in his mouth. "Why don't you throw it over here, if you want your friends to live?"

I consider his suggestion for a moment. If I throw Aaron the code, perhaps he'll let Ollinear and Emma go free, but I doubt it. And once the code is out of my hands, I'm as good as dead. So I do what any good strategist would do in my situation. I change the game.

I eat the paper.

24

"You bitch!" cries Aaron. A range of expletives, the likes of which I've never heard before, pour from the Elected's mouth. Even Dolche winces at the sound of his wrath. "Don't you know when you've lost?"

Apparently I don't, because even now I'm bargaining. "I memorized the code," I say.

"What did you say?" Aaron dares me to speak the words again, and I do, ignoring his ferocity.

"I memorized the sequence. "AUG. ACG. CUU. CGG. AGU. Just two more. Don't you want them?"

Aaron looks up to the ceiling, as if trying to remember the letters he used to know. Trying to gauge if I'm lying or not.

"I'll give you the other letters in exchange for letting Emma and Ollinear leave the building. Just let them walk down the stairs and don't go after them. Then I promise I'll tell you the other two sequence sets." For good measure, I bend down, placing my gun gently on the floor.

"Aloy, don't—," says Emma, but Dolce presses the knife harder to her throat, and Emma's voice is silenced.

"It's ok," I say, my voice quiet. "Aaron would never have let me live after all this anyway. But you have a chance." What I don't say is that I don't plan to let Aaron leave with the code either.

I won't ever see my boy again. Or Vienne or Tomlin. But maybe I'll join Griffin in whatever afterlife he may have escaped to. There is still no sign of East's men, no announcement from Ollinear that reinforcements are here.

I repeat Griffin's name in my head, a mantra, as I take this final stand and then plan to join the man I've loved.

Aaron waves his hands in the air, Ollinear's gun flashing in his right fist. "Fine!" Aaron's acceptance of my offer comes quickly. He must desperately want the code, more than he wants revenge on his former fiancée and her brother. "Who do you want to be freed first?" Aaron asks.

I stare from Ollinear to Emma and back again. I know whom Ollinear wants me to choose as his eyes slide all the way to the left toward Emma. He repeats the movement three more times, and I nod. "Emma."

"Give me the first sequence, and I'll let her leave," Aaron says.

"I don't believe you," I say.

"I swear on my mother's grave." Aaron says, rolling his eyes.

"Not good enough. You killed your own mother. Release Emma first, and then I'll tell you the letters."

Aaron runs his free hand through his hair again, looking up to the ceiling. "All right!" His answer is a snarl, and I wonder how much my forthcoming death will hurt. If I make Aaron mad enough, will he spend the extra time up here in the rocket launcher torturing me? Or will he just put a bullet in my head and run, fast as possible, back to direct his troops, giving the order for the airrides to start punishing those down below?

"Dolche," Aaron says, "put down the knife. Move away from her." Dolche follows Aaron's order reluctantly, dropping the knife to the floor so that it clatters against the smooth tiles.

Emma jumps back as soon as she's free. She grasps Ollinear's arm and then turns to me before taking two steps down the staircase. "I know now why Vienne loves you." It's almost an admission of guilt, like Emma's saying she wasn't sure of my full worthiness until now.

I blink a few times, letting the image of Vienne with her sun-kissed long hair inch its way into my head. It's comforting in a strange way to know that even as Vienne and Emma giggled behind closed doors over the last few weeks, Vienne was informing Emma how much I meant to her.

Emma takes a few reluctant steps down the stairs, and Aaron glares at me. "Well?" he says.

"UAG."

As soon as the sequence is out of my mouth, a gunshot explodes through the back of Ollinear's chest, directly behind his heart. No one is more shocked than my rebel General, who stares down at the growing red stain, his mouth open but no words escaping.

"Ollie!" Emma is running back up the stairs in a moment, catching Ollinear's faltering body as he hits the floor on his knees. Aaron releases my guard's body, letting him flop forward into Emma's outstretched arms. "Ollie!" Her cries are primitive and animalistic, as if she herself was shot, not the silent man falling forward onto the ground.

I stand there, mouth hanging wide, looking from the smoking gun in Aaron's hand back down to Ollinear in the throes of death.

"I remember the last sequence, Aloy," says Aaron, smiling wide. "It's GAG. My favorite. Like the gag I used to silence my parents as the firing squad made me Elected instead of them. Like the gag I'll use on you as I finally take what's mine." Aaron guffaws once more, his bellows creating a cacophony of noise beside Emma's shrieks.

Dolche rushes for her dropped knife, and then all chaos breaks loose. Emma launches herself toward Aaron, knocking the gun out of his hands, screaming. Aaron runs at me, barreling into my stomach with as much speed as he can muster within these tight walls. I'm scrambling for the gun I dropped to the ground just moments before, my nails scratching the tile as I try to pull away from Aaron's frame. He understands what I reach for, and then he's angling for the same weapon. Dolche brandishes the knife high in the air, screams in a high voice, and thrusts herself upon Emma.

The four of us wrestle on the fifteenth floor, rolling in a death match. Emma pulls at Dolche's hair, still shrieking like she's on fire. Dolche screeches in return, her head snapped back within Emma's grip. For a moment it's one on one. Dolche and Emma fight in an escalating tumult of scraping and knees in the guts. Aaron and I scramble across the floor, grasping for purchase on either of the two guns in the room. My hand is so close, *so close*, to the weapon while my other arm stays wrapped around Aaron's leg, holding him so he can't reach the gun. We struggle this way for what seems like eons, whipping our heads around in a sea of body parts.

Emma's foot flails, kicking at a weapon on the floor. The guns spins toward my head, and I know she's trying to get it toward me. I grunt again and reach for the weapon, but Aaron swings his body over me. We both angle toward it, Aaron's one arm pinning me down and the other groping for the gun. The sleek black weapon slides farther out of reach, and in another instant it teeters on the broken wall near us. Then it falls, the whoosh of the tiny weapon almost imperceptible on its way toward the ground, fifteen floors below.

Aaron curses, his white features red with the effort of straining against me. Emma and Dolche still roll on the ground next to us, their limbs a mess of grabbing fingers and kicking legs. Aaron lunges away from me for a second, the wind re-entering my lungs as his body lifts off my chest. He's seen the other prize across the room. Ollinear's gun, the one Aaron held just moments ago, is lying by itself on the far side of the floor, ready for its master to grasp it once again. I follow Aaron's scampering feet. He half runs, half falls, pulling himself across the floor to reach the gun, and I know in that instance that he'll reach the weapon before I can, before I have a chance to even sit up and crawl toward the same object.

I glance to my right, trying to gauge whether Emma can possibly help, but she's pinned underneath Dolche's body. The nurse pummels Emma's face with meaty fists, over and over again. The doctor's features are fast becoming mashed and bloody. Emma tries to cover her face with both hands, but it's no use. Now that Dolche has the upper hand, she's letting loose on the doctor, using every muscle in her body to enact punishment on the former soon-to-be Madam Elected, as if the offense of being Aaron's first choice of wife is reason enough for the deluge of blows. I look toward Aaron who has the gun in his hand now, fiddling with its release, and then back to Emma who issues far fewer shrieks and screams now.

I pinch the earpiece still lodged behind my right lobe and utter one furtive word into the static. "Help!" Nothing returns. Not static. Not a voice. We are alone. No one is coming to help. Not the rebel forces. Not the men from East. Not Griffin. I lift my head to see Aaron again, wondering why I don't already have a bullet in my head. Aaron still fiddles with the weapon, knocking it against the side of the wall, frustrated. Then a bullet releases from its chamber, and the sound of the blast ricochets around us, the bullet making a tiny, circular hole in the room's outer wall.

"Aha!" yells Aaron, intent again on me as his next target. In the second he advances, I realize just two inches from my hand is the surgical knife Dolche dropped earlier. She doesn't know it's near me, and she's not using it herself, having more than enough power in her hands to do the job of killing Emma. But I grope for the knife, focusing on the weapon near me instead of the one Aaron will surely fire in a second. He's right on top of me, looking down with a menacing leer.

"Shall I have my way with you before you're finished? I've always craved just a taste of my brother's finest conquests."

My hand closes on the knife at my side, which is hidden under the spread of my robes. I glance once more at the two foes, Aaron leaning over me with the gun cocked and Dolche polishing off Emma. The doctor still manages a slight kick underneath the nurse.

Before I have more time to consider the alternatives, I roll on my side, directing my knife not over me but to the right. Toward the nurse who once informed me I'd never see my son again. That she'd be the one to raise Glory. *Over my dead body.*

And then I thrust my arm outward, the arc angling straight across Dolche's back, slicing her skin from shoulder blade to spine as if the surgical knife was a sword.

Dolche's screams echo around the room, and she stops punching Emma to grab hold of her bleeding back. With her robes half hanging off, Dolche's pink and sliced skin looks like a cut of meat laid out for dinner. I see the white of her bone against the red of carved muscle. My revulsion turns from a mere gag to an eruption of bile spilling out the side of my mouth. I can't look at Dolche as she spins and rails herself against the floor.

It turns out I may not be a shooter, but I have a wicked fencing arm.

25

THE CRIES DOLCHE EXUDES are primal. She swivels on her knees, falling flat against Emma. "Elected! Help me! Help me!" She grasps onto the hem of Aaron's robes, pulling at him. Pleading.

He stares down at her, his mouth molded into something cruel and dark. "Get off me!" he roars. He kicks outward, trying to disengage Dolche's death-grip from his robes.

"My master, my lord!" she calls. "I've been hurt!" She continues to grasp at him until finally Aaron has to step off of me to deal with Dolche.

"I said, get off of me!" Aaron is sweating with bloodlust and the effort of retrieving the second gun. He kicks her with the heel of his boot, and she keels over, clutching her stomach. Her back is arched, the long knife lodged there like a third limb.

I take the distraction as my cue to escape. Turning, I aim for the stairs. I make a final glance at Emma. She's still stirring, not quite unconscious yet, and I hope that if I do make it down a few flights, I can keep Aaron's attention off her as he tries to follow me.

Aaron continues to kick Dolche, who moans plaintively in a corner, the blood leaking from her wound faster now. "I said be quiet!" he yells. Then, as Dolche's moans finally do seep into nothingness, Aaron whips his head back toward me. "Oh, no you don't!"

He thrusts himself forward, grabbing my ankle just as I'm one step down from the landing.

"No!" I scream. He still holds the gun, and I'm sure he's going to use it on me right now.

"I'm going to enjoy hurting you!" he says, close now to my ear. He throws me forward, my stomach hitting the floor tiles with a loud swoop. "On your back, Aloy! On your back!"

I know what he wants now, and I will never, *never* give it to him willingly. I expected torture, slicing of flesh, even a quick bullet to my head. But not this. Not here like this with Dolche dying in the corner, Ollinear already gone near the stairs, and Emma moaning on her way toward blackout.

I inch myself forward, feeling Aaron's eyes on my back. Every pull with my arms is one more step away from Mid's Elected. I reach the edge of the open wall, the one that's been destroyed by the enemy's bombings. I stare down, my head held over the side. The ground is deserted below us, devoid now of the fighters who ran from building to building toward the town center. Overhead the airrides still hover, and with a trickle of blood seeping from my scalp down into my left eye, I think I can see them engaging. I would rather be killed by the fall from the rocket launcher or meet my end down below in a string of bombings than stay up here and feel Aaron's body heavy against mine, his hips pressing against my torso.

I grasp onto the ledge and start to pull myself forward, but Aaron's fist wraps tight around my ankle. "No, I don't think so!" he yells. "Not before I've had my fill!"

Aaron finally does the thing I've been expecting. He points his gun at me, and a rip of pain catapults across my right shoulder. Flashes of light dance across my vision, red, gold, and bright blue. The feel of Aaron's gun wound in my flesh seers hot and all-encompassing.

"That's right. Now you can't pull yourself forward," Aaron says, a satisfied smirk stretching across his face.

But Aaron underestimates how far I'll go to keep him from touching me. And how, if I'm going down, I'm taking him with me. The energy vibrates from my belly up to my chest, through my heart and toward my good arm. Every inch of me is on fire. I hook my right foot around Aaron's ankle and with a full-body groan, I lunge forward, giving everything I have left. My eyes close, but the lack of one sense only accentuates the stinging feel of each snowflake as they land on my flailing limbs. I fall head-first out the open wall off the ledge, waiting for the inevitable impact.

$$26$$

THE CRASH DOES COME, but it's different than I expect. I fall facedown onto something smooth, like the inside of a clamshell. There's a momentary slide, as my body moves without purchase. A jolt shocks me from above, the weight of another object crushing me inside the shell. *Is this death?* My eyes stay clamped shut. *Is this what it feels like to be ripped from one world and placed into another? Soft and silky on the way in but with the other world still pressing on your back, hard and hot in its pursuit?*

I remember once before when I thought I was on the verge of death. A long arrow was aimed for my head in East Country's Ellipse where we'd just held a town hall meeting. I'd closed my eyes waiting for the pain, recognizing the familiar whooshing sound of the arrow and realizing it was too close from which to flee. But I'd wanted one more glimpse of the sky before I died. So I'd opened my eyes. Instead of billowing white clouds and periwinkle sky, I'd seen Griffin on top of me, his russet hair falling forward, almost touching my forehead. "Stop struggling and stay down!" he'd said.

I'm staying down now. I'm not struggling. I will let death come quickly this time. No need to see the sky before I go. I merely want the chance to glimpse the people I love. And since there's no way to see Vienne, Glory, or Tomlin now, I keep my eyes clamped tight. The only person I might see at this juncture is Griffin. *Griffin, where are you? I thought you'd greet me on the other side. You're here, right?*

The air pulses with an energy I can feel but not see. The clamshell envelops me, smooth on my skin. But still I feel the electricity, the heat, from my shoulder and wait for the pain to abate. Just a few more minutes now. Then I'll see him. I've waited so long. I left him behind in East Country, but I won't ever leave him again.

Minutes pass, and it feels like an eternity, but finally I hear something rich and melodic in my ears. "Aloy."

And I do see him. I finally see my love, hovering over me, the picture of health. Nothing like how I left him back in East Country. His eyes are a rich amber like molasses. His hair is tussled like the heavens are blowing a soft wind across him. He wears an inky blue, long-sleeved shirt, nothing like the standard canvas garb of Mid Country in which I last saw Griffin.

I'm ready. Come take me with you.

Griffin seems to be glancing back over his shoulder away from me. "No, she's not ready. Not yet."

No! I try to get through to him. *No! I am ready. Take me to our heaven!*

This time Griffin's face hovers right over my head, as if he's an angel flying through the air with wings. His brow is furrowed, creased in concern.

Who are you talking to? Are my parents with you?

"Aloy, swallow this." Griffin lowers down even further, so he's almost on top of me. I can smell the scent of grass and dirt on his glistening skin. I inhale deeply.

I've missed you.

"Me too. More than you could ever know. But you need to swallow this now. It'll make you feel better." He pushes something toward my lips, and I feel its tiny circular body on my tongue. "Swallow it. I'm sorry I don't have any liquid to help it down." Griffin caresses my forehead, the look of relief and happiness etched in the gold flecks of his eyes.

Around me, everything is crystalline. It's just Griffin and me on a bed of white. But when I gaze up into his face, there's darkness surrounding him in a pool.

"Where are we?" I ask. "Ama told me heaven would be all white. Not black as night. What is this place?" I feel the pain in my shoulder recede, inching its way out of the innermost muscles and evaporating off my skin in waves. I move my arm in wonder. "Heaven does cure all bodily ills. Just like Ama said."

Griffin stretches toward me, his cheek pressed against mine is pure bliss. Warm and sweet and smelling of lemons, just like I remember it. This is heaven. It's everything I've been waiting for. The curve of his arm wraps under me, pulling me forward off the clamshell into his arms. I hold him against me, returning his embrace with one of my own. I cannot be close enough to him. I bury my head in the crease between his neck and shoulder.

"Aloy," says Griffin slowly, after the effects of whatever he had me eat make my body feel all light. I feel like a child again. New body. Pain free. Simply wonderful. I can hardly make out Griffin's next words. They feel so far away, as if his very breath is the wind circling us. "Aloy. Look around. We're not in heaven. We're still in Mid Country."

$$27$$

MY PARENTS TOLD ME there was another place people went when they died. All the children heard stories of it. Brimstone. Ash. Gloom. A depth of darkness that stretched forever. But we all thought they were trying to scare us.

"This can't be *hell*," I whisper. "You're here. You'd never go to hell."

Griffin laughs a small chuckle, easy and unperturbed. "You wouldn't either, Aloy. We're not in hell. You fell from the fifteenth floor and landed in the dome's ripped fabric. Look around. You're alive, and so are your people."

I do as he says, raising my head to peer behind us. The airrides are still hovering close, but a stream of East countrymen and rebel fighters are now on the ground below us, looking up with expectation. They let out a whoop when they see me peering over the fabric's edge. We're about five stories off the ground. Still high up, but low enough to see faces. There's Ty and Vienne. Margareath too. The men from East Country are here too. Lights from the airrides swivel around to beam on us, making everything on the ground and in our white hammock as bright as day. A ladder hanging in the sky catches my eye, and I notice for the first time that Griffin holds onto it with one arm. It reaches from his hand all the way up to the lowest of the two airrides. Albine, Margareath's husband, stands at the airride's door waving to us as his wife beams up at him from below.

"But how did you . . ." I stammer out my words, so many unspoken questions sizzling in the air between my parted lips.

"There's a lot to tell you, Aloy, but first let's get you down from here." Griffin grasps me under the arms, and I help, circling my arms around his neck while he keeps hold of the ladder with one arm. The airride above us descends even further, as low as it can, and our ladder of metal and rubberized rungs inches toward the ground. It's from this vantage point that I see we weren't alone in the white fabric hammock.

My hands break out in an instant clamminess, sliding dangerously down the nape of Griffin's neck to the top of his broad shoulders. I almost lose my grip as I see the body's full outline, which lies still inside the hammock's cradle. I scramble inside Griffin's arms, like I can't get away from Mid's Elected fast enough. He's going to kill both of us with the gun! He might be lying still for a moment, but in another second, he'll be up and shooting at us. How does Griffin not see the threat? How is he so calm? "Aa . . . Aaron," I say, my eyes moving frantically between Griffin's eyes and the Elected's head.

"Aaron broke his neck in the fall," says Griffin.

He was killed, and I survived? The realization passes through my body like ice, starting at my head and moving through my limbs. I flex stiff fingertips, putting them inadvertently on my lips. Aaron's gone? Everything I worked for in the war strategies amounted to something tangible? Mid Country is free?

Aaron's body was the heaviness I felt upon landing in the white folds. It makes sense, even though the thought of heaven was divine enough to give me pause. "Emma?" I croak out the words, not knowing if anyone's yet realized she's up there in the rocket launcher, maybe already dead too.

Griffin doesn't know she was there or even who she is. I can see it in the downturn of his eyes. Instead he answers, "I'm sorry I didn't arrive sooner. Albine was convinced that if we attempted to climb down the ladder, we'd be shot by Mid's snipers. But I should have come after you, not listened to him."

I don't say anything, just continue to stare at the white fabric and the silhouette of Aaron's body lying prostrate inside it. What if Griffin had arrived earlier? Would he be dead instead of Ollinear? Or would both of them have gotten shot? Maybe if Griffin was there I wouldn't have had to jump, thinking it was to my death. I put my hand to my brow, the multiple scenarios too hard to resolve.

Griffin holds my good shoulder, as if he's trying to stop the ideas spinning in my head. "The rebels should already be up near the top to retrieve anyone left in the rocket launcher. Anyone else up there with you besides this Emma?"

The image of Ollinear's limp body clings to my mind, a thickness mixing in with the joy of seeing Griffin and East's men and the receding fear of Mid's Elected. I choke out Ollinear's name with the explanation that he's deceased. Then I add, "The nurse. The one who alerted Mid's guards when we were trying to take . . ." I can't say our son's name yet. Not now when news of his death might be enough to break me.

The ladder reaches as far as it can to the ground without the airrides hitting the buildings' rooftops. Griffin explains we have to jump, and I do so into the outstretched arms of the crowd below. They've made a sort of crisscross with their limbs, so when I make the leap, it's into almost as soft as the clamshell's white sleekness.

Vienne is upon me immediately. She holds my face within both hands, kissing my cheeks over and over again. "Thank the heavens you're alright," she says. "I saw you fall, and I just hoped—I don't know what I would have done if—" For once, Vienne can't find the right words. She just keeps kissing my face, mixing her hot tears against my cold cheeks.

I'm passed around familiar faces and even among ones I don't know. My face is kissed by countless lips, my body hugged by a seemingly unending array of arms. The exultations go on for mere minutes, but it seems an eternity to me. I close my eyes for a split second, breathing shallowly, trying to take in the odd turn of events. It seems the rebels have been victorious, but I still can't understand how. "The airrides . . ." I murmur to Griffin when I'm passed back into his grip once again.

But my thought is cut off by the scene unfolding before me. The optogenetically-cured people of Mid, the breadth of my rebel forces, are cutting the dome's fabric down. Aaron, so dangerous to me moments before, is now just a limp body being pulled down the fabric. One of the rebels grabs hold of Aaron's ankle, and the group brings him to the ground. There are shouts of fury and defiance all around us. There are dozens of hands on their former Elected's body, ridding him of his expensive velvet robes. One of his shoes is thrown up into the crowd and an angry woman catches it mid-air, giving a primal yell. Aaron is the dictator who stole these people's fertility. Their children. Their ability for human interaction and love. The crowd will devour Aaron's body in its clutches, I'm sure. I think the most barbaric part of human nature will rear its heads now. I'll be sick again if they rip Aaron's body limb from limb.

"I hated him," I say to Griffin. "But I can't watch . . ."

Griffin contemplates this for only a fraction of a second before saying, "Excuse us," firmly into the crowd. He motions with one arm and people part to create a path. "She needs to visit the hospital."

"This way." I hear Vienne's voice, but it sounds distant like she and I are in separate rooms of a large house.

My mouth is thick, and all of a sudden all I want to do is fall into the deepest of sleeps. The word *hospital* causes me to squirm in Griffin's embrace. "Not there. I don't ever want to go back to that place."

Griffin seems to understand. Maybe he's already heard from the others that it's where our women were kept prisoner. He looks around the crowd with some question, calling out his request. I don't hear his exact words, as weariness pulls at the edges of my consciousness, but a moment later I know we're deviating from our original path. I close my eyes and lean against Griffin, letting him carry me. Vienne must walk next to us because I feel her soft hand encircle mine. I squeeze it once and then just let her do the rest of the holding.

"It was right to let the crowd see her, but now she needs . . ." Vienne's sentence falls off, but I see the quick glance she and Griffin share. The way Vienne's said "see her," it makes me feel like an object, something tangible. Like I don't own myself. Thoughts slide around in my head, slick, no real definition to them.

We're almost passing the base of the two towers when I next look up from the crook of Griffin's shoulder. Through hazy eyes I see thousands of faces peering down at us from the windows of their apartments. Mid's people are spellbound, some with their palms planted against the glass. Their mouths are open, aghast. I wonder what's running through their heads. Fear? Confusion, surely. Anger? Appreciation?

I want to ask Vienne if she was able to communicate with them through the intercom, as we planned, but the words fumble in my head. I slump against Griffin again, queuing up my question in the long list I will have to remember to ask later.

It's still cold outside, but the snow stopped falling sometime while Aaron and I were swinging in the dome's fabric. Griffin's wrapped me in something warm, but my arm around his neck is uncovered. When the doors whoosh open, a soothing heat envelops me, and my whole body leans toward the warmth. We walk through a dark hallway, and it isn't until we're ushered into a blaring white, square room that I know where we are.

A rush of memories transfix me as I gaze at the plastic tiled walls on every side of us. I remember my typewritten response from last time I was here. *A forest completely surrounded by trees. An open space within the pine trees with soft needles under our feet. A warm evening, but not humid, with a crescent moon in the sky for light.* I almost wait, breathless, for the walls around us to change into my first-ever fantasy.

Griffin lays me on the floor of the Satisfaction Room. Vienne leans over me, wiping the hair off my brow. A few other people move into the room, but I don't recognize them, and I don't really try to. I just keep blinking my eyes, and each time I do, it's harder to keep them open. But there's a nagging feeling in the back of my head that I've forgotten to tell Vienne something important.

"Emma . . ." I say to her, wanting to explain everything that transpired at the top of the rocket launcher.

"She's . . ." being looked after," Vienne answers. "Don't worry."

She says the words heavily, and I realize a dead body could be looked after just as easily as a live one could. How can I not worry? The doctor who, along with her deceased brother, started this whole rebellion, was close to comatose when last we parted. What if she didn't make it? Or what if she did, only to be thrust into the realization, yet again, that her brother is dead because of me.

I nod, finding it hard once again to move the right set of words from brain to lips. Three Mid countrymen and one woman from East lean over me, entirely filling the expanse of my vision.

"Maggie!" I blurt out, putting a name to the one I recognize. Grobe's wife, Gretchen's mother, our best stargazer, smiles down at me. Her presence tells me that using the stars' positions must have worked.

"Elected, we'll get that bullet out of you. And then you'll be just fine. You hear?"

I feel two sets of hands on my shoulder, poking and prodding. My eyes wince shut, but surprisingly nothing the team of medics do hurts. It's like whatever Griffin fed me evaporated all the pain, even any new discomfort associated with this procedure.

Wisps of the medics' words pour from above. "Never seen anything like this. The tissue is repairing itself."

Griffin's voice rises above the rest, squelching their curiosity. "Yes, I know. Just keep going, please."

The medics kneel next to me for a long time, adjusting my shoulder, wrapping it, wetting it, and then drying the area. Finally, one man stands up, smiling down at me.

"You, my dear," says the man who's dressed in the standard Mid-issued medical garb, "are a treasure I'm happy to have healed. Although, I must admit, I didn't do much." He places a hand across his brow. "Just scraped out the bullet."

"Thank you for that," says Vienne. Her voice is polite but it's like she's trying to end the conversation. She moves to shake the man's hand, leading him ever so slightly toward the door.

"What I don't understand," the doctor continues, "is how her tissue rejuvenated so fast. It's like nothing—"

"She's got to rest now," says Vienne, stopping the man's question.

"Yes, yes, of course," he says. Then the doctor glances at me once again. "I heard what happened to Ollinear." At this my ears prick up. I lift my neck as high as I can to meet his gaze. How has he heard? What must everyone think—that I sacrificed my own General to save my life? The doctor's voice interrupts my thoughts, his eyes softer than I expect. "He and Emma approached me out of all of Mid's doctors. I didn't see their point of view at first, I admit, but I'm glad I came around in the end. What we were doing . . . even if it was good intentioned . . ." His voice cracks. "Now that I see how your people act, compared to ours in Mid . . ." His voice falters, and the man looks down at the floor.

The doctor moves like he's finally going to leave, but he continues to stare at me like he can't get enough of the view. I instinctively reach around with my good arm, attempting to cover myself. Hasn't he had enough of a view of my skin over the last hour? There's a blanket stretched over my entire body, though, so nothing needs covering. I fumble with the top seam, still not understanding why he stares so earnestly. Finally, Vienne puts a firm hand on his back, walking him and the two nurses out the door.

Maggie, Griffin, and I are alone in the stark Satisfaction Room. "This is a strange building," Maggie says.

I almost laugh at the absurdity of her statement. If she only knew what happened within these walls. But instead I turn to her, fear showing through pinched cheeks. "Gretchen?" The question comes out in just one word, but Maggie understands.

The stargazer pats my thigh over the blanket. "She's unhurt, thank the heavens. I saw her with the rest of East's women. After I climbed down from the airrides."

I cling to her explanation of Gretchen's safety like it's a life preserver in the middle of a frothing, dangerous sea. But Maggie's second sentence provides ammunition for my next question. "The airrides. I thought—" Griffin moves his head almost imperceptibly in Maggie's direction. It causes her to make some abrupt excuses about getting back to her daughter, and just seconds later, Griffin and I are alone in the room.

28

GRIFFIN STILL DOESN'T KNOW about the last time I visited the Satisfaction Room. I never got a chance to tell him about the simulation and how I created a robot that looked just like him.

But it's like he's playing out my fantasy anyway. Within seconds, he's holding me in a tight embrace, pulling me into his arms. The warmth of Griffin's body feels like hot chocolate sipped around a towering bonfire. All flames and sparks and need. When our lips meet, I realize it's been so long, I almost don't recognize the curve of them. Everything around me is irrelevant as I take in the feel of Griffin, his shoulders, his back within the palms of my hands. It's a good thing the box concealing us is soundproof because a moan of longing escapes my throat. I bury my face in the crook of his neck, stopping another sound from gushing out. The emotion of the last few weeks rests on the outer layer of my skin, rippling across our bodies and sticking us together. Lava against a mountainside.

Griffin kisses me but then leans back, brushing the hair off my cheeks and soaking in my image with fervent eyes. His brow furrows as if he's trying to gauge my well-being. I think about telling Griffin about this room's purpose, but there are many more important topics and questions rising to the top of the list. Now that we're alone, the impulse to hear about our baby tops everything.

"Where's Glory?" I splutter, the question erupting out of my mouth.

"He's fine. Stayed with the elderly back in East Country." Griffin's voice is husky and breathless. "You'll see him soon, I promise."

I think back to Aaron's threat to kill three men from East Country, still wondering how Griffin managed to stay unscathed. I explain Aaron's decree and watch as Griffin's face falls. This is obviously information he doesn't want to discuss at present, perhaps ever. "Tomlin?" I ask, bracing myself for Griffin's answer. I take a deep breath, knowing that if Griffin nods, confirming that the guards killed my mentor, the air will be knocked right out of my chest.

"No. They killed the three strongest men. Ze'ev, Angen, and Jock." The breath releases from my throat slowly, and I hang my head too, sorry for the three men. Mid's twisted justice makes sense. Why kill a man already dying from cancer? No, they'd want to eliminate the biggest threats. I almost ask how the three men were killed, but the ashen pallor crossing Griffin's face dissuades me. Now isn't the time to dredge up the dismal memory. Since Griffin just said "the strongest men" I realize that when the three were killed, Griffin wasn't in the "strong" category. I don't have to look up into his eyes to see the guilt there. I wonder if he would have traded spots. Or at least fought against the edict. I can't bear to think he would have left me.

So I skip the question and focus instead on the other East child. I'm sure Vienne's already peppered Griffin for information on her daughter. If Eve wasn't all right, Vienne wouldn't have appeared calm, but I want to hear something positive right now, so I ask the question anyway.

"She's good. Already crawling," says Griffin, the hint of a smile returning to his face. "And so big, I think she's outgrown all the clothes sewn for her."

I nod, and my mind whirls, shifting attention to my other questions. Strategy. The current state of Mid. How our forces overpowered the air-rides and managed to take over their cockpits. What's most important? How much time do I have to ask all my questions before someone interrupts us or I'm told to rest again?

I ask. "Are Mid's guards subdued?"

Griffin nods, curling an arm under my back and propping me up on his right leg. "They've been sequestered in the bomb shelters in the towers or back in their individual apartments."

I run my fingertips across the blank plastic tiles to my right. "They'll come around once optogenetics wears off. Just like all the rest of Mid's people. Do you know how many of our forces got hurt in the fight?"

"I'm not sure about your Mid forces. But a few of our men. For the most part, though, the airrides protected us."

I cock my head to one side, not understanding the whole story behind the airrides. How could they have protected our men when they were Mid's to control?

Before I can ask, Griffin says, "And a couple of the women imprisoned in Mid with you."

"Who?" I ask, already running through the faces in my mind. I've already seen Margareath. And Gretchen is all right.

Griffin lists off the names of the more senior women, and I bow my head in reverence. "Maybe more too. They went right up against a set of Mid guards, it seems."

I shake my head, imagining the ugly scenario as my women ran toward Mid's city gate to wait for East's men. Guns in inexperienced hands. The fighting by people who'd never known a battle, never even received a history lesson on warfare. The thought chokes me, and it takes me a full minute to keep going with my barrage of questions.

"Cole?" Part of me doesn't believe I'm asking about the clone I once despised. But now I care what's happened to him—how he's fared through all of this.

Griffin shifts, his long legs re-crossing underneath me. "I don't know about him yet. Was he part of your forces?"

"Yes, he played an integral role." I try to explain it but get caught up in the specifics, the veil of fuzziness descending across my brain once again.

"Later. You can tell me when you're feeling better. It shouldn't be too much longer now that the bullet is out." He lifts the gauze around my shoulder to peer underneath it.

"What did you give me?" I ask. "It made everything feel . . ." I mull over the right word to describe it. "Airy."

At this, Griffin smiles, his eyes creasing at the corners. "Forgotten what the purple pills feel like, have you?" He runs a hand over the top of my head, almost the same as Vienne did. He wraps a finger within one of the curly tendrils of my now long hair.

"The purple pills?" I try to imagine where he got hold of any of the miraculous drugs, the ones that cure everything from a minor cold to the onset of cancer. After our East Country cook, Dorine, took them with her into the border hills and was subsequently lost in the bombing, I thought there weren't any pills left. I say as much to Griffin and then ask if maybe they were scavenged from Mid Country's stores.

"Did Aaron have purple pills too?" he asks, confused. "The one I gave you came from a different source."

"Who?" I lean up on my good arm.

"A long story, Aloy." Griffin stops for a moment, almost as if he's contemplating how much to tell me now and how much can be saved for later. "We'll go back to East, and then you can ask Tomlin."

"Tomlin?" The events of the day overwhelm me again, and I sink down to the floor, turning onto my side within Griffin's embrace so my bad arm drifts against my stomach. "How did he have any?"

Griffin hesitates but says, "He had two of the pills left from his personal store."

"His own store of purple pills? Did he steal them from my parents?"

"No," answers Griffin. He looks away, obviously uncomfortable.

"Two left? Where's the other one, and how do you know exactly how many he has?"

"Had," Griffin corrects. "Because I gave you one just now, and the other . . . well, he made me swallow that months ago."

"I knew you were hurt badly enough that you couldn't have healed naturally!" My eyes are saucers against the backdrop of my pale face. Griffin's finally confirmed my fears—that he would have died in East Country while I was away. I feel all of the blood leave my cheeks so that everything is cold. A shiver cascades down my back. How can I ever thank Tomlin enough? He's always bolstered up East's Elected. Even as he gave Griffin the pill, was he doing it for love of me?

"I *was* badly hurt. Even though Maggie stopped the bleeding, I'd gotten some kind of infection. Tomlin stuffed one of the pills down my throat when I was hardly conscious enough to refuse."

"But it doesn't make sense," I say, my eyebrows knitting together once again. "Tomlin used to get sick all the time at home. I saw him with a cold. And he has cancer! If he had a stash of purple pills, why wasn't he using them?"

Griffin lays a hand on my knee. "There's a reason he was the oldest person in Mid, Aloy. But he'll have to explain it himself."

I shake my head so hard that the white walls seem like they're moving.

"Rest a little, ok? The pill is working in your system, and you'll get stronger, but let it take effect, will you?" Griffin chides.

I purse my lips but do as he asks, moving so that I'm leaning closer against Griffin's chest. The muscles of his stomach are hard inside the folds of his linen shirt. He takes my hands within his, and our bodies make the shape of a heart, two curves leaning against each other. My forehead touches Griffin's, the moon-like edges of his hair intermingling with mine.

"I didn't think I was leaving the rocket launcher alive," I say. "You didn't know we'd received the bee." Griffin's voice is an apology, even though there's nothing he should be sorry for. "If there was some way we could have communicated with you, without putting the operation at risk—"

I cut him off, shaking my head. He doesn't need to provide any explanation. I would have done the same thing. But I don't understand something. If Griffin received the bee and my message, why hadn't he come to the rocket launcher? My note, scrawled underneath the stars' positions, had been pretty clear. "You were supposed to meet me in the dome like last time," I say.

"I thought I'd do one better and shoot Aaron from the airride's vantage point. I just couldn't get a clear enough shot until you were pulling him out."

Griffin reaches into an inner pocket of his shirt and pulls out the mechanical bee I sent weeks ago. He unclasps the prickly body of the insect and reaches inside to extract the paper that was scrunched next to the electronics. My writing is still scrawled across the miniscule scrap of parchment, the star coordinates above my script.

We both look at the note I'd written just for Griffin. I'd hastily scratched it into the paper, hoping Griffin would still be alive to decipher it. Just as Maggie was one of the only people who could have decoded the stars' positions to tell the date and time of the coordinated coup, Griffin was the only person who would understand what my scribbles meant. I'd planned to face Aaron in the rocket launcher, and I'd saved one shred of hope that Griffin would know where I'd gone. And what I meant to do this time.

Griffin reads the phrase out loud, and the hum of his words ricochet around the white room.

"This time let him fall."

I nod at the words, and Griffin continues. "You were always planning to kill Aaron, weren't you?"

I nod again. The only problem was that I'd wanted Griffin there. To finally rectify the wrong we'd done together, saving Aaron that first time. Put the pieces back together. Rewind the effects of our past meddling.

In truth, I hadn't ever envisioned Aaron walking out of the rocket launcher alive, no matter what I'd told Vienne, Ollinear, or Emma. East's genetic code in Aaron's hands was too dangerous. Calix had been right about his brother. Aaron wasn't fit to be Mid's Elected. It had just taken me a while to agree to be the executioner.

29

"How did you get into Mid Country and overtake their airrides so fast?" I ask after another moment.

Griffin gives me a funny look. "What do you mean?"

"What was your entrance route? Through the tunnels? Across the border land?"

"We *flew* into Mid Country," Griffin says, his head giving a perplexed shake. He leans back, resting on his palms. "After we received your message, we waited for the next shipment of guards. Then we ambushed them and took control of the two airrides they'd arrived in."

If my eyes could grow wider, they'd burst out of their sockets. "The whole time I was fighting Aaron at the top of the rocket launcher, I thought those airrides would kill everyone in the square. That they were just waiting for Aaron's order." Griffin's face crinkles in an apologetic expression, his eyes turned down. "Aaron thought they were his too," I continue. "He thought he was *winning.*"

We sit for a few moments, quiet, thinking about these implications. If Aaron had been less confident, would he have killed Ollinear?

"How did you ambush Mid's guards from within the internment camp?" I ask, at last, when it just seems wrong to waste what little time we have alone. There are too many questions left unanswered, the next of which is how East Country's unarmed men overtook a crew of Mid's gun-toting guards. Even the bravest of my people couldn't have accomplished that easily.

"With a bit of help, but that's a longer story for later," Griffin says, a slight twitch to his cheek. I can't tell if he's proud or apprehensive to tell me.

"Help?" I ask, my eyebrows furrowed.

Griffin nods, but his lips don't move. What isn't he telling me?

"I should talk to Tomlin, right?" I ask, already guessing what Griffin will recommend again.

"Yes. But first rest. And I believe we need to settle a few things in Mid before leaving."

Griffin's right. There are people outside these walls who deserve more of an explanation. Plus, I find my eyes are inadvertently closing. I'm too tired to ask Griffin anything more, especially when he's being so close-lipped with the specific answers.

He helps me move from the floor of the Satisfaction Room out into the dark hallway where there's an entourage of people waiting to escort me somewhere to sleep for the night. Apparently, there's been a fuss as the group decided where best to deposit me. Not the hospital, since I'd already flatly refused to set foot in that building again. Not the Satisfaction Room as the heating units here weren't regulated for an overnight stay. Not the apartments where thousands of Mid's citizens still waited, confused at their confinement and possibly angry at the woman who organized the coup. And certainly not in Aaron and Calix's penthouse suite. It's finally Griffin who suggests the animal warehouse. Animals I can deal with. People, I'm not sure about, as the wide-eyed gaze of those escorting me from the Satisfaction Room are enough to leave me feeling exposed once again.

As soon as we leave the Satisfaction building, I feel the weight of the crowds bearing down on me. There were six thousand of Mid's people who joined our forces and another three thousand from East. When I leave the quiet of Mid's fantasy simulator, nine thousand eyes are waiting for me. Nine thousand mouths yell in my direction. Nine thousand sets of hands beat together to applaud what we've accomplished—the overthrow of Aaron's regime.

Even though I'm already mostly healed from the shoulder surgery, the amount of people all turning their attention to me is crushing. I try to wave at them with my good arm, to join in their enthusiasm, but the gesture feels wrong. Vienne is at my side instantaneously. She gives Griffin a pointed look over my head and then turns to address me. "I'd have been here sooner, but I looked in on Emma. I hope you didn't mind my absence."

"It's okay," I say. I wipe a hand across my now sweaty brow, feeling relief at hearing Emma is doing well enough to be "looked in on." "How is she?"

"Better. She wanted to know what had happened to you, actually."

"I was given a purple pill so . . ." My face blushes at my own words. The pill could have been used for other purposes. Maybe for someone in Mid who may get cancer without the optogenetics procedure. Maybe for Tomlin. Or maybe it should have been given to Emma.

Vienne reads my thoughts and says quickly, "She didn't need one. Just a few bruises on her ribs. A broken cheek bone and a concussion. Nothing that normal healing can't fix."

I look again at the crowd of faces that have just picked up my name as their new chant. It's not the fake name that I first used in Mid—Alicen. Nor the name my parents bred me for—Elected. It's my real name. The one that signifies I'm my own person. An individual. Someone who creates her own destiny. Aloy. I listen to the chanting for a couple of minutes and then turn back to Griffin and Vienne. "Should I make some sort of speech? Say something about what we'll accomplish next?"

"Not tonight," says Vienne. "Tomorrow or the next day. Tonight let them just call your name. And let yourself rest."

"Are you both staying with me in the barn?"

"Wouldn't miss the chance to have two such lovely bedmates," says Griffin, his roguish smile returning so that I can again envision the boy with whom I grew up. "We always do conduct our 'best work' in shacks and outdoor sheds, don't we?"

His teasing brings me right back to the night Griffin led me to the Technology Faction's abandoned house in the middle of the marshes. I can almost smell the scent of caked mud and see the bright circular lights of the fireflies in their glass vases. A blush rises in my cheeks. I never did tell Vienne the exact way I betrayed our marriage that night. I glance up at her face, but she doesn't seem to mind Griffin's words.

Instead she laughs outright, an airy lilt that I've missed over these past months. In fact, the only time I've heard it while we've been captives in Mid was upon interrupting Vienne in Emma's office. Ollinear had brushed off the giggling that ended once we'd opened the door, giving a brisk "Hi" and keeping his eyes firmly on the floor tiles, but I'd felt the fizzing energy in the room. At once, the memory of Ollinear creates a ball in my throat. I swallow thickly, the heaviness settling hard and lumpy in the pit of my stomach. I try to turn off my feelings, turn my attention back to my friends. I still can't believe they're here, walking side by side, just like we used to do in East Country.

Vienne is flicking Griffin on the upper arm and saying, "If by best work you mean Eve and Glory, I'll give you that."

"Of course that's what I meant." Griffin smiles broadly and rubs the crest of my good shoulder with his thumb.

We're trailed by no less than twenty guards, consisting of both East and Mid's men. But the entourage stays a respectful distance behind us, and Griffin takes the opportunity to push the conversation. His voice grows quiet, a serious tone overtaking the teasing one. "Vienne, now that everyone knows Aloy is female, I wanted to ask for your blessing that she and I marry."

Vienne returns his gaze, meeting Griffin's amber eyes with her steely blue ones. I think she's about to say something about duty and commitment to East Country and how a promise doesn't disintegrate even if it's complicated. Instead, though, she shifts her gaze toward me. "It isn't my blessing he should be asking for. Yours is the one he needs." In Vienne's own way she's asking if I've already accepted a proposal from Griffin.

How can I tell her that I said yes months ago on the very day Glory was conceived? Will Vienne think my marriage vows to her meant so little that I defiled them too easily? Will she think I'm setting her aside as Madame Elected? On the contrary, she deserves to be part of the Elected family more than I do. She was the one who stayed behind and kept up East's defenses. She was the one who rallied everyone to stay together and construct a plan of evacuation to the marshland.

What must Vienne feel hearing that our tightknit group of three would rather like to whittle down to two? What has she always felt at seeing me and Griffin together? If she truly loved me, as she always said she did, my choosing Griffin must have been a knife in her side. And she has never said one word against it.

The guilt at being together with the man I love feels like little compensation stacked against Vienne's sacrifice. I start to shrug out from under Griffin's embrace, but Vienne stops me. She puts my hand and Griffin's together within her own. Then she lets go, leaving us with our fingers intertwined. "It's all right," she says. "I know how you've always felt about each other. I watched the two of you stare at each other across the White House for years. I suppose I always knew you'd end up falling in love."

I don't say anything, just stare at my wife, trying to tell her with my eyes how much I will always care for her too. She nods at me, in effect, giving us the blessing she professed to leave in my hands.

The three of us finish our walk toward the barn where we'll sleep for the night. I lean my head against Griffin's upper arm, on the very spot where I accepted his marriage proposal over a year ago. His fingers squeeze mine harder, and I don't have to glance up to know his eyes are on me.

Truthfully, I don't mind if I never have to give Mid's people a gallant speech. I long for a couple nights just to recover from the past weeks' events. To get over the effects of planning a war. To breathe deeper, knowing Aaron doesn't have control over us anymore.

Vienne, Griffin, and I will use my convalescence in the stables as time to sketch out ideas for the future. Then we'll leave together and go see Tomlin. And our babies.

Everything is going to be all right. It's got to be.

Part 2: The Cure

30

THE NEXT DAYS PASS by faster than I'd like. We're out of the animal stables in less than forty-eight hours, and then my afternoons are spent full of speeches and explanations. Even Emma who's up and out of her hospital bed, gives long soliloquies about the wrongs of mind manipulation. Emma doesn't have the same aversion to the doctors' spaces as I do, although I've heard she won't set foot in her own yellow office anymore. I've yet to see her face to face, and I'm still nervous she'll blame me for her brother's death. Every time we're about to cross paths, I suddenly seem to take an alternate route.

It isn't until our fifth day after the coup that the new regime experiences our first disagreement within the intermingled Mid and East rebels. A heavily cloaked figure sidles next to me in the town center, causing my guards to leap in and pull the man away from me.

"Aloy, a minute of your time?" the man shouts, grasping my arm even as my guards hold him back.

"I'm sorry," I say, twisting away from the figure. "I'm about to give a speech—"

The man cuts me off, throwing back the hood he wears with a jerk of his head. I gasp and throw my arms around his shoulders, pushing my guards back with the same movement. "Cole!" I exclaim. "We didn't know where you'd gone! No one had seen you!"

The clone stands still within my embrace, not lifting his arms again, maybe in fear my guards will pull him back again.

"What's wrong?" I ask.

"I didn't know where to go," Cole says. "I've been hiding out in Aaron's apartments."

"What are you talking about? Why didn't you come find us sooner?"

Cole peers into my eyes, and I see his right brow rise. "Think what *you* did the first time you saw me. What's everyone else here going to do?"

I contemplate Cole's predicament for a moment. He looks exactly like Calix, and while the citizens of Mid have been informed what happened to their past Elected, they may be startled to see a seemingly dead man walk about, unscathed. Plus, there are many Mid citizens who now categorize Calix along the same lines as his brother—a tyrant. I hadn't thought about Cole's protection, especially as he hasn't been around for the last few days, but I have to do something to ensure his safety. He risked everything to help our cause in Aaron's penthouse suite, disposing of the guards outside the doors and then holding a weapon against the dictator.

"We're going to take care of this," I say, pulling him after me.

"I don't know," says Cole, taking reluctant steps alongside me, toward the city stage.

"Citizens!" I call out when we reach the podium. "I'd like you all to meet someone who was integral to our fight. He is nothing like who he resembles, I assure you." I place a hand on Cole's elbow and pull back the hood so our audience can see his face.

The gasps from below are not friendly. "Get him out of here!" screams one man, shaking a fist right underneath us. "Stone the clone!" yells another, and the man actually picks up a rock. All around us, the crowd thickens, as if a brewing fight is even more tempting than news of rebuilding. As if this speech is more enticing than the ones we've been giving over the last three days.

"No! He's a friend! This man is nothing like Calix or his brother!" I yell into the crowd.

"Clones are made of the same DNA as their predecessors!" yells a woman.

"This was a bad idea," Cole mumbles, his head inches from my ear. He pulls the hood back over his head and seems to be trying to disappear behind me.

I pull Cole back out from behind me, tugging on the wool sleeves of his gray robe. "This man may look exactly like Calix," I say, "and Cole does have Calix's DNA, but he has someone else's genetic code within him too." I wait for the ebb of murmurings to settle down. "My bone marrow flows within Cole too!"

The conversation reaches new heights. It appears that some of the shouting is in support of us while other exclamations still threaten Cole. I'm about to raise a hand to try and silence the crowd once again when there's a whirring sound directly over our heads that drowns out even the most boisterous of antagonizers. The crowd shelters their eyes against the sun, looking straight up. The whirring grows louder, and the sky seems to undulate before our eyes. Appearing from nowhere is a black, elongated hovercraft.

"Run!" I scream from behind the podium. Guards grab me by the arms, and I scream behind me for Cole. The mass of people gather up like sand scattering in the torrent of cresting ocean waves. I can't see the clone anymore. People scramble, gunning for cover. Margareath and her husband catch up to me, falling inside the shield of my guards.

"Where should we go, Aloy?" Albine asks above the roar of the crowd.

"To the bomb shelters!" I yell, knowing Albine and my people from East won't know the normal procedures when Mid is under attack.

The crowd is pushed forward on my orders, everyone piling into the depths of Tower One. No one stops to place a fingerprint against the scanners. People jump the turnstiles, a mess of bodies all scurrying toward safety like rats.

"What do we do with all the people up in the above-ground floors of the towers?" asks my new bodyguard, Niner. His voice is steady, but I see fear in his eyes. He's from East Country, and he's never been part of a bombing before. Only heard the stories.

I put a hand to my head, trying to create a solution out of a blinking second. "I don't know," I gasp, but Niner doesn't hear me. He's jostled by another wave of people piling downward. If I let the thousands of uncured Mid citizens out their confinement, the rebels may be flattened by the angry mob. But if I don't let them out, Mid's people might be killed. I can't have the deaths of more than thirty thousand people on my hands.

"Get them out of there!" I scream in Niner's direction. But he's gone, having been pulled away from me in the crush of bodies. I push against the streaming crowd, yelling to be let through. Some people do part ways for me, but others ignore me completely, the heat of their fear so scalding, they're blind to who's in front of them.

A familiar face rises before mine, and I call out to him. "Ty! Over here!"

Ty tries to move closer, but it's a full minute before we're near enough to clasp hands. "We have to free Mid's people up here!" I yell, pointing above me to the floors of innocent people locked within their apartments. "Do you know a way to unlock their doors?"

Ty looks from me to the bomb shelter's entrance. I see him weighing his safety against the request I've just made. After just a moment, his shoulders slump forward. "This way," he says. "I think I can unlock them from the main terminal."

We push our way upstream to the center of the first floor. A heavy console sits in the middle of the lobby, four large screens set at angles.

"You're sure you want to do this?" Ty asks. "When they're released, the people of Mid, they might—" His voice breaks, and Ty gives me a withering look.

"I know," I say, finishing his sentence. "They might revolt." Not all of them have been fully weaned off optogenetics yet. Their past treatments are still modifying many of their proteins. "It doesn't matter," I say. "I can't let them just sit there while we're under attack."

The crowd on the first floor is starting to ebb as most people are already setting up in the basement's bomb shelters. I race toward the open front doors and peer out, expecting to see more of the enemy's airrides. I wonder where Griffin and Vienne are right now. I slam my hand against the steel doorframe, feeling the jolt up my arm. Why? Why couldn't I have had the foresight to move everyone out of Mid Country back to East? I've kept us here like sitting ducks, talking about the future. What I should have been doing is making plans for anyone here to even get a future!

Ty types furiously onto the computer's port screen. I think of the tumult of people we're about to release. I've lost my guards in the commotion. Maybe they're looking for me right now underground. Or maybe they've given up protecting me. I seem like a lost cause against what'll be coming down the stairs in just a few seconds. I imagine thousands of Mid citizens crashing out of the elevators. Maybe they'll even think East Country is responsible for this latest bombing. They still don't understand East wasn't behind the previous assaults.

"You should probably hide," says Ty as the first set of locks release on the first two floors.

"In a second. I just want to see what the airrides are doing." I stare out of the main entrance, again looking for the enemy ships. But I'm surprised when I stick my head out the main door and see that the sky is clear.

"Where'd they go?" I ask, turning my head left and right, searching the horizon as far as I can see.

Ty joins me at the doors, and we both leave the shelter of Tower One to get a better look at the sky. There's nothing there. No airrides hover above us any longer.

"I didn't hear any explosions. Did you?" I ask Ty.

The teenager shakes his head. We venture out a few paces more and are met by other citizens venturing from their hideouts.

"Are they gone, Aloy?" asks a man.

I stare at the blue sky above us, half waiting for another telltale shimmer of air, another airride revealing itself. More and more people step into the town square, meeting us by the stage. After a second, I stare at Ty. "How many uncured Mid people did you release so far?"

"A thousand maybe."

"Round up as many of the rebel forces as we can. Get those people back inside their apartments! I think the attack is over." Ty and many of the people around me follow my instructions, running back to the tower. I track a course through the town square, stopping as many people as possible. I ask each of them if they've heard any explosions or saw any additional planes. No one's heard a peep. I see Griffin moving across the open space between buildings, his boots treading hard on the asphalt paths.

"Griffin!" I yell from a sizable distance away. He whirls in my direction, and I ask him the same questions I've been peppering around Mid's city streets. Did he hear any bombs? Was anything attacked?

"I don't think so," he says. "Maybe they were only trying to get our attention."

The puzzle of the enemy's here-now, gone again airride circles my head. "Attention for what purpose? What does Mid have that they want now?" It's right as I say these words, that the idea hits me square in the chest. "New leadership?"

When someone yells that the roof of building five has been disintegrated, we race up the steps of the armory. A section of the ceiling is gone inside the main room, like a laser has skewered the tiles, taking one at a time. Underneath the open sky, in the middle of the deserted floor, sits a nirogene safe with its lock cleanly severed. The metal still looks hot, red as it is around the now-displaced lock. The door swings open, the safe completely empty except for a single piece of paper laid out flat. On the middle of the heavy, white parchment is the outline of a black ship. It's the same boat with three masts as we'd seen on the bullets East found before I left the country with Griffin. The ones I'd cracked open and disposed of with Tomlin.

The threat of the picture is clear. The Ships Accord. Why didn't I realize it before? This particular law created isolation between the remaining countries. It stopped the theft of resources across boundaries. It was meant to end warfare.

The enemy is communicating with us in perfect clarity.

The Ships Accord is officially no longer in effect.

$$31$$

GRIFFIN PUTS A HAND on my wrist, his voice low. "Aloy, I think there's something you should know."

I turn my attention away from the intricately penned ship, staring at Griffin, my eyes thin lines.

"Is there something *else* about which I've been kept in the dark?" Anger bubbles just underneath my skin, raw and wounded. "Do you still not trust me with everything you know?"

Griffin shakes his head, the ends of his hair falling forward. "It's not that. Exactly. I meant for Tomlin to explain everything to you." He runs a hand through his dark hair, letting the tips bunch in his fingers. "He can do a better job than me. I don't even know all of it."

"Know what?" I ask, tightening my hold on the thick parchment. "Tell me."

"You asked how we overtook Mid's two airrides in East Country, and I said we had help."

"And you said I had to ask Tomlin," I say, frustration oozing out of my words.

"We should get you to him as soon as possible. It's imperative now."

"Now that we've been given some kind of warning? Or whatever this is?" I say, flicking the drawing in the air. I contemplate starting the evacuation of everyone in Mid Country, but when I think about the logistics of transporting thirty thousand confused and possibly angry Mid countrymen, no plan seems like it'll work.

I voice my thoughts out loud, and Griffin says, "It doesn't look like Mid's attacker is trying to kill us anymore. In fact they've tried to help."

"Help? You think these guys are the same ones that assisted you in East's internment camp?"

Griffin nods. "We've got to go. I'll tell you everything I know on the way to East."

"Can I go with you? I can fly the airride," says Cole, poking his head into the room.

Griffin and I both turn on our heels. "How long have you been there?" I ask.

Cole looks at the ground.

"Never mind," I say. "You know how to pilot one of the airrides?" I ask.

Cole squares his shoulders. "Aaron kept a lot of books in his rooms, including flight manuals." When we just stare at him, Cole says, "I had a lot of time on my hands."

"I scarcely think," starts Griffin, "that reading manuals constitutes an ability to—"

I picture Cole's face in the portscreen, aiming the gun at Aaron's head. His dedication to helping us. Then I think of Cole's wariness in front of Mid's rebel forces. How he's scared to stay here. How of everyone, I'm starting to trust the clone's loyalty to me more than even my own people. I glance at Griffin with glassy eyes. "He's coming with us and flying the airride," I say.

Griffin cocks his head, adjusting his shoulder as if stung. The two of them leave to begin preparations for our trip, mainly refueling the airride and getting Cole comfortable in the actual cockpit. As Griffin starts to walk out of the room, I grasp the sleeve of his shirt and he turns.

"If it looks like he can't fly at all, we'll figure something else out."

Griffin grins, a new, lopsided smile easing the tension I didn't even know had snaked into my chest. "Oh, I know. If Cole doesn't know what he's doing, I won't let you within a hundred yards of the airride." He leans in closer and pulls back my hair. Griffin's whisper in my ear sets my cheeks afire. "I'd carry you over one shoulder all the way to East if I had to." Then he winks, disappearing out the door behind Cole before I can even think of a protest.

I'm alone except for a group of no less than ten guards who catch up with me again outside the armory. I ask about Vienne's whereabouts and am told by Niner that she sits by Emma's bedside in the hospital. I don't want to go back into the building or see Emma, but I feel silly asking for Vienne to be brought out to me. I'm not royalty as Calix and Aaron acted. And I'm not even East's Elected anymore. I'm just a girl who wants to get back home to see her dying mentor and baby boy. So I suck up my anxiety and try to stand a little taller as I enter the hospital.

The main doors open to a hallway smelling strongly of antiseptic. There are so many words and technologies inside this building that I'd never heard of before living here. Antiseptic. Acetaminophen. Cloning. The list could go on and on. The florescent lights inside are dimmer than in most of Mid's buildings, but they're still overly bright. I look down the long corridor, expecting to find it empty with people having run for cover from the attack, but there's a line of Mid countrymen against the left wall. I suppose the hospital was as good a place as any to hunker down.

As I venture further into the hallway, eyes turn in my direction like a wave. Murmurs start before I even walk ten paces, and hands reach to meet mine. I feel like a doll, smiling at the people of Mid as they wait against the wall.

"What's the line for?" I ask Niner.

He shrugs, but another one of my guards, a man originally from Mid Country, answers instead. "They're here to speak with the Madame Elected."

"Vienne?" I ask.

The man shakes his head, correcting himself. "Mid's Madame Elected."

I nod, trying to understand. "What do all of these people want with Emma?"

Mid's guard shifts to stand at my side as I continue to shake hands with Mid's people. "You are . . . how do I say it . . . someone famous. Untouchable."

I find that last word a bit unbelievable, as I stand here letting Mid's people touch me repeatedly. As awkward as I feel, I think it would be more difficult not to accept their outstretched hands. But I'm not going to argue with my new guard over semantics.

He continues, "Emma, however, is one of us. She was also a victim of Mid's Elected, forced into a position she didn't want."

"I know she wasn't in love with him."

"Mid's people realize that now too. A lot of them owe Emma for saving them from demerits or other punishments during the brief time that she was Aaron's fiancée. She did a lot to temper his moods."

I think of Aaron's boldness when it came to my women from East—how he repeatedly wanted to watch their inseminations. I wonder what exactly Emma had to endure to calm Aaron's ferocity. Goosebumps erupt across my arms even though I'm not chilly.

"So they're giving thanks," I breathe out. I look at the many baskets held in people's hands. In one there's a small plant, not unlike the aloe plant Margareath gave Vienne a long time ago. Another woman holds the hand of a small boy. I recognize him from the children's room in the hospital. It looks like he's found his mother, as the two have almost identical features. The woman glances at me from behind long lashes, smiles shyly, and then grips the child's hand harder.

"I don't think I have time to wait in line," I say to Niner who shakes his head and pushes me onward, past all the people.

"No one expects you to," he says.

When I reach the door where Emma's apparently been staying, I think about just sending Niner to retrieve Vienne. I feel like melting into a little ball. *Have a backbone, will you? All Emma can do to you is say the very thing you're thinking. That it was your idea to meet Aaron in the top of the launcher. Your idea that eventually killed Ollinear.*

"After you," says Niner, holding the door for me. I square my shoulders and try to keep my chin parallel with the floor.

The first thing I notice upon entering the room is that it smells nothing like the rest of the hospital. Presents of all kinds are laid against the four walls, giving the illusion that Emma sits within a thicket. Baskets and trinkets are stacked on top of one another, almost spilling across the floor. The room smells like food and flowers. Striking blue orchids sit at the foot of her bed in a circle, all within clay pots of various colors.

"Aloy!" Vienne rushes to my side, her cheeks rosy. I embrace her by the shoulders, and she gives me East's customary gesture of two arms held outward, elbows bent. "I'm so glad you're here!"

"I came to . . . see if you . . ." My voice stops as I glance at Emma who's pulling the strap of her thin shirt up over one shoulder. "Did you hear the attack?"

"Attack?" Vienne asks, her head cocking to the side.

"Yes, it was a small one. Just one enemy airride that stole the last of Mid's nirogene supply. And left us a message." I show her the drawing. "No one was hurt."

Emma sits up against the back of her canopied bed, locking eyes with me. I nod at her, trying to break the eye contact quickly and ending up staring feebly at the orchids. "We heard nothing from within the hospital," she says.

"As I said, it was just a small theft." I tell them about Tomlin knowing more information—as much as I can decipher from Griffin's short explanation. "We need to leave for East," I say to Vienne at last.

My wife drops my hand that she's been holding between both of her own. Her blonde locks fall forward over her face as she looks down at the ground and then over at Emma. "I need to stay here."

The crease between my eyes deepens. "Why?"

"I've made plans for Eve to be brought here to me. I must stay and help Mid's people re-acclimate to life without optogenetics." Her explanation sounds like an apology.

"But it's not safe here," I protest. "The thief might strike again, and they might bring bombs next time!"

"All the more reason for her to stay, then," says Emma, her voice raspy but determined. "The people of Mid need leadership, of which your wife has much." She stumbles upon the word *wife*, and the pause doesn't go unobserved by either me or Vienne.

Vienne places a hand on Emma's shoulder and then walks near me again. "It won't be for too long, Aloy. Just until Emma is back on her feet and more of Mid's people are back to normal. Many of them may want to go back under optogenetics for the cancer benefits, and we'll need to broach that subject carefully."

"Yes, but, don't you want to see Tomlin?" I'm grasping at threads that might unravel her argument. "He's dying!" My hand is at my brow, and I look around the room for somewhere to sit. Vienne doesn't understand. Right when we've gotten back together, she can't separate from Griffin and me again. I won't allow it.

"I would love to see him," Vienne says, her voice barely a whisper, "but he and I had plenty of time with each other before you returned from Mid. We've already said our goodbyes."

"Aloy," says Emma, her chin jutting in my direction.

I shift my gaze back to the doctor, feeling scared of her again. Almost as if we are meeting for the first time within the yellow room. I coax myself forward, closer to the doctor.

Emma takes a deep breath, never wavering eyes from me. "I can't forgive you for what happened to Ollinear. He only went to the top of the rocket launcher to ensure your safety."

My eyes are downcast. I'm not sure I'll be able to look Emma's way again today. She speaks the very thing I imagined. The breath leaves my mouth in a sigh, almost as if it's a relief to hear Emma utter the condemnation.

"If you hadn't ventured up there, Ollie would still be alive," she continues.

Each of Emma's words are knife-thrusts to the fleshy tissue between my ribs. My body curls forward upon itself so that I'm sagging.

"But then . . . so might Aaron," Emma says.

My eyes shoot up, but I still can't meet the doctor's gaze.

"And *that* is not something my brother would have traded for his own life. You did what he would have wanted." This time I finally do swivel my head to meet Emma's. "On behalf of Ollie and all of Mid's people, we thank you for ridding us of a tyrant's heavy hand."

Emma reaches out, touching the very tips of my fingers with hers. The pink curved edges of her nails graze the top of my hands. It's a reluctant meeting in the middle, but it's more than I imagined I deserved.

"You're welcome." The words venture broken and small from my mouth.

"You say you're travelling to East to find out once and for all who's been stealing from us both. It's high time we had the answer. Take whatever resources of ours you need. But not Vienne. We need her here more than you do."

I focus on Vienne again, trying to think of some urgent need we have in East that would require her presence. Something more pressing than the psyches of thirty thousand Mid people. Nothing worthy comes to mind.

"It's not right," I say finally. I wring my hands within the folds of my robe. "Vienne, you can return to Mid when we all come back. You, Griffin, and I have been separated too much; it's time we were a team again."

Vienne's lips fold within themselves, and her eyes blink closed for four long heartbeats. When she opens them again, the blue of her irises are bright. I know from her gaze right then that I won't win. I nod once toward Emma before she can see any tears brim in my bottom lids. My hands are on the door before I can even comprehend my next move, and I'm out in the hallway with eyes on me again. I turn to the right, heading briskly in the opposite direction from the main doors and Mid's people lining the corridor. There's a steady thump of boots behind me, the guards directly at my back, but I ignore them. It's not until I'm right in front of the tall yellow door of Emma's former office that I stop, beating my fist against it.

A hand reaches up against my back, soft and gentle against the roiling I feel inside my own body. I start, as I hear Vienne's voice, a mere whisper. "Aloy. You made your choice long ago."

I turn so the yellow door is a wall to lean upon. My body slackens so that I sink to the floor. Without a word, the guards discreetly turn the corner, within earshot of us, but not within view. Vienne folds her skirts against her legs and sits on the ground beside me.

"I know it must have been hard," I say, looking away from her.

"Hard to see the woman I love in the arms of another?" Vienne asks. When I don't respond, she says, "Yes, it was. But I think I'm all right now."

"Because of *her?*" I dare to say the words that have been on the tip of my tongue for months now.

Vienne swallows, the indentation at her throat moving in and out. "Do you remember what you said to me in East's prison? That day we realized you were pregnant?"

I try to think of what she references, but Vienne proceeds. "You said when I found someone who cared about me romantically, it would feel different than how I felt for you."

I play with the tiles on the floor, my fingernails scratching against the grout as if cleaning the hospital's floor is my new occupation in life.

"Well, you were right," Vienne says. "My feelings for Emma are different. Not better or worse. Just different."

I can barely listen to Vienne's words, and I don't even know why. It's not fair that I've chosen Griffin but I still want Vienne near me too. I know this, but I can't reconcile my feelings.

Vienne continues, "It's exciting. Scary, sort of." She gives a timid laugh. "Not at all how I expected." When I don't say anything, she asks, "Don't you want me to experience what you have with Griffin?"

I nod, but shift my eyes to the floor again.

Vienne's voice is more emphatic now. "You *chose,* Aloy. You chose *him.* And I don't begrudge you that. Everyone should be allowed a choice. I need to stay here, though, to exercise *my* choice. And to help the people of Mid who are just experiencing that right again for the first time in a long while."

This time, I'm the one who's sighing. "I'll make sure Eve is brought to you safely," I say. I reach out blindly for Vienne's hand, my eyes still focused on the hospital's floor. "And come home whenever you'd like."

"I will," says Vienne, squeezing my hand harder. "Now go. You have someone waiting for you."

32

IT TAKES ALL OF three minutes to ascend into the air away from Mid, the place for which I broke my ancestors' precious Accords, trying to find a way to serve my country best. Twice now, I've been captured and held here in Mid against my will. Many times I thought of escaping this country, but never in my wildest dreams did I guess that my eventual exit would come with a crowd of well-wishers waving at me from below.

I lean against the cockpit's side window, returning the gestures, amazed at the still-amassing, sizable crowd. The vibrations at our feet are mere purrs as the airride's solar engine keeps us hovering. The controls are worked via a screen similar to that of Mid Country's Satisfaction Room. Its blue background shimmers in the morning light, causing the whole front of the cockpit to resemble sparkling diamonds. This makes me think of Dolche's limp body lying on the rocket launcher's fourteenth floor with Aaron's betrothal diamond still swinging from her neck. My palms are instantly sweaty with a pulsing heartbeat reaching up to my neck.

"All ready?" asks Griffin. I nod my head yes, and he pats Cole on the back. "Then, take us away, Captain."

Cole beams, sweeping two fingers across the top left of the screen. I walk to the closest airbag in the back of the plane, bracing myself for a rickety rise, but our acceleration forward is steady and smooth. The airbags that hold me in the back and front are similar to the ones on Aaron's airride when the women of East were transported to Mid for the first time. They feel like movable jelly, allowing me to lean in any direction I'd like while still providing support. Margareath and her husband, Albine, Gretchen and Maggie, all of the ladies from East, some of East's men, plus ten of my new bodyguards, all stand in the main hub of the airride.

It'll only take us twenty minutes to reach East, and I'm already leaning my forehead against the window for a view of my home country. Griffin's assured me that as soon as we land, Glory will be delivered into my arms, and it's all I can think about as we fly over the barren border lands.

I picture his lashes blinking open so that our eyes meet. Will he reach for me? Will he remember me?

"Glory's seven months old now," I'd said to Griffin before we left Mid. "Do you think he'll be crawling like Eve?"

Griffin had smiled his crooked grin, the light of the open sky playing against the shadows on his cheekbones. "Probably giving his minders a good run."

I roll my eyes. "He's seven months, Griffin, not years!"

"He's *my* boy, isn't he? He may even be climbing trees at this point!"

I'm smiling at the recent memory, when the real, flesh-and-blood Griffin leaves the cockpit and stands in front of me. "You and I need to talk," he says, his voice much more serious than the one in my head.

Perhaps my conversation with Vienne got back to Griffin's ears. Is he upset that I wanted her with us? I'm about to protest, to tell him that I'd rather wait and talk when we land, when a low female voice interrupts us from the left.

Gretchen reaches a hand toward the folds of my shirt, tugging it to gain my attention. Maggie is in the spot next to her daughter, and she urges her daughter on. "I know you couldn't find any purple pills for my sister," Gretchen says, reminding me of my promise from months earlier.

I nod, my face solemn. "We haven't finished scouring Mid Country. Aaron may have had a stash we haven't found yet."

Maggie nods at me, a resigned but hopeful look clouding her face. "I've been told my daughter wasn't helpful to you at first arrival in Mid Country. Disrespectful, to say the least."

"We were all just a bit anxious. I wouldn't expect—"

Gretchen breaks in, finding my eyes. "I should have believed you. You said you'd get us home, and you did."

"And you avenged my husband," Maggie says. "He wasn't your most stalwart supporter until near his end. We'll work our whole lives to make it up to you, I swear." She looks down at Gretchen who nods a slightly less enthusiastic agreement.

"Well, I appreciate that. Really. But there's no need."

Gretchen cuts me off again. "Just take our fealty already for heaven's sakes! Stop pretending we all don't owe you our lives!"

Griffin's eyebrows raise, but I just smile. Now this is the Gretchen I know. Lively and opinionated. I ignore the outburst, focusing on topics that I know are likely of more importance to her. "Did you get to say goodbye to Ty before we left?"

Gretchen's neck, underneath the collar of her East Country styled shirt, turns a light shade of red. The color travels all the way up to her cheeks. The girl swallows hard before answering, and this only makes the smile twitching on my lips split wider.

"I thought as much," I say. Then I wink at her, and Griffin guides me away. Maggie is already starting to ask Gretchen a barrage of questions that I expect will extend through the entire flight. I'm about to tell Griffin that this onslaught of motherly questions is the best payback I can give the girl who so vehemently questioned my plans back in Mid, when Griffin says my name again.

It's not so much the utterance of my informal name, but the way he says it that unnerves me once more. Griffin's voice is a mere whisper, causing the word on his tongue to sound ominous. I'm sure he'll bring up the topic of Vienne. Ask if he's really the person I want—that maybe it's been her all along. How does he not know already that I choose him? Besides my son, Griffin is the last person I want to leave my side again, *ever.*

But as soon as Griffin starts talking, I know my insecurity is unfounded. It's not love he wants to discuss, but East men's escape from the internment camp. I lean against the side of the main cabin, ready to finally hear the breath of his knowledge.

"I told you we had help in East Country, but I didn't exactly explain what kind."

"I know."

"Tomlin has a lot to tell you, but I can at least give you information about East's coup against Mid's guards in the internment camp."

We take the two outermost airbag spots on the left side of the air-ride. No one's in close proximity, but I sense that what Griffin has to tell me, most of East's men already know. I've heard a few of them, heads bent together, whispering about guns ever since I left my makeshift hospital room. I'd just thought it was condemnation about having to use the weapons we've professed to detest all our lives, but perhaps there was more.

I lean against the billowing airbag, hoping Griffin can fit his story into the next ten minutes, as we're already far over the barren border lands.

"There was a bombing in East Country a few weeks after your message arrived. We assumed it was you and your rebels in Mid, overtaking some of Mid's technology and sending in forces to help us escape. But it was mostly a distraction that left Mid's guards bewildered but not obliterated. Mid's airrides and the internment camp's fence were still completely intact, even after the bombing. The attack merely served to move us from our tents to huddle in a remote section of the campsite, awaiting the onslaught's end."

"Was it the same people who've been bombing Mid all these years?" I'm leaning forward now, half off my backrest and into Griffin's.

"Whoever it was left something extremely helpful in each of our tents."

"Guns," I say before Griffin can get the word out.

"How'd you know?" His forehead comes together in a long crease.

"A hunch." I shrug.

"So with the guns and your bee's message, we waited for the right day and then fought back against our captors a few hours before your coup. Most of Mid's guards were killed, and we secured both of their airrides."

"And you found out once you'd been in Mid for a little while, that my rebels hadn't been the bombers or the ones who gave you the guns."

"Right," says Griffin. "So there's a third party. And like you said, most likely the same one who's been bombing Mid and East all along."

"I tried to tell Mid we weren't the only countries left in the world." I flop back against my airbag. This is the same question we've been grappling with for the last year. Who's attacking Mid? And now, who helped us overthrow them?

I throw my hands over the top of my airbag, leaning my head against the silky fabric. My cheek makes an impression, and I can't help closing my eyes for a second. Already I'm feeling the dip of the airride as Cole takes us a few hundred feet lower.

"We're almost there. You want to move to the windows so we can see East?" I ask Griffin.

When he doesn't answer, I turn my head to see what holds his attention. Griffin carries a bottle of Mid Country's medicine in his palm. He stares at it, turning the capsule over and over.

"What's that?" I ask.

Griffin looks up, and I see the sadness glossing through the whites of his eyes. His mouth turns down at the sides. Griffin shakes the bottle so I can hear the array of pills hitting each other inside.

"The last thing I had to tell you about."

"Something I won't like?" I say, reading the expression on Griffin's face.

"It depends on whether you're willing to help Tomlin in the manner he'd like." Griffin hands me the bottle, and I read the label. Acetaminophen.

"This isn't so bad. It's just pain relief." I remember the pills Emma tried to give me after the first and only light pulsation I received. I open the bottle's cap and count the number of pills, estimating how many are in there. "Sixty."

It's in that moment that Cole turns from the cockpit to the main hold, letting us know we're landing.

"I'd better go up there. Cole may need some help landing. Or at least some encouragement."

I nod, squeezing my hand around the orange and white bottle. Griffin leans down and kisses me on the forehead. Before he walks away, I ask, "How many times does Tomlin envision using these?" Griffin's grave look and the way he licks his bottom lip instantly indicates what Tomlin intends. "Just once, ha?"

33

I READ THE BACK label of the medicine. Thirty doses all at once will probably kill someone. I trap the bottle inside one of my pants pockets. Whatever Tomlin intended to use them for, no one's employing any of this futuristic medicine without my express permission. We've done quite enough killing, as far as I'm concerned. It's time for healing and rebuilding.

The airride jiggles on the way down, but it's not enough to cause anyone onboard any anxiety. Everyone stares out the windows, lapping up images of our country from this unique vantage point. The fence around the internment camp is almost completely ripped down. A few tents still dot the countryside near the entrance to the nirogene mine, but it's obvious that the population moved back to the town center near the Ellipse. As we get closer to where the White House used to stand, it's also obvious there's no more Ellipse. No more Animal Remembrance monument. No more White House. There are more of the makeshift tents here, and a few people used broken pieces of building material to resurrect actual houses. One of the famous Grecian White House columns holds up an almost fully formed home in the center of the others.

People leave their shelters upon hearing the airride and cover their eyes against the glaring sun to see us land. The best sight of all is the three hundred or so children jumping up and down as we arrive. I hear a yelp from Gretchen as she sees her sister for the first time. Margareath gasps a big intake of air upon seeing her brood below. She and Albine stand side-by-side, he with his hand upon her shoulder, she with her hand over her mouth. Tears well in Margareath's eyes, and she blots them away on the cuff of one sleeve.

Finally I see two babies being escorted from the home made of the broken White House column. Glory and Eve. My two children scamper after their nursemaid, bobbing and falling, as they squeal along with the excitement, not even knowing what it's for. My heart beats so rapidly, I think I'll stumble myself.

The airbags, which kept us from jostling in-flight, deflate and are sucked upward into compartments in the ceiling. We're left, fully mobile, in the cavernous airride body. Griffin leaves the cockpit, helping Albine unhinge the main door. A whoosh of air bombards us as suction is released. I expect everyone to run toward the entrance, a tumult of bodies glad to see their families again. But the hundred or so set of eyes find mine, and one by one bodies part so there's an easy way for me to reach the doorway. I accept their generosity, exultant to see and hold my boy. Griffin holds out a palm at my first step down.

"Want me to walk out with you, or would you like to have a moment alone with him first?" he asks.

"Come with me," I say, my voice shaking. "We should meet our son as a family."

I take the four steps down as slowly as I can muster, all the while keeping my eyes on the two stumbling children. Eve crawls forward, alternating her stares at the big black machine that's just landed and on the stones that pass under her knobby knees. Glory coos as he pulls himself along, trying to walk but ending up in a crab-like crawl for most of the way. The elderly nursemaid stands farther behind, not interfering with the children's quest to reach the airride. She calls to them in a soft lilt, encouraging their advance. "There you go. That's your Ama and Apa, yes," she says.

At the words for mother and father, both babies widen their eyes, searching. I take a deep breath, knowing this is it—an answer to my questions. Will the boy I abandoned twice now remember me? Can a baby forgive if he doesn't understand all the reasons why I left him?

Glory's eyes pass over me quickly and center on Griffin's. He reaches out his hands as if to beckon Griffin over, and I look down, understanding, if not fully accepting, that it was Griffin whom Glory's grown up with over the last few months. Not me. A small sigh must escape my lips because Griffin squeezes my hand harder.

"He knows you. Just let him get closer," Griffin says. He pulls me toward my boy, and once we're in front of the twosome, he picks Glory and Eve up into each of his arms. They cling to him, Eve pressing her heart-shaped face into his shoulder. Her soft curls only fall to the bottom of her chin, but already I can see she'll have the same corn silk hair of her mother.

It takes Glory a moment, but once Griffin spins him around to face me, his eyes devour my face. He squints them, moving his mouth open and closed like a fish. Glory's face tilts, and he reaches out to pull at my hair. Eve copies him, and at once the two children have fistfuls of my locks in their grasps. Eve squeals, pulling on my curls with a strength I hadn't expected from so little a baby.

"Ow," I say, letting my reprimand come out along with a laugh. These two can pull on my hair all day, and I'd gladly let them, even if it meant I was bald by suppertime.

The nursemaid walks closer and whispers something in Griffin's ear, as if she doesn't want to intrude on our family reunion. She hands him a piece of paper as she scurries backward again.

"What is it?" I ask him. He doesn't answer, just shows me the paper. On it is a likeness of both me and Vienne, sketched in charcoal.

"She said it was the best she could do without having you right here to model for it."

I take the thin paper, holding it between me and the children. Glory reaches for it and points at the figure on the left, the one with the short, cropped hair. "Ahhh . . . ma," he says, triumphant that he's sounded out a whole word.

"He's only seen this picture of me with short hair. He doesn't recognize the long length." Griffin nods, and I gather up my locks in one hand. I tuck them under, and then point from the drawing to my chest and back again. "That's me," I say to them. "Ama." I stab my index finger into my own chest, trying to emphasize my point. "Me. Ama." Glory and Eve glance at the paper, and then try to undo the makeshift bun from my head. Glory reaches with both hands toward my neck, and before I can even blink my eyes or gasp my surprise, he's in my arms, clinging to me as Eve clings to Griffin.

I hug Glory for as long as I can. I'm barely aware of the people around me, but I hear the exultations of other families reuniting. Out of the corner of my eye, I see Gretchen throw her younger sister up into the air and point to me. I wave but keep a tight arm around my son. Margareath and Albine are in a crush of bodies with their three children.

Their youngest is sandwiched between the legs of the group until Albine hoists him onto his shoulder. I've never seen such smiles from the family.

Eve and Glory's little legs find my hips and easily fit against my body like they were made to fill in the curves at my waist. I glance up at Griffin who's standing nearby, smiling widely.

"I can't . . . I can't even . . ." I try to make out the words to tell him of my joy, but they don't come. Griffin laughs out loud, the slant of his grin starting on the left side and working its way across his whole mouth and up to his eyes. His stare makes me breathe deeper.

It's a full night of playing with the children and meeting other families inside the mud and cobbled-together house that my countrymen created for Eve and Glory. Just like in Mid Country, there's a deluge of people who want to talk to me—thank me for ridding them of Mid's oppression. But unlike in Mid, I like greeting them all. I feel rejuvenated on the soil of my ancestors. I keep digging my fingers into the soft soil, playing alongside the children in the tufts of grass and meager dandelions. I don't get tired until way past sundown when the fires are ebbing and people make their way from the city's bonfire to their tents. The nanny, who's been so shy near me, finally does come close, inching her way toward the four of us.

"Elected . . . err . . . Madame Elected . . ." She trips over the wording of my title, and finally I tell her to just call me Aloy. She bobs her head. "I wanted to know if you'd like me to stay close and keep taking care of the children, or if you'd like me to leave. Give you your privacy." I ponder her question for a moment, wanting to sleep with Eve and Griffin curled into the curve of my body, but the children reach for the nurse.

Eve yawns, her little fist knotting inside one eye. "Seep," she trills, the high pitch of her voice sounding like the beginnings of a song.

"You can sleep with me, little one," I say, but Eve yawns again, already looking for the closest lap on which to lay her head.

"Are you ready to sleep now, Aloy? Or would you like to see someone who's been waiting to talk to you alone?" Griffin asks.

"Tomlin?" I ask. In the excitement of seeing our children, I'd known Tomlin's face wasn't among the other well-wishers, but I hadn't yet asked where he was. "I shouldn't wait till morning?"

Griffin shakes his head. "If you're awake enough, Tomlin will be up," he says. I don't like the way he glances out of our home's open door toward the glowing embers of the nearby campfire. When Griffin doesn't meet my eyes, it's always bad news.

My reluctance to disengage from Glory's baby-thick arms is palpable, but he's drifting off anyway and doesn't even realize he's changed from my lap to Griffin's. Eve's already climbed into the nursemaid's lap, and she's asleep before I reach the doorway to leave.

"Where is he?" I ask Griffin.

"Out in the marshlands. The shack . . . where I kept the lightning bugs." He gives another smile, almost as if he's thinking the same thing I am. The shack is the place where Griffin and I made our son. The place where he proposed. But this time when Griffin smiles, the happiness falls just short of his eyes. I think I should hurry toward Tomlin. I don't know exactly what I'll find there, and Griffin isn't giving me the hard details. Surely someone would have told me if Tomlin had died since I arrived, right? Or with all the reverie, did his caretakers forget him?

"Take the acetaminophen," says Griffin.

I nod, patting my right pocket and take off for the marshes.

I wonder how the shack will look. It's far out, covered in swampy overhangings, but almost everything in East Country was bombed to smithereens. Maybe the shack will just be a pallet of wood at this point. I finger the bottle of medicine within the folds of my shirt so that it turns like a wheel, flipping over and over within my palm.

The walk out of East Country's center into the depths of the dark marsh isn't anything like when Griffin led me here over a year ago. I take one of Mid's solar flashlights with me, the one that's been soaking up energy all day, so that it shines like a beacon. I'm by myself now, not holding the hand of the man I love like the last time I walked this path. With the gruesome knowledge of my mentor's health in my head, I plod one foot in front of the other, wading through the thick mud and cattails.

The shack has been used for so many purposes over the years. As the Technology Faction's secret meeting place, an area in which to test their inventions away from my family's strict eyes, where Griffin and I professed our love, where the children hid as Mid's airrides took away their mothers, and now, as a final resting place for my long-time mentor. I shudder at the last thought, my skin breaking out in goose bumps.

A sound fills the emptiness, and I stop, my feet mired in a sinking inch of mud. I can hear my mentor almost before my flashlight travels across the graying outer walls of the dilapidated shack. Here in the wilderness, he doesn't try to mask the pain of his affliction. Tomlin's soft wails pour outward from the shack, a groan here, a hard cough there.

I don't want to startle him, so I call out before I advance any further. "Tomlin! It's me, Aloy!"

There are three more long coughs before he answers back with a shaky, "Come, come!"

I walk four more feet toward the shack's door and turn the knob. The fireflies I remember are mostly still in their glass orbs, hanging from the ceiling to provide glimmering light, and I can see they've been taken care of. Some of the fireflies fly freely, their bulbs flashing from on top of Tomlin's makeshift bed mat to the other side of the hut. I expect to see Tomlin lying in the bed, but a voice from the other end of the room draws my attention left.

"They're beautiful, aren't they?" I follow the sound to a far corner of the room where Tomlin sits rocking in what looks like Griffin's step-mother's former chair.

"Tomlin!" I gasp upon seeing his face. It's sunken like a skeleton. He looks so frail, he could be one of the thin rods on the back of the rocker. His hair, which used to be a glossy speckled brown and white, is now a dull color, somewhere between gray and translucent. His clothes hang off of him, and the hand that isn't grasping tightly to the rocking chair's armrest shakes.

"What's happened to you?" I can't mask my distress upon seeing him.

"My dearest girl, this is the effect of cancer when one lets the disease linger longer than advisable."

I kneel at the foot of his chair. "This isn't anything like how the other people with cancer looked. What do you have that's different from them?"

Tomlin's laugh is weak, but he manages a half-chuckle. "I've just babied the disease, letting it recede just enough to stay alive, but not destroying it completely."

"By taking some of the purple pills?" I place one hand on top of Tomlin's to let him know it's okay. I'm not upset that he took a stash from my family. I would have given him an armload myself.

"Yes, Aloy. With the miracle drugs. I have so much to tell you, my dear."

"I know. Griffin said you saved him. Gave him one pill when he was wounded and another to take to Mid."

"In case when he found you, you needed it."

"I did. You might not have heard yet—"

Tomlin cuts me off with a shaky hand lifted in the air. He coughs twice more and says, "I've had the news relayed to me by the same people who are kind enough to stock my food supplies each day." He points to a basket filled with bread. There's a cloth napkin on which a slab of dried meat sits idly by the far wall, uneaten. "They've been unnecessarily generous to an old man."

"It's not unnecessary! If I'd have been here, I'd have brought you even more."

"Nonsense. Why waste precious resources on someone who's dying? I can hardly keep anything down anyway."

"But maybe you're not dying," I say, grasping at threads. "If we could just fly you back to Mid, there've got to be some pills left in Aaron or Calix's supplies. We'd make sure you got enough to bring you back to health. You're needed, Tomlin. No resources are wasted on you."

"If there are any pills left in Mid, which I highly doubt, they are needed for younger individuals. Not me."

"What do you mean you 'highly doubt' the pills are all gone? How do you know? Aaron was using them—"

Tomlin stops me, fervently shaking his head. He reaches behind his chair, groaning with the motion.

"Let me." I crawl on my knees toward the black, shadowed spot behind Tomlin. He leans forward, letting me grasp for the object.

"I hope you're not too upset with me," he says in between a spasm of coughing.

I don't know what Tomlin's talking about. How could I be upset with my father's historian when he's two breaths away from death? How could I be upset with the teacher who imparted all of his knowledge to me over the last nineteen years, even now summoning me to his deathbed to deliver more? And how could I be upset with the man who's been like a father to me, listening to my adolescent confusion when my own father thrust a strict "no" at my seemingly harmless requests.

"I haven't always been completely honest with you, Aloy."

And that's when my hand finds the object hidden behind Tomlin's chair. It's a round, metal ball with wires jutting out from four different points. A helmet. The thing I thought I'd lost after blacking out under the oak tree. The technology that killed East Country's master chemist, Imogene. And suddenly I know why Tomlin looks shrunken and weary.

It's not just the cancer. He's been using the Mind Multiplier.

34

"Why didn't you tell me you took it from under the oak tree?" I try not to sound as accusatory as the words that fly out of my mouth.

"Ah, Aloy, there are so very many things I wish I had told you sooner."

"What have you seen in this?"

"I took it so that you wouldn't be tempted to employ the helmet anymore. At least that's what I told myself at first. It is a . . ." Tomlin searches for the right word. "An addictive machine. The very kind of technology your father warned you about. You must have guessed that I used it before you did so in the prison, right?"

I nod but let Tomlin keep talking. He'd acted so strange the day he asked me to try on the helmet. A zeal that I hadn't before seen on my mentor's face. But I'm finally getting some answers, and I don't want to interrupt Tomlin's explanation, even by asking further questions.

"Well, I kept on using it after you left East," he says. "I was trying to see you in Mid Country. Trying to determine if you were safe. But I didn't always see you. I told you that the Multiplier typically shows you things you already know. Events locked away in the recesses of your brain. Dreams you've had that you've forgotten. Conversations you overheard at too young an age to remember. It's much more difficult, more draining, to see things in the Mind Multiplier for which you haven't been present. That still uses a different part of your brain, your extrasensory perception. Which I'm afraid, even with the Multiplier, puts the synapses on overload. When I tried to see you in Mid Country, sometimes I was successful. Other times I saw different images. For instance, I saw Aaron spill a whole carton of the purple pills over the side of a faraway mountain, somewhere over the remains of West Country."

At this, I can't help interjecting. "Are you sure? He *threw them out?*" I think of all the ways those purple pills could have been used. Sickness churns inside the pit of my stomach. I'd known Aaron was affected by use of the pills-and-optogenetics combination and that I'd goaded him with talk of his memory loss, but if I was partly responsible for him throwing out the medicine . . . I look away, not willing to let any of my own guilt overshadow Tomlin's story. I'd deal with my own feelings later.

"Yes, I'm sure. There are some things in the Multiplier that show only a version of the truth, but if you use it long enough, like I have now, you start to notice the difference. When your brain is overloaded and starts fabricating images and stories, bright flashes of light pass over your eyes, almost rendering you unconscious. Which is what I imagine happened to you under the tree."

I nod, trying to discern exactly when my thoughts under the tree began to get muddled. When did I stop seeing the truth of the Mind Multiplier, and when did I start fabricating my own pictures? I can't decide right now. There's just not enough time to answer my own questions. I need to ask Tomlin what *he* knows.

"So there are no more purple pills anywhere in the three countries?" I ask. My knuckles almost pop, I'm clenching my hands together so hard.

"Well, my dear, we don't know much about West Country, if that's what you're referring to. But perhaps they are lost too. I dare say the pills on our continent are all gone. What the rest of the world is doing with theirs, though, is even harder to say."

"The rest of the world?" I sit back on the ground again with the Multiplier held within my crossed legs.

"There is so much to tell you, I hardly know where to start." My mentor mumbles to himself and then coughs so hard, he clutches at his heart. I think he'll fall forward out of the rocking chair, hitting the hard-packed ground below and breaking bones. But he rights himself, shaking his head, as if upset with himself.

"Do you remember when your parents told you to start acting like a boy? They took away your toys? They told you to grow up?"

I nod, and he continues. "Well, your mother wasn't convinced it was the right thing to do."

"My mother?" I picture her leaning over my bed, almost as if she wanted to give me a hug, and deciding against it, tucking my blankets tighter around my shoulders so that I couldn't dare move within my bed and try to hug her. "She never wanted to coddle me. She—"

"Child, hear me out." Tomlin has never called me a child before, not in all the years I've known him. And yet, here in this old shack, he's called me a child multiple times now. Perhaps everything he's saying is the ramblings of someone too far gone to be credible. Or perhaps the nostalgia is greater now than ever before.

"Aloy, your father wanted to pretend you were a boy from the day you were born, but Claraleese wished to give you at least a few years to know your true self. She thought it was the best way to preserve your psyche. It was she who bestowed upon you the fairy tales, the books, and the playthings. She wanted you to have a normal childhood before your parents overcompensated by treating you more harshly than other children. They knew it would be a difficult path they'd laid for you. No one should have to play an act for most their life. I am profoundly surprised you grew up into as great a leader, with as good a head on your shoulders, as you have now."

I make a gesture to protest, but Tomlin stops me with a raised hand.

"It was your Ama who wanted you to have something else too. Something that would typically be given to an Elected's wife to hold. But Claraleese saved it for you. And when she left, she asked that one day, when I felt you were ready, I should give it to you."

My knees knock together with all my weight on them. I'm leaning toward Tomlin so far, I feel as if I will fall forward.

Out of the folds of his tattered pants, Tomlin produces a necklace. It's a medallion, thin and gold, hanging from a linked chain. He places it into my open palm, and I read the inscription displayed along the length of the pendant in four neat lines.

Lock your strength far away;
Save it for a rainy day.
When the sun no longer shines,
That's when you'll need this little rhyme.

"I know this necklace! My mother used to wear it! And she used to sing the song to me at bedtime!"

"Did she?" Tomlin's eyebrows raise enough to show his surprise but not enough to indicate anger. "I hadn't realized that. She shouldn't have been so forthright with such an important rhyme. What if you had repeated it?"

"Why? What does it mean?" Aaron sang another stanza, so similar to this poem, on the top of the rocket launcher. My hand instinctively closes on the necklace, imagining if I clutch it hard enough, maybe I'll be able to feel my mother's heartbeat within the gold, imprinted on the very being of the pendant. I've wished for an item of Ama's, something tangible to remember her by, even though the memory of her should be enough.

Tomlin shifts in his seat, pulling a blanket full of holes over his legs. "The necklace is very old. Older than the Accords even." I stare at the pendant in my fingers, feeling the slightly sharp edge against my thumb. But I don't speak, just keep listening to my family's historian, as if this was another tutoring session in the White House.

"The world used to be a place full of technological innovation unlike anything you've ever seen before. This Mind Multiplier here," he says, pointing to the helmet I've discarded next to me on the floor, "it's just one of the remarkable scientific advancements created before the Eco Accords were enacted. Once Earth's environment turned, however, regurgitating human waste back at us in the form of toxic rain and breaking its own crust as if to reprimand humans for daring to frack for oil and water, all human scientists shifted focus to try to correct these ills. You remember the concept of money, right?"

I nod, and he continues. "Well, massive amounts of money were thrown at the problem. Countries banded together to try to fix the destruction. Satellites from many different countries looked at the ozone layer, trying to find ways to clean the sky and rid the atmosphere of all the pollution. It was only once we realized it was too little too late that the countries began turning on each other in pursuit of natural resources."

"And the wars started."

"Humans have always been a warring species. It is deep in our blood."

"And that's why the Accords mandated isolation, I know. But what does this have to do with the necklace?" I turn it over in my palm again, looking for some other embedded clue.

Tomlin takes a moment, holding his chest as if to stop a recurrence of coughing. "When I told you the scientists were too late with their fixes, I was only partially accurate."

"The scientists found something to cure the environment?" My eyes are large now, but Tomlin's don't match the size of mine. His are small, half-closed.

"Not all the scientists," Tomlin said. "One. From one of the supposedly collaborating countries. And we didn't share that cure."

"We? The former America?" I ask. "We found the cure?"

"Yes, Child."

"What's his name?" I ask. "Is he famous? Why haven't you mentioned him before? Where's the cure? Why does it still rain all toxic on us if the U.S. was cured? Why do we still all get cancer?" I'm full of questions, and they pour out of me before I can give Tomlin a moment to react to each one.

Tomlin takes a deep, labored breath, staving off another bout of coughing so he doesn't have to take a break in the story. "The scientist's given name was Gregory. And your grandfather was named after him."

"My grandfather? You mean East Country's first Elected?"

"Yes, your grandfather Gregory was named after the scientist who found a cure to heal the environment. The scientist was Gregory's grandfather. So he'd be your . . ." Tomlin thinks for a moment, taking the opportunity to wipe his mouth with the natty blanket. "Great-great-grandfather."

"It was someone from *my* family who found a cure? Is that why we got the Elected positions?"

"There is no 'got', Aloy. It was an elected role. Those left in East Country nominated your grandfather. But yes, your family has been prominent for many, many years."

"This still doesn't explain anything about my mother's necklace and why it doesn't seem like the Earth's environment got fixed. Did the cure not work in the end?"

Tomlin grasps the top of my hand, his wrinkled and frail palm covering the back of mine. "Your great-great-grandfather never got a chance to find out."

"He never tried it?"

At this, Tomlin looks away. "I don't know if he ever tried it in a small fashion or not. But he was never allowed to implement it on a global scale."

"Allowed? But I thought the countries all banded together to find a cure. They wanted to implement one, didn't they?"

At this, Tomlin looks at me, his features falling further, the lines of his face seeming to grow deeper as he locks eyes with me.

I suck in a gust of air. "They didn't," I say, breathing everything out again. "They didn't want to implement Gregory's cure."

"Not in the end, no," says Tomlin. "By the time Gregory developed the formula to heal the Earth, you have to understand, the world was under an intense amount of distress. There were massive nuclear casualties. No more allies. Every country was at war and vulnerable. The United States government made a unilateral decision not to pursue—"

I break in, standing up now and walking across the dry, creaking floorboards. My fists ball, pinning themselves to my sides. "I don't understand! If they had a cure, they should have used it!"

"Yes, I know that seems rational. However, at the time, the United States' government decided that even if the cure was implemented, human kind would return to its old ways, still hurting the environment and bringing about climate change. They felt that a cure would only hold for so long. That it would be a wasted effort if we were still using pollution-emitting machines. To create a long-term solution, the very nature of humans would have to evolve. We'd have to learn how to live without a reliance on technology."

"So they went cold turkey?" It's an expression I only ever heard Tomlin use. We don't even have turkey anymore, but I know what the animal was. When I longed to escape the White House and be with other people my own age, Tomlin said I must forget other children. *Go cold turkey.* Tomlin's eyes alight on mine, and he gives a watery half-laugh.

"Yes, the government advocated for a complete negation of technological advancement, and the Accords were enacted world-wide."

"What happened to the cure, then? And what happened to my great-great-grandfather?"

Tomlin sighs. "Not much is known about the scientist, I'm afraid. I don't believe your great-great-grandfather Gregory agreed with the decision to suspend the cure's trials. After spending much of his adult life constructing a recipe for healing, he must have been adamant against the government's ruling. Unfortunately, we don't know more because Gregory's laboratory burned down with him and the cure inside."

A gasp catches in my throat. My heart races with what this insinuates.

"I know, child, I know," says Tomlin, his fingertips rubbing the length of his forehead down to his nose and back again. "It seems strange timing, to be sure."

"But what did we do about it? Wasn't my family suspicious? Angry? Rebellious?"

"Yes, of course, but there was no proof. No way to show it was foul play. I believe the government paid your family well for their loss since Gregory was working at a federal facility when the 'accident' occurred. Your family was given more resources than others. And that may have helped them attain the Elected position. I can't be sure."

"And the cure? Is it still around somewhere?"

At this, Tomlin finally does smile. He looks over at me, across the room. I've gotten up, starting to pace, but I slow down and walk toward his chair again.

"Where is it?" I ask.

"In your hand, Aloy."

THE NECKLACE FEELS HEAVIER, all of a sudden. I open my fingers so the words on the pendant are easy to read again. The script stands out under the light of a lightning bug's orb.

> *Lock your strength far away;*
> *Save it for a rainy day.*
> *When the sun no longer shines,*
> *That's when you'll need this little rhyme.*

"This is the cure? A four line poem about *rain?*"

Tomlin smiles again until the yellow of his teeth shine through like they're individual lightning bugs that have flown inside his mouth and perched on his gums. "This is just *one part* of the formula. There are three parts. Three ingredients. Even though our forefathers decided that humankind wasn't advanced enough to use the formula and cure the Earth's ills just yet, they hoped that at some point when we'd sufficiently learned how to survive without oil or machinery and get along with each other again, the formula could be resurrected."

"Where are the other parts of the formula?" I ask.

"The United States was divided into three separate countries, small enough not to war with each other over differentiating ideals, but also so that the pieces of the formula could be divided among the three new sections and still stay within the original country. East, Mid, and West all got a piece of the cure. Each part of the formula was inscribed on a necklace and handed down from Madame Elected to Madame Elected."

"Did my father know about this?"

"The Elected family is told about the significance of the necklace when they take office, and the Madame Elected is given the pendant on her wedding day. Told to hold onto it as if her very life depends on it."

"But,"—I shake my head and screw up my eyes, rubbing them with two hands—"I wasn't told about it. And Vienne wasn't given the necklace."

"Yes, my child. That is one of the many instances where I erred. Claraleese asked me to give *you* this necklace, but I did not. There were other circumstances, other—"

"This was mine! And Vienne's!" I yell, surprised even at myself for such an outburst. "How could you keep it from me when my mother wanted me to have it? Why didn't she give it to me herself when she left?"

"It must only be given on a wedding day, as is tradition, and your parents were already gone by that time."

"Forget tradition!" I yell.

Tomlin tries to eek out a response, but it starts a fit of heavy coughing, and I think I may have gone too far in my anger toward him. I move back to his rocking chair, falling onto the floor by his feet again. "I'm sorry, Tomlin. I'm sorry. I didn't mean to accuse you. I shouldn't have—"

"You have every right, Aloy. But please, let me explain. There is more to tell you about the necklace, and I promise not to hold anything back. It's time you heard everything."

I nod and go to pour Tomlin a cup of water. The liquid sloshes in the clay pot when I walk back, I'm shaking so hard. My Ama wanted me to have this necklace, and it's part of an environmental cure. My great-great-grandfather was killed because of it. Did Ama and Apa want me to use it? Are we finally ready?

"Why didn't you give the necklace to Vienne?" I ask, as I hand Tomlin the cup and fold my legs back under themselves. My eyes close, as I regain the steady rhythm of my heartbeat. I get nothing from a fight with Tomlin.

"It is not a question of her birthplace, if that's what you're thinking. I didn't give it to either of you, because the necklace is supposed to stay in the hands of the current Elected. And I, unfortunately, held on too hard and too long to the fact that I was supposed to be Elected."

The buzz of silence in the air after Tomlin's words is almost deafening. I can't feel my fingers for a moment. My mouth falls open, and I have to lean on one outstretched arm to balance myself, even though I'm rooted to the ground. My first instinct is to get up and run, just like when Griffin told me he was the Technology Faction's lead. There cannot be another person who longs for my position. Who wants to take me out of the running. It's not possible that my own mentor can turn on me now. I look around the shack, waiting for people to jump out and attack me. After everything I've been through, everything my country has sacrificed, it's going to be Tomlin who undermines me?

But there is only quiet. The shifting of the lightning bugs as their wings beat against the sides of their orbs is the only sound that fills the room.

"I wanted to tell you for so long." Tomlin's words are slow and quiet. "But it was not right while your parents were still alive and here in the country. They didn't want you to know."

"They knew? I don't even understand. You said it was my grandfather who was the first Elected? It's my family's line. My father was the Elected. Why was it supposed to have been you?"

"Your grandfather, the first East Country Elected, was not merely your Apa's father. He was mine too." Tomlin pauses a moment to clear his throat. "Aloy, did you never, at least once, wonder why I stayed with you and your parents in the White House? Why I never married?"

I look down at the wood boards underneath my legs. I dig my free hand, the one not holding the pendant, into the wood, feeling the material give way with the scrape of my fingernails "I heard you were . . ." I can't say the word. I won't shame Tomlin by speaking it out loud, but he finishes the sentence for me.

"Impotent," he says. "There is no need to keep it a secret. We are who we are. Nothing changes it. I may be impotent, but it is not who I am inside. It does not define me." He speaks like he's given himself this speech many times before. Tomlin sits up higher in the rocker, keeping his chin level. "However, it kept me from taking my office. When your grandfather, Gregory the second, learned of my 'affliction', it was determined that my younger brother, your father, Sawyer, would take the role and marry your mother instead of me. I would step down from the position but stay within the household as the historian."

"That means . . . that . . ." Information rumbles through my head, a tumult of facts and memories, all coalescing into a soggy mass inside my brain. "You're my uncle." I stare at Tomlin in a new way, looking at the shape of his eyes and the curve of his chin. I never noticed it before, but we look alike.

Tomlin nods. "I want you to understand something. I am not upset that I didn't become the Elected. I suppose some part of me was disappointed at the time, but it was best for the country. We all make sacrifices for the things we love, Aloy. Don't we?" He looks at me, and I know he means my gender and all the play-acting I had to do to keep my family in office and the Technology Faction out of power.

But then Tomlin surprises me further. "You must understand, my child, I loved your mother. I was the one who picked her for my eventual bride. However, my betrothal to her would have begotten no offspring. And beyond everything, she yearned for a child to take the Elected reins. When my impotency was discovered, your Ama was already far into her training to be Madame Elected. Thus, she was betrothed to your father. Not me." Tomlin's voice grows even softer on this last part. His chin quivers, and I can't look at him.

My tongue feels thick in my mouth, like it will choke me with how big it is. I swallow hard, not knowing where to root my eyes. They were in love? My mother and Tomlin? He's my uncle, but he was supposed to be the Elected? My father was the second son, the one who, like Calix, was an extra insurance, but never bred for the role? I can't even picture my father without the authority of his office. He's always been the Elected. Set in his ways. Solid in his conviction. And there was a time when he was just going to be a regular boy?

"I'm not sorry, though, with the outcome," Tomlin continues, his eyes glazed. "You were born from the alternate plan. And for that I will always be grateful. Because I love East Country and your Ama, and you were the best thing for both. You were the leader that the country needed. You were the future we'd all been waiting for."

I still can't utter a word. My gut balls up in my throat and heart, sticking there like a hard lump.

"This is why I received access to the purple pills, Aloy. I did not steal them, as you may have assumed. I didn't like to waste them on myself, though. You and your parents, and your future line, needed them more than me. I only took a few when I learned of my cancer, and I wish I hadn't even taken those."

This explains why I'd seen Tomlin with colds all my life. He'd gotten sick, along with the rest of the people in East Country, and he hadn't used the pills until he had to.

"I just wish I'd taken out more before Dorine stole all of them," he says. "I had five in my chamber at the time. I took three for my advancing cancer, and I gave Griffin my last two. One for him after the bullet wound that almost killed him with infection. And one for you. I wish I'd saved all of them for you and your new family."

My mouth opens and closes like one of the surprised fish we used to capture from the Chesapeake Bay. I don't know what to say first. A thank you for saving Griffin? He didn't have to, yet Tomlin sacrificed his own health to give Griffin one of the pills. And he'd saved me with the last one.

The silence between us settles for a moment as I digest all the information and Tomlin sips water from his cup. His chair creaks back and forth like a pendulum, marking time. I close my eyes, letting my memories morph into more understandable history. Tomlin's sicknesses. The way my mother and father relied on Tomlin for so many decisions. The necklace in my hand.

"Tomlin, what do these lines on my mother's pendant mean? I don't understand what they refer to."

"I've thought about that for many years. I've come to the conclusion that it's acid rain or some form of it."

"And what happened to the other two necklaces? The other ingredients of the formula? I know for a fact that West Country fell." My eyebrows furrow with the information that I don't think Tomlin has. If that necklace is gone, then Ama's poem, this one ingredient, means nothing anymore. It's just a lone poem.

"Ah, we are finally to this point." Tomlin lays his head back against the rocking chair for a moment. "This is the last bit I must impart to you." He looks up again and clears his throat. "You once asked me what happened to your brother Evan. Do you remember?"

Of course I remember. I spent my childhood wondering where my older brother had gone. Why he'd left. I was told he lost courage and fled the role. I'd grown up thinking I must be stronger than he ever was, because there were no children in the Elected family after me. I was their last chance. I couldn't run like my brother did. I nod at Tomlin and wait for him to tell me the information I've yearned to know for years.

"I refrained from telling you all that I knew. But then, no one besides your mother knew the real reason Evan left, so it didn't seem like such a bad thing to keep from you. Now, however, it is time. Your brother did not vacate his position out of cowardice. On the contrary, he was recruited for a very dangerous, important endeavor."

Finally I find my voice, and it's rough when it does erupt. "My mother knew? She let him leave?"

"Not happily, I'm afraid. But she knew of the plans and even gave Evan the information he needed to start his quest."

"A quest?"

"Yes, Aloy. You were always so bright in our studies together. Do you not yet realize what your brother was recruited to look for?"

36

"He was looking for the other two pieces of my great-great-grandfather's formula, wasn't he?"

"Yes, and he was given the idea from your grandfather, Gregory."

I shouldn't be surprised at anything I hear anymore, but I can't help shaking my head in confusion. "My grandfather? But when Apa took office, Gregory was forced to leave, right? That's what my father always said."

"Yes, my father—your grandfather Gregory—left East Country upon your father's eighteenth birthday. He built an illicit ship and travelled into the unknown waters, hoping to sail to West Country and collect that piece of the puzzle. But he never got there. He landed instead on the shores of the former Europe, and when Evan was a teenager, Gregory came back to collect his grandson for continuance of the quest."

"So it was my grandfather's idea? Didn't he know that luring away my parents' firstborn son would take the Elected position away from the family? Didn't he care?"

"Of course he cared, but he was banking on your mother's fertility. She was still young enough to have another child." Tomlin holds his hand out toward me to show that I am evidence of Gregory's correct assumption.

"So both my grandfather and Evan believed in this recipe?"

Tomlin becomes more animated, some color pooling in his cheeks. "Wholeheartedly. They wanted to unify the world once again—to re-connect the three pieces of the formula and manufacture a cure." Tomlin's face has grown pink with the effort and exhilaration of telling me the story. His hands, which have now moved off the arms of the rocking chair, shake violently. He tries to run a hand over his scalp, but the arm won't make it up that far without flailing. "I wish I could have helped them more, but I am—" He is interrupted by the hardest coughing fit I've seen yet.

"Lung cancer," I say, the words feeling like cotton in my mouth. "That's what you have."

Tomlin manages a quick, pointy shrug. He buries his face in his sleeve, coughing more. When his head lifts, there's a splotchy stain of red blood upon the fabric. It glistens there like the pollution-filled sunset, deep and almost purple. There's an iron smell in the air, which mixes with the muddy scent surrounding the shack.

Tomlin pulls something small and white from his pants pocket, having trouble getting the item out of the folds while he shakes.

"Here, let me," I offer, but Tomlin rears back.

"No! Don't touch it!"

I fall backward as if scalded. Tomlin cups a sprig of white flowers in his hand.

"Wait. That's hemlock!" I say, staring at the lacey poisonous plant. "What are you doing? Put them down." I try to keep my voice from ascending higher.

"It's time, Aloy," he says. "I broke the Accords."

"What are you talking about?" I ask, my voice losing all control and coming out high and fierce.

"I used technology, and this is how we deal with breaking that Accord in East Country. I will abide by our rules at the very end, even if I have strayed now and then in the middle."

"What are you doing? This is ridiculous!" All of a sudden, the quiet of our conversation has become something tangible, growing in mass. Tomlin's intentions rear like a monster in the dark. "You can't mean to eat those things. Have you seen what happens?" When he doesn't answer I retort, "Well, I have. The people, they convulse. They shiver. They throw up on themselves. And they're paralyzed. No, I won't watch you do this to yourself."

"You are the Elected," he says, looking me straight in the eyes. "It is part of your responsibility to watch me ingest this."

I let his words sink in for a moment and then stare straight back at my mentor who I now know is my uncle. "Absolutely, one hundred per-cent, no. I won't."

"It is your burden. You must do as your father said. Think of my life as I take the hemlock. Keep me in your mind. Don't look away as I take it. You're the Elected, and I've used technology. I tried on the Mind Multiplier, many times. And what's more, I liked it!" Tomlin's voice has grown in degrees so this last part is a yell. An admission of which I know he is ashamed. "By law, you have to conduct capital punishment on me."

"No! Don't you know, Tomlin?" I ask, for the first time catching him off-guard with something he might not have realized. "I *break* the Accords. I set the people who should have received capital punishment free! I'm the last person who would agree to this!"

He doesn't seem fazed. "Please, Aloy." This time Tomlin's voice wavers. He beckons to me. "Help me up. I must lie down, at least."

I do as he says, and Tomlin stumbles with me to his mat across the room on the floor. I hold my mentor under his armpits, keeping him upright. When we reach his bed and Tomlin is fully adjusted onto the floor, he stares up at the lit ceiling, focusing on just a few of the lightning bugs.

"I almost forgot," he says. "I know you're upset with me. But listen, Aloy, will you?" Tomlin tries to lean forward, but he can't get more than his head off the mat, so I move closer to him. "The bombers. Through the Mind Multiplier, I saw them fly their airrides into Mid Country. You're going to have to stop whoever it is. They've bombed us too." He coughs again, a giant mass of something slippery exiting his mouth and throbbing like an organ on his pillow. "And I think I know a way to lure them here again."

"Lure them here? But why would I want to—"

"So you can then follow them and determine their origin."

"How? They come at such random times," I say. My brow furrows at the thought. "There's no rhyme or reason to the attacks."

"They almost always steal something, Aloy, right?"

"Yes, nirogene, I know, but how could I possibly . . . We don't have any—"

"You were raised to play the game, Aloy. More than anyone you know about faking your way through a situation."

"You're saying I should *pretend* to mine for nirogene to lure the aggressor into East Country?"

Tomlin just looks at me, and I know I've gotten the basics of his plan. Then he unfolds his clenched hands. The hemlock, so delicate and beautiful in his palm, shimmers in the moonlight. I can't believe he's still thinking of moving forward with his ill-fated self-punishment. I won't let him.

I'm about to say so, to grab the white, poisonous flowers from his fist, when another bout of racking coughs sends Tomlin into a fit of spasms. His whole body clenches, and he burrows in on himself. He squirms on the mat. I try to hold his head, but the sweat on his thinning scalp feels like a slick oil. My hand slides down his back instead, resting just underneath his chest.

"What can I do for you?" I ask, feeling helpless.

Tomlin rolls to his side, staring across the room at the water jug. I nod, moving quickly to the pot to pour another cupful. It only takes me a few precious seconds, but when I turn back to traverse the small room again, I realize my mistake.

My mentor—my uncle—has his hand held up to his face, the putrid, barbaric punishment of my forefathers already grinding between his teeth.

"No!" I scream, rushing forward. The cup of water falls to the floor with a sharp clatter as it breaks into pieces. I reach Tomlin and begin prying his mouth open with both hands. I pull at the hemlock leaves still on his tongue, ripping them from between his lips. I pinch one of the green stems, but there are no white flowers to be found. "Nooo" I plead again, staring at the lone stalk. My voice is a high moan on the otherwise still countryside, a harbinger of despair. Tomlin's body has already started locking up into rigidity. The hemlock is already working, in just its first moment. I didn't get enough out. My whole body falls forward over my uncle's frame. My hair splays across him like a waterfall, and I hold him against me, feeling another jolt capture his body from feet to neck.

"How could you?" I ask, moving up to look in his face again. My words are not full of anger. Just anguish.

Tomlin opens his eyes, and they're surprisingly clear. He looks from my face to my pocket where I've kept the bottle of acetaminophen.

I'd almost forgotten about the twenty doses. The stuff that will take all pain away as it also kills its victim.

I pull the bottle out, the translucent orange of the packaging shining in the half-light. Tomlin's voice, steady and clear, breaks through the silence. How is he able to speak after taking the poison?

"In pure form, not liquid, the plant isn't quite as potent. I will linger with it in my system. But it is painful, nonetheless," he says with effort.

"You tricked me." My voice cracks.

"Ah, Aloy. I hope you will not see it that way in the years to come. I hope you will remember me differently than how I am tonight." Tomlin's body spasms sharply, his torso growing rock solid for a moment before collapsing down onto the bamboo mat again. "I was already dying of cancer, my child. Please let me leave this world with dignity." At this he falters, his voice ebbing back into a soft murmur. "It turns out I am a coward in the end, though. I thought acetaminophen might reduce the effects of the hemlock's painful side effects as I go."

I plead again. "You can't leave me! You're the last family I have!" I try appealing to his emotions, but Tomlin just looks at me with milky eyes. He's already giving way, the change apparent on his slackening face. "I just found out you're my uncle!" I moan. "You can't go now. If we could just get you to Mid Country, maybe they can reverse the hemlock's effects . . ."

Tomlin gasps a long, labored breath but opens his mouth to say more. "Do you know why your mother named you Aloy? Did anyone ever tell you its meaning?"

I shake my head, letting tears cascade down my cheeks in thin lines.

"Claraleese chose it because Aloy is short for alloy. A metal made by combining two or more elements to give it greater strength. They wanted you to have your mother's compassion and your father's conviction. And above all, strength. *You* are strong, Aloy." Tomlin punctuates each word with a slight pause. I don't know if it's because of the hemlock's paralyzing effects or because he wants his message to ring clear. "And you have mettle. A bit of a play on words. But you know what mettle is, right?" Tomlin grasps onto my hand, the leathery skin brushing over mine.

"Nerve. Bravery," I say, almost choking out the words against the backdrop of my tears.

"That's right."

My tears have graduated to falling in thick streams down the front of my cheeks so that my shirt is now wet as well.

"I used to think of myself as strong too, you know," Tomlin says. "All my sacrifices. I was weak, though. I should have stood up to your father years ago. Told him about Evan's departure and imparted all of this information to you much sooner." He coughs deeply, a bubble of pinkish blood landing on his lower lip. "I wish to die as my countrymen did. Not by a debilitating cancer, but within the boundaries of our laws. At least in this I can be true to my country."

"You have been," I say. "True to your country." My legs under me are stiff, as if I've been kneeling in the same position for days. My muscles ache with the tension knotting them into ropes. "You've been East Country's biggest defender."

"No," he says, trying to smile at me. "You have." There's a pause as we look at each other. The whites of Tomlin's eyes are clear again, almost as if the hemlock is fixing the cancer inside of him, one cell at a time. But it's still killing him. Tomlin is ravaged by another round of spasms. His whole face clenches so the tip of his mouth turns white. "The acetaminophen," he says, when his mouth relaxes again.

I fetch the water, this time setting the whole jug next to my mentor. The top of the medicine bottle spins in my hand, and I hold out the open cylinder to my uncle. Tomlin tries to sit up, shifting ungracefully on bended wrists. I move behind him, propping his back against my crossed legs. He fumbles with the open container and then begins the process of easing out of life. He swallows forty pills, two at a time with six or seven small swigs of the water in between. There is no way I could save Tomlin now, even if I had a handful of purple pills.

Tomlin's eyelids flutter and a moan escapes his throat. He licks his lips and seems to focus. "Know that I love you so very much. You make me . . ." Tomlin stops for a moment, closing his eyes, his temples straining, "and your parents proud."

"I love you too," I say, between ever-increasing hiccupping sobs.

When Tomlin is done swallowing the last few pills, he leans back against my arms. I expect more convulsions, so I hold on hard to Tomlin's arms and torso. His teeth knock together once as if his jaw has lost all muscle memory. He looks at me, his eyes never leaving mine, his hand still within the confines of mine. He holds my stare as if it's his only tether to the living world, and then finally I realize I am the only one who can see the light of the room around us, even though Tomlin's eyes still catch mine, unblinking. There is no more life sparking in my uncle's body.

I try to quell my crying. If there is some kind of afterlife—if Tomlin's soul is somehow still in this room—I want him to see that he was right. That I can be strong. That I was worth his time.

"I'll fix this," I say. It's my promise to the deceased. Not just Tomlin but my parents too. I hold his thin body within my arms until the warmth has almost all left. He's the last family I had, and now he's gone too. And that's when I remember. Tomlin isn't the last family I have. There's Glory. And Griffin and Vienne are my family too.

"Thank you for everything," I say, hoping Tomlin can still hear me. "Thank you for giving me Griffin. For saving him." Tomlin's head doesn't move, and his body doesn't magically acknowledge my words in any way, but his eyes remain open. I reach up and close them, so that now my mentor looks like he's just been sleeping this entire time. "I'll do everything I can to keep our country safe. I promise." I grasp his hand, knowing I'm the only one who can feel the squeeze.

I sit like this for I don't know how long, keeping the sobs back, focusing on what Tomlin wanted from me. How he would have liked the future to play out. And then I lay my mentor down flat on the floor, the wisps of his hair tangling in my fingers. I stand upright, looking around the room, knowing this place houses my most desperate and yet meaningful of memories.

With a steeliness I didn't expect, I search the room for something I know in my flesh will be here. The goose bumps prickle on my skin when I see it. A pointed shovel. The one that moves almost like magic in my hand. Tomlin kept Cole's automated tool, and somehow I knew it would be here in this shack, waiting for me. I pick it up and walk through the shack's front door, out into the muddy bog. I slog through the marsh, trying to find moistureless dirt. It's about twelve paces from the door, the closest I can find, and when my shoes do stamp upon the mound, I notice something else about this particular area.

There's a large white, lacy plant to my right, just above the mound that I've chosen. I shake my head, a tear escaping from the rightmost corner of my eye. It would be the case, wouldn't it? That I'd lay my uncle down right next to the largest of hemlock plants I've ever seen. Almost as if he planned it.

I dig and dig, even turning off the shovel towards the end so I can feel the throb of the work in my upper arms. I want to do this on my own, without the ease of technology. When I've dug about three feet down, I stop. This is enough. The moist soil will take care of Tomlin's body, and without a coffin he will become one with the Earth again, faster than most. He'd like that, I think.

I move back into the shack, like I'm floating. All of this is surreal. Tomlin's body feels light in the hammock of my arms. I slog back into the muck, carrying my uncle with me. I couldn't bury my parents. They only received a fake ceremony when they left East Country on my eighteenth birthday. I didn't even get to say goodbye when they truly died. But now I can afford my family this one rite of passage. I can bury Tomlin's body in the ground of East, where it belongs. It may not be in the cemetery closer to town, but something about Tomlin staying here in the outskirts feels right. He didn't quite fit in, yet Tomlin was the center of everything.

The dirt and mud work between my hands. I'm almost finished when my body automatically stands up, walking into the shack once more. I grab the Mind Multiplier where I'd left it on the floor. It fits into the folds under Tomlin's arms well enough. The shovel helps me bury it beneath the last foot of dirt. I finish by packing the earth with the palms of both hands.

Dirt falls in streaks off my pants, and I brush it away as I look up to the sky. My voice sounds calm, yet older, as I speak into the air. I imagine Tomlin floating in the air right above me and the newly formed grave. "You didn't give up the Electancy for nothing. When I see you again, I will have done something to truly earn your pride. I promise."

Then I walk out of the marsh. I don't look back. I don't stop to watch the mud coalescing over my mentor's body, pushing him back into the Earth from whence we all came. Instead, I just look forward, toward East Country's camp. To Griffin, Glory, and Eve.

37

GRIFFIN SITS IN THE small living room of our makeshift house, staring at the dying embers of an almost-quiet fire, waiting up for me. I've been dry-eyed on my walk back to East, concentrating only on our future plans—how we'll start mining for nirogene, how it has to look convincing enough to lure in the bomber, and what exactly we'll do when the assailant arrives. When Griffin sees me through the entrance of the door, the knowledge of Tomlin's death apparent in the creases by his mouth, my resolve cracks, almost like I can feel the tiny fissures and burst blood vessels around my heart. All of my organs squeeze in on themselves, and I double over, wrapping both arms around myself in a tight hug.

"Tomlin . . ." I stammer. The words won't come out.

Griffin opens his arms, and I fall into them hard, curling myself between his broad shoulders. He lets my tears leak out of me until there's nothing left, and we sit in front of the last charcoal in silence. I don't have to tell Griffin what it was like to bury my mentor, or what it was like to lose someone I love. We've both seen enough death to last two lifetimes. A million lifetimes.

When the world around us is embraced in a blanket of sleep and it seems like we're the only ones in East Country still awake, I finally look up. "You were right," I say. "Tomlin did have a lot to tell." I divulge all of it to Griffin, starting with the necklace and ending with the bomber. I gloss over the fact that Tomlin ate the hemlock, mentioning it, but looking away at the part where I'd normally describe what happened next. Griffin is the last person in the world who needs to know the specifics of a hemlock death. His father's execution is still a complicated topic.

I glance at the mechanical shovel that lies next to the door where I deposited it.

"Will we need that for your next plans?" Griffin asks, following my eyes.

"Yes. We'll need it to dig a big enough cave to hide Mid's airride in East's nirogene mines."

"And what do you want to do with your great-great-grandfather's formula?" he asks.

I stare up at the mud-caked ceiling, which is reinforced by bamboo shoots and bits of leftover material from the White House. "First things first. We protect what we have. Then we go looking for this fabled cure."

Griffin turns my head. His touch is light against the side of my chin. I cock my head to the side, waiting for what he'll say next. "And look for your brother?"

Tomlin said Evan was a hero, giving up the Electancy to pursue a *higher* mission. But Evan left our family behind, and something feels wrong about that. Sure, it must have been fun to go gallivanting after some secret formula, but Evan was needed at home. Look what's become of us. If he hadn't left, and if I hadn't been the one thrown into the role, maybe things would have been different. East Country would have still been standing, not a dismal ashy mess of broken buildings and desecrated homes.

"Will Cole fly the airride for us?" I ask, ignoring Griffin's question about Evan. I'm not ready to think of the boy who abandoned his position yet, even if it was his departure that was responsible for my birth.

"I'm sure Cole will do anything you ask." Griffin runs his fingers up and down my spine. I lean into him and then pull away.

"I should go find out."

"Tonight?" Griffin's eyebrows rise, and he stares past me at the dark outside our open door. "It's three in the morning. Perhaps you'd like to rest first?"

I'm not sure I'll be able to sit still after Tomlin's admissions and then his death tonight. My body still buzzes with all of the knowledge he imparted and the helplessness at seeing his body convulse at the hemlock's onset. But I don't want to wake up Cole. He's been through enough over the past few weeks. Least I can do is let him enjoy a peaceful night's sleep before we start mining tomorrow.

"Okay," I say, "but I'm not ready to sleep yet." I pull Griffin's face closer to mine, pressing my lips hard against his. He leans backward just a fraction of an inch, as if contemplating the sincerity of my offer and the ferocity glinting in my eyes.

"Are you sure . . . after . . . ?"

"Just get my mind off things, ok?" I grasp tight to his upper arms and then dig my nails into his skin. I *need* Griffin to distract me.

He stares at me for a long moment, wary, and then says, "If this is really—"

"It was a sham," I say quickly, anger tingeing my words. "All of it. The Accords. All the death. None of it had to happen. They had the cure, and they didn't use it. Just make me forget how unfair this all is, ok? Just for tonight?" My last words are a plea, and I look up at Griffin, letting the remaining feelings I've been holding in show on my shaking lower lip.

Griffin catches his breath. His hand reaches around the back of my neck to grasp my hair. He wraps a handful around his fingers and picks my whole body up with his other arm. I'm sprawled against him, our stomachs touching. "I'll make sure you aren't thinking about anything else but us for the rest of the night." He leans down to match the strength of my first kiss.

The heat rising from the remaining coals in the nearby pit is nothing compared to the fire burning in my chest now. It's all sticky skin, flesh on flesh, as the mixing of limbs coincides with a more vigorous demand. I bury my head in Griffin's neck and shut my eyes as his hands venture lower.

Oblivion and someone to extinguish the awful thoughts swimming in my head. That's all I want now.

38

THE NEXT MORNING THE kids are wrapped up in the nurse's arms after many hugs and kisses from me and Griffin. I brush aside the fabric serving as our front door, throwing sunlight into the recesses of the hut. Cole sits outside the door on a tree stump, a basket of food ready to offer us.

His eyes alight upon seeing us. "Elected! I brought you—"

My voice is brisk. "You don't have to wait on us." Then I think better of my tone and add, "But thank you." I take the basket from his hands, and Griffin swoops upon it, devouring a slice of the bread and handing chunks back to Eve and Glory. "I was meaning to find you anyway this morning," I say to Cole. "How do you feel about piloting Mid's airride again?"

There's no hesitation in Cole's reply. "I'd love to!" He's like an eager wolf pup, lapping at the opportunity to be part of things. I nod. Cole's a symbol of my mistrust and its fallibility. I refuse to make the same mistake again. I swing an arm around his shoulder, leading Cole over to a group of my people. Cole couldn't be accepted in Mid Country because of what he looked like, but I'll be darned if he's going to be an outsider here.

"Albine," I say, striding closer to five men who lean over a small campfire, cooking their breakfast. "I'd like your opinion on something." I tell them my latest plans, leaving out the fact that they were based on Tomlin's views while using the Mind Multiplier. It's too complicated to explain fully, and none of them know what the Multiplier is anyway. The men take to the idea, and it isn't long before they're passing the plans on to the rest of my countrymen.

"Entice them into a trap, and then slam the door closed! We'll interrogate them till they're purple in the face!" says one of the women.

"Not exactly," Griffin says from beside me. "More like lure them here and then follow to see which way they go home. That way we know which country out there is attacking us."

"I'll be riding in the airride with Griffin and Cole," I say. "And we'll take whomever else wants to volunteer. With some of Mid's weapons," I add. I hate to use Mid's guns, but we don't know what we'll find at the end of the trail. In hot pursuit of an enemy country, I don't plan on being defenseless, even if I don't want to actually use the weapons we bring along.

When we're ready to leave for the mines, I kiss Glory and Eve on their foreheads, trying not to allow their whimpers to eat at my resolve as I walk away. If this goes well, it'll be the last time I *ever* leave my children. After this, no more missions. Someone else can go looking for my brother and the two other pendants. Not me. I retire after my country is safe from these invaders.

"Bring any shovels we have left! And anything else that's sharp enough to dig with," I call over my shoulder, blinking hard so that the tears in my eyes never have a chance to surface.

Three hundred people climb into the airride behind us, and another hundred start walking toward the border. Cole revs the engine, and I can tell he's getting better manning the equipment each time he sits in the pilot's chair. He eases the airride upward with a smooth acceleration, and it's not even five minutes before we're landing at the base of the old nirogene mines.

"There's nothing left in here," says a man, placing a tentative hand on my shoulder as we walk out of the plane. His eyes look sorry, like he hates to be the first one to break the bad news to me.

"I know," I say, "but the aggressor might not." I raise my voice so everyone exiting the aircraft can hear me. "First we excavate a cavern big enough to hide the airride inside the cave, then we get to work faking our mining. Got it?"

Three hundred heads nod in unison. Griffin picks up the automated shovel and leads the group inside the mine's entrance. We spend four full days cutting out a path for the airride's long wings and stout body and distributing the rock and dirt within other caverns of the border. Then we start in on mining that our attacker can view from outside the caverns.

"It may be many nights before the bomber spies us. Hunker down and find a place you'll be comfortable sleeping for a few weeks," I yell. I feel the dip in energy as my people, dirty-faced and tired, settle into the side of the mountain. We've already laid out food in a sort of kitchen, designating four of the people to work on preparations to feed four hundred. Margareath is among them.

"This is a good idea, Aloy," she says, pointing to the mountain and handing me an apple. It's plump and red, with a shiny skin I sink my teeth into.

"Delicious," I say in response, purposefully ignoring Margareath's compliment. I don't know if this is a good idea. No one might show up. Our enemy might never see us. Or they could know it's a farce—a trap we've set. Or they might come but bring a slew of bombs with them. So when Margareath tries to tell me again how smart these plans are, I look away and busy myself chomping around the apple's core, even eating the seeds, which I then spit into my hand.

I'm about to go find Griffin, to ask him how we should best stage people to fake the mining activities, when a roar and a gust of wind whips my hair around the contours of my throat. I lean my head back to see a gigantic black mass flying toward us. My people have seen it too, and they're scurrying to warn others.

"Inside the mountain!" I yell, but my words are unnecessary. Everyone is already retreating into the cavern's shelter. A few of the men keep watch outside of the hills, while a set group of twenty of us take position inside Mid's airride, as we'd originally planned. The rest of my people stand with their backs against the mine walls, flattening themselves so they won't be sheared by our airride's wings if we start moving out of the cave.

"What's going on outside?" I yell again to the sentries.

"I don't know!" one says over our airride's revving engines. Cole's in the cockpit again, starting the airride.

"There's a blue light from the center of their airride scanning over the border mountain!" The sentry spreads out his arms to describe the extent, and I look at Griffin. I can feel the skin on my forehead tighten and crease. We wanted to be seen, but certainly not scanned with some kind of advanced technology we don't understand. I don't remember anything about a blue light from my studies with Tomlin.

"A weapon?" I ask, my skin already breaking out in a sheen. Before anyone answers me, I yell, "Everyone, get deeper inside! Get ready to cross into Mid's side if you have to." Then I duck back inside the airride, closing the hatch in back of me.

Griffin's already up in the cockpit with Cole, and the seventeen others surround the windows. "Get us out of here," I say to Cole. "Let's chase the enemy airride away before it does any damage!"

"You got it!" Cole clamps a hand down on the cockpit controls. We start to push forward, and I see firsthand how close of a shave it is to drive out of the cavern. Cole tries to keep the airride perfectly straight but the tips of our wings slice through the rocky sides of the cave.

"Let's not start a collapse, for heaven's sake," I say, gripping Cole's shoulder.

"Hold on," he instructs as the nose of our airride reaches the entrance of the mine. He drives forward until we're completely free of the mountain and the aggressor airride hovers right over our head.

"Accelerate!" says Griffin to Cole. "Before they can set a mark on us!"

I know Griffin means before the aggressor can target us for a bomb's destination. The airride above us is already starting to turn. Its back engines ignite with an orange glow and then fire rips out of each in sizzling triangles.

"It's leaving!" I cry. "Go now, Cole!"

He does as I instruct, never moving his eyes off our airride's thruster levers. With four swift movements, Cole takes us from rolling to the air. We're flying right behind the other airride now, our technology keeping pace, if not gaining, on the enemy.

Everyone is quiet behind us, their eyes transfixed on the foreign airride that we follow from a distance. Cole weaves to ensure the aggressor's airride can't send a weapon along a straight path to collide with us. I don't know where he's learned this tactic, but I don't have time to ask. I'd rather his mind stay on the mission than stray to answer my questions. The bobbing makes for a nauseating passage, but I'd rather be sick than dead. We're not sandwiched in with airbags like in the body of the plane, so I hold onto the side window's edge as we rock side to side.

"There's so much water," Griffin says, transfixed to the front windows. This view is more than either of us has ever seen. At least I've had my history books. I don't know how much Griffin was informed about the rest of the world, and I can only imagine what the seventeen men and women in back of me are thinking.

"Are we heading south?" I ask Cole.

"Due east," he corrects me, pointing to a compass beside a set of numbers embedded in the console.

I stare out the window, concentrating on the world hanging below us in miniature. In the last two years I've gone from being practically locked up in the White House to venturing into unknown American territory. Now I'm seeing more than I ever imagined. We leave the edge of our shores behind, the waves farther out into the sea becoming white-capped. As we move farther from our continent we see floating debris, and I squint my eyes trying to discern if they're pieces of buildings, ships, or even the tip of former islands.

We're quiet, transferring our eyes only from the sights around us to the airride we're still following. After two hours, Cole says, "They're slowing. Just a little."

"Maybe trying to conserve fuel?" asks Griffin.

"Possibly," Cole says. "We need to think about that too."

At this, I look down. How far am I willing to take our game of cat and mouse? With us diving straight into the ocean on an empty tank? My foot shakes, and I have to stop myself from pacing around the tiny cockpit.

"Sit," Griffin says, and I know it's a demand, not a suggestion. I do as he says, dropping down into the second pilot chair.

"What's down there anyway?" I ask, looking out the front windows. All I see is water, but I know we should be coming up on Portugal from all of my studies with Tomlin. Where's the edge of Europe? Where's the United Kingdom? Maybe Mid Country was right. There's nothing out here at all. Except . . . the enemy airride must be heading *somewhere*.

We keep pace, flying directly east, feeling like we'll go on forever before collapsing into the water below.

"Land," Griffin finally whispers.

"We can't," I say, misunderstanding. And then I realize he doesn't mean we should ground ourselves but that there's land beneath us. My head jerks to the left away from my eagle eye stare on the airride still in front of us. There's a shoreline, but it's not as I would have expected from my studies on the climate. Everything below us is covered in snow. We're almost exactly due east of our home. This place should have the same climate as ours. But there's no brown dirt or green grass showing. Only ice and white for as far as the eye can see. Whereas our winter has barely started with just a few snowflakes here and there, it seems like winter's been gracing this country for a long time. There aren't any signs of life. Not people or plants. Not even any mountainous terrain.

I'm about to give up and send us home before more than half our reserves are used up, when Cole breaks in. "Their airride's starting to descend."

39

"What? Here?" I hold onto the side of the airride, at the same time calling to the people in back to inform them of the descent. "Keep your weapons close!" I face Cole and Griffin again. "Is it an unmanned airride, do you think? Is it just crashing into the snow to avoid us finding its original destination?"

"Why would it have to be unmanned, Aloy?" Griffin asks, his mouth pinched at the sides and a deep crease between his eyes.

He's right. What's to stop an enemy whose main purpose has been to steal from us and bomb our buildings from asking its people to kill themselves to avoid our pursuit? To avoid capture. I swallow, feeling the futility of the situation pump my heart faster.

We watch from a hover position as the enemy plane dives nose first, straight for the snow piles far below us.

"They're insane," I breathe. "I think we should turn back before the fires of its crash reach us."

"Wait!" exclaims Griffin. He presses his face as close as he can to the front windows, his fist making a filmy impression on the glass as he leans forward. "Something's opening on the ground!"

I join him, staring down at the scene unfolding below us. The airride isn't crashing into smithereens; it's flying toward an entrance that's been carefully masked within the snowpack.

"What do you want me to do?" asks Cole.

I look at Griffin for a second, our minds working in tandem. I can see in his eyes that he wants to finish what we started. Go after the airride. See what's down there. But who knows what's hidden in the ground. A whole colony under the earth? A million other airrides? More weapons? All of a sudden, I can't believe I didn't hide more airrides in the border between Mid and East. Here we are, about to confront an entire enemy country and all we brought was twenty people and one airride? How could I have been so foolish? We needed an army to pursue our foe. Not one lone plane.

I look at Cole, who's still gripping the pilot stick like it's a lifeline, his knuckles white against the black handle. I could order us home right now. We still have half a tank of fuel. But then we'd never find our aggressor's lair again, even if Cole marks our current coordinates. We'd never get into the hidden cove even if we did know where we should fly back to. And the enemy will never again fall for our mining ruse. This is it. Our only opportunity.

"Get us in there," I command Cole.

He doesn't flinch, just presses forward on the throttle. Our airride lurches down, racing toward the ground after the other plane.

"Do you know how to do this?" Griffin shouts toward Cole over the roar of our engine. "Can you aim while plummeting?"

Cole doesn't respond, but I see beads of sweat flowing in lines down his forehead. His hand starts shaking, but I don't tell Cole to pull up. We have mere seconds as the first airride escapes through the gap and the door of the underground complex begins closing.

"We're going in! Stay attached to the airbags!" I yell backward. I glance toward the belly of the airride and see a brigade of white faces. Everyone holds tight to their front airbags, sheltering their heads against the bulbous fabric.

I estimate we have four seconds to make it into the chamber before the whole entrance is closed off again. Griffin hooks himself to the straps of my seat with a carabiner and holds my shoulders from behind. He gets down on his knees, holding me and the entire chair from behind, like a seatbelt. His arms are hard, and I can hardly breathe, but I crook my head down into my chest, preparing for impact. There's no way we can descend this fast and not hit something.

"Closing. It's closing!" Cole half-mumbles, half-yells to himself, blinking sweat out of his eyes as the final moment comes. We plunge into the darkness just as the metal door, still moving snow out of its way, clamps shut. The back end of our airride is grazed by the shutting door, sending us careening to the right with the jolt. Cole's hand is thrown off the steering handle, and our whole plane swerves.

"I can't see anything!" Cole screeches, trying to regain control of the airride.

I think I've just made one of the worst decisions of my life as we continue somersaulting through the dark air. We're still in a nosedive with the airride's front going from spins to left and right lurches. I hear my people screaming behind us, and tears start gathering in my eyes just from the mere strain of keeping conscious. I squeeze Griffin's arms hard, feeling the flesh sink under my fingertips. His head is next to mine, and I wonder if we'll both blackout when our skulls collide together in the fall.

I've prepared for my death so many times over, it feels almost rehearsed to let the images of my loved ones go through my head in a reel of pictures. I want to imagine meeting Tomlin or my parents on whatever other side there is, or even seeing one last fleeting image of Glory's face, but all I can focus on during the free-fall is Glory's yells as he reached toward me before I boarded the airride this morning. Like he knew something I didn't.

I've left him. I've *left* him! The guilt and regret overwhelms me. I can't squeeze my eyes any tighter, but I realize the tears still have some-where to escape when I feel them draining down my cheeks.

And then everything stops. Our airride hovers. The vibration of the engine and Griffin's arms encasing me are the only feelings I register. The silence is overpowering. Or maybe it's that my ears can't recover from the rush of wind. Or is the first moment after death just filled with this much silence?

Griffin's arms release from around me and the chair, his skin peel-ing off mine as if our cells have merged and don't want to come undone. I try to turn to look at him or Cole, but my neck is so stiff, I can barely move.

"Are we on the . . . ground?" I ask, my voice a mere groan. I may throw up, I'm so numb from my chest to my feet. Darkness still sur-rounds us, enveloping everything in shadows. Our only illumination comes from the tiny red and blue lit buttons on the airride's dashboard. As I focus on the blinking lights, the controls of the plane begin moving without Cole's hand pressed against it.

"What's going on?" Griffin asks, his voice also hoarse.

Cole shakes his head, his eyes two round eggs, white and looking like they're about to crack open with fear. "Someone else is controlling the plane."

It's in that moment that we feel our airride land with a clunk on something solid below us. The soft plunk of metal echoes, and then lights around our plane buzz to life.

Griffin continues extricating himself from around me, and the three of us stand up on shaky legs. Our plane has come to rest in a deep, long room. Dark metal walls surround us and elongated light bulbs burn in sockets to our left and right. Through the cockpit's wrap-around glass windows, a sign seems to float in midair, one light eliminating it from below.

Conseil Européen pour la Recherche Nucléaire

We stare at it for a long moment, the words looking almost indiscernible.

"It's in another language," Griffin says.

"French," I respond.

"We're in French Country?" Cole asks.

I shake my head and keep staring at the words while I answer Cole. "No, the country is called France. But that's not exactly where we are."

"In some other country that speaks this 'French' language?" asks Griffin.

I nod again, glancing over the uppercase letters on the sign. C E R N. "We're in Switzerland. Or more accurately the Franco-Swiss border. The place where the Eco Accords were conceived."

Before I have a chance to further explain what CERN is and who our enemy may be, the cave wall in front of us starts to grind back, the metal and stone issuing an ear-piercing squeal against the rails on which it travels. I glance backward and see a few of my people with hands cupping their ears. At least they're still standing and not too bloodied from our free-fall down the tube.

"Weapons ready!" I call to them and then flip my head back to stare at what's advancing through the large doorway.

A booming, amplified voice echoes around us. "Put your guns down. You are sorely outnumbered." It sounds like the person is everywhere at once. Front and back of our airride. Top and bottom. Although I can see no one.

"Keep your weapons up!" Griffin yells to our people and then takes a tighter hold on his own. His brows are set. "Even if we're outnumbered, we're not going to face whatever's on the other side without a semblance of defense!"

My people do as he says, grasping onto the meager weapons we brought on board from Mid Country's stores. Everyone but Cole takes a fighting stance, stepping out from behind their airbags, which are still big and bulging, causing the body of our airride to look like an obstacle course of white pillows. Cole burrows in on himself, his knees pulled up toward his chest. He still sits in the pilot's seat, but he looks like he wishes he could crawl under the instrument panel. If there were only enough room, part of me wishes I could pull everyone underneath to hide until our enemy thinks it's a ghost ship that's flown in.

"Pry open their doors!" comes the enemy's voice over the amplifier again.

The wall in front of us finally stops its journey, and lights on the other side instantly switch on. I can't help sucking in a sharp gasp. There's an army of people staring at us through the airride's front windows, some people close enough to touch the plane's nose. They stand in an organized formation, long staffs held at an angle in each of their arms. I can't see the exact depth of the group, as the lights within their room are darker after the first few rows of warriors, but I know the booming voice overhead is telling the truth. There are at least ten times as many of them as there are of us.

We'll be slaughtered.

The first few rows of warriors march forward, their feet clattering on the ground in syncopated rhythm. It sounds like a death bell tolling.

"Stop!" I yell out. I don't know whom I'm speaking to, but I hope their leader can hear me from within the cockpit. "We only want to speak to you!"

The group converging on us doesn't halt, and no voice answers me from the walls. The army does as its leader instructed, prying open the back door of our airride. There's a loud pop, as the door's handle is wrenched off its socket. The enemy warriors are inside at once, and they grab the closest of my people, pulling the pour soul toward their ranks.

"Speak to us? With your guns drawn?" says the booming voice.

"Albine!" I call, racing out of the cockpit into the body of our airride toward the man the advancing army has taken.

Margareath's husband struggles but can't even get one shot out of his gun before the army disarms him easily. He's pulled in front of us like he's on stage. A woman in cargo pants and a thick black sweater holds her staff horizontally in front of Albine, dividing "us" and "them." She turns the staff's sides, and the weapon buzzes to life, electrifying the dark airride with a golden light. The whole rod seems to hum.

"It's heating up," says the disembodied voice from all sides of us.

I look around me, wondering if the voice emanates from one of the warriors in the crowd and contemplating if he means our fight is intensifying or if it's the weapon that's surging with heat.

"I don't believe you've seen anything like these before," says the disembodied voice before I can fully decide. "When the tip is pressed up against skin, it attracts all hydrogen and oxygen, draining a person's organs of all their water."

I start forward, but the voice speaks again. "Don't move closer unless you want all your people drying up like grapes in the sun. Or have you never seen a grape?" The voice seems to muse on this for a second. "Ah well, the disadvantages of following the Eco Accords, eh? Well, no matter. We have plenty of grapes here for you to try." The voice pauses and then says, "That is, if all of your people drop those ancient artifacts they're holding."

As if on cue, another warrior steps forward, standing parallel to the woman still holding the buzzing staff in front of Albine. He holds up a bunch of purple orbs for my people to see. He picks off one orb, deposits it in his mouth, chews, swallows, and then wordlessly sets the rest of the bunch on our airride's floor. His illuminated staff angles down so that its tip touches the fruit, and one-by-one, the tip grazes each orb. What I assume are grapes shrivel down to tiny, dry dots. When the warrior finishes the demonstration, he angles his staff the opposite way so that water leaks out the other side.

The voice speaks again, chuckling. "It's all a matter of ions, really. Drawing positives and negatives in different patterns. A simple weapon, really. The European Conglomerate used them against Russia in the fourth World War, but they were abandoned when people decided it took too long for the weapons to heat up. People were more into biological weapons at that point anyway."

We've all stayed quiet through this exhibition of strength, but finally I speak. "What do you want?"

"Drop all of your weapons, or your man will suffer as each of his organs is deprived of water. We'll start with his least important organ, if you don't comply. Give you the most time to make up your mind."

I look to my left and right. It's not a matter of defense any longer. Even if we fired our guns right now, we're not trained well on them, and my people aren't good aims. Plus, for every one of my countrymen, there are at least two enemy warriors already on our ship, ready to surround each of us. I would tell all of my troops to drop their weapons right this second if I didn't think it would signal our complete and utter defeat. I've never been one to hand my people over without a fight.

"Can't we work something out?" I ask. "All we'd like is for you to—"

"Not unless you put down your guns."

"You can't really expect us—" My words are cut off by an explosive yell from Albine. His face is taut, contorted in anguish. The tip of the electrified staff is leaned against him, barely touching his side, while three warriors hold him with thick fists. Just as quickly as the staff is placed against Albine's skin, it's lifted again. The weapon's owner tips it so a few drops of blood-tinged water drip out the other end. Albine's head falls forward, the front of his sandy hair hanging low over his eyes.

"Stop! You're killing him!" I yell.

"Truly, no," says the disembodied voice. "It isn't a fast death, so it leaves time for surrender. In fact, it's more humane than the weapons you carry."

I look at the woman who holds her staff once again near Albine, and I know that whatever will transpire from here on out, we'll need our minds to win this fight, not the weapons in our hands.

"All right," I say. I look back at my people and motion with one hand for them to drop their guns. A few of their weapons clatter onto the floor at once, while others take a moment longer, as if they're deciding to follow my orders or not. The enemy warriors walk amongst my people, moving between the bulky white airbags, collecting the guns. They pat down my troops, pulling out knives and any other sharp objects we've brought with us. A few swords and arrows are confiscated from the back of our airride. We are utterly devoid of defenses now.

I raise my head high so my chin is parallel with the floor. We are not the ones who bombed East and Mid Country and stole resources just like our warring ancestors did and like this enemy has done for the past ten years in Mid Country. We are in the right, and I have to believe that still gives us at least something to work with.

Albine is guided back toward our group. He stumbles as the warriors let go of his arms. Our people grab him up quickly, swallowing Albine back within our ranks.

"I know who you are!" I call out to the shadows.

"Do you?" says the disembodied voice again, a hint of a dare in his tone.

"Yes. You're part of CERN, the largest physics laboratory in the world. What was once the largest nuclear research facility on the planet."

"Oh, but we're not—" the voice starts to say.

"I know," I interrupt. "You're not the CERN scientists. You're the rebels who took over CERN after the Eco Accords were created here. You killed all of the diplomats who had just signed the Accords. You didn't believe in the treaties. But all the countries had already signed off on the new order, and instead of abandoning the treaties like you expected, they carried forward. And instead of coming after you, they plunged you into complete isolation. Everyone thought the rebels just died here years ago."

There's a slow clap from the back of the warriors group. I can't see the person clapping, but the army starts to part as if they're a body of water. Someone walks closer to us, out of the shadows into the dimly lit mix of our red brake lights and CERN's eerie wall sconces.

"Tomlin would have been so proud of your historic knowledge. I thought you'd have come sooner, Aloy."

A MAN WEARING DARK denim pants and a faded t-shirt with CERN's logo across the chest strides through the channel his people have opened for him. When he's left the crowd of warriors in his wake, the man halts in front of me. His honey-colored, curly hair is thinning on the top, but he doesn't look old. He wears glasses that have been taped together as if he didn't have time to construct a new pair. The leader holds a cone-like mechanism in his hand that I think has been amplifying his voice. Upon close proximity to me and my people, he sets it on the floor with a light *tink*. He holds his palms up, as if he's trying to show he means no harm—that he doesn't have any firearms with him. But I know there are other places than the hands to store a weapon.

I stand, arms at my sides, chin still up. The man is taller than me, but just barely. His nose has a slight point to the end of it, but there's a bump toward the middle that makes him look ordinary. He isn't handsome or ugly. His eyes are an icy blue, like mine, but there are flecks of green there too. The two colors cause his gaze to seem multi-dimensional, as if he can see things others merely disregard. He stares so long at me, in fact, I'm the one who turns away first, ending the silent exchange.

"Don't touch her." Griffin says, taking my obvious discomfort as his cue. His words are low snarls behind bared teeth.

The man from CERN blinks, peels his eyes from me, and instead focuses on Griffin. He reaches to place a palm on Griffin's shoulder, but Griffin backs away so that the enemy's hand hangs in midair. The leader cocks his head with a small tut of his tongue but doesn't take any further offense. "I wouldn't dream of it. But I've seen *you* touching her quite a bit. Isn't that right, Griffin?"

I twirl my head back in the man's direction. "How do you know our names?" I take a fighting stance with my feet splayed front and back as if I'm about to fence the leader, even though my sword is stowed far away, confiscated by his army.

The man leans forward, eyeing my face for just a split second longer. Then he walks in a circle around me, examining my body, front and back. I'm about to tell him to stop, that I've been through this before with Aaron, and it didn't end well for *that* tyrant, when he steps back.

"So long now. Your hair," the man says. "I always wondered what you'd look like. The cameras and microphones I dropped can only show so much. I've never gotten to see you this close before."

The air inside the cavern takes on a fizzy quality as the hairs on the back of my arm all raise in unison. I study the man's face as carefully as he's been staring at mine.

"I wondered If Ama and Apa would birth someone who looked like my twin," he says.

My mouth opens and closes once like a fish searching for oxygen before I find my voice. "Ama and Apa?" The words sound leaden even to my own ears. "What do you know of my—"

"*Your* parents?" the leader finishes for me. He gives me a moment, ending his unwavering stare by glancing over at the walls, waiting for me to mentally catch up.

"You're . . . you're . . ." I stammer.

"Yes, and I've been waiting for you, Sister."

It's dark in the cavern with only a few lights casting shadows across the faces around us. But for a moment, the world grows darker still. Tunnel vision constricts my pupils, and I can't help but squint as the man pulls at one of his earlobes, a nervous tick my mother used to do as we waited for a town hall to start in East Country. It was her way of fighting off the urge to fidget. I can't swallow the rising lump in my throat. I've been waiting so long to know my family's history, and now in the past week it's been revealed in shocking color. The milky orange color of the pills Tomlin took on his last night. The yellow sizzle of the staff used on Albine moments earlier. And the sky blue of the rebel leader's eyes.

The CERN letters on the man's shirt are all I can look at as my mind processes the information. He's been watching us? All this time? Why?

"Aren't you going to at least introduce me to your future husband and the rest of our East countrymen?" the leader asks.

I glance around to see if any of my people have picked up on what's happening. Some have. Their eyes are wide. But others still seem baffled. Griffin and Cole are among the confused, Griffin's hands at his sides in fists, still ready to attack if given the opportunity. Only the older members of my troop seem to understand.

I clear my throat, but nothing comes out.

"And some from Mid Country, too, I believe. Is that right?" the man asks.

I nod, wordlessly, looking from the leader to my people and back again. One of my hands reaches out to half-heartedly point at the warrior leader standing in front of us all. The one who has stolen from our country, bombed our nirogene supply, and attacked Mid Country countless times. The one who brought war to our peaceful countries, and the one who killed so many people in the act. He may look ordinary, but looks are deceiving. And he is no ordinary mercenary.

In the space of one breath, I manage to form the words that will explain to everyone exactly who our silent foe has been all along.

When I can't delay it any longer, I hear myself say the words as if I'm speaking from the end of a long tunnel. "This is my brother, Evan."

42

GRIFFIN STARTS FORWARD, AND the troops in back of me begin a chorus of mumblings.

"Yes, yes, I can imagine what you have heard about me, if my name was even spoken in East Country at all," says Evan. He addresses my people with his hands up, attempting to squelch their growing cacophony. "Deserter. Coward. Disloyal."

"Some of us don't know anything about you," Cole says, arriving on the other side of me. I don't know when he's gotten up enough courage to leave the cockpit and walk up here. He quivers, but I respect Cole all the more for the effort he's put into standing at my side.

"Ah, yes. The Calix look-a-like," says Evan. "You're a funny one."

"He's not *funny*," I say. "He's right. Most of my people are too young to remember you. And the ones who have heard of you don't know the real reason you left East Country."

"And you do?" Evan asks.

"Tomlin told me." I won't give Evan the thing he must want. Recognition. For his sacrifice. No matter his intentions, he abandoned us and went on a destructive rampage. The bombings. The killings. I can't believe the hero whom Tomlin told me about just this week is the same killer who's been tormenting us for so long. Evan didn't just leave East Country to follow our grandfather's quest for an environmental cure. He morphed into something evil. Or perhaps he was always self-centered and war-mongering. I want to spit the accusation in his face.

Either Evan doesn't see the vicious look I'm giving him, or he chooses to disregard it. Either way, he walks away from me, addressing my people instead. "It's true I left East Country three years before my eighteenth birthday. Of my own volition."

There are more rumblings coming from behind me, and I want to warn everyone to take care, as I cannot ensure that my brother is not so manipulative that he won't strike at them for seeming unappreciative.

"But I left for a good reason." Evan walks up and down the rows of my people, looking at each one of them like he's found a long-lost pup. He lingers in front of a few individuals, spouting their names and saying things like "how is your daughter" and "that vegetable patch you grew was just fantastic." All events that came after his time in East Country. Things he could only have known from the cameras he spoke of earlier. My people don't know how to react to his questions. Most are mute, just eyeing the warrior leader as he ventures toward them.

"East Country's former Elected," he continues, "my and Aloy's grandfather, recruited me for the most important job there ever was." He waits a moment, as if listening for clapping or other applause. When my people remain silent, Evan sighs and says, "There exists an environmental cure to the world's ills, and I've been looking for all the recipe's ingredients!" He stops again, eyes wide and a huge smile on his face. Still no one claps or rejoices. I think my people must be so confused now, they don't know how to react. Perhaps they think Evan is a lunatic.

"Well, you must be hungry," he says toward the crowd, his voice less triumphant. I bet Evan expected fanfare once East Country heard the truth of his whereabouts. Something like exultations for a long-lost prodigal son found once again. But Evan doesn't realize we've been through so much, we hardly trust anyone, let alone the man who was planning to steal more of our nirogene, caused so much pain in Mid Country, and led us on a dangerous path to his lair. "My people will feed you," he says.

On Evan's announcement, his people turn one hundred and eighty degrees on their heels with a myriad of heavy clomps. They march out of our airride, making room for all of us to exit.

"Do you expect my people to just up and follow yours?" I ask, one eyebrow raised. Evan nods, and I almost laugh at him. "After you almost killed Albine with that electric staff thing?"

"The Dehydrogenator? Oh, don't worry about that." Evan waves over the woman who had tipped the end of her weapon toward Albine's appendix. "Give him a liter of water intravenously. That should prop him back up, good as new."

"How can we be sure you won't hurt us again?" I ask, even though no matter what Evan says, we won't ever be sure.

"Your people are my people," Evan says, a whine of sincerity entering his voice. "Everything I've been doing, whatever you think, has been for them. And us. He reaches forward, grasping onto me in a sudden, sentimental hug. I'm still holding Griffin's hand, and at the fast fold into Evan's arms, Griffin pushes between us.

"You said you wouldn't touch her." Griffin's tone has turned from a warning to a snarl.

"Back off, Watchdog," Evan says. "I'm her family. You don't know the lengths I've gone to protect her."

"*Protect her?*" says Griffin. "You almost—"

"I know. I haven't been perfect," Evan says. "But I did try. Let me tell you." He pauses, a friendly look wavering over his features, softening the hard lines of his cheeks.

"I want to stay with my people," I say.

"Of course you do. But would you allow me just to show you a few things first?" He glances at Griffin and gives a slight shrug. "He can come too. I'll even let you bring a weapon, if you want."

Without waiting for our answer, Evan reaches toward one of his people and pulls two of our confiscated guns out of the warrior's backpack. He hands a gun to both me and Griffin.

"How do you know we won't use these on you?" Griffin asks, his hands already moving over the gun's casing, opening the magazine to ensure it still contains bullets.

"Once you hear what I've been doing, you won't want to shoot me. I promise."

Griffin and I share a glance. Evan sees the exchange but doesn't comment further. He points a finger to the right, gesturing for us to follow. We walk with Evan down the airride's ramp and into the cavern, along with his army and my small troop. A few of the CERN warriors carry Albine, and I hope they'll be true to their word and nurse him back to health with the fluids. The group walks around the front of the airride and then through the metal doors, which Evan says will stay permanently open.

"In case you'd like to leave at any time," he explains.

I wonder if he knows our only pilot is Cole. Or that I'm not sure if Cole knows how to fly the airride vertically so that we can actually exit this deep silo in the ground. But we have no choice at the moment but to continue following Evan into the dark, so I store those thoughts deeper in the recesses of my mind, saving them for later.

The tunnel in front of us is dimly lit, tiny wall sconces every few yards placing shadows high over our heads on the rock faces. A faint wind hits my uncovered skin, whooshing by all of us in whispers, as air seems to travel down the tunnel in sporadic gusts. I wonder how CERN manages to ventilate these deep corridors or if the technology is still working after all these years. My brother's people haven't fainted from any lack of oxygen, so our imminent suffocation isn't upon us, but still, we must be over twenty floors beneath the ground.

"We conserve energy at all times," Evan says, pointing to the closest lamp, "so please excuse the lack of light. We only use it when absolutely necessary. Or in limited quantities." The sconces are motion activated, and as we scuffle forward, the next three in front of us blink on. It gives us adequate light to see but creates the effect of continuing to walk into nothingness, it's so dark just a few yards ahead.

I'm still walking hand in hand with Griffin, as if he's keeping a hold of me so we don't lose each other in Evan's underground fortress. I squeeze his hand once, and Griffin pumps back. I can't believe I'm walking in between Griffin and my brother. My brother! A million questions tumble through my head, and I don't know whether to start ricocheting them off to Evan or wait for the gems of information he intends to reveal on his own. Sometimes remaining quiet elicits the most intelligence, so as hard as it is, I concentrate not on asking my burning questions but on keeping track of where we're being taken. So far we're just being led straight along the same corridor, but if we turn left or right, I want to remember the way out.

The tunnel is about the width of two airrides parked side by side. The walls are a dark stone that's wet every few paces with lines of water running down like tears. I reach out absently, running a finger over the tiny trail the water leaves on the stone's surface. After a few minutes of venturing farther from the cave's entrance, the walls become more industrial. Metal and plaster and other man-made materials.

"It was only a matter of time," Evan says, breaking through the sound of all our steady footsteps on the ground.

I stare at my brother, waiting for him to keep talking—to tell me why in the world he just *had* to start bringing destruction back to our homeland. Why he had to desert his duty to East Country to instead follow a fool's errand. Anything he tells us at this point will be valuable intelligence I can either use against him later or to help us escape CERN's lair.

"I didn't start out bombing Mid, if you want to know," he says, his lips curling around the last words. "We started by only taking a few things we needed to survive. Mid Country had so much, and we had so little. I was merely facilitating a bit of sharing."

"You're a saint," I say and immediately feel Griffin's hand squeeze mine in warning. I glance up at him, and he raises his eyebrows. I know what Griffin's trying to convey. Don't poke the beast. My brother's being nice right now. We don't know Evan well enough yet to test him. We're still his prisoners.

"You'll see," says Evan. "You'll thank me when you realize what I managed to find in my travels." He keeps going, not waiting for a response. "You know that each of the three former United States countries all had a part of the cure's puzzle, right?"

I nod yes, and he continues, "I can't wait to show you!" He's hopping out of his sneakers, the front of his left big toe already having worn a hole through the top leather. This fidgety excitement must be a normal hallmark of his personality. None of the CERN rebels seem pulsed by Evan's exaggerated movements or his sudden exuberance.

Evan continues, "We hadn't gotten the invisible shields working on the airrides at the start of our mission, so unfortunately we were spotted multiple times in Mid and West Countries. But it was no excuse for Mid to begin designing as many weapons as they could, don't you agree? Nuclear weapons, for heaven's sake! I couldn't let them get very far in that endeavor. You did the same thing. Dismantled their capabilities when you could." He's talking so fast, I'm surprised when he stops to take a breath of air and swallow.

"Dismantled Mid's weapons from the inside," I say. "I didn't bomb their civilians to smithereens." The contempt in my tone pours out, and Griffin coughs hard in my direction. I know, I know. I should tread lightly. But instead, I fire an emotional question toward my brother. "Do you have *any* idea what you drove Mid Country to do?"

Evan stops midstride, and the entire entourage of our two groups halts behind us. Evan's eyebrows are raised into two neat *V*'s. "Yes," he says slowly. "You merely prove my point. Mid took technology too far, just like our forefathers. They're exactly what's wrong with mankind, so if a few of their kind were destroyed, it isn't that much of a loss . . ." His voice trails off, and I bet even Evan has trouble justifying the means to his end. He raises his palms into the air. "Fine, I realize my 'dismantling' drove Mid to mistreat their people. That wasn't my intention. I merely wanted their nirogene, to hinder their nuclear capabilities, and to look for their piece of the recipe."

I shake my head. "You and the rebels," I say. "How'd you get all these people to go along with you?"

"It was our grandfather Gregory who did the convincing." Evan looks from me to the group in back of us, addressing his people. "But it wasn't hard, right? These are all ancestors of the original rebels who opposed the Eco Accords. The warriors who took over CERN after killing the Eco Accord writers. None of these people wanted to abandon technology or live in isolation. And when Grandfather told them about the secret cure, the one that was kept from them, you can imagine their response."

Griffin and I exchange another slight glance. Yes, I can imagine their response. Cut off from the outside world, left to starve for their sins against the Eco Accord creators, the rebels were probably hungry for hope. Grandfather was exactly what they needed. When he took a boat to Europe after handing the Elected reigns to my father and told the rebels how the American government was withholding a cure from everyone, they were probably livid. I know I was incredulous when Tomlin explained it all to me.

"Why nirogene?" Griffin asks, changing the direction of the conversation back to Evan's earlier statement.

Evan grins at Griffin and proceeds walking forward down the unending corridor in the semi-darkness. We rejoin Evan's side, taking long strides to keep up. My brother absently runs his hand along the left side of the wall, grazing the metal with his fingertips as he walks. "I needed so much. So *very* much for what we are trying to do. But you'll see." He bounces on the balls of his feet, his gait elongating so that I almost have to jog to keep pace.

"What happened to Grandfather Gregory after he took you from East Country?" I ask.

Evan shakes his head. "Died just a few years after I got here. Without the purple pills, and even though we try to stay indoors as much as possible, the radiation effects . . . In the water and all . . . well, you know."

I instantly look down at my hand, which had touched the wet rock behind us a few moments earlier. Remnants of the liquid are still slippery on my index finger, and I rub vigorously against my pants with a grimace.

"Did Grandfather advocate for all the carnage you caused? He was an East Country Elected, which means he advocated peace." I say.

"Not everyone is exactly what they say they are, Aloy," my brother says, his mouth tilting up on one side. "I'd have thought you of all people, would have some inkling what that's like." He looks over at my pants and male-styled uniform. It's a lot different from my mother's long skirts.

I can tell he's trying to manipulate the conversation away from his guilt, and I won't let that happen. I want to see remorse, if nothing else. "I'm sure Grandfather wouldn't have wanted you to murder so many people in Mid Country just to look for the cure and steal their nirogene."

Evan throws up his hands. "I wasn't *trying* to kill anyone. If you just wait a moment, you'll see. I'm trying to *fix* everything!" His eyes are alight with righteousness.

Griffin reaches with his other hand around to grip my shoulder, a clear warning now.

I ignore it and keep prodding. "But a couple of times. Especially that last time." My voice grows soft, remembering the carnage of Evan's last big assault against Mid. I look down at the hard rock under our feet. No one was merely dismantling Mid's weaponry or looking for nirogene that time. "The last time you struck Mid. It was all out—" My throat closes, tight against the picture of so many people injured or dead, lined up on the hospital floor. I look up again at Evan, the accusations brimming in my eyelids. "You hit indiscriminately. Women and children. Places where people lived."

Evan stops again and spins me around so both of his hands are on my shoulders. Griffin's hand is pulled out of mine in the movement. "I was just so . . . so . . . *angry*. What else could I do, Aloy? Aaron was about to *erase* your mind? Put you through the worst optogenetics procedure *ever*! I couldn't let him do that to you, my sister!"

The weight of Evan's words hit me on the shoulders as if his very touch is a hammer pummeling me deep into the earth at our feet. "So you . . . you . . . created a distraction?" My voice is thin. I don't want to say the words. Don't want to acknowledge that I was the reason for Evan's gruesome assault. I'd always known that last attack was different from the others, and perhaps a part of my brain even reconciled the coincidence that it saved me from Aaron's revenge. But hearing it outright . . . knowing that the devastation was intended for my benefit . . .

"How could you?" My words tumble out in a whisper, but there is a fire behind them that Evan doesn't yet recognize. Griffin does, though, returning his hand into mine, his fingers gripping mine in dire warning, trying to pull me closer to him and away from Evan's grasp.

Evan drops his hands from my shoulders and turns forward again, his face growing dark. "I thought you'd *thank* me when you found out. It was for the greater good. You needed to be kept alive and mentally whole." He continues walking, head straight so that our eyes don't meet.

We walk in silence like this for a few minutes. I wonder how we'll ever get out of here. How I'll ever be able to fix all the ills my brother caused. How do you fix anything once people have died? There will be no cure for them, even if Evan's quest procured any of the necessary ingredients to fix the environment's atmosphere. The destruction my brother caused is final. There's no turning back from what he's done for the "greater good."

"You were the one who gave us the guns in East Country too, weren't you?" Griffin finally says, a breath of understanding in his voice. He's been putting two and two together as we walk in the quiet corridor, and I can tell he's trying to gain back some goodwill from my brother after I just jostled Evan's composure. "Right before we needed to meet Aloy in Mid Country for the coup."

"All of it was me," Evan says, glancing at Griffin, a slight hint of hope glossing across his face again. He must think Griffin understands his motives. "We dropped the guns by each tent via a concealed airride from above." He shakes his head, looking at the ground. "There's no one else across the world who cares about curing the environment or protecting the people of East. You *needed* me to watch out for you."

"What do you mean 'across the world'?" asks Griffin, picking up on the last bit of Evan's explanation. He runs a hand through the front of his hair, a gesture I've seen him do a million times before. It makes me ache for our son who has already started showing hints of the same dark hair.

"You didn't think North America was the only continent still sustaining life, did you?" Evan chuckles at Griffin, mouth parted with his corresponding smile. "Parts of China still exist. But they're in complete isolation. Don't want to have anything to do with anyone. We've tried to fly over there a few times. But they've put up some kind of bubble. Couldn't get in, even if we wanted to visit them."

I'm still fuming at my brother's actions, but the idea that there are other parts of the world still thriving is like the pages of Tomlin's history books flapping wide open. My mouth opens once to ask a question, but Evan stops in his tracks, sending our entire procession bumping into each other.

"We're here," Evan says, pointing to the front of a dark grey door on our left. "My private quarters."

We're still within the same long corridor, but there are large doors dotting the metal walls, all of them towering over our heads, at least twelve feet tall. Evan's door looks just like the others, but there's a red letter E by the handle. I don't know if it stands for Evan's name, the word *Elected*, or something entirely different.

"Every room in our complex generates from this one corridor," says Evan. "Even the old particle accelerator from CERN is still left intact down here behind one of these doors. We haven't moved it. Thought about using some of the parts, but what if we need it again someday? You never know."

Evan's blabbering about things that Griffin and I know nothing about, but I don't care. It's giving me some time to think of what I want to say to him. How I want to tell him that he's ruined everything with his overly-confident interference, how he needs to stop. How I will stop him myself if he won't halt his meddling.

Evan pushes on the door while speaking to a few of his warriors. "We'll meet back up with you in a few minutes, if you don't mind." Then he turns to me. "There are a couple of things I want to show you."

At Evan's command and without waiting for my response, his warriors start to shuffle past us. Interspersed among the rebels are my troops, looking bewildered. As they walk by, many of my people glance toward me with worried faces, raising eyebrows when they see the anger etched into my brow. But I just nod at them and say we'll converge with the group again later. Cole stops by my side, refusing to budge, but I gesture with a jut of my head. Last thing we want is for any more of my people to feel the brunt of a Dehydrogenator again. A rebel at Cole's side pushes him forward with the unheated end of his staff in the small of Cole's back. The clone stumbles forward but keeps walking, looking back at me over his shoulder before disappearing into the darkness.

When they're all gone, just a distant sound of footsteps far away, Evan says, "After you."

Griffin is right by my side, so that the two of us peer into Evan's quarters at the same time. Could it be a trick? A way to separate me from my people just to kill me and Griffin? Are there others inside the room? But from a perfunctory first glance, all we see is a cavernous, empty room. The lights in Evan's apartment are brighter than the ones in the corridor. There's a double bed pushed up against one side of the room and a white chest of drawers a few yards to the right of it. A soft green comforter blankets the bed's surface, yellow flowers swirling in patterns across the green background.

Evan sees me staring at his bedspread and says, "It reminds me of the paradise we're seeking."

I don't respond. Just keep glancing around the room while we step inside. There are no windows, as I believe we're so far underground there will be no windows anywhere through the entire complex. But a few framed pictures dot the walls. One is of the Washington Monument before it was destroyed in the world wars. I stare at this for an extra beat, but keep looking around, not concentrating on any one thing for too long. There's a long wood table and six chairs to the left and a large white refrigerator along the wall. I'd have only recognized the contraption after living in Mid Country. Evan walks to the refrigerator first, opening the door and lifting out three glass bottles.

"Coca-Cola," he says. "From back in the day. This stuff never goes bad." He hands me and Griffin each a bottle and then unlocks the metal lid of each with a hooked tool. "Have a drink."

Griffin and I stare at the foreign object and then at Evan as he takes a long pull of the liquid. He smiles when he's done. "Love the sugar. Always get such a good rush." He scratches his neck and rests his other hand lightly on one of the nearby chair backs.

At Evan's relaxed state and his obvious lack of social perception, I can't keep my mouth shut any longer. How can Evan not realize how furious we are? Or the effects of his actions? I place my bottle down on his wooden table with a loud, deliberate *thunk*, not bothering to take a drink.

My words start as a whisper, but their tone shifts Evan's gaze to meet mine in a hurry. "Do you have *any* idea what it looks like when a woman's hand is blown off? A piece of her just lying on the ground at her side? Do you know what kind of features will show on her face as she realizes her hand is missing? *Do you?*" My whisper has quickly grown into a shout, and I yell the last words in Evan's face, moving close to him so that our faces almost touch. "You killed so many people just to save me. But you put me in that position in the first place! You made Mid think it was East hurting them for the last ten years! They *leveled* our country because of you!"

"Well, I didn't make them . . ." Evan starts. He backs up a few footsteps, but I follow, cornering him against a wall.

My brother's lack of responsibility is sickening. "You drove them to it!" I scream the words in his face, shaking with the force of my anger.

My hand leaves my side, making a trip up to Evan's neck. I think about all the blood veins there and how they will burst inside my grip. I don't need a gun. I'll do the job with my bare hands.

"Aloy?" Griffin asks, his voice at first tentative. He moves closer to me and my brother, placing a hand on my upper arm, but I don't back down.

The anger inside me feels like an animal, clawing to get out. My brother is the one who made the mistake, leaving us alone with him in here. I won't let him get away with his war crimes, no matter if he was doing everything for our country's so-called protection. "You ruined what we had in East Country," I say to Evan. "It wasn't perfect. But we were getting by. You and your stealing and your bombing. *You* and the type of person you are. You're the reason our ancestors didn't want to give the world a cure! They wanted to wait till the worst aspects of humankind were bred out of our systems. But it looks like, no matter what, there will always be people like you around. Doesn't matter how much time goes by."

"Aloy, are you sure you want to do this?" Griffin implores me. "If you anger him, our troops are out there . . . how will we explain Evan's . . ."

Evan stares straight back at me, ignoring Griffin, like my brother and I are the only two people in the room. "Are you serious, Aloy?" Evan doesn't back down, not even with my insults flying at his face and my hand dangerously close to strangling him. "You're going to get all righteous on *me?* You're the one who just *had* to sneak into Mid Country, looking for Ama and Apa. And then look what happened to them! All for your sake! Just 'cause they were trying to protect you. I was going to find a way to retrieve them. They could've lived with me here in Switzerland! But *you* ruined that!"

I shake my head. I won't be manipulated like this. "You're delusional! How do you even know they wanted to come over here with you? Maybe they planned to move back to East and tell me what was happening in Mid! Did you think of that? Maybe they'd have rather stayed with a child who didn't abandon them!" My words fly at Evan, fast and hurtful.

"Calm down," Griffin says, trying to get in between us. His body angles against mine, trying to pry me away from my brother. "Neither of you can know what your parents truly planned—"

I want to tell Griffin to stay out of this. That it's a family matter, and if I want to maim my sadistic brother, or even kill him, it's my own decision. But I don't say these things. Griffin is as much my family as Evan, if not more so. I just keep throwing words at Evan's face, my fury surely surprising him as I stand up on tip toes to meet my brother eye-to-eye. "Our parents died because you bullied Mid Country for so long, Calix thought they were the ones leading the carnage!"

"They died, Aloy, because *you* snuck into Mid, and Calix thought they were spies, same as you! Your actions, not mine, killed our parents!"

The breath catches in my throat. Could my arrival in Mid really have caused my parents' subsequent execution? Griffin manages to squirm an arm around my waist, pulling me a few feet back away from Evan. Little fissures start to crack my resolve, anger seeping like droplets of bathwater after stepping out of a tub. I feel cold and hot at the same time.

I think of the picture of my mother cutting her hair so she could impersonate me in the video in the rocket launcher. True, they were covering for me. But they didn't die because of me. And neither did all the other people in Mid and East Countries. Evan, Calix, and Aaron are the ones with blood on their hands.

"If you had your precious cameras all over the place, watching our every move, why didn't you rescue our parents?" My words bite, accusing Evan again, but this time there's less tenacity behind them. My voice cracks.

"I didn't have a chance!" Evan's losing it, his eyes clouding over with frustrated tears. "I *told* you. Things aren't perfect. I can't get my airrides over to your continent fast enough always. Sometimes there are casualties."

"Casualties . . ." I say the word dryly. Griffin wraps his arm around me tighter, and I don't think it's to prevent me from hurting Evan any longer. I think it's to hold me up if I collapse. I can feel the adrenaline slipping from my chest. Griffin knows me better than I do myself. I'm not a killer. Not even to stop my madman brother and his misguided actions.

"At least you got to say goodbye to our parents on your own terms," I say, my voice deflating. "I didn't even get to talk to them in Mid Country." I let Griffin stay close, feeling the ridges of his fingers against my spine.

Evan walks away from the back wall, pulling out a chair and dumping himself down into it. "They tried to come see you."

"What are you talking about?" Griffin asks.

"That night Aloy came back from visiting East Country and Vienne. The same night you warned Aloy about Calix's search for her." Evan looks toward me. "Our parents intended to warn you too. But Calix was in your room, and when they heard his voice inside your apartment they left."

"They came to my apartment?" My hand is at my brow. The hair there feels heavy and thick, long pieces falling over my forehead. I have an intense desire to rip it all out. To go back to my boy form when life was a lie but not as complicated as our current state of affairs.

"That wasn't the only time they tried to see you," Evan says. He rubs the back of his neck again, his head stretching to one side.

"They tried multiple times?" Now the adrenaline truly exits my body. My toes tingle as the anger seeps out, leaving me ill-prepared for the fatigue of the aftershocks. But Griffin senses my discomfort and immediately deposits me into a chair at the table and sits down in the one next to me, his arm never leaving my waist.

"The time you went to the Satisfaction Room, they were in the crowd waiting to get in," says Evan. "You didn't see them. You went inside. By the time you came out—"

"You'd started a new round of attacks on Mid," I say, my shoulders sagging.

Evan sighs. "Mid was so close to a nuclear breakthrough that time, Aloy. I had to do it. I couldn't wait."

Tears well up in my eyes, and Griffin shifts closer to me so our shoulders touch.

"They talked about convincing you to go back East," says Evan again. "I heard them from my dropped microphones."

"I wouldn't have gone back," I say, the realization sure on my tongue.

Evan wipes a hand across his brow, shifting in his chair. "I miss them, you know. When I followed Grandfather here, I expected we'd go pick up Ama and Apa when you turned eighteen. I never thought I wouldn't see them again. I didn't expect them to travel to Mid, where I couldn't extricate them. I have drop and reach capabilities from the air, but I've hardly ever landed to pick up people."

"You landed at least once before, though, right?" Griffin asks Evan. Then he looks back at me to confirm the question.

"Griffin's right." I think about what I told him about the Mind Multiplier's images. "You left a man on the ground at least once," I say.

"You saw him?" Evan asks. His hands spread on the table in front of him, flexing in and out.

"In the Mind Multiplier," I respond. "At least I think what I saw was real. One of your rebels buried bullets on East's side of the border. And then Mid's airride found and killed him. Calix told me it was his airride but not his man."

Evan's head drops. "I was leaving weapons for you. We managed to leave a man behind to hide the bullets I dropped from the sky. He was supposed to bury them and then travel to Mid to take their Madame Elected's pendant—their piece of the cure's puzzle. But obviously you know what happened to him." Evan looks down at the wood grains on the table, tracing one of them left-to-right.

"Why were you leaving weapons for us?" asks Griffin.

Evan's head bobs up again, and he shrugs. "In case you needed them against a Mid Country invasion later. I was trying to arm you. It was only a matter of time before Mid tried to take over East. I would've dropped off the guns sooner than at the internment camp, but I saw what you did with the bullets. Wasting them like that, Aloy." He shakes his head.

"And the Mind Multiplier?" I ask. "Was that you too?" Imogene said it had fallen from the sky. I'd thought she was talking nonsense in the prison cell, but maybe her gibberish was the closest I'd been to hearing the truth all those months ago.

"I wanted you to understand a few things. I tried the helmet too, and it revealed a heap of information. Like where the stores of nirogene were located in Mid and East Countries."

There are so many things I want to say to Evan. To explain that the Mind Multiplier was harmful. That it *hurt* me. That if he tried it too many times, maybe it's the thing that caused his constant jumpiness. But he thinks he was helping. And he *still* wants to help. I don't know how to convince Evan that most of what he's done has produced bad results. He may never acknowledge that fact. All I can do now is steer his intentions toward action that might actually benefit people. No more war. No more bombing.

I thump both hands, palms down, onto the table between us and lean forward. "Evan, what did you want to show us? I think it's time we saw."

43

EVAN HOPS UP FROM his seat, the metal feet from his chair skidding across the floor with a shriek. He opens the top drawer of the dresser next to his bed and brings forth a crinkled piece of parchment. Evan unfolds it on the table with reverence, careful not to rip any of the folds that have become thin and fragile. He leans between me and Griffin, gripping the back of our chairs.

"Read it," he says. "Ama gave it to Tomlin, who gave it to Grandfather, who gave it to me."

"Seems like this paper's been more places that I have," jokes Griffin. His voice is light, but his brace on my knee under the table is anything but. Evan has been on a crusade, and this artifact is the first thing that propelled him toward dangerous obsession.

My eyes scan the parchment, but after the first few words, I already know what the whole thing says. I'm mesmerized by the looping swirls of the *L*'s and *S*'s, though, so I don't stop staring at it. My mother's twirling handwriting stares back at me—another piece of her right in front of me.

> *Lock your strength far away;*
> *Save it for a rainy day.*
> *When the sun no longer shines,*
> *That's when you'll need this little rhyme.*

Griffin squeezes my hand under the table, knowing that the necklace Tomlin gave me the night before holds the same verse.

"We'll never know what other secrets Ama's pendant contained," says Evan, "but at least I have the poem from it." He moves from behind us back to his seat. "I've been trying to find the actual artifact, but Ama most likely died wearing her necklace, not having been able to hand it down to my Madame Elected."

I stare at Evan, waiting for him to mention anything about me being the Elected and having had a perfectly good wife to whom Ama could have bestowed the necklace, but he doesn't say anything about it. Perhaps Evan thinks my parents never really took my reign as Elected seriously. I'm considering piping up about his clear oversight, when he says, "I looked hard in the cameras to see if the necklace showed during footage of our parents' firing squad, but—"

"I have it," I break in, partly to shut my brother up about their execution and partly to remind him I had a role in East's Electancy after all. Evan's mouth gapes and his eyes don't move from my neck as if he's trying to see through the material of my shirt where the necklace might lay against my skin. I pull Ama's pendant from under my shirt collar, closing my hand over the scalloped gold edges. I can almost feel my mother's heartbeat in the metal this one last time. After today, I know the necklace won't just be mine anymore. My mother's jewelry will belong to all of my people, and maybe it always should have.

Evan is upon me in an instant, pulling the medallion between his fingertips even before I have a chance to fully lift the chain over my head.

"It's gold!" he exclaims, drawing the pendant and its chain away from me. Evan turns the medallion over in his palm, rubbing his fingers over the words, comparing them to the ones on the parchment. When he's satisfied they're the same, he says again, "Gold! Do you know what a breakthrough this is?"

I shake my head and look at Griffin. Both of us shrug. "What does the medallion's material matter?"

Evan shakes his head, blinking his eyes closed for an exaggerated beat. His exasperation with us steams off his features like smoke. "West's necklace was silver, so if they're different, it's got to have *some* meaning," he says. "Everything with these necklaces is a code."

"Maybe it's just a coincidence," says Griffin, his eyebrows lifting for half a second.

Evan *humphs* and directs his next comment to Griffin. "If you're foolish enough to believe that, maybe Aloy shouldn't have rescued you from East's prison. You were the Technology Faction's leader, huh? What a waste of time all that was."

Griffin gives a tolerant smile. "You think?" He leans back in his chair, one arm draped across the top, indulging my brother who thinks he truly has Griffin's ear.

"Yeah. A bunch of rebels with no backbone to fight for what they believed in. Now, the rebels here would've . . ."

I stop listening halfway through Evan's rant. My brother still stands on the side of violence, no matter what I've said to him. My words alone obviously haven't impressed upon Evan the consequences of his actions.

Our ancestors played a game with us, knowing that in the future we'd be their pawns, killing each other over these poems as we tried to piece back together the recipe my great-great-grandfather created before any of us were born. Except that we weren't supposed to *kill* for the words. We were only supposed to find them after the continent reunited in peace. It shouldn't have happened for many more lifetimes. Evan unnaturally accelerated the whole process, using violence as his means. It's not right. No one would have wanted it this way. I'm sure in West, they didn't . . .

And then it hits me. "Wait," I say, cutting Evan off in the middle of his diatribe. "What do you mean West Country's pendant was silver? How do you know?"

At this, Evan smiles, returning to his seat, letting my pendant's chain dangle back and forth between his two hands. "I told you, Aloy, you'd thank me when you found out what I accomplished." Evan reaches into his jeans pocket, pulling out an object wrapped in leather. He leans far across the table, pushing the leather satchel next to the unfolded parchment in front of me and Griffin. I can tell at once that the object contains West's pendant, as a silver chain peeks out from between Evan's fingers. It's still startling, though, to see the necklace when Griffin plucks it from the small bag. West Country's piece of the puzzle is etched onto a silver teardrop in looping script. Griffin and I bend to read the small words, Griffin's casual half-smile now erased.

> *Let the shiny metal rust;*
> *So we don't all turn to dust.*
> *Take the harvest, mix with rain;*
> *Then be free of all the pain.*

After a minute, Griffin looks up, head pointed toward Evan. "How do you know it's authentic?"

Evan sucks in his breath, smug with pride. "It's real because I took it from West Country's Madame Elected myself.

"When?" I ask. "I thought West Country was in ruins. That they were destroyed by massive earthquakes years ago."

Evan doesn't answer me, just lets the realization of his involvement wash over me in a cold sensation. Griffin's already come to my same conclusion, and when I pick up my head to look at Evan's face, Griffin is staring at him also.

"Did you steal nirogene from West too? Before or after you bombed them to smithereens?" Griffin asks.

Evan plays with the table's wood grain, his fingernail picking at the surface, still not answering us.

"Hey!" I call in his direction, rapping my knuckles on the wood table. "Did you bring on West's earthquakes with your bombs or did they just think your cloaked bombings were earthquakes?"

Evan shrugs. "Does it matter what they thought? I needed a distraction to extricate their necklace and their nirogene."

I open my mouth to say something pointed, but Evan raises a hand. "Whatever you may think about my methods, you can't deny what they achieved. I've had West's pendant, East's poem, and CERN's resources to make the recipe. I'm so close to a cure. All I need now is Mid's necklace."

The depth of my brother's folly is too difficult to grasp. He may have single-handedly killed off half of the continent's survivors looking for a way to save people from environmental devastation. The irony is astounding.

Griffin continues to stare at the teardrop with the poem from West etched into its silver surface. "This poem mentions metal rusting. So you've somehow used nirogene, the compound that stopped our bikes from rusting, in the formula?"

My brother jumps up from his seat to point at the verses. "Yes!" He taps the tip of his index finger against his temple.

I look at the two poems side by side again. First East Country's golden, scalloped pendant, and then West Country's silver teardrop, both containing one third of the precious recipe to reverse centuries of environmental damage.

Lock your strength far away;
Save it for a rainy day.
When the sun no longer shines,
That's when you'll need this little rhyme.

Let the shiny metal rust;
So we don't all turn to dust.

"We mixed nirogene with rain, and it created a chemical reaction," Evan says. "I've found a way to suck the acidic properties out of the rain, just like nirogene eats rust on East Country's bicycles. But the formula isn't perfected. I'm missing something." Evan bites his bottom lip and rubs his neck so hard I think it's actually hurting him. "We haven't found Mid's pendant yet, and it must tell of the last ingredient." He goes on before I can utter a word, not stopping even to look at our reactions. "While I use silver bowls in which to mix the formula, every time I left the acid rain in the silver, the compound evaporated into thin air. There's got to be some significance to the gold from East's medallion."

"So let me get this straight," says Griffin. "You think East's stanza tells you to use acid rain, collected in a gold bowl? And West's stanza means the second ingredient is melted nirogene that you're supposed to mix in a silver bowl? And that's why you've stolen our supplies, Mid's, and West's, so you could keep experimenting with the nirogene?"

"I knew you'd finally understand why I had to have everyone's nirogene supply!" exclaims Evan, taking Griffin's comprehension for agreement. My brother's face is blotchy with red and white patches. He's so excited, his big toe has actually popped clear out of the top of his sneaker, and he doesn't even notice. "Now that I know East's pendant is gold, I can experiment with that too!"

"Do you have any idea what Mid's piece of the puzzle says?" Griffin asks.

"Not yet. Perhaps it's another compound. Maybe even the dirt at our feet. Or carbon monoxide from the air. Or some other element from the old periodic table. I've experimented with everything I can think of, and well, you've seen what it's done to our weather."

I think of the snow laden mountains all around us, and how the flakes should just be a dusting at this point in the calendar.

"I've searched for Mid's pendant for years," says Evan, pursing his lips as if he's in actual pain at the thought. "It may have been around Aaron's mother's neck, but once he killed his parents, the necklace seems to have disappeared into thin air right along with its last Madame Elected."

"Stop," I say. I can't bear to hear Evan talk about Aaron and Calix's mother like she was a piece of dirty laundry that got lost behind a rock. Evan looks at me oddly, waiting for me to go on. But I can't tell him what I'm really thinking—that I wish our great grandfather hadn't come up with a cure at all. That we'd all have been better off without some sort of pipe dream hanging over our heads, just out of reach. That everything Evan's done, mixing chemicals and experimenting on the border of Switzerland and France, has ruined the environment even more. I know I won't change his mind, no matter what I say. I'll never be able to make him stop searching for a cure and stop killing people along the way.

"If only I could find Mid's necklace," Evan muses again, sensing that I'm not about to say anything stunning. "Now that you've taken over Mid, we can go down there, tear through people's belongings looking for the thing, inch by inch. We can *make* people talk. Some guard down there's got to know where the necklace is. How many metal pendants can be floating around their country anyway?"

It's only when Evan starts pacing across the room in rapid strides, talking about the different types of metal that could be used for jewelry, that an idea pops into my head. I put my face in my hands, leaning forward against the table with the realization. My vision swims.

I can't believe I didn't realize this before. I know how to make Evan listen to my pleas for peace. I can get my troops out from under his grasp *and* ensure Evan won't hurt anyone else in his search for Mid's necklace. I've known where Mid's pendant was this entire time. Except it's not what Evan thinks it is. It's not made out of bronze or copper or any other type of metal.

It's in the form of the largest diamond I've ever seen. And yet again, it's lying across the neck of a dead woman.

I GLANCE AT GRIFFIN who catches my eye and stands up, bending over me. I move my seat back and turn to face Griffin. Our sudden movements stop Evan's rant and he stays stock still, shifting his eyes between the two of us.

"Griffin, do you remember the three bodies at the top of Mid's rocket launcher the night of our coup?" I ask.

"Yes, Emma was still alive up there. And Aaron's guard and that nurse were dead."

"Do you know what our troops did with Ollinear and Dolche's bodies while Emma and I were being fixed up?"

"They were taken down, I'm sure, but beyond that, I can't say."

I turn to my brother who's wearing a feverish look. He can tell I know something, and he's waiting like a fox outside a chicken coop for me to explain myself. "Evan, do you know anything about Mid's burial rituals from all the time spent spying on them?"

My brother's voice is quick and to the point. "Of course. They're too pragmatic to bury their dead, so they use incineration."

That's what I thought. In no time during Margareath's tours of Mid did she ever show or point out a graveyard to me or Griffin. And I never saw one in all my rounds throughout the city center. "All right," I say, running a hand through my hair. "I may know where Mid's piece of the formula is. But it's not on a metal pendant like West or East's was. Mid's poem was inscribed inside a diamond."

Evan practically jumps with the information. "How do you know that?"

"Aaron's betrothed, Emma, had it for a while, but she didn't like to show it off. And then Aaron ripped it off her neck and gave it to the nurse who was loyal to him. That nurse, Dolche, was wearing it when Aaron killed her at the top of the rocket launcher." My voice catches when Evan starts nodding rapidly in enthusiasm. "But if Dolche's body was cremated, I'm not sure if the diamond still exists."

Evan considers this for a moment and then says, "Its existence depends on how hot Mid keeps their incinerators. A normal campfire wouldn't do anything to a diamond. It would need a temperature of seven hundred degrees Celsius to burn. And then something like over three thousand degrees to melt."

I look at Griffin, but he gives a light shake of his head. None of us knows how hot Mid's incinerator is.

"Well, we've got to go get it!" says Evan when neither Griffin nor I speak. "Right now! I'll man my airrides, and we'll rip the diamond out of Mid's hands before they can do anything else with it or hide it away for another century!"

I've been waiting for Evan's outburst, and I push my chair out of my way, approaching Evan slowly, hands at my hip. "And how do you propose to do that? Just wander in and tell them you've been the one attacking their country? And now they should just do what you want?"

"I suppose," says Evan, one of his shoulders shrugging. "We'll use my airrides and *make* them retrieve the diamond for us."

"What if the diamond was already destroyed? Or taken?" I ask, walking toward my brother. "How are you planning to wheedle the diamond out of someone's clutches, especially if they know who you are?"

Evan paces in front of his bed, frustrated. "We *cannot* let that necklace get lost again! I could just say I'm a survivor from West Country, like you did."

"I don't think so," says Griffin, picking up on my unspoken plan. "We'd tell them who you are."

Evan's hands flex and tighten into fists. "Why in the world would you do that? Do you *want* me to use force to take the diamond?" His eyes narrow into slits.

"Exactly the opposite," I say. I walk over to his dresser, resting a casual hand on its surface. I need my brother to stay calm now, not grow hopping mad and take out his fury on my troops. The only way I know how to elicit tranquility is to feign the action myself, even though my own stomach is shaking. "I can't trust that you wouldn't take out your frustration on the people of Mid if the diamond was destroyed. I don't believe that you'll search for it peaceably. So I propose to go get it for you." I stare at Evan to see if he fully understands. When he doesn't say anything, I lick my lips and take a breath. "Without you."

Evan shifts on both feet and wrings his hands together in front of his waist. "I don't know . . ." He looks up at me, searching my eyes to gauge my sincerity. "I always thought I'd be the one—" He swallows thickly and turns to face the wall.

Griffin makes a move to speak, but I put up a hand and mouth the word "wait" in his direction.

Evan shakes his head, mumbling to himself, kicking the far wall. But finally he turns around, his eyebrows knitted on his brow. "You think you'll be able to get it from them?"

"I promise I will."

Evan opens his mouth to say something else, but I break in. "On a few conditions. One, I take my people out of CERN with me. Second, you let me have Ama's necklace, now that you've seen it." Evan's already nodding yes, and flicking his hand forward like my simple requests are wasting precious time. "And last," I say, pausing to take a deep breath. "You don't ever step foot in East or Mid Country again. You stay here. In Switzerland. No matter what."

There's a beat of silence until Evan responds, "Why would I agree to that?" His head juts out from his body on a crooked angle. "Wait . . . I get it." He gives a stilted laugh. "You don't want me to take back East's Elected role. You want to keep it for yourself!" He hits a palm against his knee, guffawing louder.

"A power struggle has nothing to do with Aloy's request," says Griffin, standing at my side, his back rigid. "If she cared so much about keeping the position, she wouldn't have abdicated it to Vienne for all those months she stayed in Mid."

"Plus," I mutter, "East wouldn't take you back anyway."

Evan's face grows cold, his temples tensing. "I don't accept your conditions."

"Okay, then," I say, turning around and striding toward the door. "I'll just go get the last piece of the puzzle for myself. You don't have to be involved at all. We're leaving." Griffin turns, standing at my side as we take a few long strides toward Evan's door. I don't know how we'll get our people out if Evan doesn't accept my suggestion, but I'm banking on the fact that Evan knows Mid will do anything to stop their ten-year enemy from getting what he wants. I'm the only one who can coax the diamond away from them. If it even still exists.

"You don't know how to do anything with the formula!" Evan yells after us. "Only I know how to make the recipe. Only *I* have the resources!"

"True," I say, looking back over my shoulder. "But who says I'll try to make the cure. I might just keep all three parts of the recipe hidden for another fifty years. Maybe by that time the violence will have been bred out of people once and for all!"

"No!" Evan gasps. "You wouldn't!"

"She would," says Griffin, pursing his lips. "Aloy can be very . . . stubborn."

"But . . . I need . . . I need that cure! Now!" Evan pants.

I stop in my tracks, turning on my heel to face my brother. "Why do you need it so much? Who knows if it'll even work? It could end up further destroying the environment. Why are you in such a hurry?"

Evan looks down, stumbling over himself. I lean in when I hear him saying something under his breath. He rubs a hand over his forehead, but he won't make eye contact with me. I stare at my brother. Deep blue gullies are etched under his eyes. His hair, dirty brown, looks almost crumbly in this light. He's pale. He clutches his stomach.

I look up to the heavens and put a hand to my mouth. I hadn't realized it before, but my brother has cancer.

NOW THAT I SEE the signs of impending death on Evan's face, I understand why my brother is so determined to find the recipe. He's counting down the days until the environment's radiation claims him like it has with so many others.

"How long have you been sick?" I ask, walking toward him.

"I . . ." He tries to square his shoulders and clear his throat, but nothing comes out. Evan blinks a few times and then sighs. "The machines here at CERN show it started in my thyroid. Who knows where it's advanced to now."

"How long have you known?" Griffin asks.

Evan shakes his head but says, "Maybe a year."

"When the nirogene in East started to be stolen," I say, finally understanding another piece of the mystery. "You weren't satisfied at that point with just Mid's stores. You amped up trials of the recipe, and that's when you needed more supplies to keep experimenting."

Evan nods. "I've tried other cures. I've drunk iodine. I've had injections with alcohol." He pulls up his sleeve to show at least thirty small punctures dotting his flesh. "But nothing's working. You know, I'm not trying to stay alive just for my own sake. I need to find a cure before I die! Leave a mark on the world. Leave my legacy!"

"Why won't you accept my stipulations, then?" I ask. "I'll go get you the diamond. I promise."

"I want to trust you, but you might be exactly like Ama. She didn't want to give Grandfather the poem. She didn't think the world was ready for the cure, just as you said a moment ago." His voice falters. "If I let you out of here without me, I need some assurance you'll return with the diamond and not just hide it away."

"I won't hide it. As long as you follow my three stipulations," I say, swallowing hard.

"What I need is some collateral to ensure you'll come back," he says, half to himself.

I shake my head. "Isn't my word good enough?"

"I wish it were, Aloy." Evan looks at me with heavily-lidded yes. "But in my current state, I can't take any chances. One of your stipulations is to take all your troops back, so I wouldn't have anything here enticing you back."

Griffin breaks in, his eyes steely, changing in the light from a deep amber to an almost-gray. "I'll be your collateral," he says.

"What?" Both Evan and I spin toward him. Griffin doesn't waver or look away. "You will *not* stay here!" I say, my voice rising in pitch. "What if I'm unsuccessful?"

"See!" exclaims my brother. "I *knew* you had reservations. I *knew* you didn't think you could get the necklace!"

"Shut *up*!" I yell at Evan.

Griffin walks closer to me, placing both hands on my shoulders. "If I stay, Evan'll let you and our people leave. And I know you'll return with the diamond. I have faith in you."

I try to whisper my words, but the room is small enough that I know my brother can hear. "What happens if I can't get it? And my brother dies, Griffin? And you're stuck here with those CERN rebels and their what's-it-called weapons?" I wave my hand in the air, trying to describe the ghastly poles my brother's warriors held.

"Dehydrogenators," says Evan from across the room.

"Not *now*, Evan!" I yell, not taking my eyes off Griffin. I plead with him. "How can we be separated now when we just got back together?"

"You'll return with the diamond. I have every confidence," Griffin says, smiling down at me.

"If you want to know *my* thoughts," says Evan again, piping up from the corner, "I think it's a perfect plan. There's no way you'll leave your lover behind, am I right?"

I stare daggers at Evan, and it quiets him. He pantomimes pulling his lips closed like a zipper and walks over to his bed. "But what if I need you in Mid?" I ask Griffin. I place a hand over his on my shoulder and lean my forehead onto his chest.

"You don't. The people there love you. They'll hand the diamond over to you in an instant. And you have Vienne too, if people are in any way reluctant. The two of you can convince anyone of anything."

"I don't know . . ." I start to say.

"Aloy, you have to go. Evan's right. We do need this cure. And we need to be able to make it while Evan's still alive and can use his knowledge. Now's the time. Not fifty years from now. You and I both know that." When I don't say anything he continues, "You want Glory to grow up with the Earth in ruins like it's been for us? Always being afraid of a rain storm? Waiting for the next huge earthquake? If Evan can do anything . . ."

I keep my face against Griffin's chest. I can smell the hint of lemons on his clothes, just like I used to in East. It was common practice to mix lemon juice into the soapy concoctions to launder clothes. The hint of lemon was everywhere in East, but somehow the scent of it always smelled best on Griffin's skin. I breathe in deeply and move my hands around his waist. I pause there, burying myself inside his embrace, feeling the firmness of his chest and the way his arms move to wrap around my back. Everything feels more solid—more viable—when Griffin is close.

"Sheesh!" Evan exclaims from his seated position on the bed. "You ready to get going, or am I going to die here waiting for you to finish your love fest?"

I let go of Griffin's embrace and glance over at my brother. "I'm ready. Get my people out to my airride." Then I squint my eyes as I bore holes into Evan's forehead. "And if your rebels hurt Griffin while I'm away, if he's not here when I return, I swear to heaven I'll crush that diamond and its poem to smithereens." I ball my right hand into a fist, emphasizing my words by pounding it in the air.

"Yeah, yeah," Evan says, half-smiling, making the nervous tick with a hand on his earlobe again.

My troops and I are back inside Mid Country's airride within the next hour. It's been stocked with a few new technical advances from my brother, including a security enhancement that Evan says he'll use "just to keep us protected." I scoff at that, but I didn't really think I'd get out of CERN without some kind of tracking device embedded in our systems.

"You know how to fly this thing straight up?" I ask Cole, who's sitting next to me again in the cockpit.

"They've told me how, so I just have to remember it all."

"You'll do great," I say, trying to sound light-hearted while patting him on the back.

The CERN rebels and my brother were good on their word, healing Albine and feeding my people better than they'd eaten in a few months.

I sit in the egg-shaped seat and look at all the controls on the dashboard. There are a few more buttons there than when we set out. I want to ask Cole if he knows how they all work, but we only have a minute before we're set to leave, and all I can manage to focus on is Griffin's face through the cockpit's window. He stands next to Evan, a barrage of CERN rebels flanking both of them. They still hold their staffs, and I silently pray to the heavens that I'll prove as successful in our campaign as Griffin thinks I'll be.

"Thrusters ready," says Cole into the airrides speaker system. I don't know if he's talking to our people in the back or if he's communicating with Evan's people. Either way, a moment after he says it, I feel the airride begin to vibrate underneath me.

"Three seconds to ascension," says Cole. "Three. Two. One."

I lock eyes with Griffin, and he nods to me, keeping a smile on his face. I lean forward as we lift off the ground, trying to soak in every last moment with him. The airride begins to climb, and soon I can't see the people or the ground underneath us. Everything in the cylindrical cavity is curved brown rock. We're so close to the walls, I hold my breath as we fly straight up. I don't know how Cole manages not to knock one of our far-reaching wings against the side, but he maintains a steady gaze on the dashboard controls, his hand firm on the plane's throttle. It's dark in the cylinder for half a minute and then bright light surrounds us as the door above opens right in time for our exit. A moment later we're in open air.

I let out an elongated breath and lean back in my seat.

"That sure of my abilities, were you?" asks Cole, looking over at me for the first time since liftoff.

"I . . . well . . ." I stammer.

"It's okay," Cole laughs. "I wasn't sure I'd get us out of there safely either. This is only the third time I've flown one of these things, you know." He looks back at the controls, makes a few adjustments and then glances at me from the corner of his eyes. "Can I ask you a question?"

I turn toward Cole, surprised. "Sure, whatever you want."

"Why didn't you get one of your brother's people to fly you back to Mid? Why'd you take me?"

I think about my answer for a couple of beats before responding. "Two reasons. One is that I don't want any of the CERN rebels with us to go back into Mid. They seem, I don't know . . . hungry for bloodshed."

Cole nods, biting his lower lip. "And two?"

I grip the handles of my seat, moving my hands up and down the white edges. "You need to go back to Mid sometime, Cole. The people there, they need to know how valuable you are to them and how much you've done for them."

"I thought you'd say that."

"Oh, yeah?" I stare absently into the icy water that we've just started to transverse.

"From what I know of you so far," he says, "you don't take the easy way out. You don't hide from things."

I shake my head. "Well, then you don't know me very well yet. You know I pretended to be a boy for thirteen years, right?"

"Your parents pretended. First opportunity you had, you let the veil slip. Showed everyone who you really were."

I think about that for a few minutes, the silence between me and Cole a surprisingly easy void. We stay quiet for a while, not talking again until we're a half hour from landing. I tell him where I want to go first and that I want him with me the entire time.

"Like a bodyguard?" Cole asks, his eyes soft.

"More like an apprentice."

Cole turns toward me, a questioning look on his face. "I don't under-stand—" he starts.

"Keep your eyes on the dashboard," I say. "We're close."

46

THE VIEW OF MID from above is different than I expected. Instead of a few optogenetically-cured Mid-rebels milling around, there are thousands of people lining the streets. They're walking along the running sidewalks. They're holding hands. They're up on scaffolds repairing buildings, high in the sky.

It's only been a week or so since we left the country. I thought most of Mid's people would still be holed up in the towers while they were evaluated against their optogenetic-free rehabilitation. But it looks like Vienne's released everyone. Or she was overtaken.

"Put us down fast!" I say to Cole. "On top of that building." I point to a medium structure about ten stories high. Tall enough to keep ill-wishers away, but low enough for us to descend quickly if we need to.

I see Mid's people shield their eyes from the searing sun as they watch us land. Cole does as I command, setting us down without so much as a bump. As soon as our wheels touch, I ask Cole to release the doors, and I'm in the back of the airride with Cole hurrying to close up the cockpit and remain at my side.

"Guns away," I order my troops. "Keep them on your person, but not out." Everyone seems to understand. We don't know what's been happening in Mid, but we don't want to look unnecessarily suspicious. With a grunt, I turn the handle of the main exit door, and bright sunshine instantly hits our retinas. I'm blinded for only a split-second, blinking back a few searing tears as my pupils adjust. The roof below us is a patchy concrete, which crunches as my boots touch down upon it. I walk to the side and stare at the crowd that's gathered below us. I look for the rooftop staircase at the same time as the door flies open.

Vienne runs at me, her arms extended wide. "Aloy!" she exclaims. "You're back! So soon?"

I let my former wife crash into my arms, her kisses covering my cheeks. I let out a breath I'd been holding and take a long look at her. Vienne seems well, her white-blonde hair cascading in waves across her shoulders and down her back. She smells like a mixture of antiseptic and lilacs, a pungent scent that doesn't distract from her appeal in any way. Vienne's translucent skirts, in three different pastels—cornflower blue, yellow, and pink—sweep around her, filling the silver reflective metal of Mid's nearby building surfaces with color.

"Everything okay back in East?" she asks first. Her eyes angle down in concern, focusing on my face with intensity.

I nod, silent as I try to pick up any other emotion apparent on her face. Has she been overrun by Mid's tower prisoners or has she released them?

"I just got Eve back yesterday," Vienne says. "She's with Emma. How is Glory?"

"Good," I say. "I'm looking forward to getting back to him."

She smiles sympathetically. "The people who brought Eve said you took a ship after the nirogene thieves. You couldn't catch them?" She takes my arrival here in Mid as proof that we were unsuccessful. We'll need much more time than this rooftop exchange for me to explain everything I've learned about my family's past.

"We did, actually," I say, and Vienne's eyes grow wide. "I have a lot to tell you. But first, what's going on in Mid? Why are so many people on the streets?"

"Have you seen the progress?" she asks, beaming. Vienne grabs hold of my hand and points down to the street with her other one. "It's like the work ethic is still embedded within Mid's people, but they're functioning together like never before. It actually makes progress faster, if you can believe it!"

"So Aaron, Calix, and their parents were wrong," I say, the awe in my voice a whisper.

"Turns out people work faster when they have a common goal and *also* care about whom they're working with," Vienne muses.

"I take it you let everyone out of the towers?" I ask. My eyebrows are raised, still unsure if it was a good idea for Vienne to release everyone so soon. Who knows what optogenetics withdrawal does to individual brains.

"No one's going to be my prisoner," Vienne says, her tone cool and final. Then she sees Cole and leaves me to wrap her arms around his neck in a hug. "Cole! So glad you came too!" Vienne gives the clone a long squeeze and then steps back, raking the crowd of my troops with her eyes.

I know whom she's looking for, and I peer up at the heavens for strength before responding. When I glance back up, the question is already in Vienne's taut features.

I swallow and breathe in. How can I tell her that I've left Griffin as collateral for the enemy? The words stick in my throat. Worse, how can I tell her that our enemy's been my brother all this time? "I'll explain everything," I say, "but we need to start heading for Mid's cremation repositories. Can you lead me there, and I'll tell you along the way?"

"Griffin's okay, though?" she asks.

"I think so. For now. But it's best we hurry."

Vienne grasps my hand, leading me down the ten flights of stairs to the city center. We're led to the crematorium by a woman from Mid. As we go, I give Vienne a play by play. She remains stoic as I explain Tomlin's death, my mother's necklace, the horrifying dive down into CERN, Evan's crew of former rebels, and my brother's search for the environmental cure. In between sentences, I glance at her face. She's white when I mention Tomlin taking hemlock, but I move through the subject fast, leaving her little time to dwell on it before I elaborate on meeting Evan. Multiple times, Vienne looks like she wants to ask questions, but she bites her lip, letting me get through the bulk of the news before we arrive at the crematorium.

The incineration facilities are located inside a squat structure labeled "building eighteen." Unlike other markers I've seen so far, this one includes a symbol next to the building number. It's a small apostrophe next to a wriggling line with two legs underneath.

"Eighteen meant 'life' in past civilizations," says the woman from Mid as she sees me looking at it. "Or more exactly 'being alive.'" She points at the symbol. "That's the old biblical sign for Chai." She pronounces it like the word *hi*. "It also looks like the mathematical symbol for pi, which is a never-ending number."

I nod, surprised that Mid Country maintained any sentiments for past culture.

"Building seventeen over there," continues the woman, pointing to the long warehouse on our left. "That holds the seeds from every kind of flora and fauna known to man. The seeds all used to be housed in Norway before it got too cold there to sustain the required preservation temperatures. The number seventeen, that's significant since it literally means 'a good omen' in Japanese culture."

I look at the woman, my head cocked. I didn't know anyone in Mid, or on the entire continent for that matter, knew anything about ancient history any more. She smiles at me, pushing a lock of hair behind her ear. "Sorry. I get carried away." As if an afterthought, she adds, "You know, I almost got the historian job you took."

"What?" I pick my head up higher.

"The position that Calix granted you. The historian. I applied for it, but you know, they weren't really looking for my cultural knowledge. They wanted technical and weapon expertise more than they wanted to know about biblical references. I've remembered a lot after having been released from the monthly treatments. I speak eight languages, including Japanese. Isn't that cool?"

I stare at the woman, and she takes my silence as irritation. She shrugs. "Not that it'll come in use anymore, I suppose. But it's been fun remembering all the words, is all." Our guide leans forward, about to open the doors, but I grasp her sleeve.

I think of what my brother said about Asia staying withdrawn under an immense bubble. How the dome ensured Evan's airrides and the external environment couldn't touch them. How they haven't returned Evan's communication or put out any comms signals for the last seventy years since the Accords. What would it be like, I wonder, to reach to Asia in their mother tongue? Would they listen and respond then?

"You never know," I say to the woman. "Every skill can prove valuable."

Her smile widens, and then she parts the doors of the crematorium open for us. The walls here are white and gray, sterile and unfeeling, like so many other of Mid's buildings. A sickly sweet smell seems to drench the building's inside.

Vienne covers her nose and mouth with the back of her hand. "Is it safe in here?" she asks. "Noxious fumes?"

"I'm not sure," says the lady. "The filtration systems . . . well, you can ask the operator yourself. Harbar?" she calls out, walking forward through the first hallway. "You in here?"

"Yin?" a rough voice answers from the back. "Come on through."

Yin beckons us behind her and finds the door through which the man's voice originated. I'm surprised to see a child sitting on the floor right where we enter the room. The boy plays with a crudely whittled train set. He looks up at our group, and upon setting eyes on me, immediately scuffles across the floor to the bigger man.

"Apa! Apa! That's her! The woman who visited us in the hospital! She's the Freedom Fencer!" he exclaims, alternately pointing at my face and grabbing the man's hem.

I bend forward so I can ruffle the boy's unruly red hair. "What was that?"

"Freedom Fencer's what the children call ya," answers the man. He reaches out and grabs my hand within two of his, pumping my arm up and down like a water spigot. "Call me Harbar, ma'am. I'm indebted to ya, I know. This here's my son, Able."

"How do you do?" I ask, extricating myself from Harbar's handshake and bending down to be eye-level with the boy.

"Ty worships you," says Able, matter of factly. "He said we all owe you our freedom. And he said you know how to slash things up with a real-life sword. So we started calling you the Freedom Fencer."

"I hadn't heard that." I grin, thinking of the fictitious superheroes I'd seen in some thin-paged magazines Tomlin once showed me. The name sounds similar to the ones of the muscled men and women throwing punches with star-shaped bubbles reading "Pow" and "Boom" around their heads. Superman. The Flash. Batgirl.

"Was just reunited with my son three days ago, I was," says Harbar. "Got called up 'cause they found my name in some database. I wasn't sure at first. Thought maybe they'd gotten some wires crossed or something. See, I got no recollection of a son being born to me, but I do remember some physical exams where they gathered certain . . ." He pauses, embarrassed, looking away. "Specimens." Harbar coughs a few times, and then turns back to us. "So I went on down to the hospital, and Able was there waitin' for me."

"I look like my dad," Able says, "so he could tell right away I was his."

"That I did," Harbar responds, looking down at his son with teary eyes.

"And the mother?" asks Vienne quietly.

"I don't have one," pipes up the boy, and my eyes widen at his quick response.

Harbar gathers his son close. "What he means is, her name was in the database too, but she'd already passed. I didn't know her, so I can't really feel the loss, but it'd of course been good for Able, here, to meet 'er. Aw, well." Harbar fixes his palms on his legs, rubbing them up and down. "Wait," he says, suddenly on the defense, "You ain't here to take Able away, are ya?"

"No, no," answers Vienne. She lays a reassuring hand on Harbar's shoulder. "Aloy was looking for something of utmost importance. We thought it might be here."

"Oh ya? How can I help?" asks Harbar, stepping toward me once again.

"There was a body brought here a week or so ago. A woman. In a nurse's uniform. Her name was Dolche."

Harbar puts a hand to his chin, trying to remember. "I don't recall exactly. We've had a number of people for me to lay to rest in the last week."

I nod, about to say that I, unfortunately, understand, when he continues, "Well, let's have a look here in this computer. I keep records, ya know, just like the hospital did on my son. If this woman came through my doors, I'm sure to have a picture of her face on my screen."

Harbar leads us to a set of computers along the far wall. He points to a few black boxes on the screen, and a list of faces pop up in succinct order. They're the faces of all the dead Mid countrymen killed in our coup. Each picture captures the deceased individual's face right after death. In some, the eyes are shut, and the person looks at peace. In others, the facial features are twisted as if the agony of their death was too hard to coax out of the facial muscles. When I see Ollinear's image, I nearly gasp. His bald head shines reflectively, giving him an ethereal look, like the light of heaven is a halo around him. His eyes are closed, but he doesn't look peaceful exactly. He looks like he'll wake up at any moment and step off the screen, into the room. I don't know if Ollinear's ghost would rather congratulate me or curse me for the consequences of my actions. Vienne grips my hand, and the pictures keep coming so fast that soon my chief's face has been replaced by others. I will myself to concentrate on finding Dolche's face among the pictures, not solely on the memory of Ollinear's sacrifice.

"Stop," I say when I see the nurse's twisted smile on one snapshot. Her eyes are open wide, a look of accomplishment lingering in the grays of her eyes. I glance down, even now not wanting to look at the woman. "That's her."

"What'd ya want with her?" Harbar asks. "I don't got any remains. We spread the ashes on the harvest fields for nutrient reuse."

For an awful moment I realize that's what Mid Country must have done with my parents' remains, and my stomach clenches. I've eaten Mid's produce. Every food in Mid tasted so enriched. So sweet and tangy. My insides squeeze. Vienne seems to understand why I wince, and she speaks to Harbar for me, allowing me a moment to collect myself.

"We're looking for a large stone that was around Dolche's neck at the time of her death," says Vienne. "We're hoping you noticed it before putting her inside the . . . the . . ."

"Kiln?" finishes Harbar for her.

"Yes. Or that maybe your kiln uses a low enough temperature that the diamond didn't burn along with her body? Perhaps you found it after she was cremated? Within the ashes? It was a rather large thing that would have been hard to miss."

Harbar is already shaking his head no before Vienne finishes her questions. "We use temperatures of four thousand forty-four degrees Celsius. Nothing remains after that, not even stone."

"It was a diamond," I say, trying to clarify further. "A clear rock, with sharp, angled sides."

"Nah, I'm sorry," Harbar says, "I saw nothing like that."

My head droops. This was my big bet. The only idea I had that would stop Evan from taking out his unrelenting obsession on the people of Mid Country. My only option for freeing Griffin without a fight with my brother.

"I wish I could've been more helpful," says Harbar again, sensing my dampened mood.

"I know. Thank you," Vienne answers. She looks down at the boy again, her smile soft and warm. "Looks like you won the lottery on great fathers," she says to Able, winking. "You're a lucky boy." Vienne transfers her eyes onto Harbar, and he beams back at her. "We should leave you now. Thank you for the important work you do."

Harbar fumbles under her praise, stammering his thanks to Vienne in return.

"Apa? Can I go with the Freedom Fencer to visit the other kids in the hospital?" Able asks as we turn to exit.

"Oh," I say, "I'm not sure I'm seeing them right this—"

Able breaks in, his eyes screwing up in his small face. "They're the ones left who didn't have any parents come for them. They're still in the dorm with Ty. He's watching them."

All I want to do is get back to Switzerland to tell Evan the bad news and get Griffin out of the CERN rebels' grasp. I'm ready to put this all behind me and start rebuilding East, like Mid is doing. There is no diamond left. No poem from Mid Country to round out the other two pieces of the formula. At least not anymore. A trip to the hospital where I'd been kept prisoner, not once, but twice, isn't exactly my idea of a good time. But what can I do? The boy stares up at me with pleading eyes.

"After you, Able," I say, trying not to let the disappointment show through my voice.

"Cool! They're gonna to be so excited," he says, oblivious to my distress. "We've made up this new game they'll want to show you! Ty calls it Rollers. And it takes *forever* to play. You've got to do a round with us!"

"I can't wait," I say, my voice dismal. "I truly cannot wait one more minute." I think again of Griffin sitting in my brother's rebel's clutches with a hundred Dehydrogenators surrounding him. "Not one more minute."

T̲HE WALK FROM BUILDING eighteen to the hospital in building fifteen, just three structures away, is daunting. Hundreds of people stop what they're doing to watch me, Vienne, Cole, Able, and Harbar span the distance. I don't like the attention, as I just want to get out of the country as fast as possible. We don't need a gawking crowd to slow us down. Some people clap for us, but I also hear a disturbing echo of hisses and boos trailing after us, yelling out Calix's name, presumably at Cole. The clone looks up into the crowds of people staring at us from the scaffolds. Vienne grasps my sleeve, tugging it hard to get my attention. I turn and see she's pointing at Cole who's stopped in the middle of the city square, in the exact spot where Calix and Aaron held their firing squads.

"Hello there," Cole calls upward toward the masses of angry faces. "You think I'm just another version of Calix?" The faces staring back at him are full of bitterness. "I heard you destroyed all the other Calix clones, even the ones almost fully mature." A few more *boo*'s echo against the high-rise walls. "I may contain his DNA . . . and others," Cole says, glancing at me briefly, "but I'm not him or anyone else. I'm my own person."

A curse emits from a nearby woman. Cole holds up a hand as if he had the influence to silence her. His gesture doesn't stem the riptide of derogatory yells thrown his way, though, so he raises his voice. "You may not understand how the replicating technology works, so if you'll just allow me to tell you—" He ducks his head as a can is tossed toward him.

I catch Harbar's eye, mouthing that we'll meet him at the hospital. If there's about to be a riot, Able shouldn't be out here. The father and son scurry out of the town center, Able looking back over his shoulder, confusion spread across his features.

"I may be cloned from Calix's same DNA, but I'm my own person," says Cole again. "I have my own feelings, my own ideas. And I love Mid Country just as much as you do. I want to rebuild it so our city isn't just a shadow of what it once was. It has potential to be even more . . ." He searches for the next word, stuttering as a man thundering toward us with angry steps calls out the word "tyrannical."

"No!" Cole shouts, ducking his head against the additional pieces of trash pelted toward him.

My fingers press themselves into fists at my sides. I can't take this anymore.

Vienne raises an eyebrow and lets go of my sleeve, indicating that I can feel free to take the floor if I want to. She won't stop me.

I turn on the people in the square, looking left and right as well as up into the construction crews. "You're taking out your anger on the *wrong* person!" I yell. "Cole is not Calix! Calix is dead! He died in my arms in East Country. And while you may all hate both of your former Electeds who kept you under optogenetics, I don't believe you're not culpable to some degree, too." A mixture of surprised responses erupts from the crowd. I ignore them, shaking my head. "You broke the Accords long before you were even under the spell of optogenetics! How do you think Aaron was even able to create the treatment? Because you helped him build the technology to do so! Even before your resources began to be stolen. So take some responsibility and don't manifest your guilt . . . or whatever this is . . . on Cole!"

When there's quiet, I shout again, "Out of everyone here, he's the *most* innocent. I've never met anyone as true to his word as Cole. You should *be* so lucky to have him helping you in Mid Country!"

I catch my breath, my heart racing. I look over at Cole and see that he's gaping, a hand hovering over his open mouth. My head spins to determine Vienne's reaction.

"Not exactly what I would have said," she murmurs. "But I think it got the point across."

I *humph*, turning my back on Mid's crowd. If I'd come here hoping to garner the diamond through Mid's benevolence toward me, I've destroyed that goodwill now. But I don't care. The diamond's gone anyway. And I'm *done* letting people's biases determine our fates.

Biases like Evan's notion that I wasn't East's actual Elected because I was female and Mid's notion that Cole is bad just because of how he looks: they're all so ludicrous.

"We don't have time for this," I say, shaking my head. "Let's go."

Cole starts forward, his eyes on the ground. But after just two steps, he's confronted by the man from Mid who was thundering toward us just a moment earlier. The man in steel-toe boots lumbers over to Cole, blocking his path. The steel-toes butt up against the front of Cole's sandals, the opposite nature of the two men apparent not just in the stature of their bodies but also in the style of their shoes.

Vienne steps toward the pair, about to diffuse the situation, when the man pushes an object at Cole. "Here," he says. "I'm not going to refuse anyone's help." He thrusts a hammer into Cole's hand.

Cole's reluctant at first, but then he looks up at the man towering above him with a bursting smile. "Is . . . is . . . this an apology? I've never had anyone say they're sorry to me before."

I throw my head back, mumbling under my breath, "Cole, don't push your luck."

The man in front of Cole doesn't smile back, but he doesn't take offense either. He stands there silently as if contemplating his next move. Then he steps to the side so Cole can resume walking.

"I suppose I'll take that," Cole says. He looks up at the people who are still staring at us from above. "I have to fly Aloy back, but after that, if you're okay with it, I'd love to return and help you restore Mid." He waits for a further response, wincing slightly as if he's an abused pet who hopes to deflect another hit from its master. However, no one from above shouts anything further and no objects fly toward Cole.

"You keep that," says that man in the sturdy boots, pointing at the hammer.

Cole nods fervently, smiling so wide that I can see the molars in the back of his mouth.

When we're out of the town center, continuing on our way toward the hospital, Vienne whispers, "Well, that was interesting."

"Do you really feel that way about me, Aloy?" asks Cole, stopping again. He holds the hammer against his chest like it's something of immense value, but when he asks the question he reaches toward me, grazing my shoulder with his fingers.

I let his touch linger without baulking. "I do. But can we just get to the hospital already and back in our airride? No more delays, please. I'm not looking forward to telling Evan the last eighteen years of his life have been wasted. Putting it off isn't going to do any good."

"You want me to tell him for you?" asks Cole.

I purse my lips, trying to keep my more dangerous thoughts to myself. They blurt out anyway. "No, thanks. I'm afraid Evan might be distraught enough to kill the messenger, especially if that person isn't blood-related."

Vienne gasps. I can tell she wants to say something, maybe talk me out of going, but I shake my head. "Don't say it. You know I'm still going back to free Griffin, no matter what. Let's just get this visit with the kids over with, okay?"

"Take an army with you at least," Vienne says, ignoring my request to let the subject rest. "All of Mid's airrides. Don't face Evan alone like you did Aaron."

"You think Mid's people want to leave with me for Europe to involve themselves in yet another fight?" Vienne nods, but I continue, "You don't understand how many resources Evan has. It's like the whole world's technology converged at CERN. If Evan saw Mid's planes advancing on his lair all at once, he'd shoot them out of the sky."

"It's not a matter of Mid's people not standing behind you," Vienne says. "They're indebted to you."

"I think I just used up that goodwill back at the city square."

"You mistake their silence for dislike. I think they were just taken aback. They'd be more than happy to help you stand against a mutual enemy. They don't know yet who was behind the attacks, but once they do, I'm sure—"

"I don't want them to know!" I exclaim, keeping my eyes set on the ground. I take a deep breath and begin again. "I'm sorry. I . . . I . . ."

"I know. Evan's your brother," Vienne says. "And you don't want to start a war against him."

"It's not that I'm sentimental about him being my brother," I say, scrunching my eyes closed, trying to discern if I've just uttered a lie.

Do I want to keep Evan's secret because he's family? Will I stave off Mid's vengeance on him because of who he is? I almost wrung his neck myself back at CERN, but the idea of anyone finishing the job, having to watch another one of my family members die . . . I'm not sure I could actually be the cause of that.

At last I say, "I'd sacrifice Evan if that's what was required to stop his violent tactics. Even though he's my brother. But I think I can convince Evan not to bother Mid or East anymore. I just don't want anyone else to have to tell him about my failure."

Cole and Vienne stare at me, and I think I read pity in their eyes. I don't want sympathy, though, so I keep my head turned away until we reach the hospital. I try to wipe the image of my brother's anger out of my mind, but it keeps popping up anyway. What will he do when he finds out his quest is over? Will he use the Dehydrogenator on me? Will he kill Griffin just to show me how disappointed he is? And am I wrong about being able to convince him that the diamond is lost? Will he shred Mid to pieces still looking for it?

When we reach the hospital, I lean back to look at its exterior. The building's glass and metal walls are exactly as I remember them, and I wonder if the inside will smell the way I remember it as well. Disinfectant and the stench of death. But as Cole opens the double doors, the tang of iron-rich blood and shredded flesh don't hit me. It's only a faint chemical scent that wafts out, so I step across the threshold, vowing not to stay here long.

"It's this way," says Vienne, pointing down the hall to the left.

"I remember," I say, and the three of us plod through the hospital hallways. I can almost hear the ghosts of months past. The voice of Aaron dragging me to the yellow room. The screams of people as they were deposited here after my brother's bombing. Dolche's cruel laugh as she told me and Griffin we wouldn't be able to take Glory. My shoulders drop a little, and I keep my head down as we move further through the corridor.

I give Vienne the signal to proceed when we're in front of the children's dormitory, and she cracks open the door, addressing the people inside. "Kids," she says, "wait until you see who Able and his father brought you!" She swings the door open wide. The room is dimly lit with metal cots in rows. All of the beds are made and empty save a few that lay strewn open, the sheets haphazardly tossed into piles at the foot of the cots. The pillows are still indented where heads must have lain just hours earlier.

"You came!" Able exclaims, running to me, flinging his arms around my waist. "You guys, it's the Freedom Fencer!" Six children who were sitting on the floor jump up, their eyes little saucers. Able runs back to his father once again, as if he wants to remain only a short tether's distance away from Harbar at all times. As if he's afraid Harbar might vanish as fast as he appeared in Able's life.

Ty walks from across the room, both of his hands slid inside the pockets of his robe. He looks more mature than his fourteen years. "Hope you don't mind. But you do fence, right?"

My etched smile widens into something more sincere. "You know I do." I give him a barrel hug and then lean back, staring at the teenager's face. "You seem older."

He shrugs, a smirk fluttering across his lips. "How's Gretchen?"

At this, I laugh and give him a second, looser hug around the shoulders. "You want me to tell her you're asking?" When his cheeks go pink, I continue, "She's fine. Reunited with her mom and sister in East."

Ty nods, his raven hair brushing against my cheek with the movement. He ruffles the hair of a boy near him. "You remember Jasp, right?"

I didn't know the boy's name, but I remember his face. "Sure I do," I say, holding out my hand to touch the orphan's cheek. He's only three, a look of innocence still vivid in his features. The black curls of his hair run unfettered over his forehead and stick out at oblong angles around his ears. I have an urge to push the unruly hair behind his face, to take care of him. But I don't have the luxury of such time.

"Feedom Fence," Jasp says, dropping all of his *r*'s, "will you play 'Ollers with us?"

"That's the game I told you about!" says Able, leaving his father's side.

"I don't know," I say. "I have to get back to . . . to East Country." The lie comes out jagged and awkward, as if even my own conscious knows I should tell the people in Mid Country where I've really been.

"The kids 'ere'd love to say they played a game of Rollers with ya'," says Harbar, his smile pleading.

"Come on," whines Able. "Just one round. You promised!"

I don't remember promising any such thing, but the looks on the children's upturned faces are so expectant, I find myself uttering, "Sure, I guess just one round."

Jasp puts his tiny hand inside mine and pulls with as much strength as he can muster before I step forward on my own accord. He leads me over to a space the kids have carved in the center of the room by moving some of the unused beds out of the way. On the ground is a chalked circle with at least a dozen smooth glass balls tossed haphazardly inside its circumference.

Vienne arranges herself on the edge of an adjacent bed, smoothing the multi-layers of her skirt. I sit on the floor around the circle, cross-legged between a boy and girl.

The oldest girl of the group reaches behind herself, under a nearby bed. She pulls out a plastic bowl of additional beads, passing the set from one person to the next, offering them a choice of particular colors. Jasp takes a clear bead with a swirl of green inside its center. Able chooses purple, the color of a full moon. When the bowl is delivered to me, I already know what shade of bead I want: yellow like the lemon trees that dotted East's countryside before Mid's attacks.

But as my hand slides down into the bowl to pinch one of the beads between my fingers, I realize there's something much more enticing resting in the dish. Majestically reflecting the various other colors like a prism, right in the middle of the other beads, sits a diamond.

I PICK UP THE jewel, letting its angled sides imprint tiny points into my palm as I squeeze it. Inside the diamond are four lines of curved script, too small to read under this light.

My voice is a whisper. "Where'd you get this?"

At first the room is quiet. I look up to see Cole's surprised expression and Vienne with a hand to her mouth. The children sit like statues, our apparent shock keeping them mute. It's a few moments before one timid voice says, "It's ou' shoote'." Jasp points at the diamond, and then goes back to rolling a green bead around his hand.

"We tried to whittle it down so that it was smooth like the other glass pieces," pipes up a girl of about eight years old. "But it wouldn't file down like the others. So we used it as the central piece."

"Central piece?" She has no idea how much the gem serves as a central piece. "Yes," I say, turning the diamond over and over, "but where did you find it?"

None of the kids respond. I look from child to child and see that one girl has scurried closer to Ty's legs, almost as if trying to hide behind him. I glance at Ty who nods in return.

"Kira," he says, bending so that his knees rest on the floor, "do you know anything about the shooter piece?"

"I didn't mean to steal it," she squeaks. "I thought it'd be good for our game. That nurse wasn't going to need it anymore 'cause she was . . ." The girl sniffles and then breaks down into full sobs, burrowing into Ty's arms.

Ty holds her and looks up at me and Vienne, his face pained. "Does the gem mean something to you?" he asks.

"Yes," says Vienne. "It's something that each Elected family is supposed to pass down to future generations. People have been looking for that diamond . . . for a long time." Her voice catches on the last part.

Ty's eyes are wide as he continues to soothe the child.

"You're not in trouble for taking it," I say to Kira, touching her back with my palm.

The girl lifts her face from Ty's shirt, rubbing a tearful eye with her fist. "When all the bodies were lined up in the hospital, I was the one who was supposed to cover them with a sheet. The diamond was on this necklace." She pulls a chain out of her shirt, showing me the thin strand.

I imagine the child, having to peer upon the faces of all the dead, mangled and bloodied, after the battle for Mid's freedom. It isn't fair that she was involved. I say as much, and when she doesn't respond, I kneel next to her with the diamond cupped in my hand. "Finders keepers, Kira, but may I borrow this piece from you?"

She looks up at me with the greenest irises I've ever seen. Her eyes point downward at the corners in doubt. "I was just borrowing it too. For a little while," she says. "I was going to put it back, really."

Able looks down at her. "You couldn't have. They took her to the—"

"Material things aren't meant to stay with the dead," interrupts Cole fast, stopping Able's words from scaring the other children. "They're loaners while we're on Earth and then they pass to the next person. This stone," he says, pointing to the diamond, "it's not the nurse's anymore, no matter where she is." Cole shifts toward Kira, and when she scoots farther away from Calix's visage, Cole stops. "I just wanted to thank you," he says. "You don't even realize what you've done for Aloy." Cole lifts his head toward me. "For the Freedom Fencer."

"Does this mean the Freedom Fencer isn't going to play a game with us after all?" Able asks his father.

I turn my gaze toward the boy, thinking how just a few minutes ago I was so unwilling to spend a few extra minutes with the orphan children. How I just wanted to get back to my brother with the bad news. How all I could focus on was the failure.

I smile at Able, loosening my grip on the diamond, setting it on the ground in front of me.

"How do you play this game anyway?" I ask, crossing my legs as I reposition myself on the ground next to the children's chalked circle.

There's a *whoop* from all the children, which echoes off the concrete, filling the room with more cheer than I think have ever been felt within these particular walls. Harbar picks up the dish of beads and lets it finish its rounds, each player choosing a different color. My one yellow glass bead rolls up and down the creases of my palm as I push it with the opposite thumb.

I watch my former wife from across the circle as she picks a red bead. She lets it drop into her lap, and then she fixes the hem of her gauzy skirt where it touches the floor, her hair falling forward, a waterfall of blonde waves. I wonder how I lost her so fast. Or if she was never really mine to begin with. I wonder if she'll ever come back to East. She looks up and catches me watching her. We share a smile, and I think I can read hope in her features. Vienne doesn't look worried anymore. Happiness is more prominent in her face now than anxiety. Even the white scars dotting her cheeks seem to vanish in this dim light. I remember what it was like to meet Vienne for the first time. Before any betrayals. Before we both made sacrifices for our country and for the people we realized we loved more than one another.

Ty clears his throat. "Ready for the rules?" he asks.

"This is the shooter?" asks Cole, pointing to the diamond on the floor next to my legs. "How 'bout we use a different stone for the shooter, yes?" Everyone laughs. Cole reaches into the dish of colored beads, ready to choose a different, less special, stone for the central piece.

"Nah," I say, holding Cole's forearm. I pick up the diamond and place it in the middle of the circle. "I think we should use it. It's about time this jewel helped people win at something."

Halfway through the round, when my head should be bent over my yellow beads, my gaze instead turns toward Cole. Sometime in the last few minutes, Kira has curled herself into the space within Cole's lap and is holding his free hand. Their fingers link, and I think to myself that Cole would make a fine father. None of us will be alone for long now. I'll be heading back for Griffin soon. And then we'll return to East to join Glory. After that, I don't plan to let the two of them out of my sight ever again.

49

I DON'T KNOW IF it's the vibrations from the airride or my own shaking legs, but as Cole and I get closer to Switzerland, I begin to hear the pulse of my heartbeat in my eardrums. I ache to see Griffin and to get back to Glory, my blood boiling with my need to return us to safety once and for all.

When our airride is above the coordinates Evan gave Cole, we start our descent. The wide maw of CERN's cavern opens like a monster yawning. Long chunks of ice shift and fall when the gate pulls open. This time we don't bump and crash into the cavern walls as we fly down through the long chamber. We float like we're nestled in pillows, our thrusters turned off, as CERN's external forces take over the airride's controls. Cole and I are alone in our airride, since I'd been able to convince my seventeen troops to stay back in East. Dropping them off along the way here was the right choice, I tell myself, staring at the never-ending warriors lined up below us.

Cole clenches the airride's throttle, even though it's dead in his hands, no longer under his control.

"He'll be happy with the diamond," I say, trying to break the tension, even though the small cockpit suddenly feels too constrictive. "And then we'll go home."

Cole doesn't say anything, continuing to stare straight ahead of us through the glass windshield.

When our wheels finally land onto the ground below with a light thump, my brother peers into the airride's cockpit as if he could discern my failure or achievement just by seeing my face.

The door to the back of our airride whooshes open, the forced air sending gusts of wind through my hair.

"Did you get it?" my brother asks, boarding the plane in three fast strides.

"Where's Griffin?" I ask in return.

"Where's the diamond?"

"We can play this game forever," I say, "but someone will have to concede their hand first." I step into the belly of the plane toward my brother. "Just tell me, did you make sure your people didn't touch Griffin?"

Evan sighs and then juts his head in the direction of his troops standing just on the outside of our airride's door. "Bring him out!" he calls.

The crowd of Evan's warriors parts, and I see a body being pushed through. When at last Griffin emerges from the pack, his arms bound behind him, I gasp and run forward. The CERN warriors push Griffin toward me so that he almost falls forward into my arms. His body is heavy against mine, and his head lolls. But he's still warm. Still alive.

"What's wrong with him?" I yell at my brother.

"Aloy . . ." Griffin moans, and I turn back to him, holding Griffin's head between my two hands.

"What did your people do to him?"

"Just an extra insurance policy, is all. Give me the diamond, and I'll ensure Griffin's no longer dehydrated."

"Dehydrated? But you promised!" My voice is shrill. Cole is at our side, helping me prop up Griffin. My hands are at the nape of his neck. Griffin's hair is covered in a cold sweat, and the locks form into the shape of crescent moons, draped thick over his forehead. He moans softly, the breath ragged.

"Get him water now!" I yell at my brother.

"I will, I will, but did you get the diamond?"

I reach into my pocket and grasp the jewel within my palm so hard the points break the skin. When I pull it out, a few drops of blood run down my wrist. "Take it!" I practically throw the diamond at Evan's face.

He gives a yelp of surprise and flashes a hand into the air to retrieve the jewel before it collides with his cheek. "I didn't actually think—" he starts to say, turning the diamond over in his hand, a look of utter wonderment filling his eyes.

"You should . . . have had more faith . . . in your . . . sister," Griffin gasps, each word seeming to take enormous effort.

"Get him some water!" I yell again, frantic as I look from my brother to his silent rebel warriors. No one answers. I leave Griffin leaning on Cole and run to face Evan. My brother stoops over the diamond, a flashlight out and aimed at the jewel's poem.

"Hey!" I punch Evan on the shoulder to get his attention, and the closest warriors start forward, their weapons raised.

"No, it's all right," says Evan, waving them off but not looking up from the jewel. "Aloy, you must have looked at the poem in the ride back here. What do you think it means?"

Of course I'd looked at the inscription that was suspended inside the jewel, its spider-webbed loops now tattooed in the recesses of my brain.

"Are you kidding me? You're going to leave Griffin like this while you look at the poem? Give him some water, or I swear I will—"

Evan finally looks up, his eyes slits. "You'll do what?" He raises both eyebrows and throws a glance back at his army.

"You promised!" I yell back.

Evan raises a finger. "I swore I'd keep Griffin from getting *killed* by my army. But I never said I wouldn't hurt him myself to ensure your further cooperation."

"You already got everything I can offer!" I splutter, incredulous. "You got the diamond! I cooperated!"

"Yes, but you see, now that I've realized how good you are at eliciting cooperation from Mid and East's people, as evidenced by your retrieval of the diamond, I need to ensure you'll stay for as long as I need you."

"Evan, you can't really mean—" My voice breaks off, as I realize he surely does mean what he says. He'll keep giving and taking away water from Griffin, keeping me here infinitely if he thinks I might be of any additional help in his obsessive quest. "I . . . I . . . we have to get back to our baby, our people!" Even I can hear the desperation coating every word.

"And you will. But first I want you here as I complete the final puzzle. Shouldn't what's left of our family be together as the formula is deciphered? As our legacy—my legacy—is revealed?"

My hands are on my forehead, so angry at my brother and also at myself for not seeing this coming. How could I have been so foolish not to come back here with reinforcements? Some kind of counter-assurance? Even a way to get back in touch with Vienne and tell her I need help? I slam my fist against one of the rock walls. "And if you never decipher it?"

"Then I suppose you and I will live out our days together, trying over and over to find a path back to our ancestor's cure." He shrugs and leans back down over the diamond.

I run back to Griffin as I see him struggling against Cole's side. He trying to say something, but he's so parched, nothing comes out. "You're killing him!" I yell at Evan. "At least give him some water."

Evan snaps his fingers and a warrior walks toward Griffin with a cup of water. I snatch it from the warrior's outstretched hand and immediately put it to Griffin's mouth.

"He can have water," says Evan, "but what he'll really need is an IV of fluids to restore his hydration. And there's a time limit, Aloy. His liver and kidneys will start to cease functioning in three days. Then lungs and heart. Finally his brain. You get the picture."

I leave Griffin again and pound both hands against Evan's chest, pushing him toward wall. I don't even care when three warriors move behind me, ready to attack at Evan's slightest gesture. "Are you really this evil?" I yell in his face.

His reply is quiet. "No, not evil at all. Just desperate for a fix. As desperate as you should be if you really thought about it." He pushes me back, the diamond clenched in his fist. Evan's voice grows higher, and I realize it's not just me he's addressing. His people stand ready, their ears bent toward him, waiting for their leader to utter something inspiring. "It's high time someone hastened to fix the Earth our forefathers broke!" There's a roar from all around us. My brother lets the cavern quiet before speaking again, a wide smile spreading across his face. "We've waited so long for a way to escape this underground fortress. For a way to walk the Earth again without fear of radiation and acid rain. This is our chance for redemption! A chance to leave a legacy on this planet! What we've been waiting for ever since you stormed CERN and demanded that the past leaders rescind the ridiculous Accords!" The rebels cheer, the cacophony of noise ringing my ears. "Take them to the labs!"

I feel myself picked up from behind and held suspended off the ground by two heavily armed warriors. Griffin and Cole are likewise led behind my brother down the dark corridor into the depths of Evan's lair. We're deposited in a corner of an open room filled with a litany of machines I can't even put names to. A flurry of activity begins around us as spinning centrifuges and vats of melted nirogene are plucked off shelves and laid on a long table in the center. Evan writes the diamond's poem on a wide, rolling board, the blue marker he uses making the words appear thick and puffy, almost running together.

Cole, Griffin, and I sit in plastic chairs in a row, our hands bound behind us in thick rope. Griffin leans against me, the weight of him on my shoulder both comforting and disturbing at the same time. I find his fingers, their coldness filling me with dread.

"We need another cup of water over here!" I call out. At first I think my request will be ignored when the closest of Evan's warriors rolls his eyes at me, but a few minutes later a small water glass is laid in each of our laps and our wrists unbound. I hold my cup steady and make Griffin drink not only his water but mine too. Cole does the same, and after three glasses, Griffin's face appears less gray.

"So when do we start figuring this thing out?" I call toward my brother, the heat of anger radiating from my red cheeks.

"That's the spirit," he says from across the room. He rolls the board over to us, and the rhyme I'd memorized hours earlier, the final piece of the puzzle, is now in front of our eyes.

> *The ozone's gone; it's all a shame.*
> *Misused technology is what to blame.*
> *When people learn to use it well,*
> *Then raise these words to mend the hell.*

"What mineral do you think it's referring to?" asks Evan, staring at me. My brother rocks from the tip of his toes back to his heels, over and over again. He licks the top of his lip obsessively.

"I have no idea," I say. "Maybe the poem's just an admonishment. Some final finger-pointing from our ancestors."

"No!" My brother's anger manifests in the form of spittle toward my face. He takes a deep breath, trying to compose himself. When he speaks again, his voice is rigid. "No. The other two poems indicated some kind of ingredient to go along with its corresponding metal."

From memory, Evan writes the other two stanzas on the board so that now the whole poem is in front of us.

> *Lock your strength far away;*
> *Save it for a rainy day.*
> *When the sun no longer shines,*
> *That's when you'll need this little rhyme.*

Evan points to the second poem from West. "See, nirogene and silver. We melted the nirogene inside silver, which ensured it didn't transform chemically." He points at the first poem, the one from East Country. "This one is acid rain water in gold. We took the melted nirogene harvest and mixed it with the acid rain. The concoction rid our drinking water of its excess phosphorous and other pollutants." Evan moves to a spot on the wall that's not covered by metal. It's still a rock bed with water shimmying down its side. He allows some of the liquid to drip into a cup he holds and then shows us the specimen. "Full of cancer-inducing chemicals. See?" Evan dips a gauge into the cup, and the machine immediately flashes a red warning. Next, my brother pours some of the nirogene concoction into the water and stirs it for a minute. "Now see." He dips the gauge in again. None of its indicators light up. Evan offers Griffin the water, but when none of us jump to drink it, Evan pours the cupful into his own mouth. "Delicious," he says. "My formula works, but the water isn't the only thing polluted." Evan points to the poem in the middle of the board. "This one from Mid, it means to use diamond and something else. The *something* is what will clean the air."

Evan writes a few calculations on the board, drawing characters I've never seen before. They're all squiggly lines and numbers in rows. I'm concentrating so hard on Evan's additions and subtractions that I don't see Griffin's hand reach out and grasp Evan's sleeve until I hear my brother's exclamation.

"Get your hands off me." he says, flicking Griffin away and stepping back two paces.

"Get . . . the formula . . . up high," Griffin says with effort.

"What?" Evan bends to peer into Griffin's eyes.

"Use . . . technology. That's . . . what the poem . . . means," Griffin pants.

I stare at the words on the white board, repeating them in my head. *When people learn to use it well.* I close my eyes, letting my thoughts congeal into something solid. The former government wrote the Eco Accords, outlawing technology use, but they didn't want us to abandon technology forever. They wanted people to find middle ground. To use it sparingly, not with weapons to kill each other or with giant drills to frack the Earth's core looking for resources that the heavens never intended to be ours.

"They could have cured the environment years ago," I say, my voice low and full of amazement.

"Who's they?" asks Cole, his hand coming to rest on my shoulder as if I'm starting to lose a few brain cells and I need to be treated with caution.

"Our forefathers." I exhale. "Tomlin said as much. They didn't want us to find all three pieces of the puzzle until we had learned our lesson about technology. We were only supposed to piece the three parts of the formula together when the three areas of the former America united again peacefully. We had to somehow get to the point of communicating with each other to get all three pieces together, which would have meant breaking the Accords to stop the isolation." My words erupt in somersaults, each one running into the next. "Which would probably mean our forefathers would've assumed that we'd broken other parts of the Accords too. Like technology use."

"What are you talking about, Aloy?" my brother asks, a hint of exasperation on his tongue. But he doesn't walk away, and the way he stares at us, he knows Griffin was onto something and that I've put a few more pieces together.

"*Raise these words!*" I exclaim, pointing at the last line of the second stanza. "Get the formula up into the atmosphere!"

Evan looks back and forth at the three of us for a moment, the air heavy with anticipation. Then he stares at the ceiling and a lengthy guttural laugh bellows out from his chest. "I'll try anything. Get an airride powered up!" Evan commands the rebels dotting the room. A group of his people dash out, their excitement obvious in their abandonment of weapons. This is the first time I've seen Evan's rebels go anywhere without their long staffs.

Evan places Mid Country's diamond on the center of the table. "I need something that will cut this!" he yells at no one in particular. A few minutes later he's presented with a circular blade, its teeth tinged a gray, shiny color. The blade is affixed to a metal arm. Evan nods at the person who brought it to him, indicating that the cutting can commence. The scientist fixes goggles on his face and leans over the diamond, letting the machine start up with a jarring buzz. When the diamond has been cut, Evan picks up what's left of the jewel. It's been sawed in half with space in the center so that each side looks like a miniature bowl.

"The airride is ready for departure," says a rebel from the door, and Evan practically jumps.

"Fantastic! Load up our guests. We're going to the surface!"

Cole, Griffin, and I are prodded out of our seats. This time as we're pushed down the long, dark corridor, Griffin manages to walk on his own. His gait is limp, his eyes concentrating on each step as he moves forward, but at least he's moving.

"Hang in there," I whisper to him. "If this works, Evan will start the IV for you right away. I'll make sure of it."

Griffin gives me a slight smile, but there's no light twinkling in his eyes. He doesn't say anything, his head rolling forward again, hanging between his shoulders. But even as his head bends, I see it shake back and forth with the tiniest of movements.

It was Griffin's idea that got my brother moving. His idea to focus on use of technology. But the truth is, Griffin doesn't think my brother's formula will work.

50

Cole, Griffin, and I are guided onto a waiting airride. Evan paces around the cockpit and then back into the belly of the plane where we've been placed against three white airbags. I don't even question when Evan thrusts three parkas toward us.

"We'll watch from the ground, so bundle yourselves into these," he says.

I help Griffin into his bulky jacket, adjusting the sleeves around his arms. When my head is close to Griffin's face, he whispers in my ear. "When we reach the . . . surface . . . run. Get . . . away from here." With difficulty, Griffin reaches underneath his robes and pushes a small radio up the sleeve of my parka. "Comms device . . . set on Mid's frequency. Mid's got to . . . still . . . have someone . . . in their comms . . . rooms." His shoulders shudder with the effort to have spoken so many words at once.

Every muscle in my body is taut. Even in his weakened state Griffin was able to steal a comms radio? I feel like pressing its buttons now. Yelling for help. Getting Mid's airrides over here. My brother is crazy, and maybe it's high time they all knew.

But Griffin seems to read my mind. "When . . . the . . . experiment . . . doesn't . . . work. When Evan's distracted. Use . . . it . . . once you're far . . . away."

"Wait, but, what will you . . ." My question falls off, realizing Griffin expects me to leave him behind. To run, even if he has no chance of following. "No, I can't just—"

"You think . . . your brother . . . will ever let you go . . . if the formula...doesn't work?" Griffin takes deep, labored breaths in between every few words. "Someone's got to get . . . back to . . . Glory."

The airride jostles underneath us, and the entrance to CERN opens, light flooding through the windows so fast that we're blinded, forced to squeeze our eyes shut tight. The white snow outside reflects the sun, creating a stark backdrop.

"Out!" shouts my brother when we've landed in a snow bank. We're escorted out the back of the airride into the icy terrain. My boots create neat patterns on the ground. Even if I wanted to, there's no way I'll be able to run away from here without leaving a trail marking my exact whereabouts.

Once we're out, the back doors close again, and the airride ascends, hovering overhead. We watch, silent, as it becomes a dot in the sky above us. I hold Griffin's hand through thick mittens. Cole's breath on the other side of me escapes from his mouth in billowing gusts. The sky is a dark swatch above us, and all I can see are gray clouds and brilliant sun as I try to squint up to follow the airride. It disappears within a cloud, and I suck in a gasp as a moment later it barrels out of the sky far to the right.

"It's dropped the formula inside a storm cloud," says Evan, first listening to his ear piece and then reporting to us. "For maximum distribution."

The airride drops a few kilometers and then hovers, following Evan's instructions to wait for a sign that the formula is working before heading back to ground.

We wait, heads aimed at the cloud for ten minutes, and I try to ignore the few times Griffin tries to catch my eye. I know he's trying to tell me to leave now while Evan's so focused on the sky. But I can't. I won't leave Griffin and Cole. He shouldn't have even asked me. I think of all the times Griffin devised some outrageous plan to keep me safe, not telling me about it until the very last second. Each time I've gone along, letting Griffin's schemes play out for my benefit. In Mid as he and Margareath broke me out of the hospital prison, they risked their lives to save mine. And when Griffin pretended to drink the hemlock in East, he'd told Vienne his plans but not me, hoping my authentic tears would convince the guards of his death.

Well, not this time. I'm not following Griffin's latest plan if it involves leaving him behind. I finally let him catch my eyes. I stare back, and while everyone else is looking at the rain cloud growing darker by the second, I focus only on Griffin's amber eyes. They still look like the color of molasses. A rush of warmth fills my chest. I'd give anything to go back to the time when my worst problem was figuring out how to sneak out of the White House, affording myself another glance at the veterinarian's apprentice.

Griffin mouths the word *go*. I smile at him, and for a second I think he expects me to pick up and start running away now. But I stay still, and when I shake my head no, Griffin's eyes close and his head rears back as if struck.

"Snow!" yells Cole before I can regain Griffin's eye contact. My eyes fly to where Evan points. The smallest of flakes float down from above, their white bodies blurring with the bleached background of the horizon.

Evan scrambles to take off his mitten, fumbling with the side snaps until he manages to rip it off, the bulky fabric landing at his feet soundlessly. He reaches out, palm up, face held high. Evan opens his mouth, waiting for the snow to hit him, a large smile on his expectant face.

And when the flakes do hit, I know Griffin was right. The experiment didn't work.

The snow lands on Evan's open skin, burning the back of his fingers with tiny red pinpricks. My brother screams as the acidic rain finds his tongue and keeps coming just as it's always done before. Full of chemicals and all the world's pollutants. And holding no sign of Evan's cure whatsoever.

I DON'T THINK I'VE ever seen such rage, such disappointment. Evan is the embodiment of the phrase "hopping mad." He falls to his knees after a long bout of pounding his feet into the snow, turning to us with eyelids so widespread I wonder if eyeballs can dislodge from their sockets.

My brother points at the sky, shaking his fist alternatively upward and then back at the three of us. "It . . . it . . ." he gasps, looking at me like he expects answers.

"Let's go back in the airride," I say quietly, never taking my eyes off Evan. His face is flushed but white in spots.

"It . . . it . . . didn't . . ." My brother attempts more words, but he's too furious to say what he wants. He continues to stomp, his boots sinking with the impact.

"It didn't work," finishes Cole. My brother's crazy gaze flies to the clone. Evan grunts, stepping forward, like he might bury Cole in the burning snow right here for having the audacity to speak about the cure's failure.

I reach a hand between the two. "Let's just go back inside, all right?" I almost feel bad for my brother, in a way. All his work. Everything he's done for "the greater good." How he sacrificed his soul, killing and stealing for the recipe's pieces. It was all for this moment, and the formula didn't work. All I want to do is get out of the snow, maybe try some other formula, and keep convincing Evan to hydrate Griffin.

"Give me a Dehyrogenator," hisses Evan toward the nearest warrior, ignoring my proposal of the warmer airride.

"Why?" I ask, my heartbeat quickening.

Evan is passed a long staff, and he turns the middle so the weapon buzzes to life.

"No!" I say, my voice rising, realizing Evan means to take out his frustration on one of us.

"Hold the clone," Evan says to two of his warriors, waving his arms around like a madman even while he carries the electrified weapon.

"No!" I yell the word this time. "Evan, you don't want to do this!"

My brother ignores me, taking a step closer to Cole who now has his chin as close to his neck as possible, trying to shrink in on himself.

"You say you want to leave a legacy, right?" I yell. "Well, Glory is that legacy. If you can't cure the environment, then all you have is your offspring to leave behind. And Glory is the closest thing you have."

Evan turns toward me, his body still pointed at Cole, his head flipped in my direction. "What does Glory have to do with this mass of lab-grown skin and bones right here?" He growls the words, pointing a skinny finger at Cole. "What use does Glory have for this thing? I don't want you flying out of here, and without Cole as your pilot, you *never* will!"

I shudder at Evan's resolve to keep us prisoner. "Cole has a use!" I shout as the staff's tip comes within an inch of Cole's stomach. Evan stops moving forward, and the clone groans. "Cole's made from my DNA," I continue. "So if I ever got sick. Or Glory got sick, it would be Cole's body parts we could use!"

Evan stops mid-stride. "*Your* DNA?"

"Yes, partially. Mine and Calix's." I glance at Cole. His eyes are trained on my face, giving me an odd look. I try to give him a sign that I'm just trying to save his life, not that I *ever* imagined using his organs as a spare set for me or my son. But I can't say the words, and I don't know if Cole understands. "Can we just go inside, Evan?" I beg. "Try a different formula? Don't give up."

Evan sneers. "Oh, so now you're invested in the cure, are you? Once it's a bust?" He laughs maniacally, his head thrown back toward the heavens.

"It's . . . not . . . a bust," says Griffin from the side of us all. He's standing on his own and speaking, still with a great deal of effort. "You just didn't get it . . . high enough."

Evan stops laughing and turns his whole body toward Griffin. "Oh yeah?" he asks, his eyes thin lines.

"You . . . need . . . to . . . get it into the ozone layer, like the poem says. Not . . . the clouds."

I blink a few times. My brother moves closer to Griffin, rocking the Dehydrogenator with both hands, almost like he's about to twirl it in the air. I can see the sweat his palm prints leave on the staff. Evan could lunge at any moment, and I don't think any of us take a breath, waiting for Evan's next move. After a few tense moments, Evan drops his staff into the snow.

"That's it, isn't it?" His words are airy, full of breath. "The forefathers admired technology. They *worshipped* it!" His voice sounds shrill against the miles of flat terrain surrounding our small group. "They were still trying to land a man on *Mars* when the Accords were put in place. They would have wanted us to keep creating, no matter what they said in the Accords." He splays fingertips against both temples, thumbs resting on his cheekbones. "They just wanted to force people to create in sustainable ways." Evan paces, sliding along the surface of the snow, his boots leaving shallow gullies. "Like the rocket launcher. Our forefathers wouldn't have wanted it to drop bombs. They'd have loved it to lift things into space. If we had to find another hospitable planet to live on, for instance. Or for administering the cure!" My brother is jumping up and down now, drilling himself down into the snow pack. He's deep enough that the snow covers his calves. Evan runs a hand through his thinning hair and turns to me. "Your boyfriend is brilliant. Stupendously, ridiculously brilliant! Technology Faction Lead." He laughs out loud, throwing his head backward again, "Those people were right all along!"

I purse my lips, not willing to take my brother's leap at quite the same pace. "So you want to use Mid's rocket launcher?" I ask, one eyebrow cocked.

"Yes, the heavens help me, I want to use Mid's awful, flawed technology!"

"The one you tried to destroy?" I ask again, testing the waters with how far I can take the sarcastic tone in my voice. "'Cause they were hurting the environment by building it?"

Evan laughs. "Yes, that one!" He beckons to his rebels. "Get Griffin an IV now!" When no one moves, Evan launches himself into the face of his closest warrior. "Now!"

In minutes, Cole, Griffin, and I are back on the airride with ten of Evan's men all standing close. They've hooked Griffin up to a bag of liquid, and he's been planted in one of the cockpit's two front seats. The rest of us stand inside the belly of the vessel while Evan tells me exactly how the formula should be set inside Mid's rocket.

"You'll want to place it just so. It can't tip out of the diamond bowl until impact with the atmosphere." He motions with one hand how the cup must stay level.

"Assuming Mid Country has even fixed their rocket," I say. Part of me loves this idea of Griffin's. It's gotten him fluids. It's stopped Evan from attacking Cole, and it's getting all three of us out of CERN and away from my brother. Evan was right. Griffin is "brilliant". But I just wonder, when the formula doesn't work again, what will Evan do then? Break his promise and come to get us in Mid? Attack Mid if they refuse to fix the rocket launcher?

"Oh, they'll fix it," Evan says. "You'll convince them, won't you, Sister?" He gives me a menacing look, but it's so full of hope that it just comes off making Evan look like an addict who craves my agreement.

"She will," says Cole from my side. "Aloy is miraculous at getting people to acknowledge their potential."

I cock my head at Cole, not completely understanding his words.

"I'm staying here, Aloy," he says with a long sigh.

My mouth goes dry instantaneously. "What?"

"I'm going to stay in CERN with Evan."

"Why? What do you—" I start to say. Even Evan is staring at Cole like the clone has five heads.

Cole shakes his head. "Because you were right. My greatest asset is your DNA."

My brow furrows so deeply my eyes feel connected. "I didn't say that. I was just—"

"I know you didn't really mean it like that," he says, putting a hand on my shoulder. "You were just trying to stop your brother from killing me. But you were right. I have your DNA in me, and that means I'm the closest match Evan's going to have."

"Evan?" I ask.

My brother's already picked up on Cole's thinking. "To replace *my* cancer-ridden organs with his own," he says, his eyes wide.

"Why would you want to do *that*?" I ask Cole, pushing his hand off my shoulder like he's scalded me.

Cole takes a deep breath. "Because that's what I was born for. I wouldn't be here on this earth if not for the fact that I'm supposed to be a replacement."

"Yeah, for *Calix*, and now he's dead." I strike back, emphasizing the Mid leader's name.

"Coincidentally, a replacement for you too," he says, his eyes lowered. "And your family members."

"Interesting point," interrupts my brother, looking Cole up and down.

"Why are you volunteering for this?" I ask again. "The people in Mid want you back. They said so. You don't have to worry about fitting in any longer."

"It's not that," says Cole, shaking his head. "It's about being bigger than just my own life. In the labs, as I was growing, all I could think about was how I was half a human. Not really part of the natural order. An anomaly. Keeping your brother alive so he can continue making the formula—this is how I finally fit in. I can pick up a hammer in Mid and help them put up a building. Or I can stay and really be part of something."

I start to interrupt, my words forming bubbles on the tip of my tongue.

Evan says, "Cole's right. If this next try doesn't work, it doesn't mean the experimenting should cease. The clone's organs will keep me working."

"There's no guarantee that anything Evan is doing will *ever* pay off," I say to Cole, ignoring my brother. "You might be sacrificing yourself for *nothing*!"

"Tell us what you really think," Evan scoffs at me.

"Shut up," I retort, not even bothering to glance at my brother as I spit the words.

"Or maybe something," says Cole, the end of his sentence trailing off. He tilts his head and smiles at me. His cheeks are red inside the heated airride, giving Cole a baby doll appearance. The clone wraps his arms around me before I can say anything else, and I bury my face in his shoulder. Hiccups catch in my throat.

"What's going on?" asks Griffin as he shuffles out of the cockpit. I let go of Cole and take a small step back. Griffin walks shakily toward the back of the vessel, his IV bag gripped in his left hand, which he holds above his shoulders. I can tell by the flow of his words that the IV is already working. He hasn't had to take any big breaths while speaking. His skin tone looks better too, and his eyes are brighter.

"Cole says he's staying here," I blurt out. "To donate his organs to my *brother!*"

Griffin locks eyes on Cole. "Are you sure that's what you want to do?" he asks.

Cole nods, still not speaking.

"You know, you're not an exact match for Aloy's DNA," Griffin says to Cole. Griffin should know, as he constructed Cole's body. "You have equal, if not more, parts of Calix. Evan might reject your organs."

"I still want to try," Cole says.

"Let's get this show on the road!" yells Evan, spinning a finger in the air. I feel the vibrating tread of all his people getting busy around us. "Get one of our guys in the cockpit!" he yells to his people. And then to me, he says, "You'll need another man as your pilot."

I'm not ready to talk about leaving. Evan hasn't even given us enough time to say goodbye to Cole. But I merely say, "How will I explain who your pilot is to Mid?"

"You'll find a way," says Evan, shaking his head like that's the least of his concerns. "Say he's someone else they haven't met from East. They'll never know."

I don't respond, but I step back to Cole, wrapping my arms around his shoulders, reaching high to do so. Griffin's still at our side, but after a moment, he gently tugs Cole away from me.

"Walk me back to the cockpit, Cole? I could use a hand," he says. The clone lets Griffin's free arm rest over his neck. Griffin glances back at me, blinking his eyes closed a second too long.

I wonder if he has some idea for Cole. A way for Cole to escape Evan's lair if he should change his mind later.

"It won't be a waste," Evan says, surprising me from behind. "I wish you'd believe in me," he says with a grimace.

I shake my head, trying to blink back the tears that still stick to my lashes from Cole's goodbye. "I wish I could," I sniff. I look down, shaking my head just slightly.

"When you feel warmth on your skin in August or when you drink from a stream and it doesn't taste like soot. Just remember to tell everyone it was me who saved the world."

I glance up at Evan even though my head is still bent toward the air-ride's black floor where I've just seen Cole exit the plane. Griffin didn't convince him to come with us. My head falls farther forward in defeat. Evan's face is shrouded in the lackluster light, but I can tell he's still smiling. It's not so arrogant of a look as I might have guessed, though. He seems almost apologetic. Evan pats me on the back.

"It'll be all right, Aloy," he says. Then Evan turns and walks out of the airride, Cole and nine of his warriors with him.

I find the closest airbag to the cockpit and position myself behind it. The back doors clank shut, and I'm alone in the body of the plane. Even though Griffin isn't far in front of me, and we're heading back in the direction of Glory and Vienne, I feel like someone's scooped out my insides and laid them on the floor at my feet. Cole's gone because of something I said. And now I'm supposed to explain to Mid how I want to use their technology at the direction of their decade-long enemy. Nothing seems all right about this scenario.

52

"WHY DIDN'T YOU CONVINCE Cole to leave?" I ask Griffin the second we've landed in Mid and the CERN pilot isn't within earshot.

Griffin's IV bag and a second one are empty. They lie on the floor of the cockpit like trash, when just moments ago they were the things saving his life.

"Because everyone deserves to make their own choices. And because Evan wouldn't have let him leave at that point. Better that Cole stayed of his own accord instead of being forced."

I snort, my nose scrunching, my mouth turned down at the sides.

"Come on, let's get off this thing." He pulls me toward him, and we leave the airride on the top of the same building where we landed last time. Vienne's on the roof to greet us again, but this time she's not alone. Emma stands at her side with Eve in her arms.

"Aloy," says Emma with a nod of her head when she sees us. "Griffin." Her voice is polite but cool. Her eyes don't smile, even as her mouth makes the obligatory motion.

Griffin steps forward, enfolding Eve into his arms.

"Emma," I say, matching the guarded tone of her words.

"Did you give Evan the diamond?" asks Vienne, looking between me and Griffin to the soldier standing nearby.

"Yes, Evan has the diamond. And this is one of his—" I start to say "warriors," but then sneer at the man and choose "minions" instead. The man *humphs* and holds his staff closer to his chest.

"Where's Cole?" asks Emma, peering behind us into the depths of the airride.

I shake my head. It's too long of a story for the top of this windy roof. "We need to get to your comms room. I'll explain about Cole and the rest of our plans along the way."

"Is he hurt?" asks Vienne. Her lips are pursed, the smile having vanished from her face.

"He may be soon," answers Griffin. He hoists Eve higher in his arms, as if protecting her from the very thought of Cole's fate.

When I tell Emma and Vienne our plans on our way to building four, Vienne asks, "So you're not shielding Evan anymore?"

"I don't plan to throw him to the wolves," I say. "I'm just hoping Mid chooses peace instead of war."

Emma grimaces. "That's a tall order, Aloy. Considering what you've just told us, your brother spied on us, stole our resources, and attacked us for ten years straight. Mid's people aren't going to take that well."

"And they may not believe the formula you want to disperse over our air isn't some kind of poison," Vienne says.

I look away when Vienne says "our" like Mid is her home country now, not East. "I know," I say. "It'll be a lot to swallow. But I saw the formula work with CERN's groundwater. The people of Mid will just have to trust me." I can't believe I'm advocating for Evan's recipe, but Tomlin believed in the formula, and now that I've seen Evan's concoction work with my own eyes, I find I can't just abandon the idea of a clean environment. Not anymore.

"Trust isn't something you can just ask for," says Emma.

Our party is quiet after that, clomping forward through the streets with the eyes of Mid's people directed toward us, as always. The people are still up on the scaffoldings, repairing in groups. They stare at the newcomer behind us too, but not viciously. Maybe they do trust me. I just hope they continue to do so once they've heard what I have to say.

When we're in front of the comms building, Griffin turns to Emma, handing the baby back into Vienne's arms. He moves his arm around my waist, and I can feel the heat of each of his fingers against my spine. The shame of Emma's words are still caught in my chest, a lump that won't dissolve. I can't expect Mid's blind trust, like I can't ask for Emma's trust again after I got her brother killed.

"I think by now Aloy's *earned* everyone's trust," Griffin says, looking Emma square in the eyes.

"We'll see," says Emma before she opens the door, swinging it just a little too hard.

The comms room is exactly as I remember it, as if in all the months since I served as Calix's historian, someone came through here and froze everything in place. Headphones balance on the top of cubicle walls, and the myriad of buttons and levers still trill with the faint squeal of electricity. But the room is empty, so it feels like a ghost-town compared to last time I was here, listening to Vienne's screams as she ravaged her body looking for the microchip.

Emma leads us to the main terminal and points at the swivel chair pushed up against the desk. I lick my lips and then take a seat there. "You'll need a pair of these," Emma says, handing me a wide headset. She leans over the console, turning a few of the knobs and pushing others. "Whenever you're ready," she says, her eyebrows edging into a neat V.

I stare at the buttons in front of me and take a deep breath. Griffin's hand squeezes my shoulder from behind. "Remember, they'll always value honesty," he says. "No matter what."

I think of Griffin's bravery in telling me who he was. Who his father was. What he stood for way back in the marshland house in East Country. Back when dishonesty just meant covering up the tinkering of light bulbs. My hand curls on top of Griffin's, and then I feel another palm rest on my opposite shoulder. Vienne stands in back of me, her long hair almost falling across the console's many buttons. Emma has taken Eve and walked to the side of the room, leading CERN's warrior away too. So it's just the three of us again. Vienne, me, and Griffin.

I take another long breath, letting the air in through my mouth and out my nose. Then I punch the yellow button for the microphone that will propel my words across Mid Country.

"Hi," I say, leaning too close to the speaker. Feedback rings around us, and Vienne flinches. "Sorry," I mumble into the mic. "I know you all saw me land back in Mid again. I was hoping I could talk to you for a few minutes. It's not a real conversation, I realize, since none of you can answer back or ask me questions. But, well, that's sort of okay since I bet you'd have so many that I wouldn't be able to finish what I need to say. And I really have to finish it."

I look up at Vienne and Griffin who both give me encouraging smiles.

"I found out some information recently, and at first I didn't want to tell you. I was scared you'd resort to war again." I take another long breath. "I hope you'll see that I've had your best interests in mind this entire time." I close my eyes for a second, and then keep going. "I found out who's been attacking Mid for the past ten years. He's the reason your Electeds advocated for such an emphasis on technology and pushed you all to disregard the other facets of your life, like children, or companionship." The words exit my mouth, one syllable at a time.

"He's the one who's been stealing your resources. Your nirogene. And he's the one who bombed your rocket launcher every time you were close to repairing it. He didn't want it used for fighting, even though he was using the implements of war himself. This entire time your attacker has been looking for something in Mid Country that was buried a long time ago by a past government. It's a puzzle piece, which when placed next to the matching set from West and East Country, gives a roadmap for curing the environment. The good news is that he finally found all three pieces. He's been trying to create the serum, and it's actually worked. I saw it myself. The serum destroyed all the pollutants inside stagnant groundwater. But curing the environment isn't as easy as just spreading the serum through Earth's water supply. It has to be dispersed inside the atmosphere too. So I'm on the speaker system today to ask you for a favor. Possibly the biggest favor Mid Country has ever done for the world."

I shift in my seat. Vienne and Griffin's hands have dropped to their sides, but I still feel their body heat from in back of my chair.

"We need Mid to repair the rocket launcher one more time, and I'm asking you to trust that the attacker won't disable it again with a fresh set of bombs. He wants this serum up in the ozone layer too much to attack the machine that could do the job. So I'm asking that you trust me about the value of this cure, about fixing the rocket, and about how I can keep the attacker at bay." I sigh, the air catching in my chest. "The thing is, if I'm being completely honest, I know I'm the last person in the world who should be asking you for your support. I know I helped free you from optogenetics oppression, and I know some of you call me the Freedom Fencer because of that. But the truth is I've known who your attacker was for a while now, and I didn't tell you. I didn't want you to go after him. And it's not even because I wanted to give him the chance to create the serum."

My voice breaks for good now, and my next words come out with a sob. "It's because I wanted to protect him. Because all along your attacker was someone close to me." I shake my head. "I didn't know who he was when he bombed you, but I found out that the timing of his attacks were in large part because of me. Your attacker is part of my family. He's my brother."

I can almost hear the yells and shouting coming from the streets down below, even through the headphones. I close my eyes, letting the significance of my last words settle. Not just because I can't think of a good enough follow-up, but because I want to give the people of Mid a moment to digest what I've said.

Finally, I open my eyes, and look back at Vienne and Griffin. Griffin has moved to the surrounding windows and is looking down at the ground. Vienne's lips are pinched. I find Emma against a wall on the opposite side of the room. She's shaking her head and looking even more angry than when she found out it was my request that brought Ollinear to face Aaron in the rocket launcher.

I take another long breath. I have to say something else before the people below start climbing their way up to the comms room and over-take everything. I have to keep going.

"What my brother did was inexcusable," I say loudly. "Vile. Terrible. Utterly against humanity. No life should be sacrificed just for the hope of advancement. But what he did create is something we can all use. I sug-gest we put it up in the rocket launcher and fix our environment once and for all so our children and the generations beyond don't have to grow up with radiation looming over their heads like we've had." I think of the optogenetics procedures that staved off cancer in Mid, and realize Mid's people will all start feeling the effects of radiation soon now that no one is under the mind manipulation.

"I know you're all angry, and I don't expect you to forgive my brother," I say. "Or me. But please, try to find a peace that will allow you to use what he's created. For yourselves. For everyone."

I stop, pressing the yellow button again, and then pushing the headphones off my head, almost violently. They land on the console with a sharp clatter.

I look around, standing up. "Are we about to be mobbed?" I ask Griffin.

"I don't know," he says, still looking out of the window. I join him there and see that a crowd has formed below us. People make a semi-circle around someone. I can't tell who it is or if he's helping the people arm themselves against me. I do see a few glints of metal from below—guns and knives reflecting the sun.

"We can't hide up here," says Emma. "We have to face them. *You* have to face them," she says to me.

"Maybe if we just give them a little time," says Vienne.

"No," says Emma. "You don't want my people coming up here for you. To drag you out. You owe them a chance to respond to your statements face to face."

"But they'll lock her up again," Vienne says, her voice incredulous. "We've got to get her out of the country."

"I'm not leaving Mid," I sigh, thinking of Glory not for the first time this afternoon. "I'm not running away."

The CERN warrior leaves the window where he's been gauging the public's reaction too. "So does this mean Mid isn't going to repair the launcher?" he asks, his voice gruff.

"Don't go calling Evan just yet," says Griffin, holding up a hand.

"We're using their launcher one way or another," the warrior says.

"I know, I know," I say. "Just, please, give Mid a little time before you tell Evan." For all I know, my brother's been watching on his cameras and listening on his well-placed microphones the entire time, so he may already realize Mid's angry. But on the off chance I can buy us some time, I still have to try. "Emma's right," I continue. "I owe Mid's people a chance to talk to me in person. They should have a voice too. I'm going down there."

Griffin's continues to stare out the window, trying to determine the mood down below. But when he hears this, he comes to my side. "We'll be right there next to you."

"With the Dehydrogenator," says the warrior, angling his weapon.

"I didn't know you cared so much for me." My eyes roll at the CERN rebel, and he, in turn, *humphs.*

When we reach the first floor of building four, I see masses of people outside the glass doors. There are so many, I think our party will be swept up in a sea of bodies all scrambling to have a piece of me.

"You ready?" I ask Vienne and Griffin, and then I throw open the doors.

53

I HALF EXPECT TO be mobbed as soon as people see me emerge from the building. But instead, above the melee, I make out a voice piercing the crowd. Someone is still in the middle of the group, yelling out arguments. Most of the people are angled toward that person and away from the doors we've just exited.

"She's got a point!" the voice yells. "Don't be so stupid that you value revenge over our future health!"

A hundred voices rise to meet the one in the middle. It's a chorus of *No*'s and other exclamations. After a moment, someone on the outskirts of the group notices the four of us and yells our presence out to everyone else. The mob begins turning, a thousand sets of eyes converging on us.

"There she is!" I hear a woman yell.

"Make way!" comes the strong voice again. The person in the middle hurtles himself forward, and magically the crowd opens, letting him through.

Ty advances on us from the center of Mid's people. "Aloy!" he yells. "Come here!"

I shake my head. Why in the world does Ty want me to move into the *center* of the mob? I realize that he was the voice speaking to Mid's people, and he'd been doing it from a makeshift pedestal. Ty grasps my hand and forcefully pulls me up onto the large wooden box. He points at me from a few inches lower.

"She told you the truth!" he bellows. "More than any of your other leaders have ever done for you. And you want to hold that against her?" There's more shouting from the group. I scan over their heads for Vienne and Griffin. My friends stand at the back of the mob, looking helpless. Any moment I will be devoured by Mid's angry people.

"She didn't know it was her brother bombing us!" Ty yells. "And now that she does, Aloy's stopped him from attacking. She's what's keeping you safe, you daft imbeciles!"

I look out at the faces staring at me. The mouths are open in the midst of shouting, and I can't tell which words escape from which people. But I see a man pushing through the crowd, determined to get through. I wonder if this will be my killer. I put a hand up to my heart, like I can stave off the violence, just by holding myself close. I try to find Griffin's eyes again, but he's pushing through the crowd too, knocking elbows with people, and I can't get his attention.

The advancing man bursts through, a child wrapped around his middle. I recognize the man and boy, and take a gasp of breath knowing I've let them down.

"Ya need to spin your heads around so they're on a bit tighter!" yells Harbar. At first I think he's referring to me, Vienne, and Griffin, but he points toward Mid's people. "She's here offering ya a cure so our children can attempt to create a better life for themselves. She's handing it to ya on a silver platter, and what do ya want to do? Stone her instead of giving yer thanks!" He and the child join Ty at the ground by my feet, making a sort of fence between me and the rest of the people. Griffin arrives too, breathing hard. The four of them yell back at the mob of people.

I stay quiet, listening to the back and forth until, one by one, the anger across Mid's people dims, a light flickering out as twilight sets in. We've stood here for hours. Nothing's been shot at me, and no one's attempted to break the wall of Ty, Griffin, Harbar, and Able. In fact, no less than ten others have come to stand along that fence. Even CERN's warrior made his way to the middle, and he now stands in front of me like a sentinel.

"We're going to work on that rocket launcher. And you're all going to help!" yells Ty. "Anyone who's against it, you focus on other rebuilding. But no one halts our progress! You hear?" Ty is more forceful than I've ever heard him before. He's fourteen now, and the muscles in his shoulders and biceps bunch against the too-small shirt he wears. His voice has overcome puberty and sounds smooth and deep. I wish I could tell him how much I appreciate his defense of me, but I don't dare utter a word. I've said enough over the speakers.

As the moon climbs to hover above us, Emma finally enters the circle. "No matter what you have determined tonight," she says to her people. "It's time to rejoin your families and retire. Everyone here is hungry and tired."

People start to disperse after that. I sink down to a sitting position on the wooden box, letting my knees bend for the first time in hours. I'm famished.

"Let's go," says Vienne, and I follow her down from the pedestal. "We'll see what the mood in Mid is like tomorrow."

Griffin and I stay the night together in the bottom floor of Tower One. Ty had suggested Aaron's old quarters, but I couldn't bring myself to venture into that apartment. I'd rather take my chances among Mid's people in the skyscrapers where we used to live. Between Tower One, the hospital dormitory, or Aaron's former bedroom, I'd choose the tiny apartment any day. I stayed curled within Griffin's embrace, letting his arm grow heavy over my body until I almost lose the ability to suck in a long breath. I keep thinking about Glory and if, by telling the truth, I've robbed him yet again of growing up with his mother. Maybe I need to start thinking of my son and let everyone else rot. I squeeze my eyes shut. I *was* thinking about Glory when I told Mid the truth. I didn't want Glory growing up in the same world as I had where we worshipped weeds because they were the only foliage that continued to grow. There has to be a better existence than that.

When the sun streams in our windows the next morning, I realize I haven't slept a wink. A knock at the door rouses Griffin and sends me shuffling into the apartment's living room. Ty stands with a small group of Mid's people behind him. I stay my breathing, not knowing yet if they mean to escort me to their prison or put me back on the airride to meet my brother. But they do better than either of those options.

"I've assembled some engineers," Ty says. "Have you eaten yet? We're starting on the rocket launcher early this morning."

I shake my head but notice Griffin's already grabbing some freeze-dried packets from one of the kitchen drawers. "Won't we be stopped?" I ask.

"No. There was an automated vote from everyone's rooms last night. They'll let us work unhindered until such a point as they feel the resources need to be redirected elsewhere."

"And Aloy?" asks Griffin. "They'll leave her be?"

"Yes," answers Ty. "She's safe to walk around. No one will meddle with her."

Twenty of us work on the rocket launcher together. I keep reference books nearby and refer to them often, reminding people of Mac's work and the intricacies of past technology. The twenty people become thirty and after a week thirty becomes forty. As the walls of the rocket launcher are erected, people watch us during breaks. Welders mold the metal casing onto the rocket's skeleton. Aerospace and electrical engineers keep their heads close to the gears, configuring each mechanism so that it spins and lurches just right. People even bring us food in the afternoon so that we don't have to stop working, and light is kept on so the work can continue until we choose to be done for the day.

After a month, everything is ready for the rocket's first test. We evacuate the city center to ensure no one's hurt in a possible malfunction. We choose two people to man the controls from the console, and we stand outside the city's limits, watching to see if the rocket can make it high enough to breach the atmosphere.

The rocket breaks through the clouds but begins to break apart high in the air. We can barely make out the pieces of the rocket as it splinters, parts spewing out to the ends of the Earth. When we call back the rocket, it's a fragment of what we started with.

Another month goes by before we launch a second test. This time the structure stays intact, but the guides don't work, and the whole rocket careens haphazardly until it crashes full throttle into the Atlantic. We watch from telescopes and then only radar as the rocket falls below the horizon and our hopes plummet into the churning water.

After a third month, I'm ready to see Glory, and I'm exhausted. Our baby is brought to us from East, and at least now, at night, Griffin, Glory, me, and sometimes Eve are together, eating dinner and sleeping under the same roof like a true family.

The work continues, and after ninety days, we have a third rocket to show for our efforts. This one is launched and returns to us intact, but we couldn't guide it high enough to reach the atmosphere before it began shaking and threatening to rip apart once again.

"They're going to put an end to this at some point," says Ty the night of our latest launch attempt. "We're using too many resources."

"We know," says Griffin. We've been pooling East's supplies with Mid's for a couple of months since this is a joint endeavor, not just Mid's responsibly. But East doesn't have much to share. Just some manpower and a bit of mineral from our reopened mines.

"Does it go for vote again soon?" I ask.

"The vote's in one week," says Ty. "But a vote doesn't necessarily mean the project is finished. Mid might decide to keep going."

"Not likely," scoffs CERN's warrior. We've since gotten his name and started including him in the rebuilding so he doesn't just stand there with his staff, looking menacing but not really contributing anything. Drint still makes for an unpleasant work partner, but he's strong, and he cares about the rocket's success as much, if not more so, than we do. He says he hasn't been in contact with Evan, but as the days go on, Drint looks more antsy, almost bouncing out of his shoes, just like my brother.

"He hasn't reached out to you?" I ask, cornering Drint one day off to the side of the launch pad.

"Nope," says the warrior, looking over my shoulder into the streets of Mid. He leans with one hand in the many-pocketed pants of his CERN outfit. He has refused to garb himself in Mid's traditional robes, instead keeping himself clothed in the black military gear from Evan's lair.

"He promised he wouldn't intervene," I say, reminding Drint of Evan's oath.

"If you were proving successful," says the warrior, raising his eyebrows at me and then walking off without so much as a glance back. It's like Drint knows something, but all my further attempts at pulling the information out of him are futile.

It turns out, Mid never gets its vote.

Two days later, after everyone is holed up in the towers for the night, Mid's alarms pierce the air. They start in the apartments, causing us to jump up from our dinner tables and beds. Then as we make our ways into the hallways, not in the cool, organized way of an optogenized population, but as a country of people with feelings and concerns, the blasts of Mid's warning signals careen through the uncarpeted corridors. We hear the sirens in spades, since every open apartment door multiplies the sound.

"Bomb shelter!" shouts Griffin over the heads of people running down the halls. He carries Glory against him and grips my hand at the same time.

"It's my brother!" I say. "He's not going to bomb us. He just wants the formula back. Or maybe to take over the operation."

"Are you sure about that? Who knows how angry he is? Maybe he thinks we're purposefully failing."

"Then I've got to tell him we're not doing it on purpose!" I take two steps toward the elevator in the opposite direction from where Griffin's been leading us to the stairwell.

"Where are you going?" he yells through the screaming voices around us. Glory has tucked himself within Griffin's armpit, attaching on with all the strength a one year old can muster.

"To the rocket launcher!"

Griffin's whole face screws up. He looks at me and then at the safety of the bomb shelter beneath us. He pulls on Glory's arms, almost as if he's trying to hand Glory over to another Mid countryman, but then gnashes his teeth together. Griffin doesn't want to let Glory out of his sight. "Okay, come on," he growls, deciding to stay with me and take Glory too.

When we exit the building, I can see exactly why Mid's sirens began. There are over a dozen CERN airrides flying into Mid's territory. Some have already landed on the rooftops, and some are still hovering overhead. Mid's people run to the armory and toward their own airrides, but I know we won't even have a chance to fight, if it comes to that. We don't have as many airrides as Evan, and they've surprised us. We can't move our airrides up fast enough.

"How'd they arrive without us knowing?" I ask out loud, but I already know the answer before my own sentence finishes.

They have cloaking. Evan told me himself.

We run through the crowd, leaping between people. At one point my hand dislodges from within Griffin's, but he's back at my side in an instant, reaching for me through the throngs.

We get to Mid's rocket launcher just as Ty arrives too. "Do you hear it?" he asks.

I start to shake my head, not understanding what he means, when I hear the crackling and popping of the rocket coming to life.

We get to the launch pad, just as the whole structure starts to shake. "Drint!" I call out, seeing him directly in front of us. "What's going on?"

Drint turns toward us, but he doesn't answer. He doesn't have to. My brother emerges from next to him, responding in his stead.

"You took too long, Sister," Evan says, yelling over the rumbles. Drint shrugs at me.

"You said you wouldn't come back here! You were leaving it to me!" I yell. "You can't launch the rocket right now! Mid's people are all around!" My voice sounds manic through the combined engines of the dozen airrides and Evan's people beginning to start the launch process.

"It's not going to work!" yells Ty toward Evan. "We haven't figured out how to fix the guiders. The rocket hasn't broken through the atmosphere yet without falling."

"It needs to be manned," says a woman running up next to us. She's one of the electrical engineers. "At least get someone to man and steer the rocket it if you're going to launch it with Mid's people all over the place!"

Evan shrugs just like Drint did a moment earlier.

Ty yells from next to me again. "It needs guidance so that it can switch to manual mode before the levers freeze in the atmosphere!"

Evan seems to consider this for a moment. He steps side-to-side, weighing his options. Then he looks at Drint who swallows hard but doesn't attempt to run away.

"Why don't you—" Evan start to say to Drint, but another voice stops him.

Cole pushes out from within a set of Evan's warriors, surprising everyone by launching himself toward Evan.

"Cole!" I exclaim, blinking hard to ensure I've seen this right. The clone is still alive. It looks like Cole may be trying to attack Evan, but instead of running at him with some concealed weapon or knocking my brother down, Cole places a hand on top of Evan's outstretched one.

"I'll guide the rocket," he says.

"That's suicide!" yells Griffin, still trying to shield Glory within his robes while he leans toward Cole. "We don't have this perfected yet!"

Cole shakes his head. "I was going to sacrifice myself anyway. Why not do so as the one who cures the environment?"

My hands automatically cover my eyes before I look up again. "Do you really believe in the formula that much, Cole?"

He grants me a slight smile. "I was never supposed to be here at all, Aloy. I can't have children. I can't leave any legacy of my own. But I can be remembered for something great. Even if it was just for trying."

Evan growls next to Cole, having long ago shaken off the clone's outstretched hand. I can see my brother's cheeks turning red. "You are *not* taking this away from me, Clone!" he shouts. "Either I have the satisfaction of saving the world, or the world doesn't *get* saved!"

Before anyone can expel another word, Evan grabs the diamond and formula from out of Drint's clutches and throws himself toward a rope ladder attached to one of his hovering airrides. All around us the heat from the rocket boosters threatens to burn our exposed skin and it keeps sending us farther backward.

"You've got to get Glory out of here!" I shout at Griffin. He nods and starts to turn. Then he circles back, grabs me around the shoulders and brings my head closer to his. Griffin's kiss on my lips is urgent and hard. It tastes like the fumes around us, jet fuel and fire combined.

For a split second, I can't hear the noise emanating from all sides. The world has stopped for Griffin's goodbye.

This time I'm the one who breaks the embrace, leaning away. I plant my face within Glory's brown locks, kissing him on the top of his head, and then pull back. "Run!" I command, and for the first time ever, Griffin runs away from me, not toward me, as he tries to get our son as far away from Mid's city center as possible.

I try to talk reason to Evan as he climbs the ladder toward his airride, attempting to board the rocket's cockpit from up high. "Get down from there! What are you doing?"

Evan glances down at me, and I think I see hesitation in his eyes, but he keeps climbing, ultimately ignoring my pleas.

Everyone around me runs away too, including the CERN rebels. Some of them break rank and aim for their airrides. Some of CERN's other airrides even fly away. Ty, Cole, and I stay at the rocket's control pads, fingering the buttons. I don't know if Evan even understands how to fly the rocket, but he won't need to do anything for the first stint. It's on automatic until the guiding system starts to freeze under the intense cold from Earth's atmosphere. So far every time we've attempted a launch, those levers, among others, have been frozen solid and then charred to a melted mass as the rocket returned to Earth. Evan will have to take over the rocket's controls once we lose the ability to do so from down here. If his body can handle it. If his body doesn't freeze on the ascension or pass out from lack of oxygen.

Evan's airride almost crashes into the top of the rocket, its been flown so close to the cockpit's door. He stands, dangerously unstable, on the threshold of the airride. Evan throws himself across to the rocket, legs flailing through the doorway. CERN's airride zooms into the horizon, getting as far away as the rocket as possible.

"It's moving!" yells Cole from my left. The entire rocket is rumbling. I look up, but I don't see my brother anymore, not scrambling through the rocket's door or within the cockpit's windows. I don't see anything except the flames from the rocket's twin engines. We should be in the rocket's tower at least, but we're using controls from the launch pad, and I know we only have a second more to stay here until the roaring flames scorch us.

"On my count," I say, pressing the launch sequence, three buttons all in a row. "Three, two, one!"

Cole and Ty kick into high gear as the whole structure seems to shake on the rocket's rise. We run into the city center and then turn to watch the rocket blast through the sky into the clouds. The sound waves hit us so that I can feel the rocket rising, not just see it in the air. We haven't had the chance to armor the closest buildings against the rocket launch. Glass from the windows of the nearest buildings crack, sending shards falling toward the ground. My whole body braces itself against a nearby light post. Cole, Ty, and I hug each other, our hands finding each other's shoulders and necks. I grip them to stay upright. We try to hide underneath a small awning, but it's insufficient. I feel tiny pinpricks as the shards find my arms and hands, making tiny, exact cuts.

My hair whips around me, keeping me looking down, even after the glass has stopped falling. When I can finally force my face back up, the rocket is just a dot. Then the whole thing disappears, becoming too small to see with the naked eye.

We stand like that for minutes, just the three of us, quiet with anticipation. Our faces are still lifted toward the sky, watching, yearning for the sight of reentry. Anything that will tell us Evan completed his mission.

"He had more formula," Cole says. It's the first words since the launch. "If this didn't work, he made more. And found more diamonds from another continent."

I nod, but I don't trust my voice to say anything. I know Ty is thinking the same thing as me. Mid won't vote to build another rocket. Not after this. And there won't be any foreign force, like Evan, here to make them build it. Evan's trip into the sky right now—this was the final attempt.

Then we see it. First it's just a speck on the outermost edge of our sight. A red ball emerges into sight, picking up speed as it makes a journey back to earth. Then two more red specks alight on the sky. Then three more. I know what they are before Ty or Cole can even say it.

Debris. The rocket has broken apart. There will be no remnants this time. No guiding the skeleton back to Earth. My brother is gone too.

The whole country is in mourning. When we tell East Country what transpired, many of my countrymen join us in Mid. CERN's planes all leave without us even having to ask. The ones that were still here after Evan's joyride, that is. No one works, taking a holiday from the toil of rebuilding Mid. We stay with our families in the towers or we mill around the town center, rehashing the rocket's launch, the failure of Mid's enemy.

What I hadn't realized, though, was that Mid's people had started hoping for a favorable outcome. They'd started to root for the rocket to work.

The weather starts to change, and someone mentions that it hasn't rained in a long time. Leaves begin to fall off the couple of real trees Mid has grown in its labs and replanted in the city center. There's a nip in the air that reminds me to put Glory's jacket on before we venture out for the day.

"Gray clouds forming," Griffin warns when he sees me bundling Glory up.

"We'll hurry," I say.

"And we should start thinking about heading back East soon. The green beans here are truly magnificent, but I don't think that should keep us here, do you?"

I nod, letting the smile inch up my cheeks. "I do love a good green bean." Then I remember how Mid's produce was fertilized and my nose scrunches. "But you're right; we need to start rebuilding our own country. I wonder if Vienne will return with us. Or Cole," I add.

I'm headed out with Glory to a play date with Eve and Cole's newly adopted daughter, Kira, in Emma's quarters. Mid has divided the former Elected family's penthouse, and Emma was given one of the spacious studios. Vienne and Cole will surely be there, and I'll make a point of asking them about future plans. Maybe Vienne will agree to spend six months every year with us in East. That will be good for the siblings.

I make a point of waving to people I recognize on the walk to building thirteen. There's no reason to cower away from the gaze of Mid's people anymore. Their animosity toward me seems to have vanished along with my brother and CERN's rebels. There's still talk of bolstering Mid's defenses in case the rebels return, but chatter of taking an offensive stance doesn't reach the surface.

Glory and I are stopped along the way by one of Mid's bakers, and we're handed a soft roll. It reminds me of the time my father and I took a ride through East and a baker gave us a hot-from-the-fire pretzel.

"Mmmm," Glory says, his mouth already attached to the bread. He's started saying a few phrases over the last weeks, and I can't help repeating "I love you" to him in elongated, enunciated speech each night, hoping he'll pick up that phrase before others. It's lazy, nice days here in Mid since the rocket episode. I know we'll have to pick up the pieces of my brother's failure soon. Hold elections in Mid and East, for one. Start building some real domiciles in East instead of the mud and stick ones. But for now, I can't help just gazing at my son as he munches the roll.

Until I hear a rumble overhead and both Glory and I look to the sky.

"Thunder," I tell him. "That's warm and cold air colliding. We have to get inside before the skies open."

Glory rumples his face, looking concerned.

"Don't worry. I don't literally mean 'open.' I mean rain pelting down. We're close to Eve's house. We'll just watch the storm from her windows." Glory relaxes, his little muscles unflexing within my grip. He could walk, but I still prefer holding him.

We get inside building thirteen's lobby before the first drop lands. Everyone's ducked into the nearest building, and since Mid has so many, no one's been caught in the rain storm. We watch the storm coming through the ground windows as the clouds converge, and the sun's light is hidden. The streets grow dark, and huge droplets of water shudder down from above. It's like the heavens above us are spewing their disgust at the humans below. We, who ruined the heavens. We, who were so selfish as to create machines that spoiled our air and water.

I sigh, and watch Glory as he watches the rain. One day perhaps he'll be able to venture out into the rain and let his face and hair get drenched. Jump and splash in the puddles. Maybe his children's children will be able to do so. I'm so engrossed in my image of the future that I don't notice at first the gasps from people all around us. I look up and try to see what they're all pointing to.

A child has run out into the streets, removing his coat like he's molting skin. I cup a hand to my mouth. What's he doing? His skin will bubble and burn under the acid! I set Glory down onto the floor, squinting my eyes to see who the child is. I know all of them now. It shouldn't be so hard to see through the rain and determine whose child it is. Then I see Harbar running through the streets toward the boy, yelling his name. "Able! Able!"

"No!" I scream, as the boy goes one step further. He strips off his shirt, standing half-naked in the streets. He opens his arms wide and looks up at the sky, letting the droplets pelt his face.

"Able! Stop!" yells his father, getting closer to the boy now. But the child doesn't stop. Instead, he dances in the rain, letting it splatter all over him. The downpour is so hard I can barely see through it. I can just make out the father reaching his son, lifting him up.

And then just as fast as the rain started, it slows, siphoning to a drizzle and then extinguishing altogether. Steam rises from the asphalt outside, and I strain through the fogged windows to see Able and Harbar. I expect to see a bloody mass of a child lying face up on the ground, shrouded within his father's arms.

When we throw open the building's doors and enter into the coolness outdoors, I don't see anyone lying across the ground. I see Able standing triumphant next to his father. Harbar looks down at his boy, his mouth agape. There are no welts, red and burnt into Able's flesh. No bubbling skin, charred and raw. No screaming. Just the child standing with his soaked shirt, wringing out the water into his father's outstretched, willing hands.

I stop in my tracks, holding tight to my own child as I watch the rainwater drip down. My eyes blink a few times, adjusting to the sun peeking through the clouds, still watching the droplets in awe. They don't sizzle upon contact with the father's skin. Harbar lifts his palms to his face, splashing the water against his cheeks and eyes. The crowd rears back, aghast, but I keep walking forward. I realize before the rest of Mid's people why Able wasn't burned in the storm.

The rain is no longer acidic.

Evan left his legacy; the cure worked. I stare up into the sky, trying to discern the exact position where I last saw Evan and our rocket touch the clouds. I hold onto Glory's hand tight but lift my face up to meet the sun's peeking light. Evan is gone, but his contribution lives on. He gave everything for the formula. Not just his life, but his soul. Everything bad that he was, and the good parts too. He fixed what the world had started destroying a century earlier.

As he asked, I won't forget it.

EPILOGUE

I SIT IN THE lush green grass with my toes buried in the tendrils of some three leaf clovers and moss so fluffy it feels like the clouds above. My arms are outstretched in back of me, holding up my body. I'm staring forward at the shielded sun as it descends into the horizon, the pink and blue sky looking like whipped candy.

"I thought I'd find you out here," says a voice from behind me.

I often come to the spot where Griffin's old Technology Faction shack used to sit in the marshes. It's still far enough away from the city center that it provides some privacy. I turn and see Griffin walking forward, an apple in his left hand. I'm always surprised now to see him with gray hair. The white strands alternate between his darker ones, making his whole appearance lighter, almost like he and I now have the same coloring.

I take the apple he offers me and bite down into the crisp white inside before handing it back. A deer bounds out of the forest, sees us, stops, and then runs back into the tall brush. I still get a thrill seeing all the new animals thriving. Griffin sits down next to me, and we hold hands in silence until the sun fully melts away.

"Tomorrow is their wedding day," Griffin says. His words are soft. "Are you ready?"

Glory and Kira are getting married tomorrow morning. I don't answer Griffin's question at first, thinking instead about all the weddings I've witnessed in the last twenty years. Mine and Vienne's. Mine and Griffin's. Vienne and Emma's. Ty and Gretchen's. Eve and Able.

The weddings are different now. In some ways we've gone backward to the very distant past. There is no more branding on the upper bicep during the marriage ceremony. Instead we re-adopted the idea of rings.

I absently play with mine, turning it around in circles on my left hand. So much has happened, like the contour of the ring, constantly progressing without an end. Our world will still be here after we're gone. We're sure of that now. The weather has normalized. Births are increasing. Grass is growing. Crops are sustaining. And no one's gotten cancer in the last five years.

Finally I turn to Griffin. "Will I ever truly be ready to see Glory grow up?"

He smiles at me. "He's been a grown man for a long time."

Two years in East's Elected position, having taken it over after Vienne's long reign, should have proven it to me, but still I see Glory as my baby. Will time ever stand still long enough for me to appreciate how much we've accomplished? Two ten-year cycles of elections have gone by, but the time seems like a mere wrinkle. I could remember each moment, spreading it out until the memories are smooth, and yet they'd still seem to move too fast.

"I wish Evan could have seen the world as it is now. Peaceful and healed," I say.

Griffin nods. "He made his choices. Thank the heavens he made the right one in the end."

I think of all the people we lost since I snuck Griffin out of East's prison. Three hundred of my countrymen in Mid's war against us. Countless number of Mid countrymen in my brother's bombings and in the quest for their freedom from Aaron. Ollinear. Imogene. Brinn. Evan. Grobe. Tomlin. My parents.

"Do you think it was all worth it?" I ask, looking up at Griffin.

He shifts on the moss and wraps his arms around me. I still get flutters in my stomach being so near him. Griffin's smell, like lemons and fresh-cut grass, can still intoxicate me. I let myself sink into his hold.

"Everything was worth this, Aloy." He hugs me harder, and it makes me sigh out a deep breath. We continue sitting quietly in the twilight, the moon now showing bright against the evening sky. When I hear an owl hoot from deep within the forest, I squeeze my eyes shut, listening to the sounds of nocturnal animals waking for the night. When I open them again, there's the faintest hint of a tear suspended in their corners. I don't fight it.

"Come on," I say. "Let's go back so we're ready for tomorrow. I need to practice my blessing."

"So I take it you've already finished writing yours?" Griffin stands, then holds out an arm to me. I grasp it and pull myself up so we're facing each other.

"You're not getting any of it out of me ahead of time." I smile, my eyes slanting.

"Just a few sentences? You tell me yours, I'll tell you mine?" At our children's request, both Griffin and I are speaking at the ceremony tomorrow. "I bet I could get it out of you." He leans forward and his breath tickles the tip of my earlobe.

I giggle, feeling much younger than when I first sat down in this grass a few hours ago.

"Okay, I'll give you a hint," I say.

"I'm all ears," Griffin teases, folding a section of my long hair behind one.

"You're ridiculous. You know it's not a competition." I can't help laughing.

"I know." There's a hint of the same mischievousness I saw that very first time Griffin and I sparred in my bedroom. "I just want to know what I'm up against. You're a very good writer, you know. How can my speech compare to the written words of the New Accord's author?"

This time my laugh is louder. After Ty won Mid Country's second election, both Mid and East began reaching out to the remaining countries with the help of CERN's communication capabilities. Spoken in their mother tongue, Asia understood our message that the environment was healing. Their bubble began peeling back for short amounts of time. Then for longer. And finally for long enough that we collaborated on a set of new Accords.

Countries agreed to use technology but only for advancement that wouldn't pollute. No robbing the Earth of unreplenishable resources. There would be no more isolation. But also no more war. Guns and bombs were destroyed, the blueprints burned in a majestic ceremony on the spot where Mid's rocket launcher used to stand. We know now that there will be an abundance of children who can take the Elected role, but they won't get it automatically. Only if they want it. And only if they're truly elected. It seems the remaining countries finally understood that a person cannot be forced into a position by birth. Leadership, it turns out, does not come in a color or a gender—a Y or an X chromosome—but in the quiet confidence of the individual.

"You're an exquisite orator," I counter to Griffin, blinking hard. "How can my speaking compare to the man who read the New Accords to the public for the first time?"

"Don't change the subject." He runs his fingers through the back of my long locks. I lean my head into his hand, liking the way his touch feels on my hair.

"Fine," I say. "The last words are a homage to the traditions of our past. Not everything from that time needs to be abandoned."

Griffin stops for a moment, thinking. Then he leans down so our foreheads touch. Right before he bends in to kiss me, his words—the ones I will speak tomorrow at Glory and Kira's wedding—ring clear out of his lips.

"A new day to you."

THE END

The Game of Rollers

INSTRUCTIONS AND HISTORY

Rollers is crudely based on a mixture of old-fashioned diversions called "Marbles" and "Pool."

Pieces include one large, circular glass bead called the shooter, and ten of each set of different colored, smaller glass beads: Yellow, Blue, Green, Orange, Red, and Purple. Thus, an entire Rollers game has 61 pieces. Additionally, a game of Rollers includes a chalked circle drawn on the concrete, pavement, or any surface of your choosing. The circle has the approximate circumference of a large pizza.

The number of players can range from 2 to 6.

The object of the game is to get all of your ten colored beads to sit on the circle's circumference line first before your opponent(s) manage to do so.

To start Rollers, all players choose a unique color. All of the beads are placed in the center of the chalked circle. The player youngest in age goes first, using the shooter to hit the beads in the center or "break" the set. Moving clockwise around the circle, the second player uses the shooter to aim at one of his beads and attempts to hit it onto the circumference line without going over. If a bead is hit past the circumference line, it is moved back into the center of the circle.

Strategy comes into play when an opponent tries to hit another player's bead out of the circle or knock it farther away from the circumference line.

Once a bead lands firmly on the circumference line, the bead's owner places the bead in his lap, and that bead is out of play.

To win a round of Rollers, a player must have all 10 beads back in his/her lap.

Any number of rounds of Rollers, from 1 to infinity, can be played before determining "best of" winner.

It is said that a group of friends are still playing Rollers to this day, having chosen an infinite number of rounds "until death of one of the players" before determining the winner. The players are said to watch their backs closely, as a player in the lead may choose that particular moment to proverbially "end the game . . ."

Author's Note on The Poem

As realized by Aloy, this poem was the ancestors' way of helping future generations mend their environment after technology and the eco-system were no longer abused. Each piece of the puzzle was distributed to one of the three countries that made up the former United States. Only when the countries reunited and the Eco Accords had been abandoned, did the ancestors hope the puzzle pieces might be put back together.

Lock your strength far away;
Save it for a rainy day.
When the sun no longer shines,
That's when you'll need this little rhyme.

(East Country's piece of the puzzle. Aloy's mother wore the golden scalloped pendant around her neck and sang the song to Aloy as a child. When Claraleese left East Country, she put the pendant in Tomlin's care. Tomlin finally gives the pendant to Aloy. Puzzle pieces: Acid rain, Gold.)

Let the shiny metal rust;
So we don't all turn to dust.
Take the harvest, mix with rain;
Then be free of all the pain.

(West Country's piece of the puzzle. Evan stole it from West's Madame Elected during their catastrophic "earthquakes." Puzzle pieces: Nirogene, Silver.)

The ozone's gone; it's all a shame.
Misused technology is what to blame.
When people learn to use it well,
Then use these words to mend the hell.

(Mid Country's piece of the puzzle. Aaron and Calix's mother had this diamond pendant. When Aaron killed her, he kept the necklace and eventually gave it to Emma. Later, he placed it around Dolce's neck. Puzzle pieces: Need to get the formula up to the ozone layer in a diamond holder/bowl/etc.)

I enjoy crafting characters that aren't just all bad or all good. Almost all characters in The Elected Series, perhaps except for Cole and the youngest children, have their negative and positive attributes. This is certainly true for Evan. Even though he can be considered one of the "bad guys" of the series, he had a scientific curiosity that eventually saved the planet. Like in real life, most people are somewhat gray along the spectrum between good and evil. Perhaps, like me, many of us aim to evolve toward the light by the end of our journey.